FORTUNE'S STROKE

ERIC FLINT
DAVID DRAKE

FORTUNE'S STROKE

A Baen Books Original

Baen Publishing Enterprises
P.O. Box 1403
Riverdale, NY 10471
www.baen.com

ISBN: 0-671-31998-1

Cover art by Gary Ruddell
Interior maps by Randy Asplund

First paperback printing, July 2001
Library of Congress Cataloging-in-Publication Number 00-024712

Distributed by Simon & Schuster
1230 Avenue of the Americas
New York, NY 10020

Typeset by Brilliant Press
Printed in the United States of America

EVEN THE WORLD'S GREATEST GENERAL SHOULD HONOR THE IRON DUKE

Belisarius peered over the parapet. The Ye-Tai were very close, now. Their battle cries filled the air, thick with confidence, heavy with impending triumph. He rose, half-standing, and looked over the other parapet. The musketeers and the pikemen were just a few yards down the slope. Belisarius saw Mark of Edessa watching him, calmly waiting for the general's order.

Here goes, thought Belisarius. He gave the signal. Again, the cornicens blew. As he turned back to face the enemy, Belisarius saw small figures on nearly hilltops frantically waving banners. The scouts had caught sight of the new Roman unit surging forward, and were signaling Damodara.

Too late.

Belisarius took a deep breath, and gave a small prayer for the soul of a man he had never met, and never would. A general of a future that would never be. A man he didn't much care for, as a human being, but who had been one of history's greatest generals.

May your soul rest in peace, wherever it is, Iron Duke. I hope this works as well for me as it did for you at Busaco.

Aide's words, when they came, surprised Belisarius. He had been half-expecting some mutter reproaches to the effect that *Wellington*'s men could fire three volleys a minute, or that *Wellington* had massive fortifications to fall back on; or even—Aide had a bit of the pedant in him—that the title "Iron Duke" was an anachronism. It had been given to *Prime Minister* Wellington, years after the fall of Napoleon.

But all that came, instead, was reassurance.

It will. The reverse-slope tactic was Wellington's signature. It worked at Salamanca, too. And even against Napoleon at Waterloo.

The Belisarius Series
An Oblique Approach
In the Heart of Darkness
Destiny's Shield
Fortune's Stroke
The Tide of Victory

BAEN BOOKS by DAVID DRAKE

RCN series
With the Lightnings
Lt. Leary, Commanding

Hammer's Slammers
The Tank Lords
Caught in the Crossfire
The Butcher's Bill
The Sharp End
Cross the Stars

Independent Novels and Collections
The Dragon Lord
Birds of Prey
Northworld Trilogy
Redliners
Starliner
All the Way to the Gallows
Foreign Legions
(created by David Drake)

The General series:
(with S.M. Stirling)
The Forge
The Chosen
The Reformer
The Dance of Time
(forthcoming)

The Undesired Princess and The Enchanted Bunny
(with L. Sprague de Camp)
Lest Darkness Fall and To Bring the Light
(with L. Sprague de Camp)
Armageddon
(edited with Billie Sue Mosiman)

BAEN BOOKS by ERIC FLINT
Mother of Demons
1632
Rats, Bats, and Vats
(with Dave Freer)
The Philosophical Strangler
Pyramid Scheme (with Dave Freer)
(forthcoming)

to
John & Becky

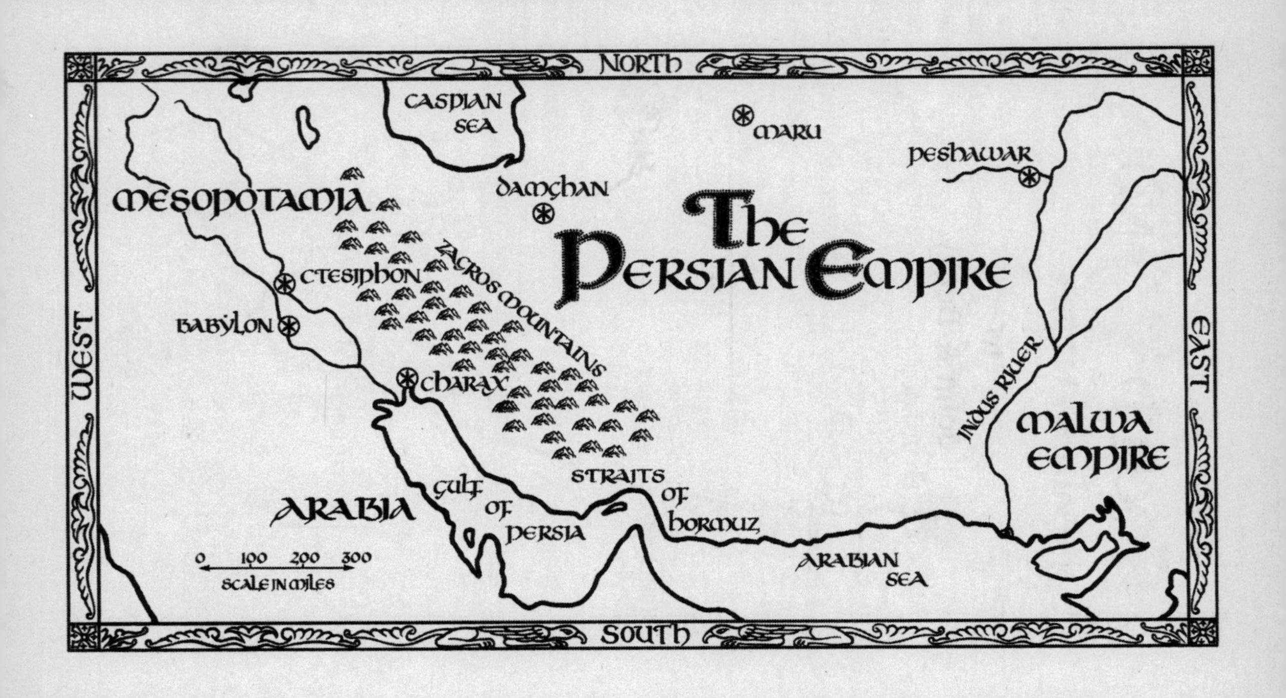
The Persian Empire
North
South
East
West
Caspian Sea
Maru
Peshawar
Damghan
Mesopotamia
Ctesiphon
Babylon
Zagros Mountains
Charax
Indus River
Malwa Empire
Arabia
Gulf of Persia
Straits of Hormuz
Arabian Sea
0 100 200 300
Scale in miles

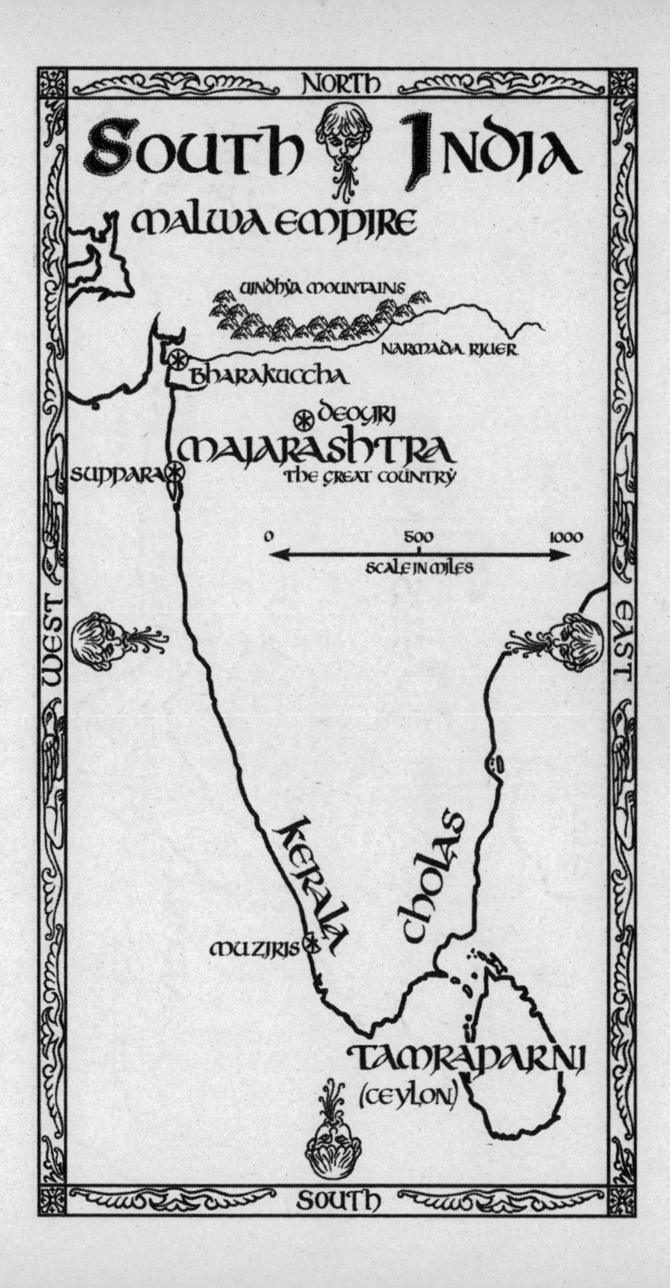
NORTH
SOUTH INDIA
MALWA EMPIRE
VINDHYA MOUNTAINS
NARMADA RIVER
BHARAKUCCHA
DEOGIRI
MAJARASHTRA
THE GREAT COUNTRY
SUPPARA
0
500
1000
SCALE IN MILES
WEST
EAST
KERALA
CHOLAS
MUZIRIS
TAMRAPARNI
(CEYLON)
SOUTH

Prologue

The best steel in the world was made in India. That steel had saved his life.

He stared at a drop of blood working its way down the blade. Slowly, slowly. The blood which covered that fine steel was already drying in the sun. Even as he watched, the last still-liquid drop came to a halt and began hardening.

He had no idea how long he had been watching the blood dry. Hours, it seemed. Hours spent staring at a sword because he was too exhausted to do anything else.

But some quiet, lurking part of his battle-hardened mind told him it had only been minutes. Minutes only, and not so many of those.

He was exhausted. In mind, perhaps, even more than in body.

In a life filled with war since his boyhood, this battle had been the most bitter. Even his famous contest against one of India's legends, fought many years before, did not compare. That, too, had been a day filled with exhaustion, struggle, and fear. But it had been a single combat, not this tornado of mass melee. And there had been no rage in it, no murderous bile. Deadly purpose, yes—in his opponent as much as in himself. But there had been glory, too, and the exultation of knowing that—whichever of them triumphed—both their names would ring down through India's ages.

There had been no glory in this battle. His overlords would claim it glorious, and their bards and chroniclers give it the name. But they were liars. Untruth came as naturally to his masters as breathing. He thought that was perhaps the worst of their many crimes, for it covered all the rest.

His staring eyes moved away from the sword, and fixed on the body of his last opponent. The corpse was a horror, now, what with the mass of flies covering the entrails which spilled out from the great wound which the world's finest steel had created. A desperate slash, that had been, delivered by a man driven to his knees by his opponent's own powerful sword-stroke.

The staring eyes moved to the stub still held in the corpse's hand. The sword had broken at the hilt. The world's finest steel had saved his life. That and his own great strength, when he parried the strike.

Now, staring at the man's face. The features were a blur. Meaningless. The life which had once animated those features was gone. The man who stared saw only the beard clearly. A heavy beard, cut in the square Persian style.

He managed a slight nod, in place of the bow he was too tired to make. His opponent had been a brave man. Determined to exact a last vengeance out of a battle he must have already known to be lost. Determined to kill the man who led the invaders of his country.

The man who stared—the *invader*, he named himself, for he was not given to lies—would see to it that the Persian's body was exposed to the elements. It seemed a strange custom, to him, but that was the Aryan way of releasing the soul.

The man who stared had invaded, and murdered, and plundered, and conquered. But he would not dishonor. That low he would not stoop.

He heard the sound of approaching footsteps behind him. Several men. Among those steps he recognized those of his commander.

He summoned the energy to rise to his feet. For a moment, swaying dizzily, he stared across the battlefield. The Caspian Gates, that battlefield was called. The doorway to all of Persia. The man who stared had opened that doorway.

He cast a last glance at the disemboweled body at his feet.

Yes, he would see to it that the corpse was exposed, in the Persian way.

All of the enemy corpses, he thought, staring back at the battlefield. The stony, barren ground was littered with dead and dying men. Far beyond the grisly sight, rearing up on the northern horizon, was the immense mountain which Persians called Demavend. An extinct volcano, its pure and clean lines stood like some godly reproach to the foul chaos of mankind.

Yes. All of them.

His honor demanded it, and honor was all that was left to him.

That, and his name.

Finally, now, he was able to stand erect. He was very tall.

Rana Sanga was his name. The greatest of Rajputana's kings, and one of India's most legendary warriors.

Rana Sanga. He took some comfort in the name. A name of honor. But he did not take much comfort, and only for an instant. For he was not a man given to lies, and he knew what else the name signified. Malwa bards and chroniclers could sing and write what they would, but he knew the truth.

Rana Sanga. The man—the legend, the Rajput king—who led the final charge which broke the Persians at the Caspian Gates. The man who opened the door, so that the world's foulest evil could spill across another continent.

He felt a gentle touch on his arm. Sanga glanced down, recognizing the pudgy little hand of Lord Damodara.

"Are you badly injured?"

Damodara's voice seemed filled with genuine concern. For a moment, a bitter thought flitted through Sanga's mind. But he dismissed it almost instantly. Some of Damodara's concern, true, was simply fear of losing his best general. But any commander worthy of the name would share that concern. Sanga was himself a general—and a magnificent one—and knew full well that any general's mind required a capacity for calculating ruthlessness.

But most of Damodara's concern was personal. Staring down at his commander, Sanga was struck by the oddity of the friendship in that fat, round face. Of all the highest men in the vast Malwa Empire, Damodara was the only one Sanga had ever met for whom he felt a genuine respect. Other Malwa overlords could be capable, even brilliant—as was Damodara—but no others could claim to be free of evil.

Not that Damodara is a saint, he thought wryly. *"Practical," he likes to call himself. Which is simply a polite way of saying "amoral." But at least he takes no pleasure in cruelty, and will avoid it when he can.*

He shook off the thought and the question simultaneously.

"No, Lord Damodara. I am exhausted, but—" Sanga shrugged. "Very little of the blood is mine. Two gashes, only. I have already bound them up. One will require some stitches. Later."

Sanga made a small gesture at the battlefield. His voice grew harsh. "It is more important, this moment, to see to the needs of honor. I want all the Persians buried—exposed—in their own manner. *With* their weapons."

Sanga cast a cold, unyielding eye on a figure standing some few feet away. Mihirakula was the commander of Lord Damodara's Ye-tai contingents.

"The Ye-tai may loot the bodies of any coin, or jewelry. But the Persians must be exposed with their weapons. Honor demands it."

Mihirakula scowled, but made no verbal protest. He knew that the Malwa commander would accede to Sanga's wishes. The heart of Damodara's army was Rajput, unlike any other of the Malwa Empire's many armies.

"Of course," said Damodara. "If you so wish."

The Malwa commander turned toward one of his other lieutenants, but the man was already moving toward his horse. The man was Rajput himself. He would see to enforcing the order.

Damodara turned back. "There is news," he announced. He gestured toward another man in his little entourage. A small, wiry, elderly man.

"One of Narses' couriers arrived just before the battle ended. With news from Mesopotamia."

Sanga glanced at Narses. There was sourness in that glance. The Rajput king had no love for traitors, even those who had betrayed his enemies.

Still—Narses was immensely competent. Of that there was no question.

"What is the news?" he asked.

"Our main army in Mesopotamia has suffered reverses." Damodara took a deep breath. "*Severe* reverses. They have been forced to lift the siege of Babylon and retreat to Charax."

"Belisarius," stated Sanga. His voice rang iron with certainty.

Damodara nodded. "Yes. He defeated one army at a place called Anatha, diverted the Euphrates, and trapped another army which came to reopen the river. Shattered it. Terrible casualties. Apparently he destroyed the dam and drowned thousands of our soldiers."

The Malwa commander looked away. "Much as you predicted. Cunning as a mongoose." Damodara blew out his cheeks. "With barely ten thousand men, Belisarius managed to force our army all the way back to the sea."

"And now?" asked Sanga.

Damodara shrugged. "It is not certain. The Persian Emperor is marshalling his forces to defeat his brother Ormazd, who betra—who is now allied with us—while he leaves a large army to hold Babylon. Belisarius went to Peroz-Shapur to rest and refit his army over the winter. After that—"

Again, he blew out his cheeks.

"He marched out of Peroz-Shapur some weeks ago, and seems to have disappeared."

Sanga nodded. He turned toward the many Rajput soldiers who were now standing nearby, gathering about their leader.

"Does one of you have any wine?" He lifted the sword in his hand. "I must clean it. The blood has dried."

One of the Rajputs began digging in the pouch behind his saddle. Sanga turned back to Damodara.

"He will be coming for us, now."

The Malwa commander cocked a quizzical eyebrow.

"Be sure of it, Lord Damodara," stated Sanga. He cocked his own eye at the Roman traitor.

Narses nodded. "Yes," he agreed. "That is my assessment also."

Listening to Narses speak, Sanga was impressed,

again, by the traitor's ability to learn Hindi so quickly. Narses' accent was pronounced, but his vocabulary seemed to grow by leaps and bounds daily. And his grammar was already almost impeccable.

But, as always, Sanga was mostly struck by the sound of Narses' voice. Such a deep voice, to come from an old eunuch. He reminded himself, again, not to let his distaste for Narses obscure the undoubted depths to the man. A traitor the eunuch might be. He was also fiendishly capable, and an excellent advisor and spymaster.

"Be sure of it, Lord Damodara," repeated Rana Sanga.

His soldier handed him a winesack. Rajputana's greatest king began cleaning the blade of his sword.

The finest steel in the world was made in India.

He would need that steel. Belisarius was coming.

Chapter 1
PERSIA
Spring, 532 A.D.

When they reached the crest of the trail, two hours after daybreak, Belisarius reined in his horse. The pass was narrow and rocky, obscuring the mountains around him. But his view of the sun-drenched scene below was quite breath-taking.

"What a magnificent country," he murmured.

Belisarius twisted slightly in the saddle, turning toward the man on his right. "Don't you think so, Maurice?"

Maurice scowled. His gray eyes glared down at the great plateau which stretched to the far-distant horizon. Their color was almost identical to his beard. Every one of the bristly strands, Maurice liked to say, had been turned gray over the years by his young commander's weird and crooked way of looking at things.

"You're a lunatic," he pronounced. "A gibbering idiot."

Smiling crookedly, Belisarius turned to the man on his left. "Is that your opinion also, Vasudeva?"

The commander of Belisarius' contingent of Kushan troops shrugged. "Difficult to say," he replied, in his thick, newly learned Greek. For a moment, Vasudeva's usually impassive face was twisted by a grimace.

"Impossible to make fair judgement," he growled. "This helmet—" A sudden fluency came upon him: "Ignorant stupid barbarian piece of shit helmet designed by ignorant stupid barbarians with shit for brains!"

A deep breath, then: "Stupid fucking barbarian helmet obscures all vision. Makes me blind as a bat." He squinted up at the sky. "It is daylight, yes?"

Belisarius' smile grew more crooked still. The Kushans had not stopped complaining about their helmets since they were first handed the things. Weeks ago, now. As soon as his army was three days' march from Peroz-Shapur, and Belisarius was satisfied there were no eyes to see, he had unloaded the Kushans' new uniforms and insisted they start wearing them.

The Kushans had howled for hours. Then, finally yielding to their master's stern commands—they were, after all, technically his slaves—they had stubbornly kept his army from resuming its march for another day. A full day, while they furiously cleaned and recleaned their new outfits. Insisting, all the while, that invented-by-a-philosopher-and-manufactured-by-a-poet-civilized-fucking caustics were no match for hordes of rampaging-murdering-raping-plundering-barbarian-fucking lice.

Glancing down at Vasudeva's gear, Belisarius privately admitted his sympathy.

He had obtained the Kushans' new armor and uniforms, through intermediaries, from the Ostrogoths. Ironically, although the workmanship—certainly the filth—of the outfits was barbarian, they were patterned on Roman uniforms of the previous century. As armor went, the outfits were quite substantial.

They were sturdier, actually, than modern cataphract gear, in the way they combined a mail tunic with laminated arm and leg protection. That weight, of course, was the source of some of the grumbling. The Kushans favored lighter armor than Roman cataphracts to begin with—much less this great, gross, grotesque Ostrogoth gear.

But it was the helmets for which the Kushans reserved their chief complaint. They were accustomed to their own light and simple headgear, which consisted of nothing much more than a steel plate across the forehead held by a leather strap. Whereas these—these—these great, heavy, head-enclosing, silly-horse-tail-crested, idiot-segmented-steel-plate fucking barbarian fucking monstrosities—

They obscured their topknots! Covered them up completely!

"Which," Belisarius had patiently explained at the time, "is the point of the whole exercise. No one will realize you are Kushans. I must keep your existence in my army a secret from the enemy."

The Kushans had understood the military logic of the matter. Still—

Belisarius felt Vasudeva's glare, but he ignored it serenely. "Oh, surely you have some opinion," he stated.

Vasudeva transferred the glare onto the countryside below. "Maurice is correct," he pronounced. "You are a lunatic. A madman."

For a moment, Vasudeva and Maurice exchanged admiring glances. In the months since they had met, the leader of the Kushan "military slaves" and the commander of Belisarius' bucellarii—his personal contingent of mostly Thracian cataphracts who constituted the elite troops of his army—had developed a close working relationship. A friendship, actually, although neither of those grizzled veterans would have admitted the term into their grim lexicon.

Observing the silent exchange, Belisarius fought down a grin. *Outrageous language,* he thought wryly, *from a slave!*

He had captured the Kushans the previous summer, at what had come to be called the battle of Anatha. In the months thereafter, while Belisarius concentrated on relieving the Malwa siege of Babylon, the Kushans had served his army as a labor force. After Belisarius had driven the main Malwa army back to the seaport of Charax—through a stratagem in which their own labor had played a key role—the Kushans had switched allegiances. They had never had any love for their arrogant Malwa overlords to begin with. And once they concluded, from close scrutiny, that Belisarius was as shrewd and capable a commander as they had ever encountered, they decided to negotiate a new status.

"Slaves" they were still, technically. The Kushans felt strongly that proprieties had to be maintained, and they had, after all, been captured in fair battle. Their status had been proposed by Belisarius himself, based on a vision which Aide had given him of military slaves of the future called "Mamelukes."

Vasudeva's eyes were now resting on him, with none of the admiration those same eyes had bestowed on Maurice a moment earlier. Quite hard, those eyes were. Almost glaring, in fact.

Belisarius let the grin emerge.

Slaves, of a sort. But we have to make allowances. It's hard for a man to remember his servile status when he's riding an armored horse with weapons at his side.

"How disrespectful," he murmured.

Vasudeva ignored the quip. The Kushan pointed a finger at the landscape below. "You call this magnificent?" he demanded.

Snort. The glare was transferred back to the plateau. The rocky, ravine-filled landscape stretched from the base of the mountains as far as the eye could see.

"If there is a single drop of water in that miserable country," growled Vasudeva, "it is being hoarded by a family of field mice. A small family, at that."

He remembered his grievance.

"So, at least," he added sourly, "it appears to me. But I am blind as a bat because of this fucking stupid barbarian helmet. Perhaps there's a river—even a huge lake!—somewhere below."

He cocked his head. "Maurice?"

The Thracian cataphract shook his head gloomily. "Not a drop, just as you said." He pointed his own accusing finger. "There's not hardly any vegetation at all down there, except for a handful of oak trees here and there."

Maurice glanced for a moment at the mountains which surrounded them. A thin layer of snow covered the slopes, but the scene was still warmer than the one below. As throughout the Zagros range, the terrain was heavily covered with oak and juniper. The rainfall which the Zagros received even produced a certain lushness in its multitude of little valleys. There, aided by irrigation, the Persian inhabitants were able to grow wheat, barley, grapes, apricots, peaches and pistachios.

He sighed, turning his eyes back to the arid plateau. "All the rain stays in the mountains," he muttered. "Down there—" Another sigh. "Nothing but—"

He finally spotted it.

Belisarius smiled. He, with his vision enhanced by Aide, had seen the thing as soon as they reached the pass. "I do believe that's an oasis!" he exclaimed cheerfully.

Vasudeva's gaze tracked that of his companions. When he spotted the small patch of greenery, his eyes widened. "*That?*" he choked. "You call *that* an 'oasis'?"

Belisarius shrugged. "It's not an oasis, actually. I think it's one of the places where the Persians dug a vertical well to their underground canals. What they call their *qanat* system."

The clatter of horses behind caused him to turn. His two bodyguards, Anastasius and Valentinian, had finally arrived at the mountain pass. They had lagged behind while Valentinian pried a rock from one of his mount's hooves.

Belisarius turned back and pointed to the "oasis." "I want to investigate," he announced. "I think we can make it there by noon."

Protest immediately erupted.

"That's a bad idea," stated Maurice.

"Idiot lunatic idea," agreed Vasudeva.

"There's only the five of us," concurred Valentinian.

"Rest of the army's still a day's march behind," added Anastasius. The giant cataphract, usually placid and philosophical, added his own glare to those of his companions.

"This so-called 'personal reconnaissance' of yours," rumbled Anastasius, "is pushing it already." A huge hand swept the surrounding mountains. A finger the size of a sausage pointed accusingly at the plateau below. "Who the hell knows what's lurking about?" he demanded. "That so-called 'plateau' is almost as broken as these mountains. Could be an entire Malwa cavalry troop hidden anywhere."

"An entire *army*," hissed Valentinian. "I think we should get out of here. I *certainly* don't think we should go down—"

Belisarius cleared his throat. "I don't recall summoning a council," he remarked mildly.

His companions scowled, but fell instantly silent.

After a moment, Maurice spoke quietly. "Are you determined on this, lad?"

Belisarius nodded. "Yes, Maurice, I am. I've been thinking about these qanats ever since Baresmanas and Kurush described them to me. They've been figuring rather heavily in my calculations, in fact." He pointed to the distant patch of greenery. "But it's all speculation until I actually get to inspect one.

This is my first chance, and I don't intend to pass it up."

Having established his authority, Belisarius relented a moment. His veterans were entitled to an explanation, not simply a command.

"Besides, I don't think we need to worry about encountering Damodara's forces yet. The battle where they took the Caspian Gates was bloody and bitter. By all accounts, Damodara simply left a holding force at the Gates while he retired his main army to Damghan for the winter. By now, they'll have refitted and recuperated—they're probably back through the Gates, maybe even as far into Mah province as Ahmadan—but that's still almost fifty miles from here."

Vasudeva cleared his throat. "Is your assessment based on reports from spies, or is it—"

Belisarius smiled. "Good Greek logic, Vasudeva."

Nothing was said. But the expression on the faces of his Thracian and Kushan companions spoke volumes concerning their opinion of "good Greek logic." Even Anastasius, normally devoted to Greek philosophy, was glowering fiercely.

Belisarius spurred his horse into motion and began picking his way down the trail. Silently, his men followed.

More or less silently, that is. Valentinian, of course, was muttering. Belisarius did not ask for a translation. He was quite sure that every phrase was purely obscene.

Halfway down the slope, a new voice entered its protest.

This is a bad idea, came the thought from Aide.

Et tu, Brute? responded Belisarius.

Very bad idea. I have been thinking it over, and Maurice is correct. And Vasudeva and Valentinian and Anastasius. This is too much

guesswork. There are only five of you. You should leave this off and rejoin your army. You can investigate that oasis later, with a much larger force.

Belisarius was a bit startled by the vehemence in Aide's tone. The crystalline being from the future had been with him for years now, ever since it was brought to him by the monk, Michael of Macedonia. Over the course of that time, in fits and starts, Belisarius and Aide had worked out their relationship. Aide advised him, and guided him, and often educated him, on matters pertaining to history and broad human affairs. And the "jewel" was also an almost inexhaustible fount of information. But, from experience, Aide had learned not to outguess Belisarius when it came to problems of strategy and tactics. In that realm, the crystalline being had learned, Belisarius was supreme. Which was why it had come here from the future, after all. To save itself and its crystal race from slavery or outright destruction, Aide had come back to the past searching for the great Roman general who might thwart the attempt of the "new gods" to change all of human history.

But, though Belisarius was startled, he was not swayed. If anything, Aide's echo of his companions' protests simply heightened his resolve.

And so it was, as Belisarius and his little troop worked their way down the slopes of the Zagros mountains onto the plateau of Persia, that another voice was added to Valentinian's muttering.

Stubborn Thracian oaf was the only one of those half-sensed thoughts which was not, technically, obscene.

Chapter 2

The trap was sprung when the Romans were less than three hundred yards from their destination. That was the only mistake the Rajputs made.

But they could hardly, in good conscience, be faulted for that error. Sanga had warned them of Belisarius' quickness and sagacity. But Sanga knew nothing of Aide, and of the way in which Aide enhanced Belisarius' hearing as well his eyesight. So his men sprang the trap at the moment when, logically, they had the Romans isolated from any retreat or shelter.

Belisarius heard the clattering of horses set into sudden motion before any of his comrades—before, even, the lurking enemy appeared out of the ravines in which they were hidden.

"It's an ambush!" he hissed.

Valentinian reacted first. He began reining his horse around.

"No!" shouted Belisarius. He pointed, with both hands, to their side and rear. "They waited until they could cut us off from the mountains!"

He spurred his horse forward, now pointing ahead. "Our only chance is to fort up!"

His comrades, from long experience, did not argue the matter. They simply followed Belisarius' galloping horse, as their commander charged forward.

Belisarius scanned the terrain ahead of him. The small "oasis" toward which they were heading was not much more than a grove of trees. Spindly fruit trees—apricots, mostly, with a handful of peaches.

Useless.

But, a moment later, his uncanny eyesight spotted what he was hoping for.

"There's a building! In the grove!" Belisarius cast a quick glance over his left shoulder. He could see the enemy now.

Damnation! Rajputs.

Perhaps a dozen. A glance over his right shoulder. *Same.*

His quick mind flashed back over his experiences in India. *The standard for a Rajput cavalry platoon is thirty. Which means—*

He turned his head back around, scanning the grove ahead. In less than two seconds, he saw what he was expecting.

"There are Rajputs in the grove, too!" he shouted. "Probably half a dozen!"

Belisarius made no attempt to draw his bow. He was not a good enough archer to handle it at a full gallop. None of his companions were, except—Valentinian already had his bow out. In less time than Belisarius would have imagined possible, the cataphract had fired an arrow. The missile sped ahead of the galloping cluster of Romans and plunged into the trees. Instantly, a cry of pain went up. Almost as instantly, five Rajputs drove their horses out of the grove, pounding toward the oncoming Romans. Belisarius could see a sixth Rajput, but the man was sliding off his horse, clutching at an arrow in his shoulder.

This was lance work, now. All of the Romans except

Valentinian already had their heavy lances in position. So did Valentinian, by the time the Rajputs arrived. With his weasel-quick reflexes, the cataphract even managed to slide his bow back in its sheath before taking up his lance. Almost any other man in the world would have been forced to simply drop the weapon.

The contest, under the circumstances—a head-on collision between an equal number of Roman cataphracts and Rajput lancers—was no match at all. Even without stirrups, the heavier Roman cavalry would have triumphed. With them, and the much heavier and longer lances the stirrups made possible, Belisarius and his men almost literally rode right over their opponents. For a few seconds, the general's world was a cacophony of shouts. The clangor of lance against shield covered but could not disguise the more hideous sounds of splitting flesh and bone. Battle cries became shrieks, fading into hissing death.

Three of the Rajputs were killed almost instantly, their bodies torn by the great spears. A fourth would die within minutes, from the blood pouring out of a half-severed thigh.

The only one who survived, suffering nothing worse than bruises, was the Rajput who faced Vasudeva. Though the Kushan was a skilled warrior, he had little experience with stirrups and lanceplay. But he was a veteran, and had the sense not to try matching the prowess of his companions. Instead of finding the gaps between armor, he simply drove his lance into his opponent's shield. The impact knocked the man right off his horse.

The Romans rode on. Belisarius could now see more of the building through the trees. It was a farmhouse, typical of the sort erected by large Persian families. Square in design, the structure was single-storied and measured approximately thirty feet on a side. The walls were heavy and solid, constructed out of dry stone.

He couldn't see the roof clearly, but he knew it would be made of wooden beams covered with soil.

Except—

There was something odd about the shape of the farmhouse. The trees obscured his vision, but it seemed as if the building sloped on one side.

A thought came from Aide. **This is earthquake country. That building is half-collapsed.**

Belisarius nodded. They were entering the small grove which surrounded the farmhouse, and he could see that the fruit trees were poorly tended. The place had all the signs of an abandoned farm.

Earthquake, probably, just like Aide says. Then— war comes. The survivors would have fled.

Belisarius cast a last glance over his shoulder. Their pursuers, he saw, were spreading out. Realizing that they had missed their chance at an immediate ambush, the Rajputs intended to surround the grove and trap the Romans in the farmhouse.

Grimly, he turned away. Five men against most of a Rajput cavalry platoon was bad odds. Very bad. But at least they'd have the advantage of being forted up rather than caught in the open.

A moment later they were through the grove and reining up next to the farmhouse.

If you can call this a "fort," he thought ruefully, examining the structure.

"There's only the one door," pointed out Maurice. "Maybe one in back, but I doubt it. Not if this is like most Persian farmhouses."

"You call that a 'door'?" demanded Valentinian. His expression was that of a man who had just eaten a basket of lemons.

Maurice managed the feat of shrugging while he climbed off his horse. "It'll do, it'll do. We can probably shore it up with beams." He glanced up at the half-collapsed roof. "Be plenty of them lying around, I should think."

Valentinian left off further comment, although his continued sour expression made clear his opinion of "forts" with collapsed roofs.

Once all five Romans were dismounted, they pried open the door and led their mounts into the farmhouse. The half-dark interior of the farmhouse was filled, for a minute or so, with the noise and dust thrown up by skittish horses, still blowing from exertion and prancing nervously. Vasudeva occupied himself with calming and tying up the mounts while his four companions spread out and investigated the place.

The investigation was quick, but thorough.

Maurice summed it up. "Could be worse. Walls are thick. The stones were well placed. Roof'll be a problem, but at least"—he pointed to the rubble filling the northern third of the farmhouse—"when it collapsed it brought down the adjoining walls. One or two Rajputs could squeeze in there, but there's no way they could do a concerted rush."

Hands on hips, he made a last survey of their fort. "Not bad, actually. Once we brace the door—"

He smiled thinly, watching Anastasius match deed to word. The giant simply picked up a beam and jammed it against the door. Then, as casually as it were but a twig, he did the same with another.

Maurice finished: "—we'll be able to hold them off for quite a bit."

Valentinian's expression was still sour. Sour, sour, sour. "That's great," he snarled. "You *have* noticed there's no way out of here? You *have* noticed there's no food in the place?"

Gloomily, he watched Belisarius pry the cover off what appeared to be a well in the southeast corner.

"At least we've got water," he grumbled. "Maybe. If that well isn't dry."

Belisarius spoke, then, with astonishing good cheer. "Better than that, Valentinian. Better than that. I do believe this leads to a qanat." He pointed down into the well. "See for yourself."

Valentinian and Maurice hurried over.

"Make it quick," commanded Vasudeva. The Kushan was peering through a small chink in the western wall. "The Rajputs are into the grove."

"Same on this side," added Anastasius, peering through a similar chink in the opposite wall. "They've got us surrounded." A moment later: "They're dismounting, now, going to charge us on foot." His tone grew aggrieved. "I thought Rajputs never got off their horses, even rode them into the damned latrines."

"Not Sanga's Rajputs," commented Belisarius idly, still staring down into the well. "He's just as stiff-necked as any Rajput when it comes to his honor, but that doesn't extend to any silliness when it comes to military tactics."

Suddenly, Vasudeva hissed. "They've got grenades!" he exclaimed.

Belisarius' head jerked up from his examination of the well.

"You're certain?" he demanded. But he didn't wait for a reply before reconsidering his plans. Vasudeva was not the man to make such a mistake.

"I thought the Malwa never let anyone but their kshatriyas handle gunpowder weapons," complained Valentinian.

"So did I," mused Belisarius, scratching his chin. "Looks like Damodara decided to relax the rules."

He resumed studying the well. "Not surprising, I suppose. He's rumored to be far and away their best field commander, and his army's based on Rajputs. Sanga's Rajputs, to boot."

As he continued his scrutiny of the well, his voice grew thoughtful. "That explains this ambush, I think. I forgot how good Sanga is. Got too accustomed to those arrogant Malwa in Mesopotamia. He knows me.

He probably figured I'd do my own reconnaissance, and set traps all along the foothills."

Belisarius looked up, finished with his examination. When he spoke, the iron tone in his voice indicated that he had reached a decision.

"No point in forting up, now," he announced. "They won't waste lives trying to force their way through the door. They'll just blow out the walls of the farmhouse."

"They're already moving in," agreed Vasudeva. "Three men, on this side, carrying grenades. I can't even fire on them. Chink's big enough to peek through, but not for an arrow."

"I've got two on my side," said Anastasius. "Same thing."

Belisarius pointed down the well. "We'll make our escape through here. Strip off your armor. It's a long, narrow climb, and I've no idea how much room we'll have below."

"What about the horses?" demanded Valentinian.

Belisarius shook his head. "No way to get them down. We'll use them for a diversion. But first—" He strode over to the horses. "Pull out our own grenades. I want to set them against all the walls. We'll do the Rajputs' work for them. Bring the whole place down. It might cover our escape."

He began digging grenades out of his saddlebags. An instant later, Maurice and Valentinian were doing the same.

"I've got fuse-cord," announced Maurice. "We can tie together all the grenades. Set them off at once."

Belisarius nodded. He carried a handful of grenades over to the west wall and began placing them, while Valentinian did the same on the east. Maurice followed, quickly tying the fuses to a length of fuse-cord.

Suddenly, Vasudeva shouted. *"Get down! Now!"*

All five Romans flopped onto the dirt floor of the farmhouse. An instant later, a series of explosions rocked the building. On the west wall, not far from Vasudeva, a small hole was blown out. Everywhere else the walls stood, although they were noticeably shakier.

"God bless good stonework," muttered Anastasius. "Always admired masons. A saintly lot, the bunch."

The horses reared up, whinnying with fear, fighting the reins which tied them to a fallen beam. Maurice, the best horse handler among them, rushed to quiet them down.

"Are they preparing a charge?" demanded Belisarius.

Vasudeva, back at his chink, shook his head. "No. They're too canny. They're putting together another batch of grenades. They won't charge until the place is a pile of rubble. Let the falling stones do their work for them." He grunted approvingly. "Good soldiers. Smart."

Belisarius nodded. "That gives us a couple of minutes." He pointed to the door. "Anastasius—pull those braces away. Then get ready to knock down the door. Maurice, as soon as the door goes, drive the horses through. That'll stop the Rajputs for a moment. They'll think we're trying a rush, and besides"—he smiled cheerfully—"Rajputs love good horses. They won't be able to resist taking the time to catch these."

He turned. Seeing that Valentinian had quietly gone about finishing the task of tying together all the grenades, he nodded with satisfaction.

"That's it, then. Vasudeva, you go first. Then Valentinian. Maurice and Anastasius, as soon as you drive the horses out, you follow. I'll go last."

Belisarius seized the heavy well cover and lifted it back onto the low stone wall which surrounded the well. Then, using a short beam, he propped it open. When the time came, he would be able to drop the cover back onto the well by knocking aside the beam.

He began stripping off his armor. Before he was

half finished, Vasudeva was out of his own armor and already clambering into the well. The Kushan grabbed a wooden peg fixed into the stonework of the shaft—the first of many which served as a ladder—and began lowering himself.

"At least I've got rid of that miserable stupid ignorant barbarian helmet and that—" The rest of his words were lost as he vanished into the darkness.

Valentinian handed Belisarius the end of the fuse cord as he began his own descent into the well. He had nothing to say. Nothing coherent, at least. He *was* muttering fiercely.

Belisarius looked up. Maurice and Anastasius were in place. They, too, had already stripped off their armor.

"Do it," he commanded. Then, remembering an undone task, shouted: "Wait! I need a striker!"

Maurice scowled, and hastily dug into one of the saddlebags. A moment later, he came up with the device and pitched it to Belisarius. As soon as Anastasius saw that Belisarius had caught the striker, the huge Thracian heaved one of the beams aside. A moment later, the other followed. And then, a moment later, Anastasius kicked open the door. One powerful blow was enough to send the half-splintered thing flying into the farmyard beyond.

That done, Anastasius lumbered toward the well while Maurice, shouting and cursing, began driving the horses through the door.

The well was a tight fit for Anastasius, but he took the problem philosophically. "There's much to be said for the Cynic school," he commented, as he began the awkward task of lowering his great form down the narrow stone shaft. "Unfairly maligned, they are."

An instant later, Maurice practically leapt into the well. "Make it quick, lad," he hissed. "None of your fancy perfect timing crap. The Rajputs are already coming." He began dropping down the shaft. "Just blow it. *Now.*"

Well said, chimed in Aide.

Belisarius was not inclined to argue the point. He just waited long enough to be certain that Maurice was far enough ahead that he wouldn't be climbing down onto his head before he struck flame to the fuse. He took a second to make sure the fuse was burning properly before tossing it onto the floor. Then, after climbing into the well and lowering himself a few feet, he reached up and knocked aside the beam. The heavy wooden cover slammed back down over the shaft opening. Belisarius barely managed to jerk his hand out of the way, saving himself from broken fingers.

The interior of the well was completely dark, now. Hastily, feeling for the wooden pegs, Belisarius began lowering himself.

He was twenty feet down when the charges went off. The force of the explosion shook the walls of the shaft. For a moment, Belisarius froze, listening intently. He could hear the slamming of stones and heavy beams on the well cover above him, and he feared that it might give way. An avalanche of rubble would sweep him off the peg ladder. He had no idea how far he would fall.

Far enough, said Aide gloomily. **Too far.**

In the event, it would have been forty feet.

When he finally reached the end of the well-shaft, his feet flailed about for a moment, searching for pegs which weren't there. A hand grabbed his ankle.

"That's it, General," came Valentinian's voice out of the darkness. "Anastasius, get him down."

Huge hands seized Belisarius' thighs. The general relinquished his grip on the pegs, and Anastasius lowered him easily onto a floor. A gravel floor, Belisarius thought, from the feel of it.

He began to stand up straight, then flinched. He couldn't see the roof, and feared crashing his head.

That brought to mind a new problem. "Damn," he growled. "I forgot it would be pitch-black down here."

"I didn't," came Maurice's self-satisfied reply. "Neither did Vasudeva. But I hope you had the sense to bring that striker down with you. It's the only one we've got."

Belisarius dug into his tunic and withdrew the striker. His hand, groping in the darkness, encountered that of Maurice. The Thracian chiliarch took the device and struck it. A moment later, Maurice had a taper burning. It was a short length of tallow-soaked cord, one of the field torches which Roman soldiers carried with them on campaign.

The smoky, flickering light was enough to illuminate the area. Belisarius began a quick examination, while Maurice lit the taper which Vasudeva was carrying.

Valentinian, staring around, whistled softly. "Damn! I'm impressed."

So was Belisarius. The underground aqueduct they found themselves in was splendidly constructed—easily up to the best standards of Roman engineering. The aqueduct—the qanat, as the Persians called it, using the Arabic term—was square in cross section, roughly eight feet wide by eight feet tall. The central area of the tunnel, about four feet in width, was sunk two feet below the ledges on either side. That central area, where the water would normally flow except during the heavy runoff in mid-spring, was covered with gravel. The ledges were crudely paved with stone blocks, and were just wide enough for a man to walk along.

Except for a small trickle of water seeping down the very center, the qanat was dry. It was still too early in the season for most of the snow to begin melting.

"What do you think the slope is, Maurice?" asked

Belisarius. "One in three hundred? That's the Roman standard."

"Do I look like an engineer?" groused the chiliarch. "I haven't got the faintest—"

"One in two hundred," interrupted Vasudeva. "Maybe even one in a hundred and fifty."

The Kushan smiled seraphically. In the flickering torchlight, he looked like a leering gargoyle. "This is mountain country, much like my own homeland. No room here for any leisurely Roman slopes." He pointed with his torch. "That way. The steep slope makes it easy to see the direction of the mountains. But we've a long way to go."

He set off, pacing along the ledge on the right. Cheerfully, over his back: "Long way. Tiring. Especially for Romans, accustomed to philosopher slopes and poet-type gradients." He barked a laugh. "One in three hundred!" Another laugh. "Ha!"

An hour later, Valentinian began complaining.

"There would have been room for the horses," he whined. "Plenty of room."

"How would you have lowered them down?" demanded Anastasius. "And what good would it have done, anyway?"

The giant glanced up at the stone ceiling. Unlike his companions, Anastasius had chosen to walk on the gravel in the central trough of the qanat. On the ledges, he would have had to stoop.

"Eight feet, at the most," he pronounced. "You couldn't possibly *ride* a horse down here. You'd still be walking, and have to lead the surly brutes by the reins."

Mutter, mutter, mutter.

"So stop whining, Valentinian. There's worse things in life than a long, uphill hike."

"Like what?" snarled Valentinian.

"Like being dead," came the serene reply.

✧ ✧ ✧

They passed a multitude of vertical shafts along the way, identical to the one down which they had lowered themselves. But Belisarius ignored them. He wanted to make sure they had reached the mountains before emerging.

Three hours after beginning their trek, they reached the first of the sloping entryways which provided easier access to the qanat. Belisarius fought off the temptation. He wanted to be well into the mountains before they emerged, away from any possible discovery or pursuit.

Onward. Valentinian started muttering again.

Two hours later—the slope was *much* steeper now—they reached another entryway. This one was almost level, which indicated how high up into the mountains they had reached.

Again, Belisarius was tempted. Again, he fought it down.

Further. Onward.

Valentinian's muttering was nonstop, now.

An hour or so later, they reached another entryway, and Belisarius decided it was safe to take it. When they emerged, they found themselves in the very same pass in the mountains from which they had begun their descent to the plateau. Night had fallen, but there was a full moon to illuminate the area.

It was very cold. And they were very hungry.

"We'll camp here," announced Belisarius. "Start our march tomorrow at first light. Hopefully, some of Coutzes' cavalry will find us before too long. I told him to keep plenty of reconnaissance platoons out in the field."

"Which could have done what we just did," grumbled Maurice. "A commanding general's got no business doing this kind of work."

Quite right, came Aide's vigorous thought.

"Quite right," came the echo from Valentinian, Anastasius and Vasudeva.

Seeing the four men glaring at him in the moonlight, and sensing the crystalline glare coming from within his own mind, Belisarius sighed.

It's going to be a long night. And a longer day tomorrow—if I'm lucky, and Coutzes is on the job. If not—

Sigh.

Days! Days of this! Slogging through the mountains is bad enough, without having every footstep dogged by reproaches and "I-told-you-so's."

"I told you so," came the inevitable words from Maurice.

Chapter 3

"I told you so," murmured Rana Sanga. The Rajput king strode over to the well and peered down into the shaft.

Pratap, the commander of the cavalry troop, suppressed a sigh of relief. Sanga, on occasion, possessed an absolutely ferocious temper. But his words of reproach had been more philosophical than condemnatory.

He joined the king at the well.

"You followed?" asked Sanga.

Pratap hesitated, then squared his shoulders. "I sent several men to investigate. But—it's pitch-black down there, and we had no good torches. Nothing that would have lasted more than a few minutes. By the time we finally cleared away the rubble and figured out what had happened, the Romans had at least an hour's head start. It didn't seem to me—"

Sanga waved him down. "You don't have to justify yourself, Pratap. As it happens, I agree with you. You almost certainly wouldn't have caught up with them and, even if you had—"

He straightened, finished with his examination of

the well. In truth, there wasn't much to see. Just a stone-lined hole descending into darkness.

"From your description of the giant Roman, I'm sure that was one of Belisarius' two personal bodyguards. I've forgotten his name. But the other one is called Valentinian, and—"

From the corner of his eye, he saw Udai wince. Udai was one of his chief lieutenants. Like Sanga himself, Udai had been present at the Malwa emperor's pavilion after the capture of Ranapur. The emperor, testing Belisarius' pretense at treason, had ordered him to execute Ranapur's lord and his family. The Roman general had not hesitated, ordering Valentinian to do the work.

For a moment, remembering, Sanga almost winced himself. Valentinian had drawn his sword and decapitated six people in less time than it would have taken most soldiers to gather their wits. Sanga was himself accounted one of India's greatest swordsmen. Valentinian was one of the few men he had ever encountered—the *very* few men—who he thought might be his equal. To meet such a man down *there*—

"Just as well," he stated firmly. "In the qanat, with no way to surround them, the advantage would have been all theirs." He turned away from the well, and began picking his way across the mound of rubble. "The ambush failed, that's all. It happens—especially against an opponent as quick and shrewd as Belisarius."

Seeing Ajatasutra standing before him, at the edge of the stone pile which had once been a farmhouse, Sanga stopped and drew himself up.

"I will not have my men criticized." The Rajput's statement was flat, hard, unyielding. His brows lowered over glaring eyes.

Ajatasutra smiled, and spread his hands in a placating gesture. "I didn't say a word." The assassin chuckled dryly. "As it happens, I agree with you. The only thing that surprises me is that you came as close as you did. I didn't really think this scheme of yours was more than a half-baked fancy. Generals, in my experience, don't conduct their own advance reconnaissance."

"I do," rasped Sanga.

"So you do," mused Ajatasutra. The assassin eyed the Rajput king. His lips twisted humorously. "You were right, and Narses was wrong," he stated. "You assessed Belisarius better than he did."

Again, Ajatasutra spread his hands. "I will simply report the facts, Sanga, that's all. The ambush was well laid, and almost succeeded. But it failed, as ambushes often do. There is no fault or failure imputed."

Sanga nodded. For a moment, he studied the man standing before him. Despite himself, and his normal fierce dislike for Malwa spies, Sanga found it impossible not to be impressed by Ajatasutra. Ajatasutra was one of the Malwa Empire's most accomplished assassins. A year earlier, he had been second in command of the mission to Rome which had engineered the attempted insurrection against the Roman Empire. Narses had been the Malwa's principal co-conspirator in that plot. The insurrection—the Nika revolt, as the Romans called it—had failed, in the end, due to Belisarius. But it had been a very close thing, and the Malwa Empire had not blamed Ajatasutra or Narses for its failure. The two men had warned Balban, the head of the Malwa mission, that Belisarius and his wife, Antonina, were playing a duplicitous game. That, at least, had been their claim—and the evidence seemed to support them.

So, held faultless for the defeat, Narses had been assigned by Emperor Skandagupta to serve Lord Damodara as an adviser. The eunuch, from his long experience as one of the Roman Empire's chief officials, possessed a wide knowledge of the intricate politics of the steppe barbarians and the semibarbarian feudal lords who ruled Persia's easternmost provinces. He had been a great help to the campaign, as Damodara and Sanga fought their way into the Persian plateau.

Ajatasutra had accompanied Narses. He served the Roman traitor as his chief lieutenant—and as his legs and eyes. The old eunuch was still spry and active—amazingly so, given his years. But for things like this sudden twenty-mile ride to investigate a failed ambush, Ajatasutra usually served in his stead. The assassin would observe, and assess, and report.

Sanga relaxed. In truth, he had found Ajatasutra guiltless of the self-serving "reports" for which Malwa spies were notorious among their Rajput vassals. He would never be fond of Ajatasutra—he had no more liking for assassins than he did for traitors, even ones on his side—but he could not honestly find any other fault in the man.

"You're lucky, in fact," remarked Ajatasutra, "that you didn't suffer worse casualties."

"Four of my men were killed!" snarled Pratap. "Two others wounded, and yet another half-crushed when the farmhouse blew up. He will lose both his legs."

Ajatasutra shrugged. The gesture was not callous so much as one of philosophical resignation. "Could have been a lot worse. Most of the stonework collapsed inward, when Belisarius blew the walls. Fortunately, he was just trying to cover his escape. If he'd been forced to make a last stand, I guarantee that half your men would be dead. And precious few of the survivors uninjured."

Pratap's eyes smoldered resentfully. "I didn't realize you were well acquainted with the man." Then, with a sneer: "Other than suffering a defeat at his hands in Constantinople."

Ajatasutra studied Pratap's angry face. His own expression was relaxed, almost bland.

"Actually, I'm not. My own contact with Belisarius came at a distance. But I am quite well-acquainted with his wife, Antonina. Balban set a trap for her, too, you know—in Constantinople, right at the end."

The anger faded from Pratap's features, replaced by curiosity.

"I never heard about that," he stated.

"Neither did I!" snapped Sanga. The Rajput king glared at the Malwa assassin. "You tried to take revenge on Belisarius by murdering his *wife*?"

Sanga's famous temper was surfacing, now. Again, Ajatasutra made the placating gesture with his hands. "Please, Rana Sanga! It was Balban's doing, not mine. And you can't even blame him—the orders came directly from Nanda Lal."

Far from placating Sanga, mention of Nanda Lal brought his outrage to the surface. But at least, Ajatasutra saw, the tall and fearsome Rajput's fury was no longer directed at him. There was no love lost, he knew, between Rana Sanga and the Malwa Empire's spymaster.

The assassin spread his hands wide. "I thought it was a bad idea, myself. And I warned Balban that he was underestimating the woman."

The hot glare in Sanga's eyes faded, as the implication registered. "The ambush failed," he stated. "Belisarius' wife survived."

Ajatasutra laughed harshly. " 'Survived'? That's one way of putting it. It'd be more accurate to say that she set her own ambush and butchered most of Balban's thugs."

By now, all of the Rajputs at the scene were clustering about—Sanga's own contingent as well as Pratap's cavalry troop. Like warriors everywhere, they enjoyed a good tale. Ajatasutra, seeing his audience—and the easing fury in Sanga's face—relaxed. He held out his hand, perhaps five feet above the ground.

"She's quite small, you know. This tall, no more.

Gorgeous woman. Beautiful, voluptuous—" He paused dramatically.

"*But*—" He grinned. "Her father was a charioteer. He was reputed to have taught her how to use a blade. And I'm quite certain her husband trained her also. Probably had that man of his—that killer Valentinian—polish her skills."

Ajatasutra paused, to make sure he had his audience's rapt attention. Then: "When she realized Balban had set a pack of street thugs after her, she forted herself up in the kitchen of a pastry shop. I wasn't there, myself—I watched from outside—but she apparently poured meat broth over the lot and began hacking them with a cleaver. Killed several herself, before one of Belisarius' cataphracts came to her rescue. After that—"

He shrugged. "One cataphract—against a handful of street toughs."

The Rajput cavalrymen surrounding him, veterans all, grunted deep satisfaction. Roman cataphracts were their enemy, of course, but—

Street toughs—against a *soldier*?

"A woman did all that?" queried one of the Rajputs. The air of satisfaction was absent, now. He seemed almost aggrieved. "A *woman?*"

Ajatasutra smiled. Nodded. Held out his hand again. "A little bitty woman," he said cheerfully. "No taller than this."

The assassin glanced at Rana Sanga. He saw that the anger in the Rajput king's face had completely faded. Replaced by something which almost seemed sadness, thought Ajatasutra.

Odd.

Abruptly, Sanga turned away and began striding toward his horse. "Let's go," he commanded. "There's nothing more to be done here. I want to make it back to the army by nightfall."

Once astride his horse, he gave the scene a last

quick survey. "The ambush failed," he announced. "That's all."

That night, standing before his tent in the giant camp of Damodara's army, Rana Sanga studied the mountains looming to the west. The full moon bathed them in a silvery beauty. But there was something ominous about that pale shimmer. Liquid, almost, those mountains seemed. As difficult to pin down as the man who lurked somewhere within them.

"I wish we had killed you," whispered Sanga. "It would have made things so much easier for us. And then again—"

He sighed, turned away, pulled back the flap to his tent. He gave a last glance at the moon, high and silvery, before stooping into the darkness. He remembered another night he had done the same, after the massacre of rebel Ranapur. Remembered his thoughts on that night. The same thoughts he had now.

I wish you were not my enemy. But—

I swore an oath.

That same moment, staring down onto the plateau from the mountain pass, Belisarius studied the flickering fires of the far-distant Malwa army camp. It was the day after the ambush, and his own army had arrived. The Roman troops were camped just half a mile below the crest of the mountains.

He was no longer estimating the size of the enemy army. He was done with that. He was simply contemplating one of the men he knew was among that huge host.

It was very nicely done, Sanga. Sorry to have disappointed you.

The thought was whimsical, not angry. Had he been in Sanga's place, he would have done the same. And he mused, once again, on the irony of the situation. There were few men in the world he dreaded as much as Rana Sanga. A tiger in human flesh.

And yet—

He sighed and turned away. He would meet Sanga again.

Picking his way down the trail in the semidarkness, he remembered the message which the Great Ones had once given Aide and his race. The secret—part of it, at least—which those awesome beings of the future imparted to the crystals they had created, when those crystals found themselves threatened by the "new gods."

Guided by that message, the crystals had sent Aide back in time to find "the general who is not a warrior." But the Great Ones had understood the entirety of the thing. Descended from human flesh—though there was no trace of that flesh remaining in them—they understood all the secrets of the human soul, and its contradictions.

Aide, in a soft mental message, spoke the words: ***See the enemy in the mirror.***

A sudden deep sadness engulfed Belisarius.

The friend across the field.

Chapter 4

AXUM

Spring, 532 A.D.

Antonina shook her head, partly in awe, partly in disbelief. "Was anyone killed when it fell?" she asked.

Next to her, Eon lifted his massive shoulders in a small shrug.

"Nobody knows, Antonina." For a moment, the Prince of Axum's dark face was twisted into a grimace of embarrassment. "We were still pagans, at the time. And the workmen would have all been slaves. We Ethiopians kept many slaves, back then"—his next words came in a bit of a rush—"before we adopted the teachings of Jesus Christ."

Antonina fought down a smile. The semi-apology in Eon's response was quite unnecessary, after all. It was not as if Roman rulers—

"Please, Eon! You don't need to apologize for the barbarity of your pagan ancestors. At least your old kings didn't stage gladiatorial contests, or feed Christians to lions."

Alas. She could tell immediately, from Eon's

expression, that her attempt at reassurance had failed of its mark.

"Not Christians, no," mumbled Eon. "But—" Another shrug of those incredible shoulders. "Well . . . There are a lot of big animals here in Africa. Lions, elephants. And it seems that the old kings—"

There came yet another shrug. But the gesture, this time, contained neither apology nor embarrassment. It was the movement of the powerful shoulders of a young prince who, when all was said and done, was not really given to self-effacement.

"It's over, now," he stated. "We instituted Christian principles of rule two hundred years ago." He pointed to the enormous thing in front of them. "We keep that here as a reminder to our kings. Of the pagan folly of royal grandiosity."

Antonina's eyes returned to the object in question. Eon had brought her here, from the royal compound a mile to the southwest—the Ta'akha Maryam, it was called—as part of his sight-seeing tour of Ethiopia's capital city. He had started off, in the morning, by showing her the magnificent churches which adorned the city. The churches, especially the cathedral which the Ethiopians had named the Maryam Tsion, were the pride of Axum. But then, in mid-afternoon, the prince had insisted on showing her this as well.

It was an obelisk, lying on its side, broken into several pieces. The huge sections were crumpled over the tombs of pre-Christian kings, leaving the obelisk a rippling monument to ancient folly. More than anything else, to Antonina, it resembled an enormous stone snake, making its serpentine way across the landscape of the Ethiopian highlands.

The obelisk had fallen, Eon explained, as it was being erected. Staring at it, Antonina could well believe the tale. It was difficult to judge, because of its position, but she thought the obelisk was far larger than any created even by the ancient Egyptians. Only a king possessed by delusions of grandeur could have thought of ordering mortal men to erect such a preposterous structure.

She shivered slightly, thinking of the men who must have been trapped by the obelisk in its ruin. When the thing fell, it crushed several of the tombs beneath it. The blood and mangled flesh of slaves, for a time, would have decorated the sepulchres where royal bones lay buried.

Eon misinterpreted the motion. "You are cold!" he exclaimed. "I have been thoughtless. I forgot that you are not accustomed—"

She waved down the apology. "No, no, Eon. I'm not really cold. I was just thinking—"

She stopped, shivering again. She *was* cold, she suddenly realized. She had always thought of Africa as the quintessential land of warmth. But the heartland of Axum lay in the Ethiopian highlands. True, the capital city was situated in the broad, fertile plain called Hatsebo, well below the mountains which towered all about in stark majesty. But it was still over a mile above sea level.

"Perhaps we should return to the Ta'akha Maryam," she admitted. A bit hurriedly, to stave off another apology: "Your father will be growing impatient with our long absence."

Actually, she knew, Eon's father—the *negusa nagast*, "King of Kings," as he was titled—would not be in the slightest bit impatient. She was quite certain that King Kaleb had welcomed her daylong absence from the royal compound. It gave him time to consult with his advisers, before making a response to the Roman Empire's proposals.

Antonina and her entourage had arrived in the Ethiopian city of Axum a week earlier. Axum—the capital had given its name to the Ethiopian kingdom, just as had Rome—had never received such a high-level delegation from the Roman Empire. Since

Ethiopia's conversion to Christianity under the tutelage of the missionaries who were revered as the "Nine Saints," the Axumites had maintained cordial relations with the great empire to their north. But, except for trade matters, there had been very little in the way of official diplomatic exchange. Until Antonina came, at the head of a small army, armed not only with the strange new gunpowder weapons but with a barrage of proposals from the Emperor of Rome.

As they began picking their way through the broken stones of ancient kings, Antonina found herself, once again, fighting down a smile. She could well understand how King Kaleb would have wanted a day—at least!—to mull over the Roman Empire's proposals.

Those proposals were, after all, hardly what you'd call vague and meaningless diplomatic phrasery.

Rome accepts Axum's offer of an alliance against the Malwa Empire. To further our joint aim of crushing that monstrous realm, we propose:

Rome will supply Axum with gunpowder weapons, and the technicians to train you in their use and manufacture.

Axum will provide the fleet necessary to keep the rebellion in southern India alive. Axumite ships will run the Malwa blockade of the Majarashtra coast, carrying arms and supplies provided by Rome.

Axum will also provide the fleet necessary to—

Her thoughts broke off. She and Eon were almost out of the ruins. As they picked their way around yet another half-crumbled structure, she caught sight of the figure lounging against one of the tombs at the very edge of the field of monuments.

Ousanas, for once, was not grinning. Indeed, he looked positively disgruntled.

Antonina made no attempt to fight down her smile, now. "What's the matter, Ousanas?" she called out. "Has your philosophical composure abandoned you, for the moment? Shame, shame! What would the Stoics say?"

Ousanas shook his head. "The Stoics advocated serenity in the face of life's tragedies and great misfortunes." Scowling: "They did *not* intend their precious teachings to be wasted on petty annoyances. Such as having to waste half a day while a fool boy prince shows a frivolous woman with too much time on her hands the inevitable results of self-aggrandizement, a lesson which"—deep scowl—"any child learns the first time they sass their elders."

Antonina and Eon reached the edge of the field. Ousanas thrust himself erect from his semi-reclined posture. There was nothing of a lurch in that movement, as there would have been for most men. On one of his powerful forearms, Ousanas bore the scar left by a panther he had slain years earlier. The tall African had triumphed in that encounter, as he had in so many others, because he shared the sinuous grace and power of the great feline hunters of the continent. For all that Ousanas derided royalty—which, as Prince Eon's dawazz, was his duty and obligation—the man was a majestic figure in his own right.

Antonina's grin was still on her face. She pointed over her shoulder with a thumb to the great field of monuments behind her.

"I would have thought you'd approve of this display," she said. "An aid to your task, showing the results of excessive royal self-esteem."

Ousanas cast a sour look at the stone ruins in question. "Nonsense," he replied forcefully. "Maintaining this grotesque and useless field is itself a testament to royal idiocy. Who but cretin kings would need to waste so much good land for such a trivial purpose? A child requires no more than the memory of his last set of bruises."

He began stalking off, headed toward the Ta'akha

Maryam. "We'd do better just to haul the negusa nagast out of his palace, once or twice a year, and thrash him soundly." He repeated Antonina's gesture, pointing with his thumb at the ruins over his shoulder. "Then we could turn this into good farmland. Raise crops for needy children. Feed poor dawazz, weak from his endless labor like Sisyphus."

Antonina glanced at Eon, walking alongside her. She was expecting to see the prince's face twisted into a scowl, hearing Ousanas' outrageous proposals. But, to her surprise, Eon's expression was one of sly amusement.

The dawazz, it seemed, had done his work well.

"And just who would do all that work, Ousanas?" asked the prince. "Hauling great stones, thousands of them, out of that field. Backbreaking work, day after day after day. Take years, probably. *You?*"

Ousanas' snort was answer enough.

"Thought not," mused Eon. "No sane man would. No *free* man, that is. So we'd have to reinstitute mass slavery. Give the King of Kings a whole army of slaves—*again*—just like in the old days."

Eon's grin did not quite match those which his dawazz usually employed, but it came close.

"So," he concluded cheerfully, "in order to accomplish your goal of abasing royalty, we'd have to elevate royalty to its grandiose status of old. Good thinking, Ousanas!" The prince shook his head in a gesture of exaggerated chagrin. "I'm ashamed of myself! All these years, I thought your obsession with philosophy was a waste of time. But now, I see—"

Ousanas interrupted: "Enough!" He stopped abruptly, and stared at the distant mountains which surrounded the Hatsebo plain. His expression, from a scowl of irritation, faded into one of thoughtfulness.

"You see those mountains?" he asked softly. "Impossible to reach, the greatest of them. Just so do men stare at justice and righteousness. An unattainable goal, but one which we must always keep in our sight. Or we will drown in the madness of the pit."

He puffed his cheeks, and then blew out the breath slowly. "It's a pity, all things considered, that democracy doesn't work," he mused. "But the Greeks proved that, along with so much else. Smartest people in the world, Greeks. Who else would be deluded enough to try running a country with no king?"

He shook his head sadly. "All they ever did was fight and bicker and squabble. Endless wars between petty states—never could run more than a city, at best!—and all for nothing. Ruin and destruction—just read Thucydides." Another shake of his head. "Finally, of course, sensible people like the great Philip of Macedon put an end to the silly business."

Still staring at the mountains, Ousanas sighed heavily. "Got to have kings, and emperors, and the whole lot of puffed-up pigeons. No way around it. Somebody's got to give the orders."

He turned to face the young prince who had been placed in his charge so many years before. Now, he smiled. A rare expression that was, for the dawazz. A beaming grin was often found on his face. But Antonina, watching, could not remember ever having seen such a simple, gentle smile on the face of the man named Ousanas.

"You are a good boy, Eon," said the hunter. "Tomorrow you will be proclaimed a man, and I will no longer be your dawazz. So I will say this now, and only this once."

Ousanas bowed his head, just slightly. "It has been a privilege to be your dawazz, and a pleasure. And I do not really think, when all is said and done, that my labor has been that of Sisyphus."

Eon stared up at the tall figure of the man who had guided him, and taught him, and—most of all—chastened and chastised him for all those years. There was a hint of moisture in his eyes.

"And I could not have found," he replied, "not anywhere in the world, a better man to be my dawazz."

Tentatively, almost timidly, Eon reached out his hand and placed it on Ousanas' arm. "You have nothing to fear tomorrow," he said softly.

The normal and proper relation between dawazz and prince returned. Ousanas immediately slapped Eon on his head. Very hard.

"Fool boy!" he cried. "Of course I have something to fear! Entire Dakuen sarwe—half of it, anyway, and that's more than enough to do for my poor bones!—will be standing in judgement. Of *me*, not you!"

He turned to Antonina, his face twisting into a grimace. His eyes were almost bulging. "Axumite sarwen most pitiless creatures in universe! Soldiers—cruel and brutal! And this—this—" He pointed an accusing finger at Eon. "This *idiot prince* says I have nothing to fear!"

He threw up his hands. "I am lost!" he cried. "Years of work—for nothing. Boy still as mindless as ever!" Again, he began stalking off. Over his shoulder: "Royalty stupid by nature, as I've always said. The Dakuen sarwe will do what it wills, cretin-maybe-someday-king! Pay no attention to *you*."

Antonina and Eon began following him. Faintly, they could hear Ousanas' grumbling.

"Idiot Ethiopians and their imbecile customs. Had any sense, they'd beat the prince instead of the poor dawazz." A low, heartfelt moan. "Why did I ever do this? Could have stayed in central Africa. Doing simple safe work. Hunting lions and elephants, and other sane endeavors."

Antonina leaned over and whispered: "Is he really worried, Eon? About the judgement, tomorrow?"

Eon smiled. "I do not think so, not really. But you know Ousanas. All that philosophy makes him gloomy." His expression changed, a bit. "And he is right about the one thing. Only the Dakuen sarwe's opinion will matter, come tomorrow morning. It is not a public ceremony. No one else will be there—not even the king himself. Only the soldiers of my regiment."

Antonina started with surprise. "But—why then was *I* invited? Wahsi asked me to come, just yesterday. He was quite insistent about it—and he's now the commander of the regiment."

Eon cocked his eye at her. "You are not a guest, Antonina. You will be there as a *witness*."

When the Ta'akha Maryam was looming before them, Antonina shook off her pensive thoughts and remembered her mission. With a few quick steps, she caught up with Ousanas.

"I really think we should go visit the Tomb of Bazen," she said, "before we return to the royal compound. And the rock-cut burial pits nearby! Eon's told me all about them."

Ousanas stopped dead in his tracks and stared down at her.

"What for?" he demanded, scowling. "They're just more graves, for ancient men possessed by ridiculous notions of their importance in the scheme of things." With a snort: "Besides, they're empty. Robbers—sane men!—plundered them long ago."

Patiently, Antonina explained.

"*Because*, Ousanas, I really think the negusa nagast would appreciate a full day to consult with his advisers, without the presence of the Roman Empire's ambassador. Two full days, actually—since I'll be tied up all day tomorrow at the Dakuen sarwe's ceremony."

Ousanas was not mollified. Rather the contrary, in fact.

"Marvelous," he growled. "I'd forgotten. One of the witnesses for the prince's sanity is a madwoman herself. Come to Axum to propose all-out war against the world's most powerful empire, for no good reason except that her husband has visions."

He resumed his stalking, headed now toward the Tomb of Bazen to the east. Antonina and Eon followed, a few steps behind.

After they had gone a few yards in their new direction, Antonina turned her head toward Eon. She was about to make some jocular remark about Ousanas, but a movement near the Ta'akha Maryam caught her eye.

Three men were racing away from the royal compound, as if being chased by a lion. Two of them were Ethiopian, but the third—

She stopped, hissed. Eon turned his head to follow her gaze.

The third of the three men fleeing the Ta'akha Maryam caught sight of them. He stumbled to a halt and stared. At the distance—perhaps fifty yards—Antonina couldn't make out his features clearly, but two things were obvious.

First, he was Indian. Second, he was cursing bitterly.

An instant later, the man resumed his flight.

"Ousanas!" called out Eon.

But the hunter had already spotted the men. And, quicker than either of his two companions, deduced the truth. Ousanas sprang on Eon and Antonina like a lion, swept them up, one in each arm, and tackled them to the ground.

The impact knocked the wind out of Antonina. The incredible explosion which followed stunned her halfsenseless.

She watched, paralyzed, as the royal compound erupted. At first, because of shock, she didn't realize what she was seeing. A paralyzing noise—rapid series of noises, actually, blurring together—was followed by a huge cloud of billowing dust. Then, within a split second, she saw great stones moving. Some of the smaller pieces were flung high into the sky, but most of the massive slabs which made up the Ta'akha Maryam simply heaved up. Seconds later, the compound began to collapse. The building which held the throne room was the first to go, buckling like a broken bridge. That set off a chain reaction, in which the toppling walls of one room or building caused its neighbor to cave in as well. The sound of screams was buried beneath the uproar of collapsing masonry. By the time the process ground to a halt, perhaps a minute later, over a third of the Ta'akha Maryam was nothing but a heap of rubble. The noise of destruction faded into a chill silence—except for one faint shriek of agony, spilling across the dust-clouded landscape like a trail of blood.

Long before that time, Antonina realized what had happened. The first billowing gust had brought a sharp and familiar smell to her nostrils.

Gunpowder. *Lots* of gunpowder.

The Malwa Empire had struck. King Kaleb, the negusa nagast of Ethiopia, was lying somewhere under those stones. So was his older son, Wa'zeb, the heir. And so—if she hadn't insisted on a last-minute change of plans—would have been Antonina herself and Eon. She realized—dimly; still half-dazed—that the men who lit the fuse had waited until they were sure that she and Eon were about to enter the royal compound.

Painfully, Antonina levered herself up. They wouldn't know until the rubble was searched, but she strongly suspected that Eon was the sole survivor of the royal dynasty. And he was not even a man yet, by the customs of his people—not until the morrow's ceremony.

Eon Bisi Dakuen, Prince of Axum, was already on his feet. He was staring at the figure of Ousanas. The dawazz, his great spear in hand, was racing after the three men who had emerged from the Ta'akha Maryam. They had a two-hundred-yard lead on

Ousanas, and were running as fast as they could, but it only took Antonina a moment to gauge the outcome.

Eon, apparently, reached the same conclusion. He took two steps in that direction, as if to follow, but stopped. "Ousanas is the greatest hunter anyone in Axum ever saw," he murmured. "Those are dead men."

He turned, stooped, and helped Antonina to her feet. His face seemed far older than his years. Bleak, and bitter.

"Are you all right?" he asked. "I must organize the search for my father and brother." A wince of pain came. "And Zaia, and our daughter Miriam, and Tarabai. And my adviser Garmat. All of them were in there."

She nodded. "I'll help. Some of my people were in the Ta'akha Maryam, too."

Eon's eyes scanned the rubble. "The Roman delegation should be safe. The section of the royal compound where you were housed is still standing."

They began making their way toward the shattered compound. Noise was returning, now, in the form of shouting commands and pleas for help. People were already moving about the ruin, beginning to pluck at the crumpled stones. One of those men, catching sight of them, cried out with joy and began sprinting in their direction.

His joy was no greater than Antonina's, or Eon's. That man was named Wahsi, and he was the commander of the Dakuen sarwe.

The prince's regiment, once. Now, in all likelihood, the royal regiment.

Wahsi reached them and swept the prince into his embrace. Other soldiers of the Dakuen sarwe were following, and their own joy was quite evident.

Antonina heard Eon's muffled voice: "Gather the regiment, Wahsi. And the Lazen and the Hadefan sarawit, if my father and brother are dead. They must sit on Ousanas' judgement also, if I am to be the negusa nagast."

He pried himself loose from Wahsi's clasp. Then, his face still cold and bleak, he issued his commands: "First, we must search the ruins. Then we will have the ceremony, as soon as possible. There is no time to waste. This will not be Malwa's only blow. We are at war, and I intend to give them no respite. *And no quarter.*"

Wahsi nodded. His own expression was fierce. So were those on the faces of the soldiers standing around.

Antonina found herself seized by a sudden—and utterly inappropriate—urge to giggle. She fought it down savagely.

Bad move, Malwa. If you'd gotten Eon also—

But, you didn't. Bad move. Bad, bad, bad move.

Chapter 5

DEOGIRI

Spring, 532 A.D.

Nanda Lal, the Malwa Empire's chief spymaster, studied Deogiri. The walled city was two miles away from the hilltop where Nanda Lal was standing, just a few yards from Lord Venandakatra's pavilion. Venandakatra had placed his headquarters on the only hill in the area which approached Deogiri's elevation. The men who built Deogiri, centuries earlier, had designed the city for defense.

And designed it very well, he thought sourly.

Deogiri, upon whose ramparts Rao's rebels held Malwa at bay, was one of the best-fortified cities in India. The upper fortress was built on a conical rock at the top of a hill that rose almost perpendicularly from the surrounding plain a hundred fifty yards below. The outer wall of the city was nearly three miles in circumference, and three additional lines of fortification lay between it and the upper fortress. Throughout, the stonework was massive and well made.

Emperor Skandagupta had sent Nanda Lal here to

determine why Lord Venandakatra was having so much difficulty subduing the Deccan rebellion. The task had not taken the spymaster long in the doing. An hour's study of Deogiri was enough, coming on top of the days which Nanda Lal had spent travelling here from Bharakuccha. Days, protected by a large escort of Rajputs, creeping through the hills of Majarashtra. Days, expecting a Maratha ambush—and fighting three of them off.

His gloomy thoughts were interrupted by a shrill scream, coming from somewhere behind him. Nanda Lal did not turn his head. He knew the source of that shriek of agony. The first of the Maratha guerrillas which his Rajput escort had captured during the last ambush was being fitted to the stake.

For a moment, the sound cheered him up. But only for a moment. Every town in Majarashtra had corpses fitted onto stakes. Still, the rebellion swelled in strength.

Silently, Nanda Lal cursed the Great Country. Silently, he cursed Raghunath Rao. Silently, he cursed the "Empress" Shakuntala. But, most of all—

Hearing the approaching footsteps, he cursed their cause.

But most of all—curse you, Venandakatra! If you hadn't let Belisarius maneuver you into giving Rao his chance, Shakuntala would never have become such a thorn in our side.

He sighed, and turned away from Deogiri. The thing was done. Much as he would have liked to curse Venandakatra aloud—fit *him* to a stake, in truth—the unity of the Malwa dynastic clan had to be maintained. That, above all, was the foundation of Malwa's success.

"You see?" demanded Venandakatra, when he reached Nanda Lal's side. The Goptri of the Deccan pointed at Deogiri. "You see? Is it not just as I said?"

Nanda Lal scowled. "Do not push the matter,

cousin!" he snapped. "Deogiri was just as strong when *you* held it."

Venandakatra flushed. But the color in his flabby cheeks was due more to embarrassment than anger. His eyes fell away from Nanda Lal's level gaze.

Nanda Lal, as was his way, twisted the blade. "Before *you*—through your carelessness, Venandakatra—allowed Rao and his rebels to take Deogiri by surprise." The spymaster sneered. "No doubt you were preoccupied, raping another Maratha hill girl instead of attending to your duty."

Venandakatra clenched his jaws, but said nothing. His thin-boned, fat-sheathed frame was practically shaking from fury. But, still, he said nothing.

Nanda Lal allowed the silence to linger, for perhaps a minute. Then, with a little shrug, he let the tension ease from his own shoulders. Thick shoulders, those were. Heavy with muscle.

"Good," he murmured. "At least you have not lost your wits." Coldly: "Do not let your kin proximity to the emperor blind you to certain realities, Venandakatra. My bloodline is equal to your own, and I am second in power only to Skandagupta himself. Do not forget it."

Nanda Lal clapped a powerful hand on Venandakatra's shoulder. Under the fat, the thin bones felt like those of a chicken. The Goptri of the Deccan flinched, as much from the force of that "friendly" gesture as surprise.

"Enough said!" boomed Nanda Lal. With his hand still on Venandakatra's shoulder, he steered the Goptri toward the pavilion.

As they neared the pavilion's entrance, their progress was interrupted by another shriek of agony. The first Maratha captive had apparently expired, and the second was being fitted onto a stake.

Venandakatra found the courage to speak. "You should have used shorter stakes," he grumbled.

Nanda Lal chuckled. "Why bother?" He stopped, in order to examine the execution. The ground surrounding Venandakatra's pavilion had been packed down. Alongside the road which led north to Bharakuccha, six stakes had been erected. The first Maratha was dead, draped over his stake. The second was still screaming. The remaining four captives were bound and gagged. The gags would not be removed until the last moment, so that the Ye-tai conducting the execution would not be subject to curses.

"Why bother?" he repeated. "The terror campaign is necessary, Venandakatra, but do not put overmuch faith in it. The Great Country is littered with skeletons on stakes. How much good has it done?"

Venandakatra opened his mouth, as if to argue the point. But, again, discretion came to his rescue.

Nanda Lal took a deep breath, and blew it out slowly through his nose. "The emperor and I will tolerate your sadism, Venandakatra," he murmured softly. "Up to a point. That point ends when your lusts interfere with your duty."

Throughout, Nanda Lal's hand had never left Venandakatra's shoulder. Now, with a shove, he forced the Goptri into the pavilion.

The pavilion's interior was lavish with furnishings. Thick carpets covered every inch of the floor. The sloping cotton walls were lined with statuary, silk tapestries, and finely crafted side tables bearing an assortment of carvings and jewelry.

With another shove, Nanda Lal pushed Venandakatra toward the great pile of cushions at the center of the pavilion. A third shove sent the Goptri sprawling onto them. Venandakatra was now hissing with outrage but, still, he spoke no words of protest.

Satisfied that he had cowed the man sufficiently, Nanda Lal scanned the interior of the pavilion. His eyes fell on a cluster of Maratha girls in a corner.

They ranged in age from ten to thirteen, he estimated. All of them were naked and chained. The current members of Venandakatra's harem. Judging from their scars and bruises, and the dull fear in their faces, they would not survive any longer than their many predecessors.

That should finish the work, thought Nanda Lal. He turned his head to the Rajput officer standing guard by the pavilion's entrance.

"Take them out"—he pointed to the girls—"and kill them. Do it now."

Seeing the rigidity in the Rajput's face, Nanda Lal snorted. "Behead them, that's enough." The Rajput nodded stiffly and advanced on the girls. A moment later, he was leading them out of the pavilion by their chains.

The girls did not protest, nor make any attempt to struggle. Nanda Lal was not surprised. Marathi-speaking peasant girls, from their look. They probably didn't understand Hindi and, even if they did—

His eyes fell on Venandakatra, gasping with outrage.

I probably did them a favor, and they know it.

Nanda Lal waited until the sound of a sword cleaving through a neck filtered into the pavilion.

"So, Venandakatra, let us deal with your duty. With no further distractions. Now that I have investigated the situation, I will recommend to the emperor that your request for siege guns be granted."

The spymaster nodded toward the north. "But you will have to be satisfied with the guns at Bharakuccha. Six of them—that should be enough. And there will be no other reinforcements. The war in Persia has proven more difficult than we foresaw, thanks to Belisarius."

He shrugged. "It would take too long to bring siege guns across the Vindhyas, anyway. As it is, hauling the great things here will take months, even from Bharakuccha."

Venandakatra's face lost its expression of outrage. Anger came, instead—anger and satisfaction.

"At last!" he exclaimed. "I will take Deogiri!" He clenched his bony fingers into a fist. "Rao will be mine! He and the Satavahana bitch! I will stake them side by side!"

Nanda Lal studied him for a moment. "Let us hope so, Venandakatra."

He turned away and strode to the pavilion entrance. There, the spymaster filled his nostrils with clean air.

Let us hope so, Venandakatra. For the sake of the Empire. Were it not for that, I would almost wish for your failure.

His eyes fell on the execution ground. The six Maratha rebels were all dead, now. Their bodies were draped over the stakes. Their heads lolled, as if they were mourning their sisters sprawled on the ground in front of them. Five heads, and five headless corpses, naked in a spreading lake of blood.

You would look good on a stake, Venandakatra. Splendid, in fact.

Chapter 6
SUPPARA
Spring, 532 A.D.

Irene Macrembolitissa, the Roman Empire's ambassador to the rebels of south India, strode down one of the corridors in Empress Shakuntala's small palace, head deep in thought. The Empress of Andhra—it was a grandiose title, for a young girl leading a rebellion against Malwa, but one to which she was legitimately entitled—had requested Irene's presence in the imperial audience chamber. It seemed that Kungas had finally returned from his long journey to the rebel-held city of Deogiri. Shakuntala wanted Rome's envoy present, to hear his report.

Irene had never met Kungas. She knew of him, of course. Kungas was one of the top military commanders of Shakuntala's small army. He bore the resplendent titles of *Mahadandanayaka* and *Bhatasvapati*—"great commandant" and "lord of army and cavalry." He was also the head of Shakuntala's personal bodyguard, an elite body made up entirely of Kushans.

Before she left Constantinople, Belisarius had provided Irene with a full and thorough assessment of Kungas. He knew the Kushan from his trip to India, and was obviously taken by him. Without quite saying so, Belisarius had left Irene the impression that Kungas' advice and opinions should be given the utmost care and consideration.

Privately, Irene had her doubts. She was one of the Roman Empire's most accomplished spymasters—an unusual occupation for a woman, especially a Greek noblewoman—and she had generally found that male military leaders were too heavily influenced by the martial accomplishments of other men. That Kungas was shrewd and cunning on the battlefield, Irene did not doubt for a moment. That did not necessarily translate into the kind of skills which were necessary for an imperial adviser.

Head down, striding along in her usual brisk and long-legged style, Irene tightened her lips. The upcoming session, she thought, would be difficult.

The young empress doted on Kungas, so much was obvious. Knowing the history of Shakuntala and Kungas' relationship, Irene did not find the girl's attitude odd. Kushans were Malwa vassals, and Kungas had been the man assigned as Shakuntala's guard and captor after the Malwa had conquered her father's empire of Andhra. He had saved her from rape, at the sack of Amaravati. Had held her safe, until Belisarius and Rao rescued her—and had then, learning the secret of that rescue, held his tongue and kept the secret from his Malwa masters. In the end, he and his men had thrown off their loyalty to Malwa and smuggled Shakuntala to south India. Since then, they had saved her life more than once from Malwa assassination teams.

The fact remained, he was nothing more than a semibarbarian warlord. Not even literate, by all accounts.

Irene was not looking forward to the upcoming session. *She would have to steer a delicate course between offending the empress and—*

Paying no attention to anything but her thoughts, Irene swept into a junction with another corridor and crashed into an unseen obstacle.

For a moment, she almost lost her footing. Only a desperate hand, reaching out to clutch the object into which she had hurtled, kept her from an undignified landing on her backside.

Startled, she looked up and found herself gazing into the statue of a steppe warrior. Into the face of the statue, more precisely. A bronze and rigid mask, apparently part of a single casting. Stiff, still, unmoving. Extremely well done, she noted, all the way down to the lifelike armor and horsehair topknot.

But the artistry of the piece did not leave her mollified.

"What idiot left a statue in the middle of a corridor?" she hissed angrily. Then, after a brief second scrutiny: "Ugly damned thing, too."

The statue moved. Its lips, at least. Irene was so startled she actually jumped.

"Horses think I'm pretty," said the statue, in heavily accented but understandable Greek. "Why else do they give me such playful nips?"

Irene gasped, clasping a hand over her mouth. She stepped back a pace or two. "You're *real*!"

The statue gazed down at its body. "So I am told by my scholarly friend Dadaji," the thing rasped. "But I am not a student of philosophy, myself, so I can't vouch for it."

For all that she was startled, Irene's quick mind had not deserted her. "You must be Kungas," she stated. "You fit Belisarius' description."

At first, Irene thought she was several inches taller than he. But closer examination revealed that Kungas was not more than an inch below her own height.

It was just that the man was so stocky, in a thick-chested and muscular fashion, that he looked shorter than he actually was. Beyond that, his whole body—especially his face—looked as if it were made of metal, or polished wood, rather than flesh. She did not think she had ever seen a human being in her life who seemed so utterly—*hard*.

His features were typically Kushan. Asiatic, steppe features: yellowish complexion, flat nose, eyes which seemed slanted due to the fold in the corners, a tight-lipped mouth. His beard was a wispy goatee, and the mustache adorning his upper lip was no more than a thin line of hair. Most of his scalp was shaved, except for a clot of coarse black hair gathered into a topknot.

Kungas returned Irene's scrutiny with one of his own. His next words startled her almost as much as the collision.

"You have beautiful eyes," he announced. "Very intelligent. And so I am puzzled."

Irene frowned. "Puzzled by what?"

"Why are you wearing such a stupid costume?" he asked, gesturing to the heavy Roman robes. "In *this* climate?"

Kungas' lips seemed to twitch. Irene thought that might be a smile. She wasn't sure.

"I grant you," he continued, "many of the Indian customs are ridiculous. But the women are quite sensible when it comes to their clothing. You would do much better to wear a sari, and leave your mid-riff bare."

Irene grinned. "I'm a diplomat," she explained. "Got to maintain my ambassadorial dignity. Especially since I'm a woman. Everybody looks at these absurd robes instead of me. So all they see is the Roman Empire, rather than the foreign *female*."

"Ah." Kungas nodded. "Good thinking."

"You must be on your way to the audience

chamber yourself," said Irene. She cocked her head to the side. "The empress will be delighted to see you. She has missed you, I think. Although she says nothing."

Now, finally, Kungas did smile. "She never does. Lest people see the uncertain girl, instead of the ruler of Andhra."

He made a slight bow. "Envoy from Rome, I must give my report to the empress. May I escort you to the audience chamber?"

Irene bowed in return, and nodded graciously. Side by side, she and Kungas headed toward the great double doors at the end of the corridor.

From the corner of her eye, Irene studied Kungas. She was a bit fascinated by the way he moved. Silently, and surely—more like a cat than a thick, stocky man. But, mostly, she was fascinated by Kungas himself. Such a thick, hard, rigid statue, he seemed. But she had not missed the warm humor lurking inside the bronze casting, nor the intelligence.

Then, turning her eyes to the front, she gave her head a little shake.

You're the envoy from Rome, she reminded herself. For a moment, her fingers plucked at her heavy robes. *So just forget it, woman. Besides, the man can't even read.*

"How long does Rao think it will take Venandakatra to bring up the siege guns?" asked Shakuntala. The empress, seated on a plush cushion, leaned forward from her lotus position. Her brow was wrinkled, as if she were a schoolgirl straining to understand a lesson.

Irene was not fooled by Shakuntala's resemblance to a young student. *That is one very worried monarch*, she thought, watching from her vantage point against the east wall of the small audience chamber.

Irene's translator leaned over, whispering, but she

stilled him with a gesture. Her Hindi had improved well enough that she was able to follow the discussion. Irene had an aptitude for languages—that skill was a necessity for a spymaster in Rome's polyglot empire—and she had been tutored by Belisarius before leaving Constantinople. In the months since her arrival at Suppara, she had been immersed in Hindi. *And* Marathi. As was true of most Indian monarchs, Shakuntala used Hindi as the court language, but Irene had begun learning the common tongue of Majarashtra as well.

"How long?" repeated the empress.

Seated easily in his own lotus position, Kungas shrugged. "It is difficult to say, Your Majesty. Many factors are involved. The siege guns were at Bharakuccha. Venandakatra has thus been forced to haul them across the Great Country. Very difficult terrain, as you know, through which to move huge war engines. And Rao has been harassing the Malwa column with his mountain fighters."

"Can he stop them?" demanded Shakuntala. "Before they can bring the guns to Deogiri?"

Kungas shook his head. As with all the man's gestures, the movement was slight—but emphatic, for all that.

"Not a chance, Your Majesty. He can slow it down, but he does not have the forces to stop it. Venandakatra has reinforced the column's escort with every spare military unit at his disposal. He cannot reduce Deogiri without those guns—and *with* them, he cannot fail. Any one of those cannons is big enough to shatter Deogiri's walls, and he has six of them."

Shakuntala winced. For a moment, Kungas' face seemed to soften. Just a tiny bit.

"There is this much, Your Majesty," he added. "The Vile One has been forced to end the punitive raids in the countryside. He cannot spare the men. Every cavalry troop he has, beyond the ones investing Deogiri, are assigned to guard the column bringing the cannons."

Shakuntala rubbed her face. For all her youth, it seemed an old, tired gesture. Venandakatra's atrocities in the Maratha countryside, Irene knew, had preyed heavily on her soul. Even by Malwa standards, Venandakatra was a beast. The man's official title was Goptri of the Deccan—the "Warden of the Marches," assigned by the Malwa emperor to subjugate his most unruly new province. But by Marathas themselves, the man was called nothing but the Vile One.

Shakuntala's face rubbing ended, within seconds. Her natural energy and assertiveness returned.

"It is up to us, then," she pronounced. "We must organize a relief column of our own."

The two Maratha cavalry officers seated next to Kungas stirred, and glanced at each other. The senior of them, a general by the name of Shahji, cleared his throat and spoke.

"I do not think that is wise, Empress. We have been able to hold Suppara, and the coast, but our forces are still not strong enough to relieve Rao at Deogiri."

"Unless we took our whole army," qualified Kondev, the other Maratha general. "But that would leave Suppara defenseless."

Shakuntala's face tightened. Kondev drove home the point:

"You have a responsibility here also, Your Majesty."

"I can't simply let Rao be destroyed!" snapped the empress. She glared angrily at the two Maratha cavalry generals.

Shakuntala's chief adviser, Dadaji Holkar, intervened. As always, the scholarly *peshwa*—"premier," Irene translated the term—spoke softly and calmly. And, as always, his tone calmed the empress.

Although, thought Irene, his words did not.

"There is the *other* alternative, Your Majesty."

Holkar's statement seemed to strike Shakuntala like a blow, or a reprimand. The young empress' face grew pinched, and Irene thought she almost recoiled.

Holkar's lips tightened, for a moment. To Irene, his eyes seemed sad.

Sad, but determined.

"If we insist, as a condition to the marriage," he continued, "I am quite certain that the Cholas will send an army. A large enough army to relieve Deogiri, without requiring us to abandon Suppara."

Holkar glanced quickly at Kungas. "At the time, I thought Kungas was unwise, to urge you to decline the offer of marriage from the Prince of Tamraparni. But his advice proved correct. The Cholas *did* make a better offer."

His gaze returned to the empress. Still sad, but still determined.

"*As you know*," he stated, gently but emphatically. "I read you the text of their offer last week. You said that you wanted to think about it. I suggest that the time for thinking is over."

Again, Holkar glanced at Kungas. More of a lingering look, actually. Irene, watching, was puzzled by Holkar's stare. It seemed more one of anger—irritation, perhaps, and apprehensiveness—than admiration and approval. And she noticed that the empress herself was staring at Kungas rather oddly. Almost as if she were beseeching him.

For his part, Kungas returned their gazes with nothing beyond masklike imperturbability.

Something's going on here, thought Irene.

As other advisers began speaking, also urging the marriage on the empress, Irene's quick mind flitted over the situation. She knew of the Chola king's offer of his oldest son in marriage to Shakuntala. Irene had learned about it almost as soon as Shakuntala herself. The Greek spymaster had begun creating her own network of informants from the moment she arrived in India. But Irene had simply filed the information away for later consideration.

Irene had realized, weeks ago, that the subject of Shakuntala's possible dynastic marriage was a source of considerable tension in the palace. Such a marriage would produce an immediate improvement in the position of the young empress. Yet, she was obviously unhappy at the prospect, and avoided the subject whenever her advisers raised it.

At first, Irene had ascribed Shakuntala's hesitation to the natural reluctance of a strong-willed female ruler to give up any portion of her power and independence. (An attitude which Irene, given her own temperament and personality, understood perfectly.) As the weeks passed, however, Irene had decided that more was involved.

The young empress never discussed the subject, except in political and military terms, but Irene suspected that her feelings on Deogiri were personal as well. Deogiri—and, more specifically, the man who was in command of the rebel forces there.

Irene had never met Raghunath Rao, no more than she had Kungas. But Belisarius had spoken about him many times, also—and at even greater length than on the subject of Kungas. To her astonishment, Irene had eventually realized that Belisarius was a bit in awe of the man—an attitude which she had never seen the Roman general take toward anyone else in the world.

Raghunath Rao. She rolled the glamorous, exotic-sounding name over a silent tongue, her mind only half-following the enthusiastic jabberings of the junior advisers. (Every one of whom, she noted, agreed with the peshwa Dadaji Holkar. But Kungas had not spoken yet.)

The Panther of Majarashtra. The Wind of the Great Country. The national hero of the Marathas, and a legend throughout all of India. The only man who ever fought the Rajput king Rana Sanga to a draw, after an entire day spent in single combat.

Raghunath Rao. One of India's greatest assassins, among other things. The man who slaughtered—single-handedly, no less—two dozen of her captors in the Vile One's palace in order to rescue Shakuntala from captivity, after Belisarius, through a ruse, saw to the removal of Kungas and her Kushan guards.

Rao, the supreme Andhra loyalist, did so in order to rescue the legitimate heir of the dynasty. Yes, of course. But he was also rescuing the girl whom he had raised since the age of seven, after her father, the Emperor of Andhra, had placed the child in the Maratha chieftain's care. The mutual devotion between Rao and Shakuntala was something of a legend itself, by now.

To all outward appearances, it was the attachment of a young woman and her older mentor. But Irene suspected that under the surface lay much more passionate sentiments. Sentiments which were perhaps all the fiercer, for never having been spoken or acted on by either person.

The junior advisers were still jabbering, so Irene continued her ruminations. Irene had her own opinion regarding the question of Shakuntala's possible dynastic marriage. That opinion was still tentative, but it seemed to her that Shakuntala's advisers were missing—

Her thoughts broke off. Kungas was finally speaking.

"I disagree. I think this is all quite premature." His words were all the more forceful for the quiet manner in which he spoke them. Kungas' voice exuded the same sense of iron certainty as his mask of a face. "The Chola offer, as I understand it, is filled with quibbles and reservations."

Holkar began to interrupt, but Kungas drove on.

"If the empress breaks the siege of Deogiri," he stated, "and thereby proves that she can hold southern Majarashtra, there will certainly be a better offer. From someone, if not the Cholas."

Holkar threw up his hands. "*If! If!*" He lowered his hands and, with an obvious effort, brought himself under control. Irene realized that—unusually, for the mild-mannered peshwa—the man was genuinely angry.

"*If*, Kungas," he repeated, through teeth that were almost clenched. "*If*." Holkar leaned forward, slapping the rug before him emphatically. "But that is precisely the point! We do not have the troops to simultaneously relieve Deogiri and hold Suppara and the coast."

Holkar sprang to his feet and strode over to a window in the west wall. He stared out at the ocean lying beyond. From her vantage point on the opposite side of the chamber, Irene could not see the ocean itself, but she knew what the peshwa was looking at.

Malwa warships, dozens of them. Holding position, as they had for weeks, just out of range of the three great cannons protecting Suppara's harbor. Each of those warships had a large contingent of marines, ready to land at a moment's notice.

The Malwa had made no attempt to storm Suppara for months now. But in the first few weeks after Irene was smuggled through the blockade on an Axumite vessel, she had watched while they made three furious assaults. Each of those attacks had been beaten off, but it had taken the efforts of all of Shakuntala's soldiers—as well as the four hundred Ethiopian sarwen under Ezana's command—to do so.

Holkar turned away from the window. He gave Kungas a hard, stony look, before turning his eyes to Shakuntala. "Shahji and Kondev are correct, Empress. We cannot relieve the siege of Deogiri without leaving Suppara defenseless. I do not therefore see—"

"We do not have to *relieve* Deogiri," interrupted Kungas. "We simply have to destroy the siege guns."

Holkar froze. Still standing, he frowned down at Kungas.

The Kushan warrior's shoulders seemed to twitch, just a bit. Irene, learning to interpret Kungas' economical gestures, decided that was a shrug. With just a hint of irony, she thought. Perhaps some amusement.

What an interesting man. Who would have expected so much subtlety, in such an ugly lump?

"Explain, Kungas," said Shahji.

Again, Kungas' shoulders made that tiny twitch. "I discussed the situation with Rao. The problem is not the siege itself. Rao is quite certain that he can hold Deogiri from the Vile One's army. You are Maratha, Shahji. You know how strong those walls are. Deogiri is the most impregnable city in the Great Country."

Shahji nodded. So did Kondev.

"Water is not a problem," continued Kungas. "Deogiri has its own wells. Nor is Rao concerned about starvation. Venandakatra simply doesn't have enough troops to completely seal off Deogiri. The Panther's men are all Maratha. They know the countryside, and have the support of the people there. Since the beginning of the siege, Rao has been able to smuggle food and provisions through the Vile One's lines. And he long ago smuggled out all of the civilians of the city. He only has to feed his own troops."

Kungas lifted his right hand from his knee and turned it over. "So, you see, the only problem is the actual *guns*. We don't have to relieve the siege. We simply have to destroy those guns, or capture them."

"And how will we do *that*?" demanded Holkar.

Before Kungas could respond, Kondev threw in his

own objection. "And even if we do, Venandakatra will simply bring in more."

Irene hesitated. Her most basic instinct as a spymaster—*never let anyone know how much you know*—was warring with her judgement.

I'm the envoy from Rome, she reminded her instinct firmly. She leaned forward in her chair—Shakuntala had thoughtfully provided them for the Romans, knowing they were unaccustomed to sitting on cushions—and cleared her throat.

"He can't," she said firmly. "He's stripped Bharakuccha of every siege gun he has. Those cannons—there are only five of them left, Kungas, by the way; one of them was destroyed recently, falling off a cliff—are the only ones the Malwa have in the Deccan. To get more, they'd have to bring them from the Gangetic plain, across the Vindhya mountains. That would take at least a year. And Emperor Skandagupta just informed Venandakatra, in a recent letter, that the Vile One will have to rely on his own resources for a while. It seems the war in Persia is proving more difficult than the Malwa had anticipated."

She leaned back, smiling. "He was quite irate, actually. Most of his anger was directed at Belisarius, but some of it is spilling over on Venandakatra. Emperor Skandagupta does not understand, as he puts it, why the 'illustrious Goptri' is having so much difficulty subduing—as he puts it—'a handful of unruly rebels.' "

Everyone was staring at her, eyes wide open. Except Kungas, she saw. The Kushan was looking at her also, but his gaze seemed less one of surprise than—

Interest? Irene lowered her own eyes, plucking at her robes. For a moment, looking down, she caught sight of her nose.

Damn great ugly beak.

She brushed back her hair and raised her head. *Envoy from Rome*, she reminded herself firmly.

The wide-eyed stares were still there.

"Is your spy network really *that* good?" asked Holkar, a bit shakily. "*Already?* You've only been here for—"

He broke off, as if distracted by another thought.

Irene coughed. "Well . . . *Yes*, peshwa, it is that good."

She gave Shakuntala an apologetic little nod. "I was intending to give you this latest information at our next meeting, Your Majesty." The empress acknowledged the apology with a nod of her own.

Irene turned her gaze back to Kungas.

"So that objection to the Bhatasvapati's proposal is moot," she said. "But I confess that I have no idea how he intends to destroy the existing guns."

Kungas began to explain. Irene listened carefully to his plan. She was required to do so, not simply by her position as the envoy of Rome, but by the nature of the plan itself. At one point, in fact, the meeting was suspended while Irene sent for one of the Syrian gunners who had accompanied her to India, in order to clarify a technical problem.

So, throughout the long session, Irene was attentive to Kungas' proposal. But there was a part of her mind, lurking far back, which focused on the man himself.

When the session was over, and she was striding back to her rooms, she found it necessary to discipline that wayward part.

The envoy of Rome! Besides, it's absurd. I'm the world's most incorrigible bookworm, and he's an illiterate. Ugly, to boot.

Not long after arriving in her quarters, a servant announced the arrival of the peshwa.

Irene put down her book, a copy of the *Periplus*

Maris Erythraei, and rose to greet her visitor. She had been expecting Dadaji Holkar, and she was quite certain why he had come.

The peshwa was ushered into her chamber. The middle-aged scholar seemed awkward, and ill at ease. He began to fumble for words, staring at the floor.

"Yes, Dadaji," said Irene. "I will instruct my spies to search for your family."

Holkar's head jerked up with surprise. Then, lowered.

"I should not ask," he muttered. "It is a private matter. Not something which—"

"You did not ask," pointed out Irene. "I volunteered."

The demands of her profession had trained Irene to maintain an aloof, calculating stance toward human suffering. But, for a moment, she felt a deep empathy for the man in front of her.

Dadaji Holkar, for all the prestige of his current status as the peshwa of India's most ancient and noble dynasty, was a low-caste scribe in his origins. After the Malwa had conquered Andhra, Dadaji—and his whole family—had been sold into slavery. Belisarius had purchased Holkar while he was in India, in order to use the man's literary skills to advance his plot against Venandakatra. In the end, Holkar had been instrumental in effecting Shakuntala's escape and had become her closest adviser.

But his family—his wife, son, and two daughters—were still in captivity. Somewhere in the vastness of Malwa India.

It was typical of Holkar, she thought, that he would even hesitate to ask for a personal favor. Most Indian officials—most officials of *any* country, in her experience—took personal favors as a matter of due course.

She smiled, brushing back her hair. "It's not a problem, Dadaji. It will be an opportunity, actually.

To begin with, it'll give my spies a challenge. The Malwa run an excellent espionage service, but they have grown too confident and sure of themselves. Quite easy to penetrate, actually. Whereas finding a few Maratha slaves, scattered across India, will test their skills."

She pursed her lips, thinking for a moment, before adding: "And there's more. I've been thinking, anyway, that we should start probing the sentiments of the lower classes in Malwa India. A very good way to do that is to have my spies scouring India looking for some Maratha slaves."

"Can you find them?" he asked, in a whisper.

"I can promise you nothing, Dadaji. But I will try."

He nodded, and left. Irene returned to her chair. But she had not read more than a page of the *Periplus* when the servant announced another visitor.

The Bhatasvapati was here.

Irene rose again. She was interested—and a bit annoyed—to find that her emotions were unsettled. She was even more interested—and not annoyed at all—to realize that she had no idea why Kungas had come.

I like surprises. I get so few of them.

When Kungas came into her chamber, Irene got her first surprise. As soon as he entered, he glanced over his shoulder and said: "I saw Dadaji leaving, just a minute ago. I don't think he even noticed me, he seemed so preoccupied."

Kungas swiveled his head back to face her. "He came to speak to you about his family," he stated. "To ask you for your help in finding them."

Irene's eyes narrowed. "How did you know?"

Kungas made the little shoulder-twitch which served him for a shrug. "There are only two reasons he would come here, right after the session in the imperial audience chamber. That is one of them. Like everyone else, he was impressed by your spy network."

"And the other reason?"

Kungas seemed to be examining her carefully. "The other reason would be to discuss with you the question of Empress Shakuntala's marriage prospects. He is much concerned with that subject, and would want to enlist the support of the Roman envoy."

Kungas' looked away for a moment, in a quick scrutiny of the chamber. The furniture he gave no more than a glance, but his gaze lingered on a chest in the corner. The lid was open, and he could see that it was full of books.

When his eyes returned to Irene, she thought there was some impish humor lurking within them.

She got her second surprise.

"But I knew that couldn't be it. He would not have left so soon. You do not agree with him, I think, and so he would have stayed to argue."

"How do you know my opinion?" she demanded.

Again, the little shoulder-twitch. "It is—not obvious, no. Nothing about you is obvious. But I do not think you agree that the empress should make a dynastic marriage with one of the independent south Indian monarchies."

Irene studied Kungas for a moment, in silence. "No, I don't," she said slowly. "I am not certain of my opinion yet, mind you. But I think . . . " She hesitated.

Kungas held up his hand. "Please! I am not prying, envoy from Rome. We can discuss this matter at a later time, when you think it more suitable. For the moment—"

A very faint smile came to his lips. "Let me just say that I suspect you look at the thing as I do. A monarch should marry the power which can uphold the throne. And so the thing is obvious—to any but these idiot Indians, with their absurd fetishes."

Irene suppressed her little start of surprise. But Kungas' eyes were knowing.

"So I thought," he murmured. "Very smart woman."

He turned away, heading for the door. "But that is not why I came," he said. "A moment, please. My servant is carrying something for me."

Irene watched while Kungas took something from the servant who appeared in the doorway. When he turned back, she got her third surprise. Kungas was carrying a stack of books.

He held them out to her. "Can you read these?"

Hesitantly, Irene took the top book and opened it. She began to scan the first page. Then stopped, frowning.

"This isn't Greek," she muttered. "I thought it was, but—"

"The lettering is Greek," explained Kungas. "When we Kushans conquered Bactria, long ago, we adopted the Greek alphabet. But the language is my own."

He fumbled with the stack of books, drawing out a slim volume buried in the middle.

"This might help," he said. "It is a bilingual translation of some of the Buddha's teachings. Half-Greek; half-Kushan." His lips twitched. "Or so my friend Dadaji tells me. He can read the Greek part. I can't read any of it. I am not literate."

Irene set the first book down on a nearby table and took the one in Kungas' outstretched hand. She began studying the volume. After a few seconds, without being conscious of the act, she moved over to her chair and sat down. As ever, with true bibliophiles, the act of reading had drawn her completely out of her immediate surroundings.

Two minutes later, she remembered Kungas. Looking up, she saw that the Kushan was still standing in the middle of the room, watching her.

"I'm sorry," she said. She waved her hand at a nearby chair.

Kungas shook his head. "I am quite comfortable, thank you." He pointed to the book. "What do you think?"

Irene looked down at the volume in her lap. "I *could*, yes." She looked up. "But why should I? It will be a considerable effort."

Kungas nodded. Then, slowly, he moved over to the one window in her room and stared out at the ocean. The window was open, letting in the cooling breeze.

"It is difficult to explain," he said, speaking as slowly as he had moved. He fell silent for a few seconds, before turning back to her rather abruptly.

"Do you believe there is such a thing as a soul?" he asked.

Somehow, the question did not surprise her. "Yes," she replied instantly. "I do."

Kungas fingered his wispy beard. "I am not so sure, myself." He stared back through the window. "But I have been listening to my friend Dadaji, this past year, and he has half convinced me that it exists."

Again, Kungas fell silent. Irene waited. She was not impatient. Not at all.

When Kungas spoke again, his voice was very low. "So I have decided to search for my soul, to see if I have one. But a man with a soul must look to the future, and not simply live in the present."

He turned his eyes back to her. He had attractive eyes, Irene thought. Almond colored, as they were almond shaped. Such a contrast, when you actually studied them, to the dull armor of his features. The eyes were very clear, and very bright. There was life dancing in those eyes, gaily, far in the background.

"I have never done that before," he explained. "Always, I lived simply in the present. But now—for some months, now—I have found myself thinking about the future."

His gaze drifted around the room, settling on a

chair not far from Irene's own. He moved over and sat in it.

"I have been thinking about Peshawar," he mused. "That was the capital of our Kushan kingdom, long ago. It is nothing but ruins, today. But I have decided that I would like to see it restored, after Malwa is broken."

"You are so confident of breaking Malwa?" asked Irene. As soon as she spoke the words, she realized they were more of a question about Kungas than they were about the prospects of war.

Kungas nodded. "Oh, yes. Quite certain." His masklike face made that little cracking movement which did for a smile. "I am *not* so certain, of course, that I myself will live to see it. But there is no point in planning for one's own death. So I keep my thoughts on Peshawar."

He studied her carefully. "But to restore Peshawar, I would have to be a king myself. So I have decided to become one. After the fall of Malwa, Shakuntala will no longer need me. I will be free to attend to the needs of my own Kushan people."

Irene swallowed. Her throat seemed dry. "I think you would make a good king," she said, a bit huskily.

Kungas nodded. "I have come to the same conclusion." He leaned forward, pointing to the volume in her lap. "But a king should know how to read—certainly his own language!—and I am illiterate."

He leaned back, still-faced. "So now you understand."

Again, Irene swallowed. "You want me to learn Kushan, so that I can teach you how to read it."

Kungas smiled. "And some other languages. I should also, I think, know how to read Greek. And Hindi."

Abruptly, Irene stood up and went to a table against the wall. She poured some wine from an amphora into a cup, and took a swallow.

Without words, she offered a cup to Kungas. He shook his head. Irene poured herself another drink.

After finishing that second cup, she stared at the wall in front of her.

"Most men," she said harshly, "do not like to learn from a woman. And learning to read is not easy, Kungas, not for a grown man. You will make many mistakes. You will be frustrated. You will resent my instructions, and my corrections. You will resent—me."

She listened for the answer, not turning her head.

"Most men," said Kungas softly, "have a small soul. That, at least, is what my friend Dadaji tells me, and he is a scholar. So I have decided, since I want to be a king, that I must have a large soul. Perhaps even a great one."

Silence. Irene's eyes were fixed on the wall. It was a blank wall, with not so much as a tapestry on it.

"I will teach you to read," she said. "I will need a week, to begin learning your language. After that, we can begin."

She heard the faint sounds of a chair scraping. Kungas was getting up.

"We will have some time, then," came his voice from behind her. "Before I have to leave on the expedition to destroy the guns."

Silence. Irene did not move her eyes from the wall, not even after she heard Kungas going toward the door. He did not make much sound, as quietly as he moved. Odd, really, for such a thick-looking man.

From the doorway, she heard his voice.

"I thank you, envoy from Rome."

"My name is Irene," she said. Harshly. Coldly.

She did not miss the softness in Kungas' voice. Or the warmth. "Yes, I know. But I have decided it is a beautiful name, and so I did not wish to use it without your permission."

"You have my permission." Her voice was still

harsh, and cold. The arrogant voice of a Greek noblewoman, bestowing a minor favor on an inferior. Silently, she cursed that voice.

"Thank you . . . Irene."

A few faint sounds of footsteps came. He was gone.

Irene finally managed to tear her eyes away from the wall. She started to pour herself another cup of wine, but stopped the motion midway. With a firm hand, she placed the cup back on the table and strode to the window.

Leaning on the ledge, she stared out at the ocean, breathing deeply. She remained there for some time, motionless, until the sunset.

Then, moving back to her chair, she took up the slim volume and began studying her new-found task. She spent the entire evening there, and got her final surprise of the day. For the first time in years, she was not able to concentrate on a book.

Chapter 7

PERSIA

Spring, 532 A.D.

"You're right, Maurice," said Belisarius, lowering his telescope. "They're *not* going to make a frontal assault."

Maurice grunted. The sound combined satisfaction with regret. Satisfaction, that his assessment had proven correct. Regret, because he wished it were otherwise.

The chiliarch examined the fieldworks below them. From the rise where he and Belisarius were standing, the Roman entrenchments were completely bare to the eye. But from the slope below, where the Rajput cavalry was massed, they would have been almost invisible.

Almost, but not quite. Again, he grunted. This time, the noise conveyed nothing but regret. "Beautiful defenses," he growled. "Damn near perfect. Pure killing ground, once they got into it." His gaze scanned the mountainous terrain around them. "Doesn't look like too bad a slope, not from below. And this is the only decent pass within miles."

Belisarius' eyes followed those of Maurice. This stretch of the Zagros range was not high, measured in sheer altitude, but it was exceptionally rugged. There was little vegetation on the slopes, and those slopes themselves, for all their rocky nature, were slick and muddy from the spring runoff. Little rills and streams could be seen everywhere.

Impossible terrain, for cavalry—except for the one pass in which Belisarius had positioned his army. He had designed his defenses carefully, making sure that their real strength was not visible from the plateau below.

The temptation, for an enemy commander, would be almost overwhelming. A powerful, surging charge—clear the pass—the road to Mesopotamia and its riches would lie wide open. The only alternative would be to continue the grueling series of marches and countermarches which had occupied both the Roman and the Malwa armies for the past several weeks.

Almost overwhelming—for any but the best commanders. Like the ones who, unfortunately, commanded the Malwa forces ranged against them.

"You were right," Belisarius pronounced again. He cocked an eye at his chief subordinate, and smiled his crooked smile. "Think I've gotten sloppy, do you, from dealing with those Malwa thickheads in Mesopotamia?"

Maurice scowled. "I wasn't criticizing, General. It was a good plan. Worth a try. But I didn't think Sanga would fall for it. Lord Damodara might have, on his own. Maybe. But it's been obvious enough, the past month, that he listens to Sanga."

Belisarius nodded. For a moment, his eyes were drawn to a pavilion on the plateau below. The structure was visible to the naked eye. But, even through a telescope, it wasn't much to see.

For two days now, while the Malwa army gathered

its forces below the pass, Belisarius had scrutinized that pavilion through his telescope. The distance was too great to discern individual features, but Belisarius had spotted Sanga almost immediately. The Rajput king was one of the tallest men Belisarius had ever met, and he had no doubt of the identity of the towering figure that regularly came and went from the pavilion. Nor of the identity of the short, pudgy man who often emerged from it in Sanga's company.

That would be Lord Damodara, the top commander of the Malwa army in the plateau. One of the *anvaya-prapta sachivya*, as the Malwa called the hereditary caste that dominated their empire. Blood kin to Emperor Skandagupta himself.

From the moment Belisarius had first seen that pavilion, he had been struck by it. It was nothing fancy, nothing elaborate, and, by Malwa standards, positively austere. The structure was completely unlike the grotesque cotton-and-silk palace which Emperor Skandagupta had erected at the siege of Ranapur. And Belisarius was quite certain that Lord Venandakatra, the anvaya-prapta sachivya whom the Roman general knew best, would have disdained to use it for anything other than a latrine.

Beyond the nature of the pavilion itself, Belisarius had been just as struck—more so, perhaps—by the use to which it was put. In his past experience, Malwa headquarters were the scenes of great pomp and ceremony. Such pavilions—or palaces, or luxury barges—were invariably surrounded by a host of elite bodyguards. Visitors who arrived were accompanied by their own resplendent entourages, and with great fanfare.

Great fanfare. Kettledrums, heralds, banners—even trained animals, prancing their way before the mighty Lords and Ladies of Malwa.

Not Damodara's pavilion. There had been a steady stream of visitors to that utilitarian structure, true enough. But they were obviously officers—Rajputs, in the main, with the occasional Ye-tai or kshatriya—and they invariably arrived either alone or in small groups. Not a bodyguard to be seen, except for the handful posted before the pavilion itself. And those—for a moment, Belisarius was tempted to use his telescope again, to study the soldiers standing guard before Damodara's pavilion. But there would be no point. He would simply see the same thing he had seen for the past two days. The thing which had impressed him most about that pavilion.

Rajput guards—always. Never Ye-tai. That single, simple fact had told him more than anything else.

The Ye-tai were barbarians. Half a century earlier, they had erupted into the plains of north India and begun conquering the region, as they had already done with the Kushan territories to the northwest. But when they came up against the newly rising Malwa realm, an offshoot of the collapsing Gupta Empire, their advance was brought to a halt. Already, Belisarius now knew, the being from the future called Link had armed the Malwa with gunpowder technology. With their rockets, cannons, and grenades, the Malwa had defeated the Ye-tai. But then, instead of simply subjugating the barbarians, the Malwa had incorporated them into their own power structure. Had, in fact, given them a prized and prestigious place—just below that of the anvaya-prapta sachivya themselves. Ye-tai clan chiefs had even been allowed to marry into the elite castes.

The move was extraordinarily shrewd, commented Aide, **and quite beyond the capacity of normal Hindu rulers to even envision. The instructions must have come from Link itself. The Ye-tai are not part of the caste-and-class structure of Hindu society—what Indians themselves call the varna system. By giving such heathen barbarians a place in the elite, Link has**

provided a powerful and reliable Praetorian guard for the Malwa dynasty which is its creature.

Mentally, Belisarius nodded his agreement. That was how the Malwa invariably used their Ye-tai forces. The barbarians were ferocious warriors in their own right. But the Malwa, instead of using them as spearhead troops, used them as security and control battalions.

Except—for Damodara.

Again, Belisarius made that mental nod. Damodara had placed his Ye-tai contingents with his fighting forces, and relied solely on Rajputs for his own protection. The Rajputs were treasured by the Malwa for their military skills, just as was true of their Kushan vassals. But they were not trusted.

Except by Damodara, Aide, just as you say. The Rajputs form the bulk of his army, and he's obviously decided to weld them to himself by giving them his final trust.

Belisarius sighed, faintly. *All of which tells me a great deal. None of which I'm happy to know.*

This had been Belisarius' first opportunity to study his opponent at close hand. Roman and Malwa contingents had clashed several times in the weeks which had elapsed since his narrow escape from the ambush at the oasis, but the forces involved had been small. For the most part, the Romans and the Malwa had kept their distance, as each army tried to outmaneuver the other through the labyrinth of the Zagros range.

The Romans had had the best of it, in a narrow sense. Belisarius was simply trying to block the Malwa from passing through the Zagros onto the open plain of Mesopotamia. He had succeeded in doing so, true. But Damodara and Sanga handled their own forces extremely well. They had not dislodged the Romans blocking their way, but they had, slowly, succeeded in forcing them back.

The Zagros was a wide range, but it was not inexhaustible. Sooner or later, Belisarius would run out of room to maneuver. So he had decided to fight a battle on his own chosen terrain. If he could badly bloody the Malwa, he would gain more time—possibly even regain some lost ground.

Against the normal run of Malwa commanders, his plan would have worked. Against Damodara, and his Rajputs, it had failed. Just as Maurice had predicted.

Belisarius raised his telescope and studied Damodara's pavilion, trying to discern anything inside the dark interior. It was a vain enterprise, more born from habit than anything else.

But, suddenly and surprisingly, Aide spoke urgent words. **There's a telescope in there! I can just barely make it out.**

Belisarius focused his own eyesight, but even with Aide's help he could not see the telescope which was apparently hidden within the pavilion. He was not surprised, however. Aide could often detect things through Belisarius' eyes which the general himself could not.

Big, clumsy damned thing, came Aide's mental sniff.

Still—nothing. Belisarius knew that Aide was using his own crystalline version of what the "jewel" called *computer image enhancement.*

Is this important? asked Aide.

In and of itself—not especially. If that telescope's as big and awkward as you say, it's not going to be much of a help on the battlefield. But the fact that Damodara has one is interesting, nonetheless. It's a reminder to us not to underestimate the Malwa.

Belisarius folded up his telescope. As so often before, in doing so, he was struck by the clever design of John of Rhodes' device. But, for all that, his motion was sharp and decisive.

"That's it, then," he announced, turning away. "Pass

the word, Maurice. We'll leave a unit here on guard, but get the army ready for another march." He gestured with his head toward the enemy below. "They'll be moving out themselves, sometime tonight. Make sure Abbu and his scouts are close enough to see which route they take."

"Won't be very close," replied Maurice grimly. "Not with Rajput flankers."

Belisarius began striding toward his own tent, some fifty yards down the trail. Over his shoulder, he said, "I'm well aware of that. Just close enough, Maurice, that's all. Just close enough. If that army ever breaks contact with us, we'll be in a sea of trouble."

A few steps away, hearing the exchange, Valentinian scowled.

"I was afraid this was going to happen. God, I'm sick of marching." He cast a half-hoping, half-skeptical eye at the Malwa army on the plateau below. "You think if I tried taunting them again—?"

Next to him, Anastasius snorted sarcastically. "And just what do you think that'll accomplish? Besides making you look like an idiot? *Again.*"

Two miles away, at the entrance to his pavilion, Lord Damodara straightened up from his own telescope. Then, feeling the usual ache, the Malwa general grimaced. "Wish I had one of *his* telescopes," he grumbled.

Standing next to him, Rana Sanga cast a glance at the optical device in question. The Malwa telescope, quite unlike the slender, handheld artifact which he had seen in Belisarius' hands, was an ungainly thing. As in many areas—steelmaking was one outstanding exception—Indian craftsmanship was not the equal of Greek. The Malwa approach to optics was much like their approach to shipbuilding: *Since we can't make it elegant, we'll make it big and sturdy.*

Big and sturdy the Malwa telescope certainly was.

So big, unfortunately, that it had to be supported on a rigid framework which could only be adjusted with great difficulty. The end result was that anyone who used the thing was forced to stoop in an awkward posture which, after a period of time, invariably resulted in back pain.

For a moment, Sanga was tempted to point out that Damodara, as short as he was, suffered less from the problem than did Sanga himself. But he restrained the impulse. Lord Damodara maintained an easy and informal bearing around his top subordinates, but he *was* anvaya-prapta sachivya. There were limits.

Instead, he opted for the bright side. "It's a better telescope than he has," he pointed out. "At least as far as its strength goes."

Judging from his snort, Damodara was not mollified. "And so what?" he demanded. He gestured through the open flap of the pavilion. "So I can discern his features, where he can't mine. On the rare occasions when he happens to wander into my field of view, that is. While he, for his part, can look anywhere he wants. *Without* breaking his spine in the process."

Damodara rubbed his back, still grimacing. "I'd trade with him in a minute! And so would you, Rana Sanga—so stop trying to cheer me up."

Sanga said nothing. After a few seconds, Damodara stopped scowling. The young Malwa lord's innate good humor returned.

"There's this much," Damodara said cheerfully. "I'm quite sure he doesn't know we have a telescope. We didn't have them when he was in India, and I'm positive he hasn't spotted mine." He glanced around his headquarters. The telescope was positioned ten feet inside the entrance, well within the gloom of his pavilion's interior. Damodara had kept it there at all times, despite the limited field of view which the position provided, precisely in order to keep Belisarius from spotting the device.

For an instant, the scowl returned. "I'm not sure that makes any difference, of course. But—" He shrugged. "With Belisarius, I'll take any advantage I can get."

Damodara turned away from the telescope and moved toward the large table located at the very center of the pavilion. Sanga, without being asked, immediately followed.

At the edge of the table, Damodara planted his pudgy hands and leaned over, intently examining the huge vellum map which covered most of it. His gaze, now, was one of satisfaction rather than disgruntlement. Whatever they lacked in optical craftsmanship, no one could fault the skill of Malwa mapmakers. He was especially pleased with the topographical information which his chief cartographer managed to include.

Damodara peered into a corner of the dimly lit pavilion. As always, his cartographer was waiting patiently, seated on a small cushion. Narses was also in the corner, available in case Damodara needed his advice. The eunuch, following Roman custom, sat in a chair.

"It is up to date, Lord Damodara," said the mapmaker. "Just this morning, I incorporated the latest information brought in by the Pathans."

Damodara nodded, and turned back to the map. For a time, he was silent, examining the terrain shown thereon. At his side, Rana Sanga did the same. Then, Lord Damodara reached out and placed his finger on a location some fifteen miles to the south.

"There, perhaps?" he asked. "Judging from the map, it seems like an obscure pass. Very narrow, but it might be enough."

Sanga studied the pass in question for a moment, before shaking his head. The gesture was more one of slow consideration, however, than firm judgement. "I don't think so, Lord." He hesitated, tugging at his rich beard. "I am not sure of this, you understand, but it seems to me that Belisarius has been especially keen to thwart us from making any headway to the *south*. I suspect that he already has scouts watching the approaches to that pass."

Damodara looked up, his eyes widening. He seemed slightly startled.

"To the south—*especially*? I hadn't—" He frowned, thinking; then, chuckled ruefully. "It seemed more to me that he was thwarting us *anywhere* we went."

Sanga's shoulders lifted in a small shrug. "That is true, Lord. But I still think that he has been quickest of all to prevent us from going south."

Damodara spread his hands on the table, staring at the map. It was obvious to Sanga, watching the movement of his eyes, that Damodara was retracing every step of the past month's maneuvers.

"I think you're right," he murmured, after a minute or two. Damodara straightened up, staring now at the bare leather of the pavilion wall across from him.

"Why is that, do you think?" he mused thoughtfully. His gaze turned to Sanga. "It doesn't make any sense. What difference does it make, whether we bypass him to the north or the south? So long as he can keep us from making westward progress, he keeps us out of Mesopotamia. Tied up here, in these miserable mountains."

Damodara's eyes returned to the map. "If anything," he added slowly, "I would think he'd prefer to maneuver us south. That way he can keep us following the Zagros range—all the way to the Gulf." He pointed to the southern reaches of the mountains shown on the map. "In the end, we might find ourselves emerging into Mesopotamia down at the delta. Near Charax."

He laughed sarcastically. "Where he already has our main army bottled up! With Emperor Khusrau and his lancers to keep the cork in the bottle."

Sanga's beard-tugging grew more vigorous. "There *is* one possible explanation. Especially dealing with Belisarius."

Lord Damodara cocked his head, peering up at the tall Rajput next him. "A trap," he stated. Sanga nodded.

Damodara began pacing back and forth slowly. His hands, in one of the Malwa lord's characteristic gestures, were clasped in front of him as if he were in prayer. But the short, jabbing, back-and-forth motion of the hands conveyed concentration rather than piety.

"You could be right," he mused. A sudden bark—half-humorous, half-exasperated. "Subtle bait! But that is the way the man thinks."

Damodara suddenly stopped his pacing and turned to face Sanga squarely. "What do you advise?" he demanded.

Sanga stopped his beard-tugging, and took a deep breath.

"Go north," he said firmly. "It may be a trap, Lord Damodara. He may be laying an ambush for us. But traps can be turned against the trapper. A trap designed for a wolf will not necessarily hold a tiger. Our troops are excellent, and our army outnumbers his by two to one."

Damodara nodded. "Closer to three to one, I think." The Malwa lord's eyes grew a bit vacant. Again, his hands were clasped before him in the gesture of prayer. But there was no emphatic jabbing, this time. The hands were still, except for a slight flexing of the fingers.

Sanga, recognizing the signs, waited. As usual, Damodara did not take long to make his decision.

"I agree," the Lord said firmly. "We will go north." He barked another laugh. "With our eyes wide open! And—"

There was a sudden commotion at the entrance to the pavilion. Damodara and Sanga turned. They saw that two of the Lord's Rajput guards were barring the way of a Ye-tai who, for his part, was expressing his anger in no uncertain terms.

It was General Mihirakula, the commander of Damodara's Ye-tai troops.

"Let him in!" called out Damodara. The guards stepped aside, and Mihirakula stormed into the pavilion. He cast an angry glance at Rana Sanga before coming to a halt in front of Lord Damodara.

"What is this nonsense I hear?" demanded Mihirakula. "I was just informed by one of your"—another angry glance at Sanga—"Rajput dispatch riders that we are to make preparations for a march. *Is this true?*"

The question was obviously rhetorical. Mihirakula did not wait for an answer before gesturing angrily at the mountains visible through the open flap of the pavilion.

"Why are we not charging the stinking Romans?" he demanded. "We will brush them aside like flies!" Again, Mihirakula glared at Sanga. "If the Rajputs are too fearful, then my Ye-tai will lead the way!"

The Ye-tai general was a big man, heavy in the shoulders and thick in the chest, but Sanga was as much taller than he as Mihirakula was than Damodara. The Rajput drew himself up to his full towering height. His hands were clasped tightly behind his back, but it was obvious from the tension in Sanga's powerful arms that he was barely controlling his anger.

Damodara intervened quickly. He placed a slight, restraining hand on Sanga. To the Ye-tai general, he stated firmly: "The orders were mine, General Mihirakula." Damodara made his own gesture toward the mountains. "The Roman fieldworks here are too powerful. *But*," he added, overriding the Ye-tai's gathering splutter of protest, "my scouts tell me that we may find a way to the north."

Again, he overrode Mihirakula's protest. This time, saying with a cheerful smile: "The scouts think there will be opposition, of course. So I was thinking of using you and your men as my vanguard element in the next march."

The smile Damodara was bestowing on Mihirakula was positively a beam, now. "To clear the way for us, of course. So that we can finally be done with these damned mountains."

Mihirakula relaxed, a bit. He glanced at Sanga, once again, before replying to Damodara. But the glance had more of satisfaction in it than anger.

"Soon, do you think? My men are very restless."

Damodara shrugged. "Soon enough. Within a week, I imagine." He made a little, apologetic grimace. "Marching through these mountains, as you know, is not a quick business."

All apology and goodwill vanished. Damodara's next words were spoken in a tone of steel: "And *now*, General Mihirakula, you will carry out my commands. *At once*."

The Ye-tai commander knew that tone. For all his barbarous nature, Mihirakula was not a fool. He bowed his head, stiffly, and departed from the pavilion.

After he was gone, Sanga let out a short, angry grunt. "My Rajputs can lead—" he began, but Damodara waved him silent.

"I am well aware of that, Sanga. But the Ye-tai *are* getting restless." He gave Sanga a shrewd glance. "So are your Rajputs, for that matter, even if they control their impatience better."

Damodara pointed at the map. His finger made little wandering gestures, as if retracing the tortuous route of the past weeks. "Good soldiers grow impatient with this kind of endless maneuvering. Sooner or later, they will demand action. You know that as well as I do."

Grudgingly, Sanga nodded.

Damodara spread his hands. "So let the Ye-tai lead the way, for now. If there is a trap, they will spring it. To be frank, I'd rather see them bloodied than you."

It was plain enough, from the look on his face, that Sanga found his commander's cold-bloodedness distasteful. But Damodara took no offense. He simply chuckled.

"I am Malwa, Rana Sanga, not Rajput. *Practical.*"

Two days later, Belisarius was studying a map spread across a table in his own field headquarters. All of his top commanders were joining him in the enterprise. Those included, in addition to Maurice and Vasudeva: Cyril, who had succeeded Agathius in command of the Greek cataphracts after Agathius had been crippled at the Battle of the Nehar Malka; and Bouzes and Coutzes, the two young Thracian brothers who commanded the Syrian contingents in Belisarius' army.

Abbu entered, pushing his way through the leather flaps which served as an entrance. The chief of Belisarius' Arab scouts did not wait for an invitation to speak before advancing to the center of the tent and giving his report.

The old bedouin did not give the map so much as a glance. Abbu was a stern traditionalist. Despite his deep (if unspoken) admiration for Belisarius, the Arab considered the map an alarming omen—either of the Roman general's early senility, or of his rapid descent into modern decadence.

"The Malwa are heading north," he announced, "toward that saddle pass I told you about. It is obvious they are expecting an ambush. They have their Ye-tai contingents leading the way." Abbu grunted approvingly. "He's no fool, that Malwa commander. He'll feed the barbarians into the fire—good riddance—before following through with his Rajputs."

"Before *trying* to follow through," said Cyril.

Abbu shook his head. The bedouin's countenance, always dour, grew positively gloomy. "They will succeed. The pass is too wide, and the slopes on either side not steep enough. The north slope is especially shallow. They will be able to use their numbers against us. It won't be easy, but they'll force their way through."

Cyril began to bridle at the Arab's easy assumption of defeat, but Belisarius intervened.

"That's just as well," he stated forcefully. "I *want* to steer them north. So we'll put up a stiff resistance at the pass itself, but withdraw before our men get mangled." He bent over, studying the map; then pointed with his finger.

"If this is accurate, once they get through the pass their easiest route will be to follow this small river to the northwest." He cocked an eye at Abbu. The Arab scowled fiercely, but said nothing—which was his way of admitting that the newfangled absurdity could not be faulted.

Belisarius kept his eye on Abbu. "And if I'm reading this map correctly," he added, "when we fall back and set our positions *southwest* of the pass, our fieldworks will be too strong for the Malwa to take any other direction."

Abbu's scowl deepened. But, again, he said nothing.

"If you don't want to hold the pass, general," asked Bouzes, frowning, "then why even put up a fight at all? Seems like a waste of good soldiers." The young Thracian did not bother to add: *which is not your usual style*. Like all of the men in that tent, he had become very familiar with Belisarius' tactical methods. One of those methods—a very important one—was to be sparing with his men's lives, whenever possible.

Belisarius shook his head. "I don't have any choice, Bouzes. I can't afford to make it *too* easy, not for commanders like Damodara and Sanga. If we fight like lions whenever they move south, but stand aside when they move north, they'll start to wonder why. Doesn't make sense. Strict military logic would be the other way around—I should be more than happy to steer them down the Zagros, toward Pars." He winced. "I do *not* want Sanga and Damodara spending much time contemplating my bad logic."

Maurice interrupted. His own expression did not exude any great happiness. "They're probably already doing that," he growled.

Belisarius heaved a sigh. "Yes, I'm sure they are. But as long as they don't think too much about the qanats, and don't know about the Kushans, I think we'll be all right."

He cast a quick glance at the helmet which Vasudeva had placed upon the table. As always, the Kushan had removed the detested monstrosity as soon as he entered the tent and was safe from spying eyes. Belisarius' expression resumed its usual calm serenity. He even managed a crooked smile.

"My plan *is*, after all," he said cheerfully, "a bit on the crazed side."

That announcement did not seem to bring any great cheer to the other men in the tent. But they did not protest—not, at least, beyond thinking private dark thoughts. Those men were all very familiar with Belisarius' tactical principles and methods. Many of those methods struck them as bizarre, but not the one which—*always*—stood at the very center.

Win the war. That's all that matters.

Chapter 8
AXUM
Spring, 532 A.D.

Eon's regimental ceremony did not take place until days after the bombing of the Ta'akha Maryam. Initially, the prince had insisted on doing it at once. But calmer voices—older ones, at least—prevailed.

Foremost among those voices had been that of Wahsi, the commander of the regiment itself.

"There is no time now, King of Kings," he insisted.

"I am not the negusa nagast!" roared Eon. "I cannot be—not until I am accepted into the Dakuen sarwe!"

The prince—king, now; his father and brother's corpses had already been found—rose from his labors. Eon had worked through the night, along with his soldiers and most of Axum's populace, clearing away the rubble and debris. It was now mid-morning of the next day, and there was still much work to be done. The royal quarters themselves had been excavated, but the Malwa explosives had shattered well over a third of the great complex. Hundreds of corpses had been found, and as many survivors. The rescue workers could hear the faint moans of a few victims who were still alive, buried beneath the stones.

Wahsi placed a gentle hand on Eon's shoulder. "The Dakuen can wait, King."

The Dakuen commander gestured with his head, indicating the knot of soldiers standing just a few feet behind him. Those men were all of the officers of the regiment, other than the ones who were with Ezana in India. "None of us are concerned about the matter."

Hearing Wahsi's words, the regimental officers growled their agreement. Several of them glanced at the figure of Ousanas. The dawazz was just a few yards away, oblivious to the exchange. He was too busy pulling away stones.

Not even Eon failed to miss the obvious approval in those glances.

"There is no need," repeated Wahsi softly. Then, very softly, in words only Eon could hear: "No need, Eon. There is no question of the regiment's approval of Ousanas, and you."

Wahsi chuckled but, again, so softly that only Eon could hear. "They will have harsh words to say, of course, about the hunter's ridiculous philosophies, and will relish every detail of your childhood follies. But that is just tradition." He cast a glance at the distant figure of Antonina, who was directing her own soldiers in the rescue operation. All of the Roman troops had survived the explosion, and they had immediately pitched into the work. "They are especially looking forward to hearing about all the times Ousanas was forced to slap you silly, until you finally learned not to ogle the wife of Belisarius."

Eon managed a smile. It wasn't much of a smile, but Wahsi was still relieved to see it. For just a fleeting instant, Eon's was the face of a young man again. For hours, since the bodies of Zaia and Tarabai had been found, his face had been that of an old man broken with grief. Zaia had been his concubine since Eon was thirteen years old. If the passion had faded, some, from their relationship, he had still loved her deeply. And he had been almost besotted with Tarabai, since he met her in India.

"You lost everyone yesterday, Eon," said Wahsi gently. "Your women and your only child, along with your father and brother. No man in the world—prince or peasant, it matters not—can think clearly at such a time, or deal with anything beyond his grief. So let us simply concentrate on the work before us. There will be time, soon enough, for the ceremony."

He stepped back a pace, and raised his voice slightly.

"For the moment, you are the negusa nagast. That is the opinion of the Dakuen sarwe, as well as the Lazen and the Hadefan."

Wahsi gestured toward two of the officers in the cluster. They were named Aphilas and Saizana and were, respectively, the commanders of the Lazen and the Hadefan sarwe. The Lazen had been the regiment of Kaleb; the Hadefan, that of Wa'zeb. Along with the Dakuen, they constituted the current royal regiments of the Ethiopian army.

"That is correct, King," said Aphilas. Saizana nodded, adding: "And we have spoken to all of the other sarawit. The soldiers are of one mind on this matter. All of them."

Then, almost in a snarl: "We will have our vengeance on Malwa. And you are the King of Kings who will lead us to it."

Eon wiped his face with a hand, smearing dirt and rock dust. It was a weary, weary gesture. "How is Garmat?" he asked. "Will he survive?"

Wahsi broke into a smile of his own. And not a thin one, either.

"Be serious, King! If twenty great stones falling on

that old Arab brigand couldn't kill him outright, do you really think he would die of lingering wounds?"

One of the officers—an older man, well into his fifties—laughed. "I remember when we were chasing that bandit through the desert, years ago. Never could catch him, no matter how many ambushes we laid."

Another officer, also middle-aged, grinned. "Personally, I think he's malingering. Lazy half-breed! Just doesn't want to haul stones."

A little laugh swept the small crowd. Even Eon joined in the humor, for a moment.

Finding Garmat had been the only brightness in a long, dark night. The adviser had apparently been standing some distance away from the throne, when the bombs went off. The Malwa saboteurs, of course, had set the main charges in the walls near the throne itself. When the explosion took place, King Kaleb and all of the people in his immediate vicinity—including his oldest son and heir, Wa'zeb—had been pulverized by the great blast. The rest of the people in the throne room, except for Garmat and a servant, had been crushed by the falling roof and walls. But, by a freak of fortune, some of the Ta'akha Maryam's great stones, in their collapse, had formed a sort of shelter for Garmat and the servant. The servant, in fact, had been almost unharmed, other than being frightened half out of her wits. Garmat's injuries had been severe—several broken bones, along with innumerable bruises and lacerations—but his life had been spared.

The news of Garmat's survival, as it spread, brought cheer to everyone—especially to the sarwen. Partly, that was due to fondness for the man himself. King Kaleb's rule had been good, so far as the people of Axum were concerned. Much of that they ascribed to the sage, and usually gentle, advice of Garmat.

But, mostly, the news brought cheer to the soldiers

laboring in the wreckage because it stirred flame in their fierce hearts. The sarwen had not forgotten that Garmat was the same wily half-Arab bandit who had eluded the Ethiopian army for years—until, finally, he had accepted their offer to become Kaleb's own dawazz, when Eon's father was still a boy. After Kaleb succeeded to the throne, Garmat had been his chief adviser for years, until Kaleb assigned him to serve Eon in the same post.

Gentle, the man Garmat had often been, in his advice to Ethiopian royalty. But always shrewd, always cunning, and—when he felt it necessary—as savage and pitiless as the Arabian desert which had shaped him. More than one Axumite soldier, hearing the news that Garmat still lived, silently repeated Antonina's own thought.

Bad move, Malwa. Bad news, you bastards. You'd have done better to toy with a scorpion, after tweaking its tail.

Ten days after the explosion, the regimental ceremony was finally held. The fact that the Ta'akha Maryam was a ruin did not impede the proceedings. By tradition, the ceremony was never held in the royal compound. It was always held on the training fields where, Ethiopians never forgot, the real power of Axum was created. The army's training fields were located about half a mile west by northwest of the royal compound, at the base of one of the two great hills which overlooked the capital. This hill, which formed the eastern boundary of Axum, was called the Mai Qoho. The one on the north, the Bieta Giyorghis.

Standing to one side, in the group of witnesses who were not members of the regiments, Antonina surveyed the scene. She was impressed, more than anything, by the open—almost barren—nature of the grounds. Other than the row of open-air thrones on the north end of the field, butted against the slope of the Mai Qoho, the training grounds were completely bare except for a handful of wooden spear targets.

That was the Axumite way of looking at things, she realized. When she first arrived in Ethiopia, Antonina had not noticed the absence of fortifications until the officers of her army began pointing it out to her. They had been quite impressed. None of Axum's towns—not even the capital city of Axum itself, nor the great seaport of Adulis—were surrounded by walls. Not one of the many villages through which they passed, on their long trek upcountry, had so much as a small fortress to protect it.

The ancient Athenians had placed their faith in the wooden walls of their ships. The Axumites, in the spears of their regiments.

That was not from lack of ability. Axumites were quite capable of massive stonework. The Ta'akha Maryam and, especially, the glorious cathedral of Maryam Tsion, were testimony to the skill and craftsmanship of Ethiopian masons. But those edifices were for pomp, display, ceremony, and worship. They had nothing to do with *power*.

Power came from the regiments. They, and they alone.

She brought her eyes back to the thrones at the north end of the field. Those, too, she thought, testified to the same approach.

The structures were identical, and quite small—nothing like Kaleb's great throne in the Ta'akha Maryam had been. Each throne rested on a granite slab not more than eight feet square. A smaller slab atop the first provided the base for the throne itself, which was a solid but simple wooden chair. Four slender stone columns, rising from each corner of the upper slab, supported a canopy which sheltered the occupant from the sun. A gold cross—very finely made; Axumite metalsmiths were as skilled as their masons—

surmounted the entire structure, but the canopy itself was made of nothing fancier than woven grass.

Those thrones were for the commanders of the Axumite sarawit, the regiments into which their army was organized. It was typical of Axumite notions of rule that those commanders, taken as a collective group, were called "nagast"—kings.

None of them, as individuals, enjoyed that title. Unlike the vassal states of the Ethiopian Empire, whose rulers retained their royal trappings (so long, of course, as they acknowledged the suzerainty of the King of Kings), the regimental commanders derived their authority entirely from the army itself. But, in the real world, the attitude of the regiments was considered far more important than the vagaries of sub-kings.

Only three of the thrones were occupied, this day. Even that was unusual. According to tradition, one man alone should be sitting on a throne today—the commander of the Dakuen sarwe. Even the king himself, though he was not present, was required to vacate his throne in the royal compound until his son's regiment had passed its judgement.

But Wahsi had bent the custom, today. With the murder of Kaleb and Wa'zeb, the Lazen and the Hadefan sarawit had lost their own royalty. Wahsi had offered, and they had accepted, to share the prince. For the first time in Axumite history, a man would ascend the throne with the approval—and the name—of three regiments.

The ceremony was beginning. Eon was taking his own place, standing alone to one side. At the very front, before the assembled regiments themselves, Ousanas was being brought forward.

Antonina struggled mightily against a giggle. The dawazz was positively festooned with chains and manacles. The servile devices looked about as appropriate on him as ribbons on a lion.

And probably, she thought, eyeing Ousanas' tall and heavily muscled figure, *just about as effective, if he decides he's tired of the rigmarole.* Belisarius had told her once, after returning from India, that Ousanas was probably the strongest man he had ever met in his life. Even stronger, he suspected, than the giant Anastasius.

But Antonina's humor faded quickly enough. The chains and manacles might seem absurd, but there was nothing absurd-looking about the squad of soldiers who surrounded Ousanas. There were eight of them, and all were holding weapons in their hands. These were not the usual stabbing spears and heavy, cleaverlike swords with which Axumites went into battle, however. The soldiers were holding clubs, inlaid with iron studs.

Weapons to beat a slave who had failed in his duty. Beat him to death, easily enough, if he had failed badly.

Antonina, staring at those cruel implements, had no trouble with giggles. Not any longer. She knew the clubs were not ornaments. It had happened, over the past two centuries, that a regiment had beaten a dawazz savagely—fatally, on two occasions—because they judged that he had failed in his duty to educate his prince.

She tore her eyes away, and looked at Eon. The sight of the young royal's upright and square-shouldered stance reassured her. The calmness in his face, even more so.

Not today. Not that prince.

A minute later, the ceremony itself got underway.

Five minutes later, Antonina was fighting giggles again.

Ten minutes later, she stopped trying altogether, and joined in the general hilarity. She spent most of the day, in fact, laughing along with everyone else.

Antonina had forgotten. There was a serious core—deadly serious—at the heart of that ceremony. But Axumites, when all was said and done, did not hold solemnity in any great esteem. The best armor against self-aggrandizement and pomposity, after all, is always humor.

By and large, the ceremony proceeded chronologically. Eon's prepubescent follies were dismissed quickly enough. Everyone wanted to get to the next stage.

Antonina learned, then, the reason for the other women standing in her group. All of them, it seemed—except for three old crones whose testimony had to do with Eon's pranks in the royal kitchen—had been seduced by the young prince at one time or another.

It was quite a crowd. Antonina was rather impressed.

But she was more impressed, *much* more, by what followed. Most of the women were—or had been—servants in the royal compound, while Eon was in his teens. The kind of women, in every land, who were the natural prey of young male nobles feeling the first urges of budding sexuality.

But they were not there, it developed, to press any grievances against the prince. They simply recounted—either volunteering the information, or responding to one of the many questions shouted out by soldiers in the ranks—the ways in which Eon had finagled his way into their beds. Their statements were frank, open, usually jocular—and often at the expense of Eon himself. It became clear soon enough that, especially in his earlier years, the prince's skill at working his way into their beds had not been matched by any great skill once he got there.

Several of the tales were downright hilarious. Antonina was especially entertained by the account of a plump, older woman who had once been a cook in the royal compound. The woman—she must have been a good twenty years older than Eon—recounted in lavish detail her patient, frustrated attempts to instruct a headstrong fifteen-year-old prince in the basic principles of female anatomy. Not with any great success, it seemed, until she discovered the secret: *slap the fool boy on his head!*

That produced a gale of laughter, sweeping across the entire training field. The soldiers guarding Ousanas grinned at him with approval.

Unfortunately, Antonina could not follow all of the woman's tale. Her own knowledge of Ge'ez, the Axumite language, was still very poor. Menander, one of the cataphracts who had accompanied Belisarius on his trip to India, was serving as her translator. He had become good friends with Wahsi and Ezana during that long journey, and was quite fluent in the language.

Alas, Menander was also young, and he still bore the imprint of his conservative village upbringing. So, whenever the story got especially juicy, he fumbled and stumbled and—Antonina had no doubt—was guilty of excessive abridgement.

"And what was *that* about?" Antonina demanded, once the roaring laughter had subsided a bit.

Menander fumbled and stumbled. Abridged.

"Ah," said Antonina, nodding her head wisely. "Yes, of course. It *is* difficult to teach a thick-headed male how to use his tongue for something more useful than boasting."

But, for all its salacious humor, there was still a deadly serious purpose to the business. As she listened to the questions which the soldiers asked of the women, Antonina understood that they were probing for something quite important.

The soldiers were not concerned—not in the least—with Eon's amatory habits. Young lads, of any rank in society, are always randy. A prince, because of his prestigious position and the self-confidence which that position gives him, will be much more successful than most teenage boys in the art of seduction. That much was inevitable, natural, and no concern of the soldiers. Rather the contrary, in fact—no one wanted a shy, self-effacing king in charge of a country, especially one who might have difficulty perpetuating the royal line.

And if a particular prince proved to be particularly adept at the skill—as Eon obviously was—so much the better. A glib tongue was a useful attribute for a good monarch.

What the soldiers *were* concerned about were Eon's methods. Charm is one thing; bullying is another. If Eon could use his prestige as a prince to sweet-talk his way into a hundred servant girls' beds, that was a source for nothing beyond amusement. But if he used that royal position in order to threaten his way to the goal, that *was* regimental business. A prince who would rape his servants would not hesitate, as a king, to rape his country.

But there was no trace of that in Eon's past. The questioning of the women went on as long as it did, Antonina decided, simply because everyone was enjoying the affair. Everyone except Eon, at least, although Antonina noticed that the prince himself was not reluctant to join in the laughter, even when he was the butt of the joke.

Soon enough, it was Antonina's turn to be a witness. Wahsi led the questioning, as he had since the beginning of the ceremony.

It did not take him more than a minute to clarify the issue involving Antonina. A randy prince was fine, so long as he could keep it under control. But a prince who would jeopardize important political affairs because of his unbridled lust would make a disastrous ruler.

Here, Wahsi glowered fiercely, leaning forward in his throne.

Isn't it true that during his trip to Constantinople, the fool boy prince could not stop ogling the wife of Rome's greatest general?

Antonina was not even tempted to deny the charge. Wahsi himself, along with Ezana, had been Eon's bodyguards during that time. But she managed to toss the thing off easily enough.

Well, yes, I suppose, for the first few days. But I was not offended. It's not as if I'm unaccustomed to it, after all—

Here, she drew herself erect, swelling her chest a bit. Antonina had deliberately worn the most revealing costume she had brought with her on this expedition. The outfit was not really very provocative, in all truth—nothing like the costumes she had worn in her days as a courtesan—but it didn't need to be. With her figure, she could attract men wearing a sackcloth.

An appreciative murmur rose from the ranks of the watching soldiers.

—and Eon was perfectly courteous in his actual conduct. A most proper young prince.

So much for that.

Menander was summoned next. The questioning here had no sexual overtone, but the issue was the same. Wasn't it true, during Eon's trip, that he behaved overbearingly toward Roman soldiers? Mention was made, in particular, of an arm-wrestling match in which the arrogant prince could not resist showing off his grotesque musculature.

Menander did not handle the thing as smoothly as Antonina. But, in its own way, his stubborn and vehement—almost resentful—defense of Eon was even more effective. No one watching the young foreign soldier, stammering his admiration for the prince, could fail to be impressed with the way in which Eon had obviously won over his allies, whatever might have been his initial blunders. And, again, laughter swept the field when Menander described Ousanas' methods of correcting Eon's behavior.

The rest of the ceremony was much of a piece. Every aspect of Eon's character was probed—with humor, more often than not, but relentlessly nonetheless. The dawazz was on trial, not the prince. But the real issue was Eon's suitability to assume the throne.

By mid-afternoon, the question was settled. In truth, Antonina realized, it had never really been at issue. The soldiers in the gathered regiments had followed the tradition scrupulously, but they had long since made their own private judgements. And it was not difficult for her, watching those soldiers, to come to the conclusion that they would not only accept Eon as their monarch, but were fiercely looking forward to his rule.

Bad move, Malwa.

The ceremony ended. The shackles were removed from Ousanas. Following custom, Wahsi offered the former dawazz a choice. He could return to his homeland, laden with riches; or he could choose to stay in Axum, where the new king would doubtless find a suitable post for his talents.

Ousanas' answer brought the last roar of laughter to the field—and a roar of fury with it.

"I shall stay here," he announced. "My own folk are too practical. Here, I will have great opportunity to contemplate philosophy. Especially the dialectic, which teaches us that all things are a contradiction."

He gave Eon a stony look. "As the fool boy king will prove soon enough."

When the laughter faded, he said: "But the dialectic also teaches us that all things change. *As the Malwa are about to discover—even quicker!*"

Chapter 9

The following day, Eon began his duties as negusa nagast. By tradition, he would have spent the evening carousing with his soldiers and the townsfolk of Axum. But Eon had been in no mood for festivity. His personal losses were too recent, and too deeply felt. His soldiers understood, and did not begrudge their new King of Kings spending the night in the cathedral of Maryam Tsion, praying for the souls of his family.

But by the morning, Eon had assumed his post. Whatever grief he still felt—and no one doubted it was there—he kept it locked away. The struggle against Malwa took center stage.

As it must. Just as Eon had predicted, the Malwa had struck again.

"Abreha is leading the rebellion," stated Wahsi. Sitting on his little stool, the Dakuen commander planted his hands on his knees. "And apparently the entire Metin sarwe has decided to accept their commander's claim to being the new King of Kings."

"The Falha sarwe has done the same," chimed in

Saizana. The commander of the Hadefan leaned forward on his own stool, adding: "But they will only support Abreha as the king of Yemen. According to our spy, at least, they will not support Abreha if he tries to cross the Red Sea and invade Ethiopia itself."

Garmat, lying on an elevated pallet near Eon, raised his head. "What of the Halen?" he whispered. The old adviser was on his way to recovery, but he was still very weak. "And do we know what happened to Sumyafa Ashwa?"

"The Halen regiment," replied Saizana, "is apparently torn by dissension. They are forted up in Marib, and—so far—seem to be adopting a neutral stance." He shrugged. "As for Sumyafa Ashwa, his fate is unknown at the moment. But I think we must assume he was murdered. The viceroy was resident in Sana, after all, which is the hotbed of the rebellion."

Garmat lowered his head. For a few seconds, his eyes closed. There was no visible expression on his face, but Antonina, seated next to him, thought that Garmat was allowing himself a moment of sorrow. She knew that Sumyafa Ashwa had been a close friend of Garmat's for many years. It had been at Garmat's recommendation, after Axum conquered southern Arabia, that King Kaleb had appointed the Christian Arab as viceroy of Yemen.

Others in the room apparently shared her assessment. No one spoke, allowing Garmat to grieve in peace.

Antonina used that moment to inspect the room, and its occupants. Eon had begun the session by asking her to present the Roman Empire's proposals. Preoccupied with that task, and with the discussion which had immediately followed concerning the rebellion in Arabia, she had not had the opportunity to assess the new circle of royal advisers.

It was a small circle. Except for Garmat, none of the Ethiopian kingdom's top advisers had survived the bombing. The royal council was being held in the only audience chamber of the Ta'akha Maryam which had escaped unscathed. The room was quite large. Even the heavy wooden columns which were scattered throughout, supporting the stone ceiling, could not disguise the fact that most of the chamber was empty.

Antonina's eyes, scanning the room, fell on one of the windows which were situated along the eastern wall. The window was sturdily built, in the square stone-and-timber style favored by Axumites. There was no glass in that window. The cool highland breeze came into the chamber through the stone crosses which were the window's structure and decoration. Antonina's view of the Mai Qoho and the mountains looming beyond was filtered through the symbol of the Christian faith.

She found strength in that symbol, even more than the majesty of the mountains, and turned her eyes back to the circle of advisers.

Small, yes. But rich otherwise.

Garmat was there, after all. And all of the regimental commanders except the three who had been stationed in Yemen. And—most important of all, Antonina suspected—Ousanas was there.

Her gaze came to rest on Ousanas. In times past, the former dawazz would have squatted on a stool behind the prince. Ready to chastise him, when necessary, but otherwise keeping his place.

Ousanas was no longer a slave, however. He had no title, now. But Antonina did not miss the significance of his position in the circle. Axumites, like Romans, reserved the place by a monarch's right hand as the place of ultimate respect. And there Ousanas sat—on a cushion, not a stool, in that peculiar cross-legged position which he had learned in India. "The lotus," he called it, claiming that it was an aid to meditation.

A bizarre man, in so many ways, given to fancies

and philosophies. But Antonina was reassured by his presence.

Eon cleared his throat, indicating a resumption of the discussion. The young king squared his shoulders against the wooden back of the massive chair which was serving him as a throne, and turned to Antonina.

"We will have to deal with this rebellion first," he stated. "You know I agree with Rome's proposals, but I cannot—"

Eon spoke in Ge'ez, but Antonina did not wait for Menander's interpretation. She understood enough of the words, and she had been expecting the sense of them anyway.

Waving her hand in a gesture of agreement, she said: "Of course, Your Majesty. Axum must set its own house in order, before it can even think of striking at Malwa. Besides, this rebellion was certainly inspired and organized by the Malwa espionage service. It is no accident that the rebellion broke out *the very same day* that the Ta'akha Maryam was destroyed. There is no way the rebels in Yemen could have known about the bombing, unless they had been told in advance. It takes at least a week to travel from Axum to Sana, using the fastest horses and ships."

After Menander interpreted, she continued. "I do not think the Malwa suspect my husband's strategy. But they had good reason to strike at Axum, anyway. Ethiopians played a key role in rescuing the Empress Shakuntala and setting in motion the rebellion in the Deccan. The Malwa obviously decided to pay Axum back in the same coin—and throw in regicide for good measure."

She nodded at Eon. "So far as I am concerned, crushing the rebellion in Yemen is part of the war against Malwa. My own army is therefore at your disposal, for that purpose."

One of the officers—Gabra, commander of the Damawa regiment—began to protest. "This is an internal affair. I am not sure that using foreign troops wouldn't make the problem worse. The Halen regiment has stayed neutral, this far. If we use—"

Ousanas interrupted him. "Be damned to all that! Abreha and his rebels are using foreign troops, aren't they? According to our spy"—he glanced to a corner of the room, where the man recently arrived from Sana was standing—"Abreha is surrounded by half a dozen Malwa agents, everywhere he goes. He is publicly boasting that Malwa military units will soon be arriving in Yemen."

The hunter slapped the floor. "And most of his forces *now* are not Axumite! Abreha's regiment and the Falha—put together—are less than two thousand men." His eyes swept the room, scanning the row of regimental commanders seated before the negusa nagast. "On their own, they would stand no chance. So—according to our spy—most of Abreha's forces consist of Arabs. Bedouin tribesmen from the interior."

Again, he looked in the corner. The regimental commanders twisted their heads, following his gaze. Seeing all eyes upon him, the spy stepped forward a few paces.

"Most of them," the man stated. "Some of the Arabs of the towns have declared for Abreha. But most of his support comes from the bedouin."

Garmat levered himself up. "What about the Quraysh?" he asked.

The spy made a fluttering motion with his hand. "So far, Mecca has remained loyal. That could change, of course—*will* change, soon enough—if the rebellion is not crushed."

Hearing this news, several of the commanders grunted. The sounds were inarticulate, but full of import.

Antonina understood the meaning. The great Arab tribes centered in Mecca and the other towns of western Arabia—among which the Quraysh were dominant—were traders, not bedouin. It was they, not the nomads of the interior, who chafed most under Ethiopian rule. The bedouin of the interior did not really care who ruled fertile Yemen. Those nomads who had given their allegiance to Abreha would have done so for immediate bribes—and the hope of possible loot, if Abreha set out to conquer Ethiopia.

But the commercial interests of the tribes in Mecca often clashed with those of Axum. Axum's control of the great trading route which passed through the Red Sea rested on its navy's ability to suppress piracy. The Quraysh, on the other hand, *depended* on piracy. It was not that they themselves were pirates—although the accusation was often made—so much as the simple fact that no one used their more expensive camel caravans unless the sea route was infested by pirates.

For years now, since Axum under King Kaleb had conquered southern Arabia and clamped the iron grip of its navy on the Red Sea, the traders of Mecca had suffered greatly. By all logic, it should have been they—not bedouin nomads—who were flocking to Abreha's banner. The fact that they weren't—

"They've always been smart," said Garmat, now sitting erect. For the first time since the session began, the old adviser's face was animated and eager. He seemed like the Garmat of old, and Antonina was not the only one in the room who felt their spirits rise.

"Mecca is the key," said Garmat emphatically. "Mecca and Yathrib, and the whole of the Hijaz. I have said this before, and I will say it now again: control of Yemen depends on our control of the western coast."

Garmat stuck out his thumb. "We will always have the allegiance of the Arab townsmen of Yemen. Most of them, at least. Those people are farmers. They want stability and order, and no power in this region can provide it as well as Axum. True, they chafe a bit, because we are foreign. But not much, because Ethiopians are not *very* foreign, and—" He made a quick little flip of his hands, indicating himself. A small laugh rose in the chamber. Garmat was the product of a liaison between an Arab woman and an Ethiopian trader.

The adviser grinned. "I am by no means the only half-breed in Arabia—or in Axum." The assembled commanders grinned back. From their appearance, at least two of them had obvious Arab ancestry. Antonina, knowing of the long and intimate contact between Ethiopia and Arabia, suspected that most Axumites had Arabs perched in their family trees. Whole flocks of Arabs, more often than not.

Garmat continued. "The towns of Yemen will support us, given a choice. The bedouin mean nothing. They will bow to whoever has the power, and will not rebel so long as their customs are not meddled with." He shrugged. "Of course, their allegiance is casual. If there is unrest, they will look to take advantage. But so long as Axum is firmly in control of Yemen—*and the Hijaz*, the western coast—the bedouin will tend to their own affairs."

He leaned forward, looking intently at Eon.

"I said this to your father, and I will say it to you. *Mecca is the key*. Weld the Hijaz to Ethiopian rule, and you will hold all of southern Arabia in a solid grip. But so long as the Quraysh are discontent, your rule is based on sand."

For a moment, his eyes closed. "I was never quite able to convince Kaleb. He did not disagree, exactly, but—" The eyes reopened. "He was never willing to pay the price."

Garmat's tone hardened. "*The price must be paid. Now.*"

A murmur of protest began to rise from the military officers. Garmat eyed them stonily.

Antonina hesitated. She agreed with Garmat, but was unsure if she was in position to intervene in what was a delicate matter for Ethiopians.

Her hesitation was made moot, almost at once.

"What is your advice, Ousanas?" asked Eon.

The former dawazz spoke forcefully. "Pay the price. Immediately—*and in full.* I agree completely with Garmat."

The murmur of protest was swelling. Ousanas fixed the assembled regimental commanders with his eyes. If the gaze of Garmat was stony, his was that of a basilisk.

"These sounds of protest you hear, King of Kings," said Ousanas, indicating the officers with an accusing finger, "are the sounds of petty greed. Nothing more."

The officers—most of them, at least; not Wahsi—glared at Ousanas. The former dawazz glared back. And made instantly clear, whatever his official status was now, that a former slave was not hesitant to clash with army commanders.

"Stupid boys," he sneered, "coveting their stupid little marbles, and unwilling to share them with the other boys on the playground."

Antonina took a deep breath. She understood what lay beneath this quarrel. She had been well-briefed by her own excellent advisers, one of whom—the Armenian cataphract Ashot—was very familiar with Ethiopia and the complexities of Red Sea trade and politics.

Unlike Rome, Axum made no distinction between its army and its navy. Each of the regiments had its own fleet of ships, which were manned by its soldiers. For all that they were highland-born-and-bred, Ethiopia's soldiers were as much seamen as they were infantry. Seamen—and traders. Whenever the navy was not at war, or not on patrol, the regiments' ships carried trade goods. *And* took a percentage of the profits from civilian ships, on the grounds that their suppression of piracy was all that enabled civilian merchants to prosper.

Ethiopia's army, in short, had an immediate and vested interest in maintaining the supremacy of seaborne trade in the Red Sea—which was precisely the condition that squeezed the camel caravans of the Quraysh and the other trading tribes of Mecca and the Hijaz.

Antonina realized that she was holding her breath. This quarrel had the potential to erupt into a bitter brawl which could be disastrous for her plans. Belisarius' strategy depended on the support of a strong—and united—Axum.

When Eon spoke, his voice was low. Like a lion, growling at cubs.

"You—will—obey—me."

Startled by the majesty in that voice, the eyes of the officers left Ousanas and settled on the negusa nagast.

Eon sat in his throne, almost unmoving. In the time which followed, he used no grand gestures to give emphasis to his words. It was quite unnecessary. The words themselves seemed carved in stone.

"Do not forget, commanders of the sarawit, why Ethiopia is ruled by me—and not you. You are the nagast, but I am the *negusa* nagast. King of Kings. Our ancestors realized that kings are prone to folly, and thus they instituted the dawazz and required the approval of the regiments before a prince could become a king. But they also realized that officers—nobles of all stripes—are prone to a different folly. They forget to think of the kingdom, and think only of their own little piece of the realm. And thus the *negusa* nagast was set above you."

He stared down at them, like a sphinx. "You think only of your profits, as if they were the sum of things. But I was at Ranapur, where Malwa butchered two hundred thousand people. Flayed them, fed them to animals, trampled them under elephants, tore them apart with oxen."

He was stone, stone: "*Two hundred thousand*. Can you comprehend that number—you *coin-counters*? All the towns in Ethiopia and Arabia, put together, do not contain half so many people. You think Malwa will not do the same to Axum and Sana? Do you?"

Finally, he moved. A finger lifted from the arm of the throne and pointed to Ousanas.

"My dawazz, at my command, took the Talisman of God in his own hand and saw Axum's future, if Malwa is not crushed. By the time of his death in battle, we were nothing but refugees fleeing into central Africa—and with no great hope of finding a haven there."

He leaned forward, just a bit. "What use will your treasure be in central Africa, *merchants*? Do you plan to buy the finest grass huts, and sleep on the best dirt?"

Eon stared at his commanders. After a moment, they lowered their heads.

All but Wahsi, who growled: "I was at Ranapur, also. I did not try to count Malwa's murders. I could not even count the rivers of blood."

Eon let the silence last for a full minute, before he spoke again. Stone became iron.

"There will be no quarrel over this matter. I will tolerate no dispute. I will order the immediate execution of any officer who so much as utters a word of protest in private conversation with his soldiers. I will perch the heads of every commander of every regiment on the crosses of their thrones in the training field. If you doubt me—if you think the sarwen will follow you rather than the negusa nagast—then test me now. Before I smash rebellion in Arabia, I will smash it here."

Silence. Eon let it stand, for two full minutes.

Iron became steel.

"My commands are as follows. We will send a delegation to Mecca immediately, riding the fastest horses in Axum and taking the fastest ship in Adulis. If Garmat is strong enough for the journey, he will lead the expedition. If he is not—"

"I am well enough, King of Kings," said Garmat.

Eon nodded; continued: "Our delegation will meet with the leaders of the Quraysh and all the other tribes of the Hijaz. They will offer the following. Henceforth, the tribes will be entitled to a share of the profits from the seaborne trade. They will also be granted access to all caravan trade anywhere in the realm of Axum—here in Ethiopia as well as in Arabia. And finally—"

The young king took a little breath of his own. For just a second, a shadow seemed to cross his face.

"The delegation will offer marriage to the negusa nagast—to me—for one of their princesses. Whichever one they select. The blood of Arabia will henceforth flow into Axum's ruling dynasty."

Eon smiled, finally. It was a small, wan smile. "Legally, and officially. It has already flowed into it often enough otherwise."

Antonina was not fooled by that smile. She understood how little Eon cared, so soon after the death of Tarabai and Zaia, to even think of marriage. But the young king, here also, was showing that he could put the needs of his kingdom first.

"*Negusa nagast*," she murmured, under her breath.

Or so she thought. Perhaps she spoke louder than she intended, because the words were almost instantly echoed by others in the room. By all in the room, within seconds.

"*Negusa nagast*," repeated the regimental commanders. The two words, alone, were the token of their submission.

Ethiopia's new King of Kings had established his

rule. In what mattered, now, not in the formalities of ritual and custom. The regiments had raised him to the throne, but he had shown that he could break them to his will.

At first, as she carefully studied the faces of the commanders of the sarawit, Antonina was surprised that she could see no signs of resentment. To the contrary—for all their impassivity, she was sure she detected an underlying sense of satisfaction in those hard, black faces.

But, after a time, she realized that she had misunderstood those men. Traders and merchants they might be, in some part of their lives. But at the heart of those lives lay spears, not coins. When all was said and done, those warriors counted victory as the greatest treasure of all. And, like all such men, they knew that triumph was impossible without sureness of command.

Sureness of which they had just been given evidence. With their own heads offered, if need be, as the proof.

There was no need. In the hours which followed, as the session relaxed and delved into the specifics of war, and campaigns, and negotiations, and trade privileges, Antonina witnessed the forging of Ethiopia's new leadership. It centered on Eon, of course; but Ousanas was there also, and Garmat and Wahsi, and, by the end of the day, every single commander of the sarawit except those in rebellion in Arabia.

Watching the easy confidence with which those men planned their next campaign—participating in it fully, in fact, for her own forces were integral to the plans—Antonina found herself, again and again, forced to suppress an urge to giggle.

Bad move, Malwa. Oh—bad, bad move.

Chapter 10

DEOGIRI

Spring, 532 A.D.

Raghunath Rao finished his bowl of rice and set it down on the stone floor of the rampart. Still squatting on his heels, he leaned back against the outer wall. His head, resting against the rough stones, was only inches from one of the open embrasures in the crenellated fortification. The breeze coming through the gap in the wall helped to ease the heat. It was the middle of *garam*, India's dry season, and the land was like an oven.

Rao exuded satisfaction. "It's nice to get rice for a change," he commented. "I get sick of millet."

Squatting next to him, Maloji nodded cheerfully. "We should have enough for several days, too. That was a big shipment smuggled in from the coast."

Rao turned his head, peering through the embrasure at the distant lines of the Malwa besieging Deogiri. "Was there any trouble?"

Maloji grinned. "Not the least." He jerked his head

toward the Malwa. "Half of those wretches, by now, are simply trying to stay alive. The Vile One isn't sending out many patrols any longer, and most of those keep their eyes closed. We let them pass unmolested, they don't see anything. That's the unspoken agreement."

Rao smiled. His eyes scanned the enemy trenches and fieldworks. That was simply habit. The Malwa besiegers were not trying to advance their lines any longer. They were simply waiting for the siege guns to arrive and break Deogiri's huge walls.

The walls of Deogiri had shrugged off Venandakatra's light field artillery, and they had been the doom of thousands of Malwa soldiers. The enemy had not tried to assault the city for weeks, now. Not even Venandakatra, who cared as much for the lives of common soldiers as he did for insects, would order any more charges.

Maloji continued. "If the Rajputs were still here, of course, we'd have a problem. But they've all been sent north. Our spies in Bharakuccha say the Malwa are having nothing but grief with the Romans in Persia." He spit on the floor. "Not even the Vile One's Ye-tai can force the regular rabble to conduct serious patrols any longer."

Both men fell silent, for several minutes. Then, clearing his throat, Maloji spoke again.

"Have you received word from the empress?"

Rao nodded. "Yes. A letter arrived yesterday. But she said nothing concerning the siege guns. I didn't expect her to. If Kungas was able to convince her of our plan, she would not send any message to us. For fear of interception. The plan can only succeed if absolute secrecy is maintained."

Maloji hesitated, then scowled. "I still don't like it. How can you trust that man so much? He betrayed Malwa once. Why would he not betray us? Everything depends on him, and his fellow traitors."

Rao's eyes left the enemy and settled on Maloji. His expression was utterly serene.

"Words, Maloji. Those are just words. The veil of illusion. How can the man be accused of betraying Malwa, when he never gave his loyalty to them in the first place? He was born into their world, he did not choose it freely."

"He worked for them," countered Maloji stubbornly. "All the Kushans did."

Rao smiled. "Tell me, Maloji. Did you ever catch wild animals—cubs—when you were a boy, and keep them in a pen?" His friend and subordinate nodded. "Did they escape?"

Maloji chuckled. "The mongoose did."

Rao nodded. "And then? Did you denounce the mongoose for a traitor?"

Maloji laughed. After a moment, he made a little gesture with his hand, opening the palm. It was not the first time in his life he had made that gesture, nor, he knew, would it be the last. The student, acknowledging the master.

Rao's eyes grew slightly unfocused. "I know that man, Maloji. Better, perhaps, than I know any other man alive. I spent weeks studying him, outside the walls of the Vile One's palace, while he was still Shakuntala's captor. My enemy, he was then. I hated him with a pure fury. But I never misunderstood him."

Rao rolled his shoulders against the stone wall, pointing to the south.

"I will never forget the day I saw Kungas coming through that gate, bringing word from the empress that she had taken Suppara. I fell to my knees, I was so stunned. I knew Belisarius must have found Indian allies, to smuggle Shakuntala out of captivity, but I had no idea it was him."

Rao's eyes closed, as he savored the memory.

"On my knees. He came up to me and extended

his hand, but I refused the offer. I stayed on my knees for several minutes, not because I was still shocked, but because I was praying."

He opened his eyes and stared at the blinding sky of India. "I understood, then—*I knew*—that God has not forsaken us. I *knew* the asura was doomed."

He brought down his eyes to meet those of his friend. "Trust me in this, Maloji. If the thing can be done, Kungas will do it."

Silence reigned for several minutes. Then, with a little shake of his head, Rao spoke again. His voice was perhaps a bit harsh.

"The empress wrote the letter to ask for my advice. The Cholas have offered marriage to her. The eldest son of the dynasty."

Maloji studied Rao intently. "And what did you say?"

Rao flexed his hands. He spent a few seconds examining the opening and closing fingers, as if they were objects of great fascination.

"I urged her to accept," he said forcefully. "The Cholas are the most powerful independent kingdom of south India. Their proposal was full of quibbles, of course, but they are still offering a genuine alliance. A marriage between Shakuntala and the Cholas would strengthen us like no other. I am in full agreement with Dadaji Holkar on that matter, and I told her so very clearly."

Maloji looked away. "That must have been a difficult letter for you to write," he said softly.

Rao's eyes widened. "Why?"

Maloji snorted. A moment later, he brought his gaze back to Rao. It was a sad gaze.

"Old friend, you cannot fool me. Others, perhaps. But not *me*."

He said nothing else. For a moment, Rao tried to meet Maloji's level gaze with one of his own. But only for a moment.

"It is dharma, Maloji," he murmured, studying his flexing fingers. "I have lived my life by duty, and discipline. And so has—"

He took a deep, almost shuddering breath. A faint sheen of moisture came to his eyes.

"And so has she." Another breath—he made no attempt to control the shudder, now—and he finally, to another man, spoke the words. "She is the treasure of my soul, Maloji. But I have my duty, and she has hers. We will both be faithful to our dharma."

His fingers became fists. "That is the way it must be. *Will* be."

Maloji hesitated. He was perhaps Rao's closest friend, but this was a subject they had never discussed. With a little shrug, he decided to widen the crack.

"Have you ever spoken to her?"

Rao's back stiffened. "Never!" he exclaimed. "That, alone, would be a betrayal of my trust. She was given into my care by the Emperor of Andhra himself, to safeguard the dynasty. It would be the foulest treason for me to betray that trust."

Maloji shook his head. "You are not her father, Rao. Much older than she, true. So what? If I remember right, the oldest son of Chola is no younger than you."

Rao made a short, chopping motion. "That has nothing to do with anything. She is the purest blood of India. The heir of ancient Satavahana. I am a Maratha chieftain." For a moment, he managed a grin. "It is true, I am considered kshatriya—by Marathas, at least. But my mother's father was a peasant, and no one even knows the name of my paternal grandfather, although he is reputed to have been a tinker."

His powerful hands relaxed. A great sigh loosened his muscular body. "The world is what it is, Maloji. We must be true to our dharma, or we lose our souls."

His whole body seemed to ooze against the stones of the wall, as if he were seeking to find oneness with the universe.

"We must accept, that is all." Rao turned his eyes to his friend. The moisture was gone, along with any outward sign of pain. Suddenly, he grinned.

"It has been difficult, I admit. I remember, the first time—" He chuckled wryly. "She was thirteen, perhaps fourteen years old. She had done especially well in one of the exercises I set her to, and I praised her. She laughed and embraced me, pressing herself close. Suddenly—it struck me like a bolt of lighting, I will never forget the moment—I realized she was a woman now. And not just any woman, but—"

He groped for words. Maloji provided them: "She has been called the Black-Eyed Pearl of the Satavahanas since she was twelve. There is a reason for it, which goes far beyond her eyes. I have not seen her since Amaravati, but even then she was beautiful."

Rao closed his eyes again. "I try not to think about it," he whispered. "It is difficult, but I manage. Since that day, years ago, I have kept myself from looking at the beauty of her body. Other men may do so, but not I." His eyes reopened. "But I cannot blind myself to the real beauty. I have tried—so very hard—but I cannot. I simply try not to think about it." He smiled. "Perhaps that is why I meditate so often."

Abruptly, he rose. "Enough. We will not speak of this again, Maloji, though I thank you for your words." He stared at the Malwa enemy over the battlements. "We have a war to fight and win. A dynasty to return to its rightful place. An empress to shield and protect—and cherish. That is our dharma."

He pushed himself away from the stones and turned toward the stairs leading to the city below.

"And now, I must be about my tasks. I have my duty, she has hers. She will marry Chola, and I will dance at her wedding. The best dance I ever danced."

Seconds later, he was gone. Maloji, watching him go, bowed his head. "Not even you, Raghunath Rao," he whispered. "Not even you—the Great Country's best dancer as well as its soul—can dance that well."

Chapter 11
PERSIA
Spring, 532 A.D.

The first Malwa barrage came as an unpleasant surprise to the Roman troops dug in on the crest of the saddle pass. Instead of sailing all over the landscape, a majority of the Malwa rockets landed uncomfortably near their entrenchments. And the fire from the small battery of field guns which Damodara had placed on a nearby hilltop was fiendishly accurate. The Roman fieldworks were partially obscured by small clouds of dust and flying dirt.

There was not much actual damage, however. Two cannon balls landed in trenches, but they caused only one fatality. Solid cannon shot was designed for field battles, where a ball could bounce through the packed ranks of advancing infantry. Even when such a solid shot struck a trench directly, it usually did nothing more than bury itself in the loosened dirt. The man killed just had the misfortune of standing on the wrong patch of soil. His death was almost silent, marked only by a sodden thud; and then, by the soft and awful sounds of blood and intestines spilling from a corpse severed at the waist.

Worse casualties were created by the single rocket which hit directly in a trench. Rocket warheads were packed with gunpowder and iron pellets. When such a warhead exploded in a crowded trench, the result was horrendous.

"*Damn*," hissed Maurice, watching the survivors in the trench frantically trying to save the wounded. The shouts of the rescuers were drowned beneath the shrieks of dying and injured men. "They've got impact fuses."

Belisarius nodded. "*And* they've refitted their rockets with proper venturi," he added. "You can tell the difference in the sound alone, leaving aside the fact they're ten times more accurate."

Frowning, he swiveled his telescope to point at Damodara's pavilion, erected just a few hundred yards behind the front lines of the Ye-tai who were massing for a charge.

Through the telescope, Belisarius could see Damodara standing on a platform which had been erected in front of the pavilion. The platform was just a sturdy framework of small logs, but it was enough to give the Malwa commander a good field of view. It was typical of Damodara, thought Belisarius, that he had not even bothered to have the logs planed. Most anvaya-prapta sachivya would have insisted on polished planks, covered with rugs.

"How did he do it?" the Roman general muttered. "I knew the Malwa would come up with impact fuses and venturi soon enough. But I didn't expect to see them appear in Damodara's army, as isolated as they are from the manufactories in India."

Belisarius lowered the telescope, still frowning.

"They must have hauled them here," said Maurice. The gray-haired veteran frowned as well. "Hell of a logistics route! I'd hate to be relying on supplies that have to be moved through the Hindu Kush and—all that."

The last two words were accompanied by a vague little wave of Maurice's hand, indicating the entire broken and arid terrain between the lush plains of north India and the Zagros range. Mountains, hills, deserts—some of the roughest country in the world, that was. More suited for mountain goats than supply trains.

"It *could* be done," mused Belisarius. "Trade caravans have made it all the way to China, when you think about it. But not often, and not carrying anything more cumbersome than luxury goods."

Aide amplified. **Gold coins, crystal and red coral from the Roman Empire, in exchange for silk from China. Some jewelry, both ways.**

Belisarius scratched his chin, as he invariably did when deep in thought. "Damodara would have one advantage," he added slowly. "He wouldn't have to worry about brigands. No hill bandit in his right mind would attack a Malwa military caravan."

"Pathans would," countered Maurice, referring to the fiercest of the mountain tribes. "Those bastards—*down!*"

He and Belisarius hastily crouched in their trench. Nearby, Anastasius and Valentinian did the same. A volley of Malwa rockets sailed overhead, passing no more than ten feet above them. A few seconds later, they heard the explosive sounds of the rockets landing somewhere on the back slope of the saddle pass.

As soon as Belisarius was certain that the volley had ended, he rose and peered behind him. He had taken position in a trench at the very crest of the pass, allowing him as good a view of the back slope as the foreground. Leaning over the log parapet, he studied the scene intently.

His brow was creased with worry. Belisarius had positioned his handcannon troops just behind the crest of the pass. They would—he thought—be out of danger there until he needed them. *And* out of sight of the enemy. The handcannons were Belisarius' own little surprise for the Malwa. He had not used them yet, in this campaign, and he hoped that Damodara and Sanga were still unaware of their existence.

Maurice joined him. The chiliarch, after one quick look, verbalized Belisarius' own thoughts.

"No damage. The rockets passed over them too." Maurice's face broke into a grin. That was a rare expression, on *his* face. Belisarius was amused to see that it was probably the least humorous grin in the world. Wintry, you might call it.

"But I'll bet they're not whining anymore about all the digging you make them do," chuckled Maurice. He and Belisarius could see the first heads of the handcannon troops popping up from their trenches. Those soldiers were not more than fifty yards away, and their expressions caused Belisarius to break into his own grin. Worry, fear—combined with more than a dose of outrage.

What the hell is this? *Here we were, enjoying a pleasant moment of relaxation, engrossed in cursing that damn fool General Pick-and-Shovel who makes us dig trenches every time we take two steps, and—*

What the hell's going on? It's not fair*!*

Still grinning, Belisarius turned around and resumed his study of the enemy. After a moment, he picked up the broken thread of their conversation.

"Pathans wouldn't attack Damodara's supply trains. Don't forget, Maurice, those caravans would be protected by Rajput troops. *Sanga's* Rajputs, to boot. And I'm sure Sanga would see to it that the information was passed on to the tribesmen. He has his own Pathan trackers, you know."

Belisarius looked at the large body of Rajput cavalry that formed the right wing of the enemy's formation. There were a smaller number of Rajputs on the Malwa left wing, but Belisarius had spotted Sanga earlier through his telescope. In this coming battle, the Rajput king had been assigned to the right. With his naked eyes, Belisarius couldn't distinguish Sanga any longer from the thousands of other Rajputs massed on that side of the battlefield. But he was certain that Sanga was still there.

"Sanga led the last punitive expedition which the Rajputs sent against the Pathans," he said, speaking softly. "That was years ago. There haven't been any since because Sanga ravaged them so badly—" Belisarius broke off, with a little grimace. "Bloody business, that is."

Maurice gave his commander a quick, shrewd glance. Belisarius, in the past, had led his own punitive expeditions against barbarians. In the trans-Danube, several times; and, once, against the Isaurians in Asia Minor. Even as young as he'd been then—and Belisarius was still shy of thirty—his campaigns had already been marked by sagacity and cunning.

They'd also been brutal and savage, as campaigns against barbarians always were. Belisarius had a detestation of cruelty which was unusual in soldiers of the time. Some of that aversion, thought Maurice, was simply due to the man's nature. But that natural inclination had been hardened and tempered by the sight of Goth and Isaurian villages visited by his own troops.

Seeing beneath Belisarius' now-expressionless face, Maurice turned his eyes away. He was quite sure, in that moment, that he knew what Belisarius was thinking. An image came to Maurice, as vividly as if it had just happened yesterday. He remembered seeing Belisarius standing over the body of a child in one of those villages. The young commander—still in his teens, he'd been—had just arrived, with Maurice and some of his Thracian cataphracts. The village was in flames, but the main body of the army had already passed through, rampaging on ahead.

Judging by the size of the pitiful little corpse, the Goth had been not more than five years old. Belisarius' soldiers had set a sharpened stake in the ground, impaled the boy, castrated him—and cut off his penis for good measure—amputated his arms, and then, mercifully, cut his throat. But neither Belisarius nor Maurice, surveying the scene, doubted the sequence in which the soldiers had committed their atrocities. For minutes which must have seemed an eternity to their victim, Roman troops had subjected a helpless child to the cruelest tortures imaginable.

The naked and disemboweled body of a girl had been lying nearby. The boy's mother, perhaps, but more likely his sister. The corpse's face was nothing but a pulp, covered with half-dried, crusted blood. It was impossible to discern her features, but the body itself seemed not far past puberty. The girl had obviously been gang-raped before she was murdered.

Remembering, Maurice could still hear Belisarius' quiet and anguished words. "*And these men call themselves Christians?*"

Prior to that day, Belisarius had simply tried to restrain his army. Thereafter, he instituted the draconian policy regarding atrocities for which he was famous—notorious, from the viewpoint of some soldiers and all mercenary troops. As it happened, by good fortune, the men responsible for that particular atrocity had been identified and arrested within a week. Belisarius immediately ordered their execution. The army had almost mutinied, but Belisarius already had his corps of hand-picked Thracian bucellarii to enforce his orders.

Still, the atrocities continued, if not as often. It was almost impossible to restrain troops completely in war against barbarians, since so many of the soldiers in the campaigns were borderers. Barbarians were guilty of their own brutal practices, and the soldiers burned for vengeance. In the dispersed nature of such combat, troops soon learned to keep their savageries hidden.

Maurice banished the memory. Again, he glanced at Belisarius. The general's gaze was still on the Rajput troops, where Sanga commanded, and his lips were moving. Maurice could not hear the words he spoke, but he thought he knew what they were. Belisarius had told him of the message which the Great Ones of the future had given to Aide, to guide the crystal in its search for help in the ancient past of humanity.

Find the general who is not a warrior, had been part of that message. But there had also been: *See the enemy in the mirror, the friend across the field.*

Belisarius emitted a little sigh, and shook his head. The motion was quick and abrupt, as if he were tossing something off. When the general turned back to Maurice, there was no sign of anything in his brown eyes but the calm self-control of an experienced commander on a battlefield.

"We've got some time," Belisarius pronounced. As if to verify his words, the distant Malwa batteries erupted in new salvos. After a quick glance, Maurice ignored them. From their trajectories, none of the missiles would strike in their vicinity. He gave his attention back to the general.

"At least an hour," continued Belisarius, "before they start their first assault." He began walking toward the cross-trench which gave access to the back slope. From habit, Belisarius stayed in a semicrouch, but it was obvious from the casual way he looked back at Maurice that he had come to the same assessment of the current barrage's accuracy.

"Kurush should still be in the field headquarters. I want to talk to him." Belisarius pointed to the enemy. "There's a bit of a mystery here that I'd like to clear up, if we can. I don't like bad news of any kind, but I *especially* don't like surprises."

As Belisarius had hoped, Kurush was in the field headquarters. The young Persian nobleman had arrived just the day before, accompanied by three subordinate officers. He had been sent by Emperor Khusrau to reestablish liaison with the Romans. Since Belisarius had led his army into the Zagros, in hopes of delaying Damodara's advance while Khusrau set Mesopotamia in order, the Persian emperor had had no contact with his Roman allies.

Khusrau Anushirvan—Khusrau of the Immortal Soul, as the Aryans called him—had not chosen Kurush for the assignment by accident. Partly, of course, his choice had been dictated by the prickly class sensitivities of Aryan society. Kurush was a sahrdaran, the highest-ranked layer of the Persian aristocracy. To have sent a lesser figure would have been insulting—not to Belisarius, who didn't care—but to other members of the sahrdaran. Faced with his half-brother Ormazd's treasonous rebellion, Khusrau could not afford to lose the loyalty of any more Persian aristocrats.

But, for the most part, the Emperor of Persia had sent Kurush because of the man's own qualities. For all his youth, Kurush was an excellent military commander in his own right. And, best of all, he was familiar to Belisarius. The two men had worked together the year before, during Belisarius' campaign in northern Mesopotamia.

When Belisarius strode through the open flaps of the field headquarters' entrance, he saw that the four Persian officers were bent over the table in the center of the tent, admiring the huge map.

"This is marvelous!" exclaimed Kurush, seeing Belisarius. The nobleman strode forward, gesticulating, with the nervous energy that was always a part of him.

"Where did you get the idea?" he demanded. He shook his head vigorously. "Not the map itself. I mean the—" Kurush snapped his head around, looking toward the Syrian craftsman whom Belisarius had trained as a cartographer. "What did you call it? Tapo—*something*."

"Topography," said the mapmaker.

"Yes, that's it!" Kurush's head snapped back to Belisarius. "Where did you get the idea? I've never seen any other maps or charts which show elevation and terrain features. Except maybe one or two prominent mountains. And rivers, of course."

Belisarius shrugged. "It just came to me, one day." His words were abrupt, even a little curt.

Typical, groused Aide. **I never get any credit. Glory hound!**

Belisarius pursed his lips, trying not to smile. This was a subject he did not want broached. Belisarius had once told Kurush's uncle, the sahrdaran Baresmanas, the secret of Aide's existence. But he didn't think Kurush knew, and he saw no reason to change that state of affairs. The fact was that Aide had given him the idea, just as he had so many others that Belisarius had implemented.

Toil, toil, toil, that's all I do. A slave in the gold mines, while you get to prance around in all the finery. Good thing for you trade unions haven't been invented yet, or I'd go out on strike.

Wanting to change the subject—as much to keep from laughing as anything else—

The eight-hour day! For a start. Wages, of course. Not better wages, either—*any* wages. I'm not getting paid at all, now that I think about it. Exploiter! Then—

—Belisarius drove over Aide's witticisms—

—there's the whole matter of benefits. I'll let the medical slide, seeing as how the current state of medical practice makes me shudder, but—

—along with Kurush's onrushing stream of questions.

I demand a pension. Thirty-and-out, nothing less!

"Are any Persian towns in your eastern provinces centers of artisanship?" asked Belisarius. "Especially metalworking?"

Kurush's mouth snapped shut. For a moment, the Persian nobleman stared at Belisarius as if he were a madman. Then he burst into laughter.

"In the *east*?" he cried. Kurush's laughter was echoed by all three of his officers. One of them snorted. "Those hicks can barely manage to rim a cartwheel."

"Do they even *have* carts?" demanded another.

Kurush was back to vigorous headshaking. "The eastern provinces are inhabited by nothing besides peasants and petty noblemen. They know how to grow crops. And how to fight, of course—but even that, they do poorly."

He rocked his head back and forth, once, twice, thrice. The quick little gesture was by way of qualification. "I should be fair. The eastern dehgans are as good as any, in single combat. But their tactics—"

"*Charge*," sneered one of his officers. "If that doesn't work—*charge again*." His two fellows chortled agreement. "And if that doesn't work?" queried one. He shrugged. "Charge again. And keep doing it until your horse has the good sense to run away."

Kurush grinned. "If you want Persian artisans, Belisarius, you have to go to Mesopotamia or Persarmenia for them. Except in Fars province. There are some metalsmiths—armorers, mostly—in Persepolis and Pasargadae."

He cocked his head quizzically. "Why do you ask?"

Belisarius walked over to the table and stared down at the map, scratching his chin. "I ask because the gunpowder weapons Damodara's army is using are quite a bit more sophisticated than anything I expected them to have." He gestured with his head toward the east. The sound of the Malwa barrages carried clearly through the leather walls of the tent.

Still scratching his chin, he added: "I thought it might be possible that Damodara established a manufacturing center somewhere in Hyrcania or Khorasan. But that's not likely, if there are no native craftsmen to draw on. I doubt he would have brought an entire labor force with him all the way from the Gangetic plain. A few experts, maybe. But not the hundreds of skilled workers it would take to manufacture—"

Again, he gestured toward the east wall of the tent. Again, the sound of Malwa rocketry and cannon fire pierced the leather.

A new voice entered the discussion. "It *is* possible, General Belisarius. He could have set one up at Marv." Vasudeva rose from a chair in a corner of the tent and ambled toward the table. "Marv is a big enough town, and it's well located for the purpose."

Vasudeva reached the table and leaned over, pointing to Marv's location on the map. His finger then moved east to the river Oxus, and then, following the river's course, southeast to a spot on the map which bore no markings.

"Right about there is the city of Begram," said the Kushan general. "The largest Kushan city, after Peshawar. Our kings, in the old days, had their summer palaces at Begram." A bitter tinge entered his voice. "Peshawar is nothing but ruins, today. But Begram still stands. The Ye-tai did not destroy it, except for the stupas."

For all the calm in Vasudeva's voice, Belisarius did not miss the underlying anger—even hatred. When the Ye-tai conquered the Kushan kingdom, a century earlier, they had singled out Buddhism for particularly savage repression. All the monks had been murdered, and the stupas razed to the ground. Like most

Kushans Belisarius knew, Vasudeva still considered himself a Buddhist. But it was a faith he practiced in fumbling secret, with no monks or learned scrolls to guide him.

Vasudeva's finger retraced the route he had indicated a few seconds earlier. "As you can see, travel from Begram to Marv is not difficult. Most of it can be done by river craft."

"And what's in Begram?" asked Kurush.

Vasudeva smiled thinly. "Kushans. What else?" The smile faded. "More precisely, Kushan *craftsmen*. Even in the old days, Begram was the center of artisanship in the Kushan realm. Peshawar was bigger, but it was the royal city. Full of soldiers, courtiers, that sort of thing." With a chuckle, as dry as the smile: "And a horde of bureaucrats, of course."

Vasudeva fingered his wispy goatee. "If Damodara had the good sense—*if*, General Belisarius; the Malwa, as a rule, don't think of Kushans as anything other than vassal soldiers—he could have easily transplanted hundreds of Kushan craftsmen to Marv. There, he could have built up an armament center. Close enough, as you can see from the map, to supply his army once it passed the Caspian Gates. But far enough away, in a sheltered oasis, to keep it safe from Persian raiders."

He's right! said Aide to Belisarius. **Marv would be perfect. The Seleucids walled the city eight hundred years ago. The whole oasis, actually. The Sassanids made it a provincial capital and a military center after they conquered the western part of the Kushan Empire. And Marv will become—would have become—the capital of Khorasan province after the Islamic conquest.**

The Persian officers were staring at Vasudeva as if he were babbling in an unknown tongue. One of them turned his head and muttered to another: "*I've* never thought of Kushans as anything but soldiers."

Vasudeva heard the remark. His smile returned. It was a *very* thin smile.

"Nobody does," he said. "The fact remains that Kushans have been skilled artisans for centuries. Appearances to the contrary, we aren't barbarian nomads." He looked down at his hands, flexing his fingers. "My father was a very good jeweler. I wanted to follow in his footsteps. But the Malwa had other plans for me."

Belisarius felt a sudden rush of empathy for the stocky Kushan mercenary. He, as a boy, had wanted to be a blacksmith rather than a soldier. Until the demands of his class, and Rome, decreed otherwise.

"Damodara is smart enough," he mused. He leaned back from the table. "More than smart enough."

Belisarius began slowly pacing around. His softly spoken words were those of a man thinking aloud. "*If* he had good enough intelligence, that is. The Malwa spymaster, Nanda Lal, is a capable man—very capable—but I never got the sense, in the many days I spent in his company, that he thought much about manufacturing and artisanry. His orientation seemed entirely political and military. So where would Damodara have learned—?"

Narses!

"*Narses*," snarled Maurice. "He's got that stinking traitor working for him."

Belisarius stopped his pacing and stared at the Thracian chiliarch. His own eyes held nothing of Maurice's angry glare. They were simply calm. Calm, and thoughtful.

"That's possible," he said, after a few seconds. "I've never spotted him, through the telescope. But if he's with Damodara's army, Narses would be sure to stay out of sight."

Belisarius scratched his chin. "Possible, possible," he mused. "Narses was an expert on central Asia." He gave Kurush a half-rueful, half-apologetic glance.

"We always let him handle that side of our affairs with the Aryans. He was—well, I've got to be honest: *superb*—when it came to bribing and maneuvering barbarians into harassing Persia's eastern provinces."

For a moment, Kurush began to glower. But, within a couple of seconds, the glower turned into a little laugh.

"I know!" he exclaimed. "The grief that man caused us! It wasn't just barbarians, either. He was also a master at keeping those damned eastern noblemen stirred up against imperial authority."

Kurush took four quick strides to the entrance. He stared out and up, toward the crest of the pass. To all appearance, he was listening to the sound of the Malwa barrage. But Belisarius knew that the man's thoughts were really directed elsewhere, both in time and space.

Kurush turned his head. "Assuming that you're right, Belisarius, what's the significance of it?"

"The significance, Kurush, is that it means this Malwa army is even more dangerous that we thought." The Roman general moved toward the entrance, stopping a few feet behind Kurush. "What it means is that *this* army could ravage Mesopotamia on its own, regardless of what happens to the main Malwa army in the delta."

Startled, Kurush spun around.

"They're not big enough!" he exclaimed. "If Emperor Khusrau wasn't tied up keeping the Malwa in Charax—" He stumbled to a halt; then, glumly: "And if we didn't have the traitor Ormazd to deal with in upper Mesopotamia—" His words trailed off again. Stubbornly, Kurush shook his head.

"They're still not big enough," he insisted.

"They *are*, Kurush," countered Belisarius. "*If* they have their own armament center—and I'm now convinced they do—then they are more than big enough."

He stepped up to the entrance, standing right next

to Kurush. His next words the general pitched very low, so that only the Persian nobleman could hear.

"That's as good an army as any in the world, sahrdaran. Trust me. I've been fighting them for weeks, now." He hesitated, knowing Kurush's touchy Aryan pride, but pushed on. "And they've defeated every Persian army that was sent against them."

Kurush tightened his jaws. But, touchy or not, the Persian was also honest. He nodded his head curtly.

Belisarius continued. "I thought they'd be limited by the fact that Emperor Skandagupta sent Damodara and Sanga into eastern Persia with very little in the way of gunpowder weapons. But if that's *not* true—if they've created their own weapons industry along the way—then we are looking at a very different kind of animal. A tiger instead of a leopard."

Kurush frowned. "Would Skandagupta permit Damodara such freedom? I always got the impression, from what you told me of your trip to India, that the Malwa gunpowder industry was kept exclusively in their capital city of Kausambi—right under the emperor's nose."

Belisarius stared at the pass above them, as if he were trying to peer through the rock of the mountains and study the enemy on the other side.

"Interesting question," he murmured. "Offhand, I'd say—*no*. But what does Skandagupta know of things in far-off Marv?" Belisarius smiled himself, now—a smile every bit as thin as Vasudeva's had been.

"*Narses*," he said softly, almost lingering over the name. "If Damodara does have Narses working for him, then he's got one of the world's supreme politicians—and spymasters—helping to plan his moves. Narses is not famous, to put it mildly, for his slavish respect for established authority. And he worships no god but Ambition."

Kurush stared at Belisarius, wide-eyed. "You think—"

Belisarius' shoulders moved in a tiny shrug. "Who knows? Except this: if Narses is on the other side of that pass, then I can guarantee that he is spinning plans within plans. Never underestimate that old eunuch, Kurush. He doesn't think simply of the next two steps. He always thinks of the twenty steps beyond those."

Kurush's smile was *not* thin. "That description reminds me of someone else I know."

Belisarius did not smile in return. He simply nodded, once. "Well, yes. It does."

For a few seconds, the two men were silent. Then, after a quick glance into the interior of the tent to make sure no one could overhear, Kurush whispered: "What does this mean—in terms of your strategy?"

Again, Belisarius made that tiny shrug. "I don't know. At the moment, I don't see where it changes anything." He thrust out his chin, pointing at the enemy hidden from their sight by the pass above. "I can delay that army, Kurush, but I can't stop it. So I don't see that I have any choice but to continue with the plan we are already agreed on."

Belisarius gave his own quick glance backward, to make sure no one was within hearing range. Kurush was familiar with his plans, as were Belisarius' own chief subordinates, but he knew that none of the other Persian officers were privy to them. So far as they knew, Belisarius and his Roman army were in the Zagros simply to fend off Damodara's advance. He wanted to keep them in that happy state of ignorance.

"I do know this much," he continued, turning his eyes back to Kurush. "The rebellion in south India is now more important than ever. If our strategy works, here, and we drive the main Malwa army out of the delta—and *if* the rebellion in Majarashtra swells to gigantic proportions—then the Malwa will have no choice." Again, he pointed with his chin to the pass. "They will have to pull that magnificent army out of

Persia. And use *it*, instead of Venandakatra's torturers, to crush the Deccan."

Kurush eyed him. He knew how much Belisarius liked and admired the Marathas and their Empress Shakuntala. "That'll be very tough on the rebels."

Belisarius winced, but only briefly. "Yes—and then again, maybe not."

He paused, staring at the mountains. "Those men are far better soldiers than anything Venandakatra has. And there's no comparison at all between their leaders and the Vile One. But that army is Rajput, now, at its core. And Damodara has welded himself to them. Rajputs have their own hard sense of honor, which fits their Malwa masters about as well as a glove fits a fish tail. I'm not sure how good they'll be, when the time comes for murder instead of war."

Kurush scowled. The expression made clear his own opinion. *Malwa was Malwa.*

Belisarius did not argue the point. He was not at all sure that Kurush was wrong. But, inwardly, he made another shrug. As much as Belisarius prided himself on his ability to plan ahead, he had never forgotten that the heart of war is chaos and confusion. Between the moment—now—and the future, lay the maelstrom. Who could foresee what combinations, and what contradictions, that vortex would produce? In the months—years—ahead?

Now intervened, breaking his train of thought. The sounds of the Malwa barrage abruptly ceased. Looking up the slope, Belisarius saw a courier racing toward the field headquarters. One of Bouzes' Syrians, he thought.

Belisarius did not wait for the man to arrive. He turned back into the tent and announced, to the Roman and Persian officers who had remained by the table: "Gentlemen, there's a battle to be fought."

Chapter 12

On his way back up the slope, Belisarius stopped when he came to the trenches where the handcannon soldiers were dug in. He turned to Maurice, waving his hand.

"Go on ahead, and see to the rest of the army. I want to go over our plans one last time with Mark and Gregory."

Maurice nodded, and continued plodding toward the crest of the pass. His progress was slow. The trench through which he was moving had been recently dug. The soil was still loose, making for unfirm footing. His biggest difficulty, however, came from the sheer weight of his weapons and armor. Cataphract gear was heavy enough, sitting on a horse. For a man on foot, climbing uphill, the armor seemed made of lead ingots instead of steel scale. The weapons weighed more than Nero's sins.

Belisarius felt a moment's sympathy for Maurice—but only a moment. He was wearing his own cataphract gear, and would be making that trek himself soon enough. If the war against Malwa dragged on for years, Belisarius thought the day would come when Roman soldiers could finally be rid of that damned armor. In visions which Aide had given him of gunpowder armies of the future, soldiers had worn nothing but a plate cuirass and a helmet. Just enough to stop a bullet, except at close range.

He sighed. That day was still far off. Belisarius had spent hours—and hours and hours—studying the great generals of the future, especially those of the first centuries of gunpowder warfare. Aide knew all of human history, and the crystal had shown Belisarius the methods and tactics of those men. Jan Zizka; Gonzalo de Cordoba and the Duke of Parma; Maurice of Nassau; Henry IV of France; Tilly and Wallenstein, and Gustavus Adolphus; Turenne and Frederick the Great; Marlborough; Napoleon and Wellington; and many others.

Of all those men, the only one Belisarius truly admired was Gustavus Adolphus. To some degree, his admiration was professional. Gustav II Adolf, King of Sweden, had reintroduced mobility and fluid tactics into a style of war which had become nothing more than brutal hammering. Massive squares of musket and pike slamming into other such squares, like the old Greek phalanxes.

But, for the most part, Belisarius was attracted by the man himself. Gustavus Adolphus had been a king—a very self-confident and ambitious king, in point of fact—who was by no mean immune from monarchy's vices. Still, he had been scrupulous about consulting the various estates of his kingdom, as he was required to do by Swedish law. He had managed to win the firm loyalty of his officers and soldiers by his fair and consistent conduct. He was as good a king as he was a general—Sweden was, by far, the best administered realm of his time. He had been the only king of his day who cared a fig for the needs of common folk. And his troops, when they entered the Thirty Years War under his command, had been the only soldiers who did not ravage the German countryside.

I would have liked to meet that man, he mused.

Aide's voice came into his mind. The crystal's thoughts were hesitant, almost apologetic.

He will never exist, now. Whatever happens. If Malwa wins this war, and Link establishes its domination over mankind, there will be no kings like that. Not ever.

Belisarius' face tightened. Link, the secret master of the Malwa dynasty, was an artificial intelligence sent back in time by the "new gods" of the future. Belisarius had met the creature, once, when he was in India. It had taken the form of Great Lady Holi, the aunt of the Malwa emperor. Aide called it a cybernetic organism.

Belisarius' eyes drifted across the landscape of the Zagros, as if that rugged mountain range was a metaphor for human destiny. The slopes of those mountains were rocky, treacherous, and at least half-hidden by spurs and crests. Belisarius had learned much, over the past four years, about mankind's future—it would be better to say, *futures*, because the "new gods" had their own plans for shaping human destiny. But he still did not know much about the "new gods" themselves. Aide, he was sure, was not withholding information from him. The crystal was simply incapable of understanding such mentalities.

Belisarius thought he understood them. They reminded him of religious fanatics he had met. Orthodox or Monophysite, it mattered not. All such men were imbued with the certainty that they—and they alone—understood the Will of God. Those who opposed them were not simply in error, they were the minions of Satan. To be scourged, that others might be cleansed.

That was the vision, he thought, which animated the "new gods" of the future. Outraged by the chaotic kaleidoscope of humanity, as it spread through the stars, they were seized by a determination to *purify the race*.

There had been no conceivable way to accomplish that goal, in their future time. Humanity had settled throughout the galaxy, and all the galaxies nearby. Isolated by incredible distances and the speed of light, each human planet went its own way. The human species was evolving in a million different directions, like the branches of a great tree, with nothing to bind it but a common heritage and the slender threads of the Great Ones in their travels.

So, the "new gods" had sent Link back in time, to alter history when humanity was still living on a single planet. To crush the mongrel empire called Rome, and to build a world state centered in north India. The "new gods" intended to use the Hindu caste system as the germ for what they called a "eugenics program." They would *purify the race*—and if, in the doing, they slaughtered millions, they cared not the least. Those were cattle, at best, if not outright vermin. Only the "new gods," and those they would shape in their image, were truly human.

Aide was right. If Malwa won, there would be no kings in the future like Gustavus Adolphus.

And if we win? he asked. But he knew the answer, before Aide even gave it.

Then you will have changed history also. The course of it will remain, like a broad river, but the banks will be altered. There may not even be a country called Sweden, in that future. There certainly won't be a man named Gustavus Adolphus. Or, if there is, he's as likely to be a peasant or a glassmaker as a king.

For a moment, the thought saddened Belisarius. The Roman general had no doubt of the righteousness of his cause. None at all. But even the most just war causes destruction. Saving that great, flowering tree of humanity's future, Belisarius would crush many of its buds. There would be no Gustavus Adolphus. No Shakespeare; no Cervantes; no Spinoza and Kant; no Sir Isaac Newton.

The moment passed. *But there will be others, like them.*

Yes, came Aide's reply. Quietly: **And there will be a place, too, for others like me. We are also people, with our own rightful place in that great tree.**

Belisarius' musings were interrupted by a voice.

"How soon do you want us ready, general?"

Belisarius snapped out of his reverie and focused his eyes on the speaker. It was Mark of Edessa, the commander of Belisarius' new unit of handcannon soldiers.

An idle thought crossed Belisarius' mind. *I have* got *to come up with a new name for them. "Handcannon soldiers" is just too much of a mouthful.*

Belisarius took a moment to examine the man. Mark was in his early twenties. He was a Syrian, of predominantly Arab ancestry. That was useful, given that most of his men were of similar stock. Like all Roman soldiers, the men spoke Greek—or learned to, at least, shortly after enlisting. But Mark's fluency in Arabic and several of the Aramaic dialects had proven valuable many times.

But that was not the principal reason Mark had been given this new command. The young officer, during the course of the previous year's campaign in Mesopotamia, had shown himself to be resourceful and reliable. He also—this was quite unusual for a cavalryman—had no objection to fighting on foot, and had proven to have a knack for the new gunpowder weapons.

Belisarius remembered the first time he met Mark, almost four years earlier. The general had just taken command of the army at Mindouos. His predecessor had let that army rot, and Belisarius had found it necessary to purge many of the existing officers. A number of men had been promoted from the ranks. Mark had been one of them, recommended by Belisarius' cataphract, Gregory.

He saw two more figures scuttling up the trench.

"Speak of the devil," he murmured. Gregory himself was arriving. He and Mark had become good friends, and had shown they could work together well in combat. That was one of the reasons that Belisarius had put Gregory in command of another new unit, the pikemen who served as a bulwark for the handcannon soldiers.

Call them "musketeers," came Aide's thought. **Technically, it would be more accurate to call them arquebusiers, but—**

"Arquebusiers" is ridiculous. Musketeers it is!

Belisarius broke into a smile. The new name was a minor triumph, true. Picayune, perhaps. But he was a firm believer in the axiom that large victories grow out of a multitude of small ones.

Gregory had arrived, now. He and Mark were eyeing their general quizzically, wondering why he was smiling. Almost grinning, in fact.

"I've got a new name for your men, Mark," he announced. "From now on, we'll call you musketeers."

Mark and Gregory looked at each other. It was almost comical the way each began mouthing the word.

"I like it," pronounced Gregory, after a moment's experimentation. Mark nodded his head. "So do I!"

The third man came up, and now Belisarius did break into a grin.

"And what have we here?" he asked. "The three musketeers?"

Oh, that's gross! There followed a mental, crystalline version of a raspberry. **Low, low.**

Gregory gave the new man, whose name was Felix Chalcenterus, an unkind look. The same little glare was transferred to Mark of Edessa.

"Give me a break, general," he growled. "You won't find me fighting with these new-fangled gadgets. Cold steel, that's still my business."

Mark and Felix matched Belisarius' grin. "He's hopeless, General," stated Mark. "Set in his ways, like an old village woman."

Belisarius chuckled at the quip, even though it was quite unfair. For the past year, Gregory had served as Belisarius' chief artillery officer. In this campaign of fluid maneuver, Belisarius had left his cumbersome artillery behind, so Gregory had been free to take on another assignment. The main reason Belisarius had put the man in charge of the new unit of pikemen was that Gregory was one of those officers who seemed almost infinitely flexible. He was one of the very few Thracian cataphracts who didn't squeal like a stuck pig when asked to fight on foot, with a pike instead of a lance. The pikemen were an elite unit, true, but Gregory had still been hard-pressed to find enough Thracians to volunteer. In the end, he had relied heavily on the new Isaurians who were enlisting into the general's corps of bucellarii.

Belisarius got down to business. "Are *you* ready?" he asked. The question was directed at all three men simultaneously. Felix Chalcenterus served Mark as his executive officer.

"We're set, general," came Mark's reply. Gregory and Felix nodded their agreement.

"Good. Remember—don't start up the slope until I signal for you." Belisarius made a little head toss toward the east. "You can be damned sure that Sanga will have some of his Pathan scouts perched on the nearby hilltops, watching everything we do. They'll have some means of signaling Damodara—mirrors, if the sun's right. If not, they'll have something else.

Banners, maybe smoke. It's essential that they can't see you until the time comes for your countercharge."

Belisarius gave the three men a quick scrutiny. Satisfied that they understood the point, he added: "You'll have to come up the hill in a hurry, mind. I won't give the signal until the last minute. In a hurry—*and* in good formation. Can you do it?"

There was no verbal reply. Just three self-confident smiles and nodding heads.

"All right," said Belisarius. He gave out a little sigh. "The moment's come, then. It's my turn to climb that damned hill."

He turned and set off, slogging his way. Every step forward was marked by half a step backward, sliding in the loose soil. Progress was marked by the soft, crunching sounds of semifutility. Within a few yards, his armor and weapons felt like the burden of Atlas.

"Some day," he muttered. "If this war goes on long enough. I'll be skipping through the meadows with nothing but a helmet and a linen uniform. Not a care in the world."

Except frying in napalm, or being shredded by high explosive shells, came Aide's unkind thought. **Not to mention being picked off at five hundred yards by a sniper armed with a high-velocity rifle. And while we're at it, let's not forget—**

Not a care in the world! insisted Belisarius. His thought was perhaps a bit surly. *Death is a feather. Cataphract gear is the torment of Prometheus.*

Then, very surly: *Spoilsport.*

By the time he reached the trench at the crest of the pass, Belisarius was exhausted. He half-collapsed next to Maurice. Valentinian and Anastasius were still in the trench, a few feet to his right.

Maurice gave him no more than a cursory glance before resuming his study of the enemy troops on the slope below. "You'll get over it soon enough," he said. The words were unkind but the tone was sympathetic. "You'd better," added Maurice grimly. "The Ye-tai aren't wasting any time."

Wearily, Belisarius nodded. Fortunately, his exhaustion was simply due to heavy, but brief, exertion. It was not the kind of fatigue produced by hours of relentless labor. He knew from experience that his well-toned muscles would recover in a few minutes—even if, at the moment, he didn't feel as if he could ever walk again.

The general's head was below the parapet, resting against the sloped wall of the trench. He was too tired to lift it. He could hear the faint sounds of orders being shouted in Hindi, coming from far down the slope.

"What are they doing, Maurice?" he asked.

"The Ye-tai will be making the main assault. Nothing fancy, just a straight charge up the slope. On foot. They've just about finished dressing their lines." He gave a little half-incredulous grunt. "Good lines, too. Way better than I've ever seen barbarians do before."

"They're not exactly barbarians," said Belisarius. He made a brief attempt at raising his head, but gave it up almost instantly. "They act like it, sure enough. The Malwa encourage them to behave barbarously, not that the Ye-tai need much encouragement. But they've been an integral part of the Malwa ruling class for three generations, now. All of their sub-officers, to give you an idea, are literate. Down to a rank equivalent to our pentarchs."

Maurice emitted another grunt. From Belisarius' other side came Valentinian's half-incredulous (and half-disgruntled) exclamation: "You've got to be kidding!"

Belisarius smiled. Valentinian's attitude was understandable. Even in the Roman army, with its comparatively democratic traditions, not more than half of the sub-officers below the rank of hecatontarch could read and write.

Valentinian himself carried the rank of a hecatontarch. That was the modern Greek equivalent of the old Latin "centurion"—commander of a hundred. But in his case, the rank was a formal honor more than anything else. Valentinian didn't command anyone. His job, along with Anastasius, was to keep Belisarius alive on the battlefield.

Valentinian was literate, just barely. He could sign his name without help, and he could pick his way through simple written messages. But he had never even thought of trying to read a book. If someone had ever suggested it to him—

"You should read a book sometime," commented Anastasius mildly. "Be good for you, Valentinian."

"You've got to be kidding," came the instant, hissing response.

He's got to be kidding, echoed Aide.

Listening to the exchange, Belisarius' smile widened. Anastasius *was* literate—and not barely. The giant Thracian cataphract read any book he could get his hands on, especially if it dealt with philosophy. But his attitude, for a Roman soldier, was unusual—it might be better to say, extraordinary.

Anastasius himself ascribed his peculiarity to the fact that he had a Greek father. But Belisarius thought otherwise. There were plenty of Greek soldiers in the Roman army who were as illiterate—and as uninterested in literacy—as any Hun. Belisarius suspected that Anastasius' obsession with philosophy was more in the nature of a personal rebellion. The man was so huge, and so strong, and so brutal in his appearance, that Belisarius thought he had turned to reading as a way of assuring himself that he was a man and not an ogre.

The thought of ogres brought his mind back to the moment. Literate they might be, but the Ye-tai were the closest human equivalents to ogres that Belisarius had ever met.

Speaking of which, muttered Aide, **you'd better gird your loins, grandpa. The ogres are coming.**

Belisarius heard the sound of kettledrums. "They're coming," said Maurice. He spoke softly, as he usually did, but his tone was as grim as a glacier. "Fierce bastards, too. Nobody's got to drive *them* forward. They're coming on like starving wolves after a crippled antelope."

Belisarius had recovered enough. With a little grunt of effort, he heaved himself half-erect and looked over the parapet.

He gave the Ye-tai charging up the mountain pass no more than a quick, almost perfunctory, study. He had seen Ye-tai in action before, and was not surprised by anything he saw—neither the vigor of their charge, nor the way they still managed to keep their lines reasonably well dressed even while storming up a rock-strewn slope. It was impressive, to be sure. But there was nothing in the world as sheerly *impressive* as a charge of Persian heavy cavalry. Belisarius had faced Persian charges, in the past, and broken the armies who made them.

He spent a little more time gauging the kshatriyas who were accompanying the Ye-tai. In the Malwa Empire, unlike other Hindu realms, the warrior caste was devoted almost exclusively to gunpowder weapons and tactics. Except in Damodara's army, in fact, they had a monopoly on such weapons.

There were a number of kshatriyas dispersed through the ranks of the oncoming Ye-tai. All of them were carrying grenades—one in the hand, with several more slung from bandoliers. Their free hands held the strikers to light the fuses.

None of the kshatriyas, of course, were in the first few ranks. As lightly armored as they were, the grenadiers could not hope to match Roman soldiers in hand-to-hand combat. But Belisarius was impressed to see that the kshatriyas were not, as he had observed in other Malwa armies, hanging far back in the rear.

Here, too, Damodara's style of leadership was evident. Over time, Malwa's pampered kshatriyas had lost much of the martial rigor which that warrior caste possessed in other Hindu societies. They were held in open scorn by Rajput kshatriyas. Damodara, it seemed, had reinstituted the old traditions. Those grenadiers storming up the hill alongside the sword-wielding Ye-tai bore no resemblance to the arrogant idlers whom Belisarius had seen while he was in India.

But there were still not many of them, he was relieved to see. Not enough to change the equation in the immediate battle. No more than one in twenty of the enemy soldiers in the oncoming charge were carrying grenades. That was an even smaller percentage than usual. Whatever armaments complex Damodara had succeeded in creating, it was apparently still small. Belisarius suspected that Damodara was doing what he would have done himself—*had* done, in fact, when Belisarius created his own weapons industry. Concentrate on quality, not quantity. Build a few good cannons, and improve the rocketry, rather than try to churn out simple grenades.

So, the general's eyes were soon drawn to the enemy's flanks, where the Rajput cavalry were massed. *That* was the real threat. Belisarius was confident that he could handle the Ye-tai charge. He had his own surprise waiting, on the back side of the slope. But, no more than Damodara, had Belisarius been able to produce gunpowder weapons in great quantity. His one thousand musketeers could break the Ye-tai but—

Aide's voice interrupted his train of thought. There was a tinge of annoyance in the crystal's words. A tinge of annoyance—and more than a tinge of worry.

They're *not* musketeers. Not really. Eighteenth-century musketeers could fire three volleys a minute. But they had flintlocks. You don't even have arquebusses as good as Gustavus Adolphus' soldiers, and they couldn't fire more often than—

Aide broke off, with the mental equivalent of a sigh of exasperation. He and Belisarius had already had this argument. As always, when the dispute involved purely military affairs, Belisarius' opinion had carried the day.

The general did not bother with a reply. He was too preoccupied with studying the Rajputs.

Not to his surprise, Belisarius saw that most of the Rajput cavalry—two out of three, he gauged—were now concentrated on the enemy's right flank, under Sanga's command. The pass in which Belisarius was making a stand was saddle-shaped. The flanks of the pass were not sheer cliffs, but rounded slopes. The slope on Belisarius' left was almost gentle. If the Ye-tai could pin the Roman center, Sanga would have no real difficulty leading a mass cavalry charge against the Roman left.

Belisarius, of course, had read the terrain the same way as Damodara and Sanga. And so he had positioned his heaviest troops, the Greek cataphracts under Cyril's command, on his left. He would hold the center and the right with the lighter Syrian forces, and the new units of musketeers and pikemen.

The fact remained that he was badly outnumbered, and the ground was open enough that the Malwa could bring all their forces to bear. Not easily; not quickly—but surely, for all that.

Belisarius shook his head a little, reminding himself that he was not trying to *win* this battle. He just needed to put up enough of a fight so that his retreat to the south, when the time came, would not seem too puzzling to his opponents. Belisarius could afford the tactical setback involved in giving up this battlefield, as long as his troops weren't badly mauled. He could *not* afford the strategic defeat which would be certain, if Damodara or Sanga—or Narses, if the canny eunuch was with them—ever figured out what Belisarius was planning for, months from now.

Maurice verbalized Belisarius' own thoughts.

"It's going to be a bit touch-and-go," growled the chiliarch. "More than a bit, if your little surprise doesn't work as well as you think it will. Which it probably won't," he added sourly. "Nothing ever works the way it's supposed to, on a battlefield."

Belisarius started to respond, but fell silent. The Ye-tai were almost close enough—

Time. Belisarius gave the hand signal, and the small group of cornicenes just a few yards away immediately began blowing on their horns.

The peal of the cornicens immediately brought thousands of Greek cataphracts and Syrian archers to their feet, standing hip-high in their trenches with bows already nocked. A volley of arrows swept down the slope.

Like a scythe, came the simile to Belisarius' mind, but he knew it was inappropriate. Plunging fire was difficult. He was not surprised to see many of the arrows sail right over the approaching mass of Ye-tai. And it was often ineffective even when it struck, against experienced troops.

The Ye-tai were veterans, and had been expecting the volley. As soon as they saw the cataphracts rearing up, the Ye-tai crouched and sheltered behind their shields. The shouted orders of their officers were quite unnecessary. Because of the angle, they presented smaller targets to begin with, and each Ye-tai was experienced enough to keep his shield properly slanted.

Those were good shields, as good as Roman ones. Laminated wood reinforced with iron—nothing like the flimsy wicker shields with which the Malwa Empire armed its common soldiers. Most of the Roman arrows which hit their targets glanced off harmlessly.

The Ye-tai immediately resumed their charge, bellowing their battle cries. Another volley; another shielded crouch; another upward surge. They lost men, of course—plenty of them—but not enough. Not for *those* warriors. Ye-tai had many vices; cowardice was not one of them.

"Not a chance," grunted Maurice. There was no amazement in those words. Not even a trace of surprise. Maurice sounded like a man remarking that there was no way a sand castle was going to hold back the tide.

The chiliarch glanced at Belisarius. "You'd better see to your gunmen. We're going to need them."

Belisarius was already turning. As he began giving the new signal, he heard Maurice mutter: "Oh, marvelous. The Rajputs are already starting *their* charge. God, I hate competent enemies." A few seconds later, hissing: "*Shit.* I can't believe it!"

Belisarius had been watching the musketeers climbing up the slope. Hearing the alarm in Maurice's voice, he immediately turned around.

Seeing the speed with which the Rajput cavalry was charging up that side of the saddle, Belisarius understood Maurice's shock. Belisarius himself had never seen cavalry move that quickly in mountainous terrain.

Silently, he cursed himself for an idiot. He had forgotten—it might be better to say, never understood in the first place. Belisarius was accustomed to Roman and Persian heavy cavalry, whose gear and tactics had been shaped by centuries of war on the flat plains of Mesopotamia. But the Rajputs were *not* heavy cavalry—not, at least, by Roman and Persian standards—and they were unfazed by rough terrain.

Rajputana is a land of hills, chimed in Aide. **The Rajput military tradition was forged in expeditions against Pathan mountaineers, and battles fought against Marathas in the volcanic badlands of the Great Country.**

"Like a bunch of damned mountain goats," growled Maurice. He cocked his head. "You do realize, young man, that your fancy battle plan just flew south for the winter." For all the grimness of the words, there was a trace of satisfaction in the voice. Maurice was one of those natural-born pessimists who took a strange pleasure in seeing the world live down to their expectations.

Belisarius had already reached the same conclusion. The weakest part of his tactical plan had been its reliance on close timing. The Rajputs had just kicked over the hourglass. Shattered it to pieces, in fact. Sanga's forces would strike the Roman left long before Belisarius had expected them to.

"Get over there quick, Maurice," he commanded. "Work with Cyril to get the Greeks reoriented. They'll have to hold off Sanga now, as long as they can. Forget about any countercharge against the Ye-tai." He pointed to the large force of Thracian cataphracts positioned halfway down the back slope, as a reserve. "And send a dispatch rider to the bucellarii, telling them to move left. We're going to need them."

"What about the Mamelukes?" asked Maurice. He looked southwest, to where the Kushans were holding the fords at the river half a mile below. "Do you want them up here, with you?"

Belisarius shook his head. "Not unless I'm desperate. I can't risk having any of them captured. Even a dead Kushan body could give the game away."

Maurice gave a skeptical glance at the musketeers who were nearing the crest.

"Do you really you think you can hold—" he started to say, but broke off. A second later, the chiliarch was scuttling down the trench, toward the Roman left. For all Maurice's frequent sarcasms on the subject of Belisarius' "fancy damned battle plans," the Thracian veteran was not given to arguing with him in the midst of actual combat. A general's willingness to *command*—instantly and surely—was more important in a battle than whether the command itself was wise. Maurice had seen battles won, more than once, simply because the commander had stood his ground and given clear and definite orders. *Any* orders, just so long as the troops felt that a steady hand was in control.

Belisarius peered over the parapet. The Ye-tai were very close, now. Their battle cries filled the air, thick with confidence, heavy with impending triumph. They had been bloodied by the Roman archery, but not badly enough. Several thousand would still reach the crest, where outnumbered and lightly armed Syrian infantry would be no match for them.

He rose, half-standing, and looked over the other parapet. The musketeers and the pikemen were almost at the crest, just a few yards down the slope. They had stopped, actually, to make a final dress of their lines. Belisarius saw Mark of Edessa watching him, calmly waiting for the general's order.

Here goes, thought Belisarius.

He gave the signal. Again, the cornicens blew. As he turned back to face the enemy, Belisarius saw small figures on nearby hilltops frantically waving banners. The Pathan scouts had caught sight of the new Roman unit surging forward, and were signaling Damodara.

Too late.

Belisarius took a deep breath, and gave a small prayer for the soul of a man he had never met, and never would. A general of a future that would never be. A man he didn't much care for, as a human being, but who had been one of history's greatest generals.

May your soul rest in peace, wherever it is, Iron Duke. I hope this works as well for me as it did for you at Busaco.

Aide's words, when they came, surprised Belisarius. He had been half-expecting some muttered reproaches. Something to the effect that *Wellington's* men could fire three volleys a minute; or that *Wellington* had the massive fortifications of the Lines of Torres Vedras to fall back on; or even—Aide had a bit of the pedant in him—that the title "Iron Duke" was an anachronism, in this context. The nickname was political, not military. It had been given to *Prime Minister* Wellington by English commoners, years after the fall of Napoleon, when he responded to a mob breaking his windows by installing iron shutters on his mansion in London.

But all that came, instead, was reassurance.

It will. The reverse-slope tactic was Wellington's signature. It worked at Salamanca, too. And even against Napoleon at Waterloo.

Belisarius was grateful for that quiet voice of confidence. He needed it. This battle was shaping up to be the worst fight of his life, rather than the simple cut-and-run he had anticipated. Once again, he had underestimated the Rajputs.

The musketeers reached the crest of the pass, and leveled their handcannons at the Ye-tai storming forward. Belisarius rose to join in his world's first use of a musket volley in battle, but not before giving himself a small curse.

Don't ever do that again, you jackass. Just because you've got brains, and a friend who can show you the future, don't ever forget that other men have brains too. And damned good ones, with the will to match.

The muskets roared, all across the line. Instantly, the crest of the pass was shrouded in gunsmoke. It was impossible to see more than a few feet through those acrid billows. Impatiently, while his musketeers went through the practiced drill with their clumsy muzzle loaders, Belisarius waited for the smoke to clear.

There was a good breeze coming through the pass. The clouds of gunsmoke were swept away within seconds. And Belisarius, seeing the havoc wreaked by a thousand .80-caliber smoothbores firing at close range, felt himself relax. Just a bit. The Ye-tai army was like a bull, half-stunned by a hammer blow between the eyes.

He raised his eyes, staring across the mounded heaps of Ye-tai corpses to his opponent's distant pavilion. Belisarius had just sent his own message—to himself, as well as Damodara. Reminding them both that if Belisarius had no monopoly on intelligence, neither did he have a monopoly on overconfidence.

And don't underestimate me *again, Lord of Malwa,* he thought. *Better yet*—do *underestimate me again.*

The Ye-tai, stubborn and courageous, were pushing forward. They clambered up and over the corpses and hideously shattered bodies of their wounded comrades, roaring with rage and hefting their swords. The Ye-tai were no longer trying to maintain formation. They were just a mob of enraged berserks, burning to reach their tormentors. The bull was half-stunned, but it was still a bull.

The second line of musketeers stepped forward and fired. While the smoke cleared, the third line took their place. Behind, the first line had already finished reloading and was preparing for a second volley.

It was true that Belisarius' musketeers, with their awkward matchlocks, could not match Wellington's three volleys a minute. The guns themselves were not much better than sixteenth-century arquebusses. John of Rhodes, working with sixth-century technology, couldn't possibly match the precision of nineteenth-century gunmaking. But Belisarius had all of Aide's encyclopedic knowledge to draw upon, so he had been able to leap over centuries of military experimentation in other ways. It *was* within the capacity of the Roman Empire to manufacture the prepared cartridges which Gustavus Adolphus had introduced. The muzzle loaders themselves were clumsy things, but there was nothing clumsy about the way they were being used.

His musketeers couldn't manage more than one volley a minute, but Belisarius could *rely* on that rate. And, as the smoke cleared, and he saw the carnage which the second volley had created, Belisarius knew that would be enough.

Wellington's reverse-slope tactic depended as much on the shock of surprise as it did on rates of fire, said Aide.

Belisarius nodded. An enemy storming forward in expectation of furious victory had its spirits shattered, along with its bodies, when it was struck down by a hail of bullets. Not even warriors like the Ye-tai could withstand such a blow.

No more than Napoleon's Imperial Guard at Waterloo.

The third line stepped forward, their weapons ready. There was no need for plunging fire, now. The vanguard elements of the Ye-tai had reached the crest and were not more than ten yards from the trenches. Felix Chalcenterus, the executive officer, was in charge of fire control. He called out the orders, in sure sequence.

Level! The guns came up like so many blunt lances.

There was no command to aim. Belisarius' musketeers, like Wellington's, were simply trained to fire in the general direction of the enemy. The weapons were so inaccurate, beyond fifty yards, that marksmanship was pointless.

Fire! The handcannons erupted. Another cloud of smoke obscured everything.

Obscured sight, that is, not sound. Belisarius could hear the bullets slamming into the struggling mass of Ye-tai. The sounds had a metallic edge, where bullets impacted armor, but he knew the armor was irrelevant. At that range, the murderous lead pellets punched through the finest plate armor as if it were mere cloth. The muzzle velocity of a matchlock arquebus was extremely high—supersonic, more often than not. The high-velocity rifles which would replace them in the future would do no more than double that, even after centuries of arms development and refinement. An arquebus' round shot lost its muzzle velocity very quickly, of course—far sooner than the spinning bullets of rifles. But at *this* range, the heavy-caliber arquebusses were probably even more effective than rifles.

The shrieks of wounded Ye-tai began to fill the pass, like the wail of a giant banshee. The Ye-tai were tough—as tough as any soldiers Belisarius had ever seen. But no soldiers are *that* tough.

The bull was on its knees, now. Bellowing, still, but dying for all that.

Their bloody work done, the third line retired. Even with the breeze, the pass was still half-obscured with smoke. But Belisarius could hear Felix commanding the first line back to the front. Chalcenterus' voice still had the timbre of his youth, but the voice itself was relaxed and confident.

I didn't make any mistake there, at least, Belisarius consoled himself. Felix had first caught the general's eye at the battle of the villa near Anatha, the previous year. Belisarius had been impressed by the Syrian soldier's alert calmness when the Roman army was subjected to its first experience with rocket fire. He had kept an eye on the youth, and seen to his rapid promotion.

The first line, back in position, went through the sequence. Another roar of handcannon fire. The pass was completely shrouded in smoke. Even with their clumsy weapons, the men could still keep up a rate of fire that outmatched the breeze.

The sound of bullets slamming into the enemy had a sodden quality, now. Belisarius was thankful that he couldn't actually see the results. This was sheer slaughter. He knew that the rear elements of the Ye-tai would already be staggering back in defeat. But the barbarian soldiers trapped at the front were helpless. Immobile targets. The bull was no longer even bellowing. It was just a dying beast, dumbly waiting for another blow of the hammer.

The second line returned, and the blow came. Belisarius heard Gregory calling out an order. His pikemen had been in position since the first line of musketeers stepped forward, ready to fend off any Ye-tai who made it through the gunfire. But they had not even been needed. Gregory had obviously come to the conclusion that they wouldn't be, and so he had called on his men to use their grenades.

The pikemen lowered their twelve-foot spears and plucked grenades from their bandoliers. Each pikeman carried only two of the devices. More would have impeded them in performing their principal duty. But these were special grenades. The pikemen had been equipped with the new grenades which John of Rhodes had developed—the ones with impact fuses.

The grenades had a simple "potato-masher" design. A strip of cloth was attached to the butt of the wooden handle. Like the cloth strips often attached to javelins, it would stabilize the grenade in flight and ensure that the weapon would strike in the proper orientation to set off the fuse. There was no need to fumble with a striker, or cut a fuse to proper length. Each pikeman simply yanked out the pin which armed the device, and sent it sailing down the slope.

The grenades disappeared into the clouds of smoke which were wafting down the pass. Before they hit,

Felix had ordered another round of gunfire. Not more than a second after that roaring lightning, Belisarius heard the sharp claps of the grenades exploding down the slope. The sounds harmonized like music composed by a maniac. A homicidal maniac. Those Ye-tai at the rear, trying to retreat, were being savaged by the grenades even while their comrades at the front were being hammered into pulp by the guns.

For an instant, Belisarius was seized by a savage urge to order a countercharge. That had been his plan from the beginning. The Ye-tai were already broken—as badly as any army could be, driven back from an assault. A rush of pikemen now would complete their destruction. The fierce army which had charged up the slope not minutes earlier would be as thoroughly beaten as any army in human history.

Mark and Gregory were at his side now, awaiting the order. Their faces were tense and eager. They knew as well as Belisarius that they were on the verge of total victory.

Fiercely, Belisarius restrained himself. Yes, the enemy was beaten *here*. But—

Distantly, he could hear wails from another direction. To his left. Wails of pain, and the steel clash of weapons. He couldn't see anything through the wafting clouds of gunsmoke, but he knew the Rajputs were already hammering his left flank.

All ferocity and sense of satisfaction fled. His counterstroke at the saddle had worked, just as it had worked in another future for a man named Arthur Wellesley. But battles are rarely neat and tidy affairs which go according to plan. Not against well-led enemies, at least.

This battle could still wind up a disaster, came Aide's forceful thought.

Belisarius had won the struggle at the center, true. But if he didn't withdraw his army quickly, and in good order—which was the most difficult maneuver of all, in the face of the enemy—Sanga and the Rajputs would roll up his flank.

"No," he commanded, pointing toward the slope of the saddle to their left. Only the crest of the pass was still visible, due to the gunsmoke, but they could see hundreds of Rajput cavalry pouring across the terrain. Ten times that number would be hidden in the clouds below, on the lower part of the slope. *Twenty* times, more likely. There had been at least ten thousand Rajputs massed on the Malwa right, under Sanga's command.

Mark began to argue—respectfully, but still vehemently, but Gregory restrained him with a firm shake of the shoulder. The Thracian cataphract was older than the Syrian, more of a veteran—and more familiar with Belisarius.

"Shut up, youngster," he growled. "The general's right. If we charge down that slope, we'll be completely out of position when the Rajputs hit us. They'll turn us into sausage."

Belisarius didn't pick his officers for reticence and timidity. The young Syrian flushed, a bit, from Gregory's rebuke, but plowed on. "The Greeks'll hold them! Those are Cyril's men—and Agathius', before him. The same cataphracts who broke the Malwa at Anatha, and then at—"

"There are only three thousand of them, Mark," said Belisarius mildly. He wasn't going to spend more than a few seconds, arguing with a subordinate in the middle of a battle. But he *was* prepared to spend those seconds. There was no other way to train good officers.

"They're facing four times their number—probably five," he continued. "They're splendid troops, yes. But they don't have as good a position as we did here in the center. There's no one protecting *their* flank. Sanga will just send enough men to keep them pinned while he sweeps around them. He won't even try to crush the Greeks, not now. He'll bypass them and fall on us."

He pointed to the line of musketeers. The men had ceased firing now, and the pikemen had used up all their grenades. The center of the battlefield was almost quiet, except for the cries of wounded Ye-tai.

"How do you expect to form a defensive line against that charge—*here*? Straddling a mountain pass, with the enemy coming *down* the slope?"

Mark fell silent. His face still had a stubborn look to it, but Belisarius knew that the young Syrian was—not convinced, perhaps, but ready to obey.

Satisfied with that, Belisarius turned to Gregory and said: "Fall back southwest, toward the river. Upstream." He pointed to a location where the narrow river below the pass broadened a bit. "Where Vasudeva's guarding the fords. Set your men, and the musketeers, to hold the river after I get the rest of the army across."

Gregory nodded. A moment later, he and Mark were shouting commands to their men.

And now, thought Belisarius, looking toward his left flank, *I've got to try to get those men out of here. Which is not going to be easy. Sanga will be like a tiger, with me trying to pry meat from his jaws.*

Belisarius heard Valentinian and Anastasius stirring behind him. As the general's personal bodyguards, they hadn't been expecting to do much in this current battle beyond looking grim and fearsome. But they were veterans, and could recognize a battle plan in tatters when they saw one.

"Looks like we're going to have to work, after all," groused Valentinian. Anastasius was silent. "What's the matter, large one?" came Valentinian's sarcastic voice. "No philosophical motto for the occasion? No words of wisdom?"

"Don't need 'em," rumbled Anastasius in reply. "Even a witless weasel can see when he's in a fight for his life."

Chapter 13

By the time Belisarius reached his left flank, where the Greeks were holding back the Rajputs, his bucellarii were already arriving. He was deeply thankful for their speed in responding to his orders, but he took a moment to give himself a mental pat on the back.

His tactics for this battle were at least half ruined, but Belisarius thought he could still pull his army out before disaster struck. If he did, it would be because of his past foresight. His Thracian cataphracts rode the finest heavy chargers in the world. Half the money for those magnificent and expensive warhorses was provided by Belisarius out of his own purse. Only the best steeds in the world, coming from halfway down the slope and carrying their own armor and armored cataphracts, could have reached the crest so quickly.

And they would be needed. It took only the sight of Cyril's exhausted face for Belisarius to know that his Greek cataphracts were on the verge of collapse. They'd held off the Rajput charges, so far. But they would break under the next one, or the one after that. Sanga had taken full advantage of his numerical superiority on the Roman left. His Rajputs outnumbered the Greeks five or six to one, and Sanga had sent them up in swirling waves—one after another, with hardly a moment's pause.

The Rajput king had not made the mistake of trying to hammer the Greeks under. The cataphracts were more heavily armed and armored than Rajputs, and they were fighting dismounted from behind fieldworks. If the Rajputs had tried a simple and direct assault, their numbers would have been nullified by the inevitable jamming up at the fieldworks. Instead, Sanga had used his own variation of "Parthian tactics," except that his sallies were as much lance-and-sword work as archery. Cut, slash, and whirl away. Repeat; repeat; repeat; repeat; repeat.

With his advantage in numbers, Sanga had been able to rotate his units. His cavalrymen had had time to rest and tend to their wounded. But for the Greeks defending, there had been no respite at all. It was like holding back waves from the ocean. As soon as one ebbed, another came.

The best soldiers in the world are only flesh and blood, and muscle. The Greeks were so weary that it was an effort to even lift a sword—much less swing it properly. Men at that stage of exhaustion are almost helpless against a good opponent. Lance thrusts strike home, that could have been parried by fresh arms. Sword strokes kill, that should have been easily deflected with a shield.

Half the Greeks had dropped their shields, by now. They needed both hands to hold their weapons. And the hands themselves, often enough, were trembling with fatigue.

"Get them out, Cyril!" called Belisarius. "Pull them out of the fieldworks—*now.*" He twisted in his saddle and pointed to the river below. Vasudeva and his Kushans were clearly visible, in well-ordered formations, guarding the fords.

"Get them across the river," he commanded. "Don't even try for an orderly retreat. Just get them mounted and down there, as fast as you can. The Syrians will cover your flank and the musketeers will hold the river against any Malwa pursuit."

Cyril reached between the flanges of his helmet with a thumb and two fingers, wringing the sweat off his brow and down his nose. He staggered half a pace.

"The Rajputs'll be coming again," he started to protest. "In a minute, no more. You'll need us—"

"I'll take care of the Rajputs with my Thracians," snapped Belisarius. "*Do as I say, Cyril.* Get your men out of here!"

The Greek commander stopped arguing. As Cyril began calling out orders to his men, Belisarius took the time for a quick study of the enemy.

The Rajputs massed on the northern flank of the pass had paused in their attacks, he saw. They had seen the Thracians coming, and were taking the time themselves to gauge the new situation. The reinforcements would strengthen the Roman left, but—

Not enough. That would be Sanga's conclusion, Belisarius knew, within less than five minutes. He was certain the Rajput king was already organizing a new wave of attacks. Sanga was not one to waste time at the climactic moment of a battle.

Neither was Belisarius. Five minutes would be enough. More than enough—and less. Before that time was up, Sanga would realize the truth. Belisarius had no intention of shoring up his left flank. He was going to use his Thracians to cover a general retreat.

Once Sanga understood what Belisarius was doing, all hell would break loose. There would be no careful, calculated sallies. Just a great smash of armies, as Sanga tried to shatter the Roman army's last shield—using fifteen thousand Rajputs against less than three thousand Thracian cataphracts.

The bucellarii were pouring up onto the crest, now.

Maurice was already organizing the charge, without waiting for Belisarius' command.

Belisarius took another moment to study the rest of the battlefield. The gunsmoke had all cleared away, and he could see the center. For one of the few times in his bloody life, Belisarius saw a battleground that was literally covered with bodies. The Ye-tai had been shattered. Hundreds of them—perhaps even as many as two thousand—were staggering away down the slope toward their own camp. But those men were out of the battle. Satan himself couldn't have rallied them, not after that butchery.

The Roman right wing, and the enemy facing them—not more than five thousand Rajputs, now—had hardly fought at all. A few probes and skirmishes, nothing more. The southern flank of the pass was much steeper than the northern one. Sanga—or Damodara—had not made the mistake of trying to duplicate the Malwa charges which had been so successful on their right. The Rajput left wing had been there simply to keep the Romans from counterattacking.

Not that Belisarius had ever intended to send his lightly armed Syrians in a counterattack, unless by wild fortune the entire battle had turned into a Malwa rout. He had stationed them there to do the same thing as their opponents—keep them from reinforcing the other flank.

That was another part of Belisarius' tactics which had not worked as well as he had planned. Judging from what he could see, Belisarius thought Damodara had steadily drawn troops from his left in order to reinforce Sanga's hammer blows on the right. The Malwa lord had judged Belisarius' Syrians correctly. They would be fearsome opponents, defending a steep slope against cavalry. But almost useless, in a sally. So he had moved thousands of his Rajput cavalrymen from one end of the battlefield to the other. Belisarius could see large contingents of them cantering across the small valley below the pass, going to reinforce Sanga. And even as he watched, another unit of five hundred Rajputs broke away from their lines on his right and did the same.

Belisarius almost laughed, then. He had never seen a better illustration of Maurice's conviction that battles are by nature an unholy, contradictory mess, in which nothing ever works the way it's supposed to. This time, however—*and thank God for that!*—it was his enemy who had fallen into the quagmire.

Ironically, Damodara's best move was also his worst. *If* Belisarius had been planning to make a stand, Damodara's transfer of forces would have been a masterstroke. But the Roman general had no intention of doing so. Instead, he was going to pivot his army in a retreat to the southwest, using his right flank as the hinge. His biggest fear had been that Damodara would break the hinge. But now, having depleted his left wing, Damodara had not a chance of storming the Syrians on the southern slope of the pass. Bouzes and Coutzes would be able to withdraw their men in an orderly manner, after covering the retreat of the rest of the army.

Marvelous, marvelous—assuming, of course, that Belisarius could blunt Sanga's coming charge with his Thracians. And that—

He eyed the huge mass of Rajput cavalry on the northern slope.

That's going to be—

"This is going to be fucking dicey," growled Maurice. Belisarius turned in his saddle. Unnoticed, Maurice had already brought his horse alongside.

"It's still a mountain pass, broad and shallow as it is, Maurice," pointed out Belisarius. "It's not a level plain. Sanga won't be able to send more than five thousand at a time. Six at the most."

Peering between the cheekplates of his helmet, Maurice's eyes did not seemed filled with great cheer at this news. He could count just as well as Belisarius. The Thracians were still facing two-to-one odds, against an enemy with plenty of reserves.

"If we didn't have stirrups," said the chiliarch bleakly, "this'd be pure suicide." He frowned. "Now that I think about it—why *don't* the Malwa have stirrups? You'd think they would, by now." Maurice glanced at Belisarius' chest plate, below which Aide nestled in a leather pouch. "They've got their own visions of the future, don't they?"

Belisarius shrugged. "Link's mind doesn't work like Aide's. Aide is a—an *aide*. Link is the Supreme Commander of the Universe. I suspect the thing is so bound up with its great plans for future weapons that it didn't think to build on the little possibilities which are already here. It certainly wouldn't have thought to consult with its human tools—any more than you'd ask a hammer's opinion if you were wielding it properly."

Not likely, remarked Aide. **For Link, people barely even qualify as tools. Just so much raw material.**

Belisarius began to add something, but broke off. He could see the Greeks were ready to mount. And all of his Thracians were here, and in formation.

"May as well do it," said Maurice, anticipating his general's thought. Belisarius nodded. A moment later, Maurice passed on the command. The cornicens began to wail.

The Greeks surged out of the trenches and began clambering aboard their horses. They were tired, tired, but they found the strength regardless. *They* were getting out of here, and only had to make it down to the river below.

The Thracians began moving forward, toward the Rajputs. They were slowed a bit, making their way through the narrow spaces between the fieldworks which had been left open for sallies. By the time the bucellarii made it onto the open and relatively flat northern part of the saddle, Sanga had realized the truth. His own horns began blowing. The sound was different, in pitch and timbre, from that made by Roman cornicens. But Belisarius did not mistake their meaning.

Attack! Now! Everyone!

The huge mass of Rajput cavalry surged toward them. Belisarius ordered his own charge. There was no room here for the usual Roman tactic of preceding a lance charge with a murderous volley of arrows. No room—and no time. The Thracians were so badly outnumbered that Belisarius could only try to use their greater weight in a single blow of the hammer. The saddle was wide and shallow, for a mountain pass, but it was still not a level plain. If his cataphracts, with their heavier armor and lances—and stirrups—could smash the front ranks of the Rajputs into a pulp, that would stymie the rest. Long enough, hopefully, for the Thracians to be able to beat their own retreat.

The distance between the two armies vanished in seconds. The hammer fell.

The Rajputs did not break—quite.

Belisarius had shattered a Malwa army once before, with such a charge, on the first day of the battle at Anatha. But that Malwa army had been arrogant, and unfamiliar with Roman heavy cavalry tactics.

For the Rajputs, too, this was their first time facing Roman cataphracts in a lance charge. But *this* Malwa army had fought its way across the entire Persian plateau, against Aryan dehgans. They had faced heavy cavalry before, and won. Every time.

Still . . . The Persians had not been equipped with stirrups, and that was the deciding difference. A long, heavy lance braced by feet in stirrups is simply a far more effective weapon than the shorter, much lighter spear used by cavalrymen without stirrups. In the relatively narrow confines of the saddle pass, the Rajputs could not avoid those lances. And the lances ripped them apart.

But not completely. Not enough to allow the Romans to simply turn and break away. Hundreds of Rajputs in the front ranks survived the first clash, and were immediately tying up the cataphracts with their swordplay. Within seconds, the saddle pass was filled with the sounds of steel meeting steel.

We can't afford this, thought Belisarius, as he jerked his lance out of the belly of a Rajput cavalryman. For a moment, he was able to survey the battle scene in reasonable safety. Anastasius and Valentinian were keeping most of the enemy in his vicinity from getting near him.

It took less than five seconds for Belisarius to make his decision. *Enough. It's more ragged than I would have liked, but—enough.*

He shouted new orders to the small unit of cornicenes who were trailing him. The horns began blowing the call for retreat. The Thracians obeyed immediately, even though—for the moment—they were winning the battle. Maurice had long since purged the ranks of Belisarius' bucellarii of any arrogant hotheads. *If the general says you retreat, then you retreat. Forget about the guy in front of you, and the fact that you're beating him into a pulp. The general sees the whole battle. You do what* he *says. At once.*

Belisarius himself began moving away from the front line. He swept his eyes back and forth, gauging the progress of his troops. It was uneven—there were still knots of Romans and Rajputs flailing at each other with swords—but most of the cataphracts were falling back well enough. The Rajputs were trying to pursue, of course, but the piled-up bodies of the men and horses driven under in the hammersmash were delaying them badly. Badly enough, Belisarius thought, for most of his men to make their escape.

Within seconds, in fact, Belisarius realized that he and his little cluster of soldiers were almost at the very rear of the Roman retreat. A bit isolated, actually. He had been so preoccupied with watching the rest of the army that he hadn't paid attention to his own situation.

Valentinian brought the point home. "We're sticking out like a thumb, general. Everyone's ahead of us. We ought to pick up the pace a little or—"

A swirl of motion caught the corner of Belisarius' eye. He turned his head and saw that a small group of Rajputs had forced their way over the barricade of bodies. The enemy was charging toward them, now, with not more than thirty yards to cover.

Belisarius didn't even think of fleeing. Against enemies like these, running was sure death. He reined his horse around and set his lance. Alongside him, he sensed Valentinian and Anastasius doing the same.

The Rajput in the lead was very tall. As he reared up, holding his spear in the overhead position of stirrupless lancers, he loomed like a giant.

Belisarius looked up—and up—at the man's face. Rajput helmets were visorless, beyond a narrow noseguard.

The face was Rana Sanga's.

Belisarius' own helmet was a German Spangenhelm. The heavy, curving cheekplates covered much of his face, but there was no noseguard. And so, in that instant, he knew that Sanga recognized him as well.

The friend across the field. But the friend had crossed the field, now, and was no friend here. Belisarius was about to fight a man who was counted one of the greatest warriors of India.

He braced his feet, set the lance, and spurred his charger forward. Valentinian rode alongside, perhaps a pace behind. Anastasius tried to do the same, but was intercepted by two other Rajputs.

Two seconds later, Belisarius learned why Sanga was a legend.

Since he first discovered stirrups, Belisarius had never failed to defeat an enemy lancer without them. Until Sanga. The Rajput king avoided the longer and heavier Roman lance by a quick twist in the saddle, and then plunged his own lance downward with all the power of his mighty arm.

Into the neck of Valentinian's horse. The spear tip penetrated unerringly between two plates in the armor and ruptured arteries. The horse coughed blood and collapsed, spilling Valentinian to the ground.

As always in battle, Aide was augmenting Belisarius' senses and reflexes. The general's mind seemed to move as quickly as lightning. But it was ice, not fire, which coursed through his nerves now. Sanga's stroke, he realized, had been completely purposeful. The Rajput king had seen Valentinian in action, and had obviously made his own estimate of which enemy needed to be taken out first.

Which does not, thought Belisarius grimly, *speak well for* my *prospects*.

The Roman general reined his horse around. In the corner of his eye, he saw that Anastasius was now facing three Rajputs. The giant was hammering one of them down, but he would be no immediate help to Belisarius.

Sanga was also wheeling around, ready to charge. He was too close for the heavy lance to be more than a hindrance. Belisarius dropped the weapon and drew his long cavalry saber. He spurred his mount forward.

An instant later, his sword stroke was deflected by Sanga's shield. Belisarius barely managed to get his own shield up in time to meet Sanga's counterstrike.

The power of that blow was shocking, especially

coming from a man riding a horse without stirrups. Unlike Belisarius, Sanga could only grip his horse with his knees. That incredible sword stroke had been delivered with upper-body strength alone.

Belisarius was a strong man himself, but he knew at once that he was hopelessly outmatched. Fortunately, most very powerful men are slow, and Belisarius hoped—

The next stroke came so quickly that even Belisarius' Aide-augmented senses could barely react in time to block it. The third blow—Belisarius was not even trying to strike back—was aimed at his thigh. Only Aide's help allowed Belisarius to interpose his shield quickly enough to keep from having his leg amputated. But the leg went numb. Sanga's sword had driven the shield into his thigh like a sledge. And had also, judging by the sound, cracked the shield itself.

The next sword cut broke his shield in half. Only the iron outer rim was still holding it together.

Finally, Belisarius swung his own blade. Sanga blocked the cut with his shield and then, with a flashing sweep, hammered the sword right out of Belisarius' hand. In the backstroke, the Rajput king drove Belisarius half out of the saddle. The Roman's shield was practically in tatters, now.

Never in his life had Belisarius faced such an incredible opponent. He saw another stroke of that terrible sword coming, and knew he was a dead man. Off balance, with a shredded shield, he had no hope of blocking it.

His mind, Aide-augmented, was still racing. His body could not react in time, but everything seemed to move as slowly as blood in winter. He even had time to find it odd, that his last thought should be:

I can't believe Raghunath Rao faced this man—for an entire day!

The sword descended. But, at the last instant, veered aside. Not much, but enough to simply knock

Belisarius off his horse instead of cutting him in half. The shield absorbed most of the blow, splintering completely, but Belisarius knew his arm was broken. He was half-stunned before he even hit the ground, and that impact dazed him completely.

His eyes were still open. But his mind, for a few seconds, was blank.

He saw Sanga's horse buckle. Saw the lance jutting into the mount's throat. Saw Valentinian, on foot, holding the lance and bringing the beast down. Saw Sanga leap free before the horse could pin him, sword still in hand. Saw Valentinian's first sword stroke, quick as lightning. Saw Sanga parry it, just in time. Saw—

Nothing more, but a horse's flank. A huge hand seized him by the collar of his tunic and hauled him up. Hercules plucking a fruit. He was hanging across a saddle like a sack of flour.

His brain began to work again. *Anastasius' saddle*, he realized. He realized, too—dimly—that he could hear Maurice's shouting voice. And the voices of other Thracians. He could hear the sound of pounding hooves, and feel the horse beneath him break into a gallop.

"Valentinian," he croaked.

"Valentinian will have to do for himself," rumbled Anastasius. "I'm *your* bodyguard, not his."

"Valentinian," he croaked again.

The giant's sigh was audible even over the sound of thundering horses. Then: "I'm sorry, general. I'll miss the bastard. I surely will, not that I'd ever say it to him."

Then, only: "Not that I'll ever have the chance. He's on his own now, against that demon Sanga and twenty thousand of his Rajputs."

Chapter 14

Valentinian did not have to face twenty thousand Rajputs. Only their greatest king.

By the time the battle between Rana Sanga and Valentinian ended, every one of the Rajputs in Damodara's army was on the crest of the saddle, watching. All except the men too badly injured to be moved—and many of those, in later years, counted that loss worse than their scars and severed limbs.

In the annals of Rome, it would be named the *Battle of the Pass*. But for the Rajputs, it would always be known as the Battle of the Mongoose.

In part, the name was given in Belisarius' honor. The Rajputs had won the battle, insofar as possession of the field counts as victory. (Which it does, in every land.) But even on their day of triumph, they knew that the Roman general had yielded little but the blood-soaked ground itself. A pittance, really, when the disparity in numbers was counted—and the butcher's bill paid.

True, they had driven him off, and seized the pass, and cleared their way to yet another range within the Zagros. But there were many more passes to come, before they finally broke through to Mesopotamia. And the Roman general had shown them, in rack and ruin, just how steep a price he would charge for that passage.

For the most part, however, the name was given in honor of Valentinian.

Indians have their own way of looking at animals, and incorporating their spirits into legend. Western folk, seeing Valentinian, were often reminded of a weasel. But there are no weasels in India. There are mongoose, instead. As quick; as deadly—but admired rather, for their cunning, than feared for their bloodlust.

Like Westerners, Indians are familiar with snakes. But they do not share the occidental detestation for serpents. Rather the opposite. There are few of God's creatures, in their eyes, as majestic as the king cobra.

It was those eyes which watched the battle, and gave it the name. Valentinian, much smaller and less powerful than the great king, was the quickest and most agile swordsman any of those Rajputs had ever seen. A battle which most of them expected to last for three minutes—if that long—lasted instead for three hours.

The Roman army watched also, from a much greater distance. By the time the battle was well underway, every surviving Roman soldier had forded the river. On the relative safety of the far bank, Belisarius' officers drew the army into formation while the general himself had his broken arm tended to.

At first, the Roman troops were tense. They were half expecting the enemy to launch a new attack. There was still time, after all—it was no later than mid-afternoon—and this Malwa army had proven its mettle.

Tense, but not worried. The Roman soldiers, in fact, were almost hoping their enemies would try to force their way across the river. They were quite confident of their ability to beat back the assault, and with heavy losses.

But, soon enough, it became obvious that the Rajputs had no intention of making any such foolish gesture. They were too battlewise, first of all. And, secondly, they were completely preoccupied with watching the single combat on the crest between Sanga and Valentinian.

By the time Belisarius emerged from his tent, his arm splinted and bound to his chest, the Roman troops themselves had settled into the relaxation of watching the match. More accurately, they listened to the news brought by dispatch riders. Only Maurice, using Belisarius' telescope, was actually able to see much.

When Belisarius came up to Maurice, the chiliarch lowered the telescope.

"You heard?" he asked. Belisarius nodded.

"Craziest damned thing I've ever seen," muttered Maurice.

His attitude did not surprise Belisarius. Nor Aide: **The custom of single combat between champions is no longer part of Graeco-Roman culture. Hasn't been, for over a millennium—not since the days of Homer. But it's still a living part of India's traditions, at least among Rajputs. Not even two decades of Malwa rule has broken that romantic notion of chivalry.**

Belisarius' eyes studied the pass above. There seemed to be Rajputs covering every inch of the slopes which provided a view of the battle. Even the Rajput units standing guard, assigned to watch for a possible enemy counterattack, had their heads turned away from the Roman army.

If anything, added Aide, **their time in the Malwa yoke is making them treasure this moment even more. There has been nothing like this in years, for Rajputana's warriors. Just the butchery of Ranapur, and Amaravati before that.**

Maurice extended the telescope to its rightful owner.

Belisarius shook his head. "One of two men I treasure is going to die, today. I have no desire to watch it."

Aide's voice, soft: **I am sorry for it, too.**

Maurice brought the telescope back to his eye and resumed observing the battle. He had expected Belisarius' response. His offer of the telescope had been more in the way of a formality than anything else.

But he was still astonished by the Malwa commander.

"Craziest thing I've ever seen," he repeated. "What the hell is Damodara thinking?" He pulled the telescope a few inches from his eye and used it to point at the huge force of Rajputs covering the entire pass. "All he has to do is give the order, and Valentinian is a pincushion. You couldn't see him, for all the arrows sticking out of his body."

Belisarius shook his head. "No Rajput would obey that order, and Damodara knows it. If he sent anyone else, the Rajputs would kill them. And Damodara himself, most likely, if they thought he'd given the command. Besides—"

Belisarius stared across the river, and up the slope. He was not trying to watch the battle between Sanga and Valentinian. He was simply searching, in his mind's eye, for Damodara.

Aide verbalized his thoughts. **A man who rides a tiger long enough begins to think like a tiger himself.**

"This is utter madness!" snarled the Malwa spymaster. He glared down at Damodara, and pointed to the enemy army across the river half a mile distant. "While you waste time in this frivolity, the Romans are making their escape!"

The Malwa commander, squatting comfortably on a cushion, did not respond for a few seconds. His eyes remained fixed on the two men battling fiercely a few dozen yards away. When he did reply, his tone was mild.

"It's a moot point, Isanavarman." Damodara glanced down the slope. "Under no circumstances would I order my army to force the river against *that* opponent." His tone hardened. "I certainly have no intention of giving such an order today. Not after the losses we've taken, from those infernal handcannons."

His eyes moved to the spymaster. They were hard, cold eyes. "Of whose existence I was not informed, by men whose duty it is to know such things."

The spymaster did not flush. But he looked away. Behind him, his three top subordinates tried to make themselves as inconspicuous as possible.

"The best spies in the world," muttered Isanavarman, "cannot discover everything."

The spymaster gave Narses a sour look. The eunuch was squatting on his own cushion next to Damodara. At Damodara's *left* hand—the position allotted, by Indian custom, to a lord's chief civilian adviser. "Did your Roman pet warn you?" demanded Isanavarman, almost snarling. "He has his own spies."

"Not more than a few," responded Damodara. The Malwa commander was back to watching the battle. "Nothing like the horde of spies which Nanda Lal placed at your disposal."

The spymaster gritted his teeth, but said nothing. What was there to say?

Nanda Lal was the chief spymaster for the entire Malwa Empire, and considered Isanavarman his best agent. Nanda Lal had assigned him to be the spymaster for Damodara's army for that very reason. By the simple nature of geography, Damodara was operating an independent command. His was the only army not under the immediate and watchful eye of Malwa's rulers. So Nanda Lal had sent Isanavarman—with many spies, if not quite a horde—as much to keep an eye on Damodara as his enemies.

So what was there to say?

Damodara found words. "Make yourself useful for a change, Isanavarman. Interview the surviving Ye-tai. Find out as much as you can about the handcannons."

Isanavarman began to say something, but Damodara cut him short. "*Do it*. I am the commander of this army, spymaster, not you."

The Malwa lord lifted his finger in a little gesture at the troops surrounding them. Rajputs, all of them, except a few hundred kshatriyas—those whose proven valor had made them welcome. Most of the kshatriyas were in the camp, knowing full well the Rajputs would not permit their presence.

Isanavarman scanned the mass of soldiers. There were perhaps a thousand Ye-tai there also. But the spymaster did not fail to notice that the Ye-tai were scattered through the mass of Rajputs in small groups. Individuals, often enough, chatting amiably with their Rajput companions. Rajputs had a certain scorn for Ye-tai barbarity. But this was a day of manliness, and no one questioned Ye-tai courage.

"Do it," repeated Damodara. Again, cold eyes went to the spymaster. "Leave now, Isanavarman. This is not a place for you."

The spymaster left, then, trailed by his three subordinates. Nanda Lal's agents did not flee, exactly, but neither did they amble. They were not oblivious to other hard, cold eyes upon them. The eyes of thousands of Rajput warriors, who had no love for Malwa spies at any time or place—and certainly not here, on this day of glory.

When they were gone, Damodara leaned toward Narses. The commander's eyes were still fixed on the combat between Valentinian and Rana Sanga, but his gaze seemed a bit unfocused. As if Damodara's thoughts were elsewhere.

"I trust he no longer has a horde of spies," he murmured.

Narses' sneer, as always, was magnificent. "He's got the three who came with him, and two others. The rest are on my payroll."

Damodara nodded. "Tonight, then. I think that would be best."

"It'll be perfect," agreed Narses. "A pitched battle was fought today. A great victory for Malwa, of course, but not without its cost. The cunning Roman general sent a cavalry troop raiding into our camp. Terrible carnage. Great losses."

Narses crooked his finger. Ajatasutra, squatting ten feet away, rose and came over.

"Tonight," whispered Narses. "Do it yourself, if possible."

Ajatasutra did not sneer. He never did. That was one of the reasons, oddly, why Narses had grown so fond of him. But the assassin's thin smile had not a trace of humor in it.

"Those arrogant snobs haven't used a dagger in years," he said softly. "Years spent lounging in Kausambi, reading reports, while poor downtrodden agents like me were having hair-raising adventures with tired old eunuchs."

Narses had a fine grin, to match his sneer. It was not an expression often seen on his reptilian face—and no more reassuring, come to it, that a cobra's yawning gape. But the grin stayed on his face, for minutes thereafter.

He was amused, thinking not of serpents but of different animals. Tigers, and men who choose to ride them.

He glanced at Damodara. The Malwa commander's eyes were riveted on the combat, now, and there was nothing unfocused in the gaze.

He might as well have stripes himself, thought Narses.

✧ ✧ ✧

In the tales of bards, and the lays of poets, truth takes on a rosy tinge. More than a tinge, actually. The reality of a single combat between two great warriors becomes something purely legendary.

There is little place, in legends, for sweat. Even less for thirst and exhaustion. And none at all for urination.

But the fact remains that two men do not battle each other, for hours, without rest. Not even if they were fighting half-naked, with bare hands—much less encumbered by heavy armor and wielding swords. Single combat between champions, other than a glancing encounter in the midst of battle, is by nature a formal affair. And, like most formalities, has a practical core at the center of its rituals.

After the first five minutes, Sanga and Valentinian broke off, gasping for breath. By then, the area was surrounded by Rajputs. Sanga's cavalrymen were still astride their mounts, holding their weapons. One of them, seeing the first open space between the two combatants, began edging his horse toward Valentinian. The man's lance was half-raised.

Sanga bellowed inarticulate fury. The Rajput shied away.

Sanga planted his sword tip in the ground—carefully, making sure there were no stones to dull the blade—and leaned upon it. After gasping a few more breaths, he pointed at Valentinian.

"Give the man water," he commanded. "Wine, if he prefers." The Rajput king studied his opponent, for a few seconds. Valentinian was still breathing deeply, and leaning on his own sword, but Sanga saw that he was no longer gasping.

"And bring us food and cushions," added Sanga. He smiled, quite cheerfully. "I think we're going to need them."

For the next few minutes, while Sanga and Valentinian rested, the Rajputs organized the necessities. A dozen Rajputs clustered around Sanga. Four began moving toward Valentinian, after lowering their weapons. One of them carried a winesack; another, a skin full of water; the third, a rolled-up blanket to serve Valentinian as a cushion whenever he rested; the fourth, some dry bread and cheese.

Sanga nodded toward them, while keeping his eyes on Valentinian. "They will assist you," he called out to the Roman. "Anything you need."

Sanga straightened. "You may surrender, of course. At any time."

For a moment, Valentinian almost gave his natural response—*fuck you, asshole!*—but restrained the impulse. He simply shook his head. A gesture which, at the end, turned into a little bow. Even Valentinian, hardbitten and cynical as he was, could sense the gathering glory.

In the hours which followed, as a lowborn Roman cataphract fought his way into India's legends, the man's mind wondered at his actions.

Why are you doing this, you damned fool?

All his life, Valentinian had been feared by other men. Feared for his astonishing quickness, his reflexes, his uncanny eye—most of all, for his instant capacity to murder. Precious few men, in truth, can kill at the drop of a hat. Valentinian, since the age of ten, could do it before the hat was touched.

And so men feared him. And found, in his whipcord shape and narrow face, the human image of a vicious predator.

Because I'm tired of being called a weasel, came the soul's reply.

The end came suddenly, awkwardly, unexpectedly—almost casually. As it usually does, in the real world. The bards and poets, of course, would have centuries to clean it up.

Sanga's foot slipped, skidding on a loose pebble. For a moment, catching his balance, his shield swung aside. Valentinian, seeing his opening, swung for the Rajput's exposed leg. No Herculean stroke, just Valentinian's usual economic slice. The quick blade cut deeply into Sanga's thigh.

The Rajput fell to one knee, crying out in pain. Pain—and despair. His leg was already covered with blood. It was not the bright, crimson spurting of arterial blood, true, but it was enough. That wound would slay him within half an hour, from blood loss alone. Sooner, really. Within minutes, pain and weakness would cripple him enough for his enemy to make the kill.

Then—

All other men, watching or hearing of that battle in years to come, would always assume that Valentinian made his only mistake.

But the truth was quite otherwise. For hours, Valentinian had avoided matching strength with Sanga. He had countered the king's astonishing power with speed, instead. Speed, cunning, and experience. He could have—*should* have—ended the battle so. Circling the Rajput, probing, slashing, bleeding him further, staying away from that incredible strength, until his opponent was so weak that the quick death thrust could be driven home. Killing a king, like a wolf brings down a crippled bull. Like a weasel kills.

Something inside the man, buried deep, rebelled. For the first time since the battle began—for the first time in his life, truth be told—Valentinian swung a heroic blow. A mighty overhand strike at the Rajput's head.

Sanga threw up his sword, crosswise, to block the cut. Valentinian's sword, descending with the power of his own great strength, met a blade held in Rajputana's mightiest hand.

The finest steel in the world was made in India.

The impact snapped the Roman sword in half, leaving not more than a six-inch stub in Valentinian's fist.

Six inches can still be enough, in a knife fight. Valentinian never hesitated. Weasel-quick, he flung himself to his own knee and drove the sword stub at Sanga's throat.

The Rajput king managed to lower his helmet in time. The blade glanced off the noseguard and ripped a great tear in Sanga's cheek. More blood gushed forth.

It was not enough. No cry of despair escaped his lips, but Valentinian knew he was finished. Facing each other at close distance, both on their knees, the advantage now was all Sanga's.

Sanga was never one for hesitation himself. Instantly, the Rajput king swung a blow. Valentinian interposed his shield. The shield cracked. Another blow. The shield broke. Another blow, to the head, knocked the Roman's helmet askew. The final blow, again to the helmet, split the segmented steel and sent Valentinian sprawling to the ground. Senseless, at the very least. Probably dead, judging from the blood which began pouring through the sundered pieces of the Spangenhelm.

Sanga raised his arm, to sever Valentinian's neck. But he stopped the motion, even before the sword finished its ascent.

He had won a glorious victory, this day. He would not stain it with an executioner's stroke.

Sanga sagged back on his heels. In a daze, he stared up at the sky. It was sunset, and the mountains were bathed in purple majesty. Around him, vaguely, he heard thunderous cheers coming from thousands of Rajput throats. And, seconds later, felt hands laying him down and beginning to bind his wounds.

A glorious victory. He had not felt this clean—this Rajput pure—for many years. Not since the day he fought Raghunath Rao, and first entered himself into Indian legend.

In the river valley below, the Romans also heard the cheer. The mountains seemed to ring with the sound.

Maurice lowered the telescope. "That's it," he said softly.

Belisarius took a deep breath. Then, turning to Coutzes: "Send a courier, under banner of truce. I want to know if Valentinian's dead, so that the priests can do the rites."

"And if he's alive?" asked Coutzes.

"See if they'll accept a ransom." Belisarius' crooked smile made a brief appearance. "Not that I think I could afford it, even as rich as I am. Not unless Damodara's truly lost his mind."

"Not for all the gold in Rome," was Damodara's instant reply. "Do I look like a madman?"

When Coutzes brought back the news, Belisarius lowered his head. But his heart, for the first time in hours, soared to the heavens.

"He might still die," cautioned Coutzes. "They say he's lost a lot of blood. And his skull's broken."

Anastasius snorted. So did Maurice.

"Not Valentinian," said Belisarius. He lifted his head, smiling as broadly as he ever had in his life. "Not *my* champion. Not that great, roaring, lion of a man."

The following morning, the Malwa army began moving along the river. To the northwest, away from the Romans. Belisarius' army, still holding the fords, made no effort to block them.

Not a single soldier, on either side, thought the matter odd.

"Let's hear it for maneuvers," said a Rajput to a Ye-tai. The barbarian nodded quick agreement.

"God, I love to march," announced a Greek cataphract. His eyes swept the mountains. "Gives us a chance to admire the scenery. For weeks, if we're lucky. Maybe even months."

"Beats staring at your own guts," came a Syrian's response. "Even for a minute."

Chapter 15
YEMEN
Spring, 532 A.D.

"It'll be tonight, for sure," stated Menander.

Ashot wobbled his hand back and forth, in a gesture which indicated less certainty. "Maybe. Maybe not."

Menander stood his ground. "It'll be tonight," he repeated confidently. The young cataphract took two steps to the entrance of the field headquarters and pulled back the flap. The Roman army's camp had been set up half a mile east of a small oasis. Menander was staring in that direction, but his eyes were on the horizon rather than the oasis itself.

A moment later, Euphronius joined him. The young Syrian—he was Menander's age, in his early twenties—took one look at the sky and nodded.

"Sundown in less than an hour," he said. "Moonshine, after that, until midnight. The Arabs will wait until the moon goes down. Then they'll attack."

Antonina, seated in a chair near the center of the

tent, found herself smiling. As soon as she realized what she was doing, she removed the expression. But not soon enough for it to have escaped Ashot's attention.

Ashot grinned at her. She returned the grin with a look of stern admonition, like a prim schoolteacher reproving an older boy in a classroom when he mocked the youngsters.

With about the same success. True, Ashot had the grace to press his lips together. But he still looked like the proverbial cat who swallowed a canary.

Ashot commanded the five hundred cataphracts whom Belisarius had sent along with Antonina on her expedition. Her husband had selected the Armenian officer for the assignment because Belisarius thought Ashot—after Maurice, of course—was the best field commander among his bucellarii. For the most part, Belisarius' decision had been due to Ashot's innate ability. But he had also been influenced by the man's experience. Even though Ashot was only in his mid-thirties, the Armenian was a veteran of more battles and campaigns than any other officer in Belisarius' household troops. (Again, of course, leaving aside Maurice.)

From her own experience over the past year, Antonina had come to understand why Belisarius had counted that so heavily in his decision. She was still herself something of a novice in the art of war. Time and again, Ashot's steadying hand had been there, when Antonina's assumptions proved incorrect.

The enemy didn't do what you expected them to do? Yeah, well, they usually don't. No problem. We'll deal with it.

Euphronius and Menander turned away from the entrance. With the absolute surety possessed only by young men, they made their pronouncements.

"Tonight," predicted Menander.

"Right after the moon goes down," decreed Euphronius.

"The main attack will come from the east," ruled Menander.

Euphronius nodded his head. Solon approving a judgement by Hammurabi. "Only possible direction. They'll be able to use the setting moon to guide them in the approach. And they won't get tangled up in the oasis."

Antonina squared her shoulders. "Very well, then. See to the preparations."

The two young officers swept out of the tent, brushing aside the flap as if they were the trade winds. When they were gone, Antonina eyed Ashot. The Armenian's grin was back in full force.

"All right," she growled, "now tell me what *you* think."

Still grinning, the Armenian shrugged. "I don't know. And for that matter, I don't care. The attack *might* come tonight—although I'm skeptical—so we need to be prepared anyway. It'll be good drill, if nothing else."

Ashot pulled up a chair and lounged in it. His grin faded into a smile of approval. "I like cocky young officers," he said. "As long as they're men of substance—which those two certainly are." He shrugged again. "They'll get the silly crap knocked out of them soon enough. In the meantime, I can count on them to stand straight in the storm. Whenever it comes, from whatever direction."

Antonina lifted a cup from the table next to her chair and took a sip. The vessel was filled with water from the nearby oasis, flavored with just a dash of wine.

"Why don't you think it'll be tonight?" she asked.

Ashot stroked his cheek, running fingers through his stiff and bristly beard. "It just doesn't seem likely to me, that's all. We'll be facing bedouin nomads. They're quite capable of moving fast, once they've made their decision. Fast enough, even through the desert, that they *could* be in position by tonight."

He leaned forward, planting elbows on knees. "But

I know that breed. I can almost guarantee that they'll spend two or three days quarreling and bickering before they decide what to do." He chuckled. "That's the whole point of this exercise. That's why we landed north of Sana, instead of right at the coast with Eon and his sarawit."

Antonina nodded. The tactics of this campaign had been primarily worked out by Ashot and Wahsi. Antonina and Eon, of course, had approved the plan. But neither had felt themselves qualified to develop it in the first place.

And if they had, she knew, they wouldn't have thought to come up with *this* plan. Ashot and Wahsi, veterans of campaigns and not just battles, had immediately seen the weakness in the traitor Abreha's strategic position. His problem was political, more than purely military.

Abreha was holding Yemen with only two rebel regiments from the Ethiopian army. Those two regiments, the Metin and the Falha, were forted up in the provincial capital of Sana. The third regiment stationed in Arabia, the Halen at Marib, was still maintaining neutrality in the civil war.

The bulk of Abreha's forces, therefore—well over three-fourths of them—consisted of Arab irregulars. Warriors from the various bedouin tribes in southern Arabia, under the shaky command of an unstable cluster of war chiefs. As individuals, the Arab nomads were ferocious fighters. But their discipline was almost nonexistent, and their concept of war was essentially that of brigands and pirates. They had flocked to Abreha's banner, not because they cared which faction of Axum ruled southern Arabia, but because they saw a chance for loot.

So, Antonina was offering them a juicy plum—her small army of Romans, detached and isolated from the main body of Ethiopian sarwen who had landed on the coast near Sana. Rome was the land of wealth, in that part of the world. What few gold coins the Arabs possessed were solidii minted in Constantinople. The streets of the fabled city, capital of the Roman Empire, were reputed among those tribesmen to be paved with gold. (There were a few skeptics in their midst, of course, who thought the tales unlikely. Silver, certainly, but not gold.)

Now, this day, ready to be plucked, was a force of rich Romans not more than two thousand strong. Less than that, really, in the eyes of the bedouin. At least five hundred of those Romans were *women*.

And that, of course, was another inducement to attack. The tribesmen would capture concubines along with treasure. Roman women, to boot, who were reputed to be the most beautiful women in the world. (Again, of course, there were skeptics. But they were all women themselves, driven by spite and jealousy.)

It was a cunning plan. Even if Abreha tried to restrain them, his Arab irregulars would ignore his orders. But Ashot and Wahsi thought that Abreha, in all likelihood, would not object. From a purely military standpoint, attacking the Romans would seem to be a good move. By approaching Sana from the north, in a separate column, the Romans were isolated from the Axumite army under Eon. Abreha would see the chance to defeat his enemy in detail.

A cunning plan—and risky. There were at least five thousand bedouin under Abreha's banner. They would outnumber the Roman forces by a factor of almost three to one.

Antonina's eyes drifted to a corner of the tent. There, resting on a small table, was her own handcannon. Much as she detested the thing, the sight of the weapon helped to restore her confidence.

The handcannon was smaller than the heavy smoothbores carried by her Cohort, and much more finely crafted. John of Rhodes had made it for her personally. It was the prototype of a line of weapons he planned to develop for cavalrymen. He called it a *pistol*.

"An over-and-under double-barreled caplock, to be precise," he'd told her, when he handed her the weapon a week before her departure from Alexandria. "It's the first gun made using the new percussion caps. Beautiful piece, isn't it?"

Antonina, handling the device, had privately thought the term "beautiful" was absurd. To her, the grotesque-looking weapon was ugly, awkward—and God-awful *heavy*. Her small hand could barely hold the grip.

"No, no, Antonina!" John exclaimed. "You've got to hold it with *both* hands. Here—put your left hand under the stock. That's why the wood's there." His expression shaded from pride to half-apology. "It's not really a true handgun, yet, except for a big man. But it's the best I could come up with this soon."

Despite her private reservations, Antonina had thanked John for the gift. Quite profusely, at the time he gave it to her. Two days later, after spending several hours on the practice range—John had been adamant on the point—her thanks were less heartfelt. She had no doubt the damned thing would do its lethal duty, if and when the time came. But her hands ached and her butt was bruised from the times she had been knocked off her feet by the recoil. She darkly suspected, moreover—damn what the doctors said—that at least one of her shoulders was dislocated. Permanently, from the feel of it.

Ashot's eyes followed hers.

"Ugly damned thing," he grunted. "Glad I don't have to shoot a handcannon. Even that one, much less the bonebreakers the Cohort uses."

For all the sourness of the words, however, his expression was cheerful enough. He leaned back in his chair and planted his hands on his hips.

"Relax, Antonina. The plan'll work. It looks a lot riskier than it really is, unless we screw up."

Antonina blew out her cheeks. "You're that confident in the handcannons?" she asked.

Ashot snorted. "Antonina, I don't have any confidence in *any* weapons. Weapons are just tools, I don't care how newfangled and fancy they are. No better than the men who use them."

He waved his hand. "I *do* have confidence in those Syrian boys out there. And their wives. But most of all, I've got confidence in the general."

"The general," to Ashot, meant Belisarius. Like most of the bucellarii, it was a title which Ashot bestowed on no one else. So Antonina was surprised, when Ashot added: "*Both* generals."

She gazed at him quizzically. Ashot chuckled.

"Didn't your husband ever mention him to you? I'm sure he must have."

Antonina understood the reference, then. Belisarius had done much more than "mention" that other general to her, in point of fact. In the weeks leading up to his departure for Persia, the year before, Belisarius had spent half his time preparing his wife for her own expedition. He had drilled her for hours, day after day, in that other general's tactics. He had even insisted—the only time he ever did so—that she take Aide in her hand and enter the crystal's world of visions.

She almost shuddered, remembering those scenes of ghastly slaughter. But she took heart, as well, remembering the battle of Waterloo. Where the French cavalry broke—again and again—against Wellington's infantry at the ridge of La Haye Sainte.

"Maybe tonight," she heard Ashot murmur. "And maybe not. Doesn't matter. We'll break the bastards, whenever they come."

He barked a harsh laugh. "The only thing I know for sure is this, Antonina. A month from now, those bedouin hotheads will be sulking in their tents. Calling you the Iron Dyke."

Chapter 16

The attack came two nights later, long before the moon went down, and from the south. Menander and Euphronius were both exceedingly disgruntled. The tactics of their enemies made no sense at all!

They got over it, quickly enough. Very quickly. Whatever the Arabs lacked in the way of tactical acumen, they made up for in other ways.

Ashot was not surprised—neither by the Arabs' tactics nor by the vigor of their attack. The timing was about what he had guessed, so far as the day was concerned. He had not really expected bedouin irregulars to be patient enough to wait until midnight. South was the direction from which they had come, and they had the advantage of moonlight to guide them. True, the same moonlight made them easier targets, but the desert warriors sneered at such unmanly concerns. There was a hill to the south, moreover, almost next to the Roman camp. The hill would disguise the Arabs' approach, and give them the advantage of charging downhill.

None of it, as Ashot had foreseen, made any difference. The Theodoran Cohort was prepared, as they had been for three days. As soon as the sun went down, the troops were on full alert. The matchlocks were loaded and the matches themselves were lit. The musketeers buckled on their short swords. The wives laid out the grenades, cut the fuses, prepared the cartridges. Sharpened stakes were set in the ground at eighteen-inch intervals, making for additional protection for the musketeers. The Thracian cataphracts, dismounted, took up their pikes.

The smell of smoldering slow match blew across the camp on the ceaseless breeze. The cataphracts and the Cohort waited. Ashot waited. Menander and Euphronius polished their certainties. Antonina mouthed a silent prayer for the soul of a general she had never met and never would, wherever that soul might be.

Two hours after sundown, the attack started. With a sudden whoop, several thousand Arabs on camelback surged over the hilltop and began charging down onto the camp. Most of them were holding swords, but many brandished torches.

"What the hell?" demanded Menander.

"What's wrong with those stupid—" began Euphronius. But the young commander of the Cohort broke off. He had immediate duties to attend to.

"Sling-staffs!" he shouted. "To the south! As soon as the enemy's in range!" He raced off, seeing to the disposition of the musketeers.

Menander stayed behind, standing next to Antonina and Ashot. He was in direct charge of the cataphract pikemen, but he really had nothing to do. The cataphracts, veterans all, were no more surprised by the illogic of the enemy's attack than Ashot. And, unlike the musketeers, they did not have cumbersome supplies and equipment to move around. The units, without waiting for orders, simply shifted their positions slightly.

They didn't have far to go. Ashot had set the camp in such a way that the Roman troops formed a tightly packed square. The musketeers formed the front line, on all four sides, protected by the palisade of sharpened stakes. The pikemen took position just a few yards behind, ready to form an additional bulwark where needed. The grenadiers, along with the hundred cataphracts whom Ashot was keeping as a mounted reserve, were positioned in the center of the camp.

"Range," for grenadiers wielding sling-staffs, meant a hundred and fifty yards. By the time the first wave of Arabs reached that distance, the wives had cut and lit the fuses. The grenades were sent on their way.

Ashot mounted up. He managed the task unassisted, and with relative ease. Like the rest of the cataphracts, he was wearing half-armor instead of full gear. He had felt that would be enough, against lightly armed irregulars. Mobility would be more important than protection and weight of charge, in this battle.

Ashot was not planning any thunderous sallies, in any case. His relative handful of cavalrymen would be swallowed up in a sea of swirling bedouin, if they ever left the safety of the camp. Their role was to provide a sharp, quick counterpunch wherever the enemy might threaten to break through the front lines.

Menander and Euphronius, of course, had argued with him.

"Can't destroy an enemy without cavalry pursuit," Menander had sagely pointed out. Euphronius nodded firm agreement.

"Don't need to," had been Ashot's sanguine reply. "We're not facing disciplined regulars, who'll regroup after a defeat. The bedouin haven't got any staying power. They'll attack like maniacs, but if they bounce off, good and bloodied, they'll decide the whole business is not favored by the gods. They'll melt into the desert and go back to tending their flocks. That's good enough, for our purposes. Abreha won't have them, at his side, when Eon and Wahsi storm into Sana."

Menander and Euphronius, of course, had not been convinced. But the youngsters had satisfied themselves, in the days thereafter, with lengthy exchanges on the subject of senility.

Antonina did less than anyone, waiting for the charge. She simply followed Ashot's advice—say better, *instructions*—and stood firmly in her place. Right at the center of the camp, where everyone could see and hear her.

"Your job," Ashot had explained cheerfully, "is simply to give the troops confidence. That's it, Antonina. Just stand there, looking as resolute as Athena, and shout encouragement. And make sure you wear that obscene breastplate."

Antonina donned the cuirass, with the help of her maid, Koutina. Looking down at her immense brass mammaries, she had her usual reaction.

Ashot's good cheer faded. "And *try* not to giggle," he grumbled. "That looks bad, in a commander, during desperate battle."

Antonina giggled.

Now, as she waited for the charge, Antonina had no trouble restraining her giggle. She maintained her outward composure, but she was quite scared. Terrified, if truth be told.

Ashot could make his veteran pronouncements, and her young officers could decree the certain future. But all Antonina could see, staring at the horde of shrieking nomads coming down the hill like an irresistible force of nature, was a wave of rape and murder.

Cursing at the weight of her awkward firearm, she shifted the strap which held the thing over her shoulder. Her hand groped for the hilt of her "sword." Once her fingers curled around the plain wood of the blade's utilitarian handle, she felt her confidence return. She had used that cleaver before—and used it successfully—to defend herself against rape and murder, when Malwa-paid thugs attacked her in Constantinople. Maurice had purchased the cleaver, afterward, and given it to her for her personal weapon in the battle at the stadium.

Ask any veteran, Antonina, he'd told her at the time. *They'll all tell you there's nothing as important in a battle as having a trusty,* tested *blade.*

The cleaver brought confidence. And so, even more, did Ashot's whispered words: "It's just another knife fight in a kitchen, Antonina. Like you've done before."

The grenades began landing among the Arabs. Few of them missed. The Syrian slingers were combat veterans themselves, now. The confidence which that gave them, added to their own skill, made for a murderous volley.

As before, against cavalry, the main effect of the exploding bombs was moral. Not many of the Arabs themselves were killed, or even seriously injured, by the crude devices. Most of the casualties were sustained by their mounts, and even the camels did not suffer greatly. The year before, when used against Ambrose's rebel cataphracts on the paved streets of Alexandria, shrapnel from exploding grenades had wreaked havoc on the unarmored legs of their horses. But here, on desert sand, there were no ricochets to multiply the damage.

The camels did not suffer greatly from *physical* damage, that is. But the beasts were completely unaccustomed to artillery fire, and immediately began to panic. The sound and fury of the explosions caused most of that terror. But even the sputtering flare of a burning fuse caused camels to stumble and shy away.

Camels are large animals, heavier than horses. Once started on a charge down a hill, they were impossible to stop. But the charge, as hundreds of camels either collapsed from wounds or simply stumbled from fear, turned into something more in the nature of an avalanche. An avalanche is a fearsome thing, true. But it has no brains at all. By the time thousands of bedouin piled up at the foot of the hill, not fifty yards from the Roman front lines, they had about as much coordination and conscious purpose as a snowdrift blown by the wind.

Euphronius gave the order. *Level!* Antonina held her breath. *Fire!*

Fifty yards was within range of the smoothbore arquebusses. Some of the bullets went wide, and many simply buried themselves in the sand. But of the hundreds of rounds fired in that first volley, almost a fourth found a human target.

It mattered hardly at all whether the bullets struck a head, a torso, or a limb. Round shot loses muzzle velocity quickly. But, within fifty yards, the loss was not enough to offset the weight of the .80-caliber lead drop shot. The heavy projectiles, at that range, caused terrible wounds—and struck with incredible force. Arms were blown off, not simply wounded. Thigh bones were pulverized. Men died from shock alone.

The first line of musketeers stepped back, replaced by the second. Antonina expected Euphronius to give the order to fire immediately, but the Syrian waited for the dense cloud of gunsmoke to clear away. She began dancing impatiently, until she realized what she was doing and forced herself to stand still.

Restraint was difficult, even though Antonina understood Euphronius' inaction. It was impossible to see more than a few yards from the front line—and would have been, even in broad daylight. Even the crest of the hill was obscured by the gunsmoke. Until the smoke cleared, the musketeers would be guessing at their target.

A few gaps began appearing in the clouds. Enough, apparently. Euphronius gave the order, and the arquebusses roared again.

The second line stepped back, and the third line came forward. By now, Antonina saw, the first line was already reloaded and ready to fire again.

She felt a certain female smugness. *Her* troops could manage a much better rate of fire, she knew, than those of her husband. Despite the fact that they were using the same type of firearms, *her* troops had wives, standing with the men. The Theodoran Cohort carried twice as many handcannons as they had gunners. The women kept the spares ready and loaded. As soon as the men stepped back, a freshly loaded gun was in their hands, while their wives set to work reloading the fired pieces.

With that advantage, Antonina's cohort could manage a rate of fire which approached that of Wellington's men. As a battle wore on, of course, the rate would drop quickly. After a few rounds had been fired through the crude arquebusses, gunpowder residues fouled the bores. The weapons had to be cleaned before they could be reloaded, and even efficient Syrian wives could not do that instantly.

Still—

Fire! she heard Euphronius shout. The third line discharged their pieces.

The only reason her troops were not maintaining a faster rate of fire was simply to let the clouds of gunsmoke clear away sufficiently to aim. Had there been a strong wind blowing, they could have been hammering the Arabs almost ceaselessly.

Antonina cursed the light desert breeze. The curse

seemed to be effective. A sudden gust blew a great hole in the clouds.

The gap was closed, within seconds, by the first rank's second round of fire. But in those seconds, Antonina saw the carnage.

By now, just as she had experienced in her fight in the kitchen, Antonina was feeling nothing beyond controlled fury. But even with battle-lust burning in her veins, she was glad that the scene was filtered through dim moonlight. The shrieks coming out of that murky mass of struggling men were bloodcurdling enough.

That's got to be pure horror.

The thought was at the edge of her mind, however. At the forefront came recognition that the enemy had recovered enough to change tactics. Wails of agony were overridden by frantic shouts and commands. Murky movement blurred, poured to the sides.

"They're going to the flanks!" bellowed Ashot, loud enough to be heard all through the Roman camp. On the heels of that baritone shout, Antonina heard Menander's high tenor. The young cataphract was shifting his pikemen, shoring up all four sides of the camp.

Seconds later, Euphronius did the same. The commander of the Cohort had concentrated half his musketeers on the southern flank of the camp, facing the hill. Now, he began moving units to the other three sides.

Within two minutes, the Roman formation was that of a classic infantry square, bristling like a hedgehog with muskets and pikes. The Arabs were swirling all around the camp, attacking on every side in small lunges and sallies.

For the first time, the pikemen went to work. Euphronius, for all his youth, was too canny to waste entire salvoes on small clots of enemy cavalry. The threat of those shattering salvoes, in the long run, was all that was holding the enemy at bay. If the Roman musketeers fired too often, their weapons would become hopelessly fouled.

So he waited, patiently, until he saw a large enough cluster gathering. Then, and only then, did the gunsmoke clouds fill the air. In the meantime, the pikes were busy, keeping at bay the small groups of Arabs—sometimes one man alone—who tried to rush the Roman lines.

"Keeping busy" meant, for the most part, simply standing their ground. Not often were the blades of the pikes actually needed.

That was not due to cowardice on the part of the men facing those pikes. No one doubted the courage of the bedouin, or their willingness to hurl themselves onto the Roman lines. But it is a simple fact, often glossed over by historians and *always* by poets and bards, that horses and camels—level-headed, sensible, sane, rational creatures—can not be forced onto a wall of spears. Any number of camels, either from accident or from being half-crazed by wounds, did stumble against the pikes. The pikes brought them down, and their riders with them. But the great mass of the beasts shied away, despite the shrieking commands of their supposed masters.

Antonina, after a few minutes, felt her tension easing. She had been told—*assured*—by her husband, and by Maurice and Ashot, that this would be true. Still, seeing is believing.

Stand your ground, love, her husband had told her. *Just stand your ground, with pike and handcannon. No cavalry in the world will be able to break you, unless they break your will. Artillery could, but you won't be facing that where you're going.*

Many things about herself Antonina had doubted, over the years. Never her will. She was a small woman, but she had a spine to match Atlas.

So, as the battle raged, Antonina found herself

doing exactly what Ashot—and her husband and Maurice before him—had told her to do. Just stand there, looking calm and confident. Shout the occasional words of encouragement; whistle a tune; whatever—as long as it's not a giggle.

She only had to fight down a giggle once. Her maid, Koutina, having no duties of her own in battle, had still insisted on staying at Antonina's side. The time came when Koutina nodded sagely, as if some inner suspicion had been confirmed.

"I knew it," she said. The young Egyptian maid glanced at the wall of pikes and muskets, dismissing them serenely. "They're scared of your giant tits, is what it is. That's why they won't come any closer."

At the very end, Antonina learned another lesson. Her husband—and Maurice, and Ashot—had told her of this one, too. But she had forgotten, or never quite believed.

Battles are unpredictable things. Chaos incarnate.

The bedouin finally broke, screaming their frustration. Thousands of Arabs pounded away from the camp, fleeing into the desert. But, by some strange eddy, a large cluster of enemy cavalrymen suddenly hammered into the southern flank of the Roman square.

Since the first few moments of the battle, when the soldiers facing the hill had borne the brunt of the attack, their fight had been easy. If nothing else, the great mound of human and camel bodies in front of them kept most of the Arabs at bay. Now, coming from God-knows-where-or-how, a knot of some twenty bedouin thundered at the line.

The line had been thinned, too far. The Roman flank did not break, but it did crack. Three bedouin made it into the camp itself. Ashot's cataphracts, mounted and held in reserve, started moving toward them.

Before the cataphracts could reach them, two of the Arabs were felled by gunshots. The third Arab's mount was brought down by a pike. The bedouin warrior sprang off the collapsing camel, like a nimble acrobat, and rolled to his feet.

Not six yards from where Antonina was standing, alone except for Koutina.

The maid screamed and scuttled behind Antonina. Drawn by the sound, the nomad turned his head. An instant later, he bounded toward them, his curved sword held high. The man was shrieking like a berserk.

Antonina never even thought to draw her cleaver. Against street thugs, that trusty blade had done wonders. But it would be as effective as a whittling knife against the man charging her now.

She snatched the handcannon off her shoulder. For a moment, she fumbled with the dual hammers and triggers, until John of Rhodes' endless hours of training bore fruit. With her finger firmly on the rear trigger, she cocked the left-side hammer, leveled the gun, and fired.

As always, the blast was deafening and the recoil half-spun her around. But she ignored the pain—was not even aware of it, in truth.

Frantically, she brought the weapon to bear again. She was astonished to see that the Arab was still standing. Her first shot had smashed his rib cage. The man's right side was covered with blood. Antonina could *see* a jagged rib protruding, glistening in the moonlight.

The bedouin did not even grimace. He had stopped shrieking, now. His face seemed calm, like a death mask. The man reached across his body with his left hand and pressed the horrible wound, holding his ruptured side in place. Then he began plodding toward her. His sword was still in his right hand.

For an instant, Antonina was paralyzed by the incredible sight. Then she went berserk herself.

"Fuck you!" she screamed. She sprang forward and jammed the muzzle against the Arab's chest. The fury of her charge was so great that the small woman actually forced the man back two paces. Driving him with the handcannon by rage of body, while her mind—as cold as a kitchen icebox—went through the trained sequence.

The bedouin raised the sword. *Finger on front trigger. Cock the right-side hammer.*

She pulled the trigger. Again, the recoil hammered her aside.

Antonina was oblivious to the pain. Still shrieking obscenities, she spun back and swung the heavy barrel at the Arab's head.

The gun swept through thin air. The momentum of the frenzied swing spun Antonina clear around. She stumbled, off balance, and fell on her butt. The heavy cuirass drove her down.

She stared at her opponent. The man was lying on his back, just a few feet away. She had swung at nothing, she realized. The second shot had ruptured the Arab's heart, and probably his spine with it. He had fallen even before she spun around.

Finally, pain registered. Her hands hurt. Her arms hurt. Her shoulders hurt. Her ass hurt. Even her breasts hurt, where the brass armor had impacted them in her fall.

"Ow," she muttered. A moment later, Koutina was at her side, kneeling, clutching her. The clutch, unfortunately—the desperate squeeze of a terrified kitten—was right across her breasts, pressing the armor further into the poor bruised things.

"Ow." Almost desperate herself, she tried to pry Koutina loose. Or, at least, to shift the girl's anaconda grip a little lower down.

Ashot loomed above her. Antonina stared up at him.

"Well, the battle's won," announced the cataphract. "Total victory. We won't see those Arabs again. Neither will Abreha."

Ashot did not seem ecstatic at the news. To the contrary. His expression was grim and condemnatory. "I *told* you so," he snarled, glaring at the body of the dead Arab.

Two more cataphracts came up behind Ashot. They seemed to loom over the stubby Armenian as much as he loomed over Antonina. Huge men.

Antonina recognized them. They were named Matthew and Leo. They were the two cataphracts whom Ashot had proposed as her bodyguards, when the expedition left Alexandria.

Antonina had spurned the proposal. She had not been able to explain why, at the time, even to herself. Or had not wanted to, at least. She knew that her husband had bodyguards. Valentinian and Anastasius, as a matter of fact, who were universally considered the best fighters in the Thracian bucellarii. But for Antonina—

No. It had not been necessary, she felt. Unlike Belisarius, who led his men in combat, Antonina had no intention of actually fighting. And there was a stubborn, mulish part of her which had resented the idea.

What am I, a little girl who needs chaperones?

"Does that offer still stand?" she croaked.

Ashot snorted. He gave Matthew and Leo a wave of the hand. "You've got a new job, lads."

" 'Bout time," she heard Matthew mutter.

Leo said nothing. He almost never did. He just reached down his bear-paw-sized hand and lifted Antonina to her feet.

Antonina stared up at him. Leo was the ugliest, scariest-looking, most brutish man she—or anyone else—had ever seen. His fellow cataphracts called him "the Ogre." When they weren't calling him "the Ox," that is, on account of his extremely limited intellect.

But they never called him either name to his face.

Such a handsome man, thought Antonina. *I can't think of better company.*

Antonina's maid was still clutching her. Leo had lifted both of the women, with one hand. Koutina's grip shifted again.

"*Ow*," hissed Antonina. But she didn't pry the girl off. She just patted her hand reassuringly, while she took her own comfort staring at an ogre.

Her ogre.

Chapter 17

KAUSAMBI

Summer, 532 A.D.

"You are disturbed, Nanda Lal," said Great Lady Sati. The young Malwa noblewoman leaned back in her plush, well-upholstered chair. Her ring-heavy fingers stroked the armrests, but her austerely beautiful face was completely still. "Something is troubling you."

The Malwa emperor started, hearing those words. Skandagupta rolled his fat little body side to side on his ornate throne, shifting his eyes from Lady Sati to Nanda Lal. As always when the Malwa Empire's highest council met, the room was unoccupied except for those three people and the special guards. The guards, recruited exclusively from the distant land of the Khmers, were all devotees of Link's cult. Seven of them were giant eunuchs, kneeling in a row against a far wall of the chamber. Their immense bodies were naked from the waist up. Each held a bare tulwar in his hands. The remaining two guards were assassins. Those, garbed in black shirts and pantaloons, stood on either side of the chamber's entrance.

Nanda Lal was frowning, but silent. Emperor Skandagupta prompted him. "If something is troubling you, cousin, speak up," he commanded. "I can't imagine what it is."

Skandagupta reached for the cup of tea resting on a side table next to his throne. "Best news we've had in months. Belisarius has finally been beaten!"

Lady Sati shook her head. The gesture carried a certainty far beyond her years—as if she were already possessed by the divine being which would someday inhabit her body. But the certainty was simply born of habit and training. Sati had spent more time in the company of Link than any other person in the world. (Other than her aunt Holi, of course. But Great Lady Holi was no longer a human being. Holi was nothing, now, beyond Link's sheath.)

"He has not been *beaten*," she said. "Simply driven off, for a time. There is a difference."

Finally, Nanda Lal spoke. "Quite a difference," he growled in agreement. The spymaster took a deep breath. "But it is not Belisarius who concerns me, at the moment. It is Damodara."

The emperor's eyes widened. Lady Sati's did not. "You are concerned about the arms complex in Marv," she stated.

Nanda Lal extended a thick hand, wobbling it back and forth. "In itself—no. Not much, anyhow. We discussed that matter weeks ago, you recall, when we first discovered the fact."

"Yes, we did," interrupted the emperor. "And we agreed that it was not worth making an issue over." Skandagupta shrugged. "It is against Malwa law, true. But we gave Damodara a most thankless task, and can hardly complain when he improved his odds."

The emperor fixed narrow, fat-shrouded eyes on Nanda Lal. "So why the sudden concern?" Forcefully:

"I myself am very partial to Damodara. He is far and away our best military commander. Energetic and practical."

"Which is *precisely* what bothers me," countered Nanda Lal. "Your Majesty," he added, almost as a casual afterthought.

Nanda Lal reached to another side table and picked up a scroll. He waved it before him.

"This is a report from a man named Pulumayi, which supplements Lord Damodara's account of the recent battle in the Zagros where Belisarius was beaten."

The emperor frowned. "Pulumayi? Who is he? Never heard of him." He raised his cup toward his mouth.

Nanda Lal snorted. "Neither had I! I had to check my records, to verify his claim." He drew air into his nostrils. "Apparently, Pulumayi is now my chief spy in Damodara's army."

Skandagupta's cup paused before reaching his lips. "What happened to Isanavarman?" he demanded.

"He is dead," came Nanda Lal's harsh reply. "Along with all my top agents. Pulumayi succeeded to Isanavarman's post because he is the most highly ranked survivor—" Again, that deep-drawn breath. "It seems that Belisarius' cavalry raided Damodara's camp during the battle."

Nanda Lal tapped the scroll in the palm of his left hand. "So, at least, this report claims. I do not doubt the claim—not insofar as the casualties are concerned, that is. Their actual cause may be otherwise."

Lady Sati's fingers came to a stop. They did not clench the armrests. Not exactly. But the grip was very firm.

"You suspect Damodara," she stated. Her quick, Link-trained mind sped beyond. "Narses."

"Yes. The entire affair is too convenient." Again,

Nanda Lal lifted the scroll. "This, combined with the arms complex, is making me uneasy."

Abruptly, Skandagupta drained his cup and set it down, rattling, on the side table. "I still think it's nonsense! I've known Damodara since he was a toddler. That's a practical man if you'll ever meet one. And he's not given to ambition, beyond a reasonable measure."

Slowly, Nanda Lal shook his head. "No, Emperor, he is not. But practicality is a malleable thing. What is impractical one day, may be practical on the morrow. As for ambition—?" He sniffed. "That, too, changes with the tide."

When Sati spoke, her voice was low and calm. "Your fear is for the future, then. Not the immediate present. A possibility."

"Yes." Nanda Lal paused. "Yes, that. I do not propose to take action, at the moment. But I think we should not close our eyes to the—possibility, as you call it."

Lady Sati shrugged. "It's a simple enough matter." She leaned toward the Emperor. "Bestow great honors on Damodara, Skandagupta. And riches. Hold a ceremony within a week. Among those riches will be a mansion here at the capital. Very near to this palace." She smiled, thinly. "Among those honors will be the expectation that Damodara's entire family will take up residence therein. And stay there."

Skandagupta squinted; then, smiled his own thin humor. "Hostages. Yes. That should do nicely. Damodara dotes on his children."

Still, Nanda Lal seemed unhappy. But, after a moment, he shook off the mood. His next words were almost cheerful: "Venandakatra's siege guns should be arriving at Deogiri very soon. Within two weeks, three at the most."

"Finally!" exclaimed the emperor. His eyes narrowed. "That should do for Raghunath Rao. I look forward to seeing his skinsack suspended in my feast hall." Fat folded further; the eyes became mere slits. "*And* Shakuntala's. I will hang her right next to her father."

"Shakuntala will take a bit of time," cautioned Sati. "Even after we take Deogiri."

She looked to Nanda Lal. "We must tighten the blockade of Suppara. Make sure the rebel empress does not make her escape."

The spymaster scowled. "I'm afraid that's impossible. We don't have the naval forces available—not with Axum to contend with."

"A pity," muttered Skandagupta, "that we didn't catch Prince Eon with the rest." He shrugged. "But I don't see where it matters. Even if Shakuntala escapes after we take Deogiri, where can she go? Only to Ethiopia, or Rome. Where she will be nothing but an impoverished exile."

The emperor nodded toward Sati. "Just as Link said, long ago. Without Majarashtra, Shakuntala is nothing but a nuisance."

Sati nodded grudging agreement. "True. Although I *would* prefer to see her flayed."

"Whatever we do," sneered Nanda Lal, "we certainly won't make the mistake of handing her over to Venandakatra again. Dead—or exiled. That's it."

The spymaster reached up and stroked his nose. As always, the feel of that crushed and mangled proboscis stirred his fury. Belisarius had done for that.

Since there was no way, at present, to vent his feelings for Belisarius, Nanda Lal transferred his cold rage elsewhere. "One last point," he snarled, "before we end this meeting. The rebel bands in Bihar and Bengal are growing bolder. I recommend—"

"More impalings!" snapped the emperor. "Line every road with the bandits!"

"I agree," chimed in Great Lady Sati. "The male ones, anyway. Better to turn their women over to the soldiers, before auctioning them to the whoremasters. Add defilement to destruction. That will cow the peasants."

Nanda Lal's snarl of fury slid into something resembling a leer. "Not enough," he demurred. "It's too hard to catch the bandits in the forests."

He bestowed the leer on the emperor. "Since all the news is good—Belisarius defeated; Deogiri about to fall—I see no reason that half your Imperial Guard can't be released for a campaign."

The emperor smiled. Grinned. "Excellent idea! The Ye-tai are getting restless, anyway, from garrison duty here in Kausambi. A campaign in Bihar and Bengal would do them good."

Skandagupta leaned forward, planting his hands on his knees. "What do you have in mind? A punitive campaign, right through the countryside?" He barked a laugh. "Yes! Sweep everything, like a knife. Cut a swath twenty miles wide—from Pataliputra to the Bay of Bengal. The hell with hunting for bandits! Just burn everything, kill everyone." Another barked laugh. "Except the women, of course. My Ye-tai will have a better use for those."

Nanda Lal leaned forward to match gazes with the emperor. "I was thinking of two swaths, actually. One—just as you say—starting at Pataliputra. The other—"

There came a knock on the door. Nanda Lal paused. One of the assassins opened the door and peered through. A moment later, he turned to the emperor and announced: "Sire, your lunch is here."

"Ah!" exclaimed Skandagupta. "Excellent." He smacked his hands together. "Let us eat. We can develop our plans over the meal."

"Food will sustain us," concurred Sati. "This will be a long session."

Nanda Lal's leer returned. "Yes—but the discussion will season the meal. I like my food hot and spicy."

Chapter 18

MAJARASHTRA

Summer, 532 A.D.

Irene stared nervously at the Malwa milling around the impromptu field camp which Ezana's soldiers had set up alongside the road to Deogiri. There appeared to be thousands of them—especially leering Ye-tai, who were making no attempt to hide their ogling of her. Muttered phrases swelled from the mob. The content of those coarse words was not quite audible, but their meaning was more than clear enough—like surf, frothing lust. Ezana's four hundred sarwen, standing guard with their spears in hand, reminded her of a pitiful dike before a surging ocean. A child's sand castle, with the tide about to come in.

Why did I ever agree to do this? Irene demanded of herself.

Herself babbled reassurance: "Seemed like a good idea at the time."

That was then; this is now.

"Get a grip on yourself, woman. The whole idea was to distract them, which has definitely been done."

Sure has. I'll bet they'll be even more distracted when all four thousand of them start gang-raping me. Wonderful!

"You and your husband, Ezana, are supposed to be envoys from the King of the Vandals, seeking an alliance against Rome. Surely they wouldn't—"

Surely, my ass! Do those drooling thugs look like diplomats to you? Whoever came up with this insane scheme?

"Well, actually—*you* did."

Thanks for reminding me. I forgot I'm an idiot.

"It's a good plan," herself repeated stubbornly. Herself reminded Irene of one child reassuring another that there really aren't any monsters, as the ogre stuffs them into his gullet.

I'm an idiot. Idiot—idiot—idiot! This is the stupidest plan—

Ezana entered the small pavilion—not much more than a canopy, really, shielding the richly garbed "Vandal" noblewoman from the blistering sun. Her "noble African husband" had to stoop, in order to keep his elaborate ostrich-plume headdress from being swept off.

"Good plan!" he grunted, as soon as he straightened. Ezana gazed placidly on the Malwa soldiery swarming around them. In the far distance, to the north, the first of the siege guns in the column was now visible, being painfully hauled another few feet south to Deogiri.

"Will you look at that rabble?" he demanded. "They make bedouin look like a Macedonian phalanx. The officers are worse than the men."

"Don't remind me," snarled Irene. She glanced apprehensively at the cluster of officers sitting their horses nearby. The officers were perched a few yards up a slope, giving them a better view of Irene than that enjoyed by the common troops. Behind them reared the crest of one of Majarashtra's multitude of ridges.

The officers were ogling her even more openly than the Ye-tai. She saw one of them say something, followed by a round of leering laughs.

"What is *wrong* with these animals?" she demanded, half-angrily and half-nervously. "Haven't they ever seen a woman before? If I looked like Antonina, I might understand it. She could make the sun stop in its tracks. But I'm—"

She gestured at herself. Again, anger was mixed with apprehension. "I'm not ugly, I suppose. But with my big nose—"

Ezana chuckled. "You are quite an attractive woman, Irene, in my opinion. But it really doesn't matter."

He hooked a thumb toward the Malwa. "This is why we agreed to the plan, Irene. If you hadn't volunteered to come, we never would have considered it. Kungas and I both knew what would happen, if the Malwa encountered a large party of foreigners claiming to have been shipwrecked on the coast. They are not diplomats. They would have just attacked us, on general principle. Even if they weren't guarding their precious siege guns."

He gazed at her with approval. "But with *you* here, all dressed up in such finery—" His gaze, falling on her bosom, became very approving. "Such *provocative* finery—scandalous, the way foreign women dress! And they're all sluts, those heathens, everybody knows it."

Irene scowled. "Those monkeys know as much about Vandals as I do about—" She groped for a simile, but couldn't find an appropriate one. With her voracious reading habits, Irene couldn't think of any subject that she didn't know more about than Ye-tai and Malwa soldiers did about the people and politics of North Africa.

Ezana grinned. "They know Africa is a land of black people." He cupped his hand under his chin, as if presenting his ebony face. "And if the woman is pale, and beautiful, so much the more exotic!"

"I am *not* beautiful," insisted Irene.

Ezana, still grinning, shook his head. Then, nodding toward the Malwa soldiers gawking at her: "You look beautiful to *them*, woman. After weeks on the road, struggling through India's heat and dust, you look like Aphrodite herself."

Again, he admired her bosom. "Especially your tits."

Even as nervous as she was, Irene couldn't help but chuckle. She glanced down at the objects in question, which were almost entirely visible due to the cut of her tunic. She had overseen the seamstresses in Suppara herself, blending Roman style with what she remembered of the costumes of Minoan women painted on vases. The small amount of skin still covered—a fifth, at most—simply framed, supported, presented, and emphasized the splendid remainder.

"It *is* impressive, isn't it? Makes me look like Antonina, almost."

Ezana's grin faded to a simple smile. "It was bound to happen, Irene. You've never been a soldier, on a long and arduous march. Even disciplined sarwen or Roman cataphracts would be ragged in their ranks, with every man eager to get a look. Hot, tired, aching feet and butts—most of all, *bored.* Especially since Rao stopped attacking the column many days ago."

The smile became a sneer, cheerfully bestowed on the mob surrounding the Ethiopian camp. "*Those* soldiers? Ha!"

He rubbed his hands with satisfaction. "No, no. It worked just like you planned. Four hundred sarwen, some Syrian gunners disguised as slaves, and one Roman woman have completely distracted an army ten times their number. Stopped them in their tracks, diverted their attention, disintegrated their formations—"

His eye caught movement to the north. He barked a laugh. "Look! Even some of the troops dragging the guns are trotting our way."

"*Oh, marvelous,*" hissed Irene. Gloomily: "At least I'm not a virgin." She eyed the leering mob, and the artillery soldiers hastening down the road to join them. "Step aside, Messalina," she muttered. "I think I'm about to exceed your exploits. Put them completely in the shade, in fact."

Ezana chuckled. "I'm not sure who Messalina was, but if—" Humor remained, in his eyes, but Ezana's face was suddenly stern and solemn.

"You are a bold woman, Irene Macrembolitissa. Hold fast to that courage, and set aside your fears. No one will harm you. Kungas would never have agreed to this, if he did not think we Ethiopians could shield you when the hammer falls." The stiff face became a black mask; as hard and unyielding as Kungas' own. "Which it will, and very soon."

Irene's eyes began to move toward the ridge above them, but she forced them aside.

Ezana, seeing the movement, nodded. "He will be there, Irene. Kungas will come."

Irene, trying to settle her nerves, fastened on that image. Kungas, and his hard face, coming toward her. Kungas, smiling with his eyes as she corrected his grammar. The little twitch in his lips, before he made a jest about thick-headed Kushans, even though she herself had been astonished by his ability to learn anything quickly. Kungas, day after day after day, sitting by her side in a chamber, learning to read. Never complaining, never grumbling, never angry at her for his own shortcomings.

The memory of a hard face, and clear almond eyes, and a heart beating hidden warmth and humor, and a mind like an uncut diamond, steadied her. She took a few deep breaths. *Kungas will come.* A few more breaths. *He will.* A few more. *Kungas.*

She felt herself return. To the memory of a hard face she added her own irrepressible humor.

"What do you think, Ezana?" she asked, gesturing with her chin toward the cluster of officers not more than thirty yards away. The Malwa were still staring at her, exchanging unheard quips. "Will they start the seduction with fine wine? Some music, perhaps?"

Ezana chuckled. Irene snorted. "Not likely, is it?" Her sour gaze fell on one particularly gross Malwa officer. The man had his tongue sticking out, wagging it at her.

"Will you look at—"

The officer's eyes bulged. Blood coughed out of his mouth, coating the obscene tongue. An arrowhead was protruding through his throat.

An instant later, the clustered officers were swept off their horses as if struck by a giant sickle. Irene gaped. Part of her mind identified the objects which had turned men into shredded meat. Arrows. But most of her brain simply went blank.

Dimly, she heard Ezana shouting. Her mouth still wide open from shock, she turned her head. The Syrian gunners had abandoned their servile toil and were already hurling grenades. The missiles were joined in mid-flight—and then overtaken—by four hundred javelins. Ethiopia's spearmen were also in action.

The javelin volley swept the front ranks of the Malwa mob like another great sickle. The second volley was on its way before the grenades even landed. Again, Death swung its sickle—and then *again*, as the grenades began exploding in the packed crowd. Some of the grenades were smoke bombs. Within seconds, the bloody scene began to disappear behind streaked and wafting clouds.

She was in a daze. Irene had never been in a battle before. She had never been *near* a battle before. Part of her shock and confusion was produced by simple fear. But most of it was an even simpler collapse of intelligence.

Irene's well-trained, logical mind stumbled and tripped, trying to find order and reason in the bedlam around her. Everything seemed pure chaos. An inferno of unreason. Through the eddying smoke, she caught glimpses of: men dying; sarwen locking their shields; the flight of arrows and javelins, and grenades; yelling Kushans charging down the slope; bellowing Ye-tai, desperately trying to rally confused troops. Shouts of confusion; shrieks of agony; screams of death and despair; cries of victory and triumph.

Noise, noise, everywhere. Steel and wood and flesh breaking. She clapped her hands over her ears, in her own desperate struggle to rally intelligence. Half in a crouch, sheltered under a canopy, she forced her eyes to watch. Desperately—*desperately*—trying to find a place where reason could set its anchor.

The anchor scraped across stone, finding no place.

How can men stand this? she wondered. Her eyes recognized purpose in the chaos. Her eyes saw the discipline of the sarwen, the way their shield wall held like a dike—and no pitiful child's castle of sand, this, against the coming tide. Her eyes saw—she had been told, but had never really believed—how the Malwa broke against those shields and spears. Men—enemies, yes, but still men—using their own flesh like water, trying to break the reef. Flesh became red ruin; blood everywhere; a severed arm, here; a coil of intestines, there; a piece of Malwa brain, crushed under an Ethiopian sandal.

Irene's eyes watched Satan spread his carpet across a dusty road in India. She *saw*, but her mind could not encompass the seeing.

A powerful hand seized her shoulder and drove her to her knees.

"*Down,* woman!" Her ears heard Ezana's voice, shouting further commands. Her eyes saw five sarwen, surrounding her like a wall. Her mind understood nothing. She was no more than a child, now, recognizing shelter.

She closed her eyes and pressed her hands over her ears. Finally, darkness and relative quiet brought back a modicum of reason. In that small eye of the storm, Irene sought herself.

After a time—seconds? minutes? hours?—she began to recognize herself.

Courage, foundation of all virtues, came back first.

I will not do this. Firmly, she opened her eyes and removed her hands from her ears.

She could see nothing, on her knees, except a few glimpses through the legs of the sarwen standing guard over her. And what little she could see was still obscured by smoke. After a moment, she stopped trying to make sense of the battle. She simply studied the legs of the soldiers shielding her.

Excellent legs, she concluded. Under the black skin, powerful muscles flexed calves and thighs. The easy movement of men watching, not fighting themselves, but ready to spring into action at an instant's notice. Human leopards. Horny, calloused feet rested firmly in sturdy sandals. Toes shaped in Ethiopia's mountains fit stony Majarashtra to perfection.

She listened to their banter. Her Ge'ez was good enough, now, to understand the words. But her mind made no attempt to translate. Most of the words were profanity, anyway—nothing more than taunting curses hurled down on the invisible enemy. She simply listened to the confidence in those voices. Human leopards, growling with predator satisfaction.

Two phrases, only, did she ever remember.

The first, howled with glee: "And will you look at those fucking Kushans? God—*damn*!"

And the response, growling bemused wonder: "I'm glad Kungas is on our side, boys. Or we'd be so much dog food."

So am I. Oh, dear God, so am I.

In the time which followed, as a Malwa army was ripped to pieces between Ethiopia's shield wall and a Kushan avalanche, Irene went away. This was not her place. She had no purpose here.

She needed to find herself, again. For perhaps the first time in her life.

Herself appeared, and demanded the truth. *Don't ask why you came, woman. You know the answer. And don't tell me lies about clever stratagems, and ruses, and battle plans. Tell others, but not* me. *You know why you came.*

"Yes," she choked, closing her eyes. Tears leaked through the lids. "I know."

A sarwen, hearing the soft sobs, glanced down at her. For a moment, no more, before he looked away. A woman, her wits shattered. Nothing to puzzle over. Women were fragile by nature.

But he was quite wrong. The tears streaking Irene's cheeks were tears of happiness, not fear. Fear there was, of course, and fear aplenty. But it was not fear of the moment. No, not at all. It was the much greater fear—the deep terror, entwined with joy—of a human being who had finally, like so many others before her, been able to give up a hostage to fortune. A woman who, finally, understood her friend Antonina and could—finally—make the same choice.

"He would have gone into the fire, anyway," she whispered to herself. "No matter what I did."

Herself nodded. *And you could not bear the thought. Of staying behind, staring at a horse.*

✧ ✧ ✧

Then, he was there. She saw the legs of the sarwen around her ease and stretch. Saw them move aside. Heard the shouts of greeting and glee. In the distance, a muted roar. The first of the Malwa guns was being destroyed—overcharged powder blowing overcharged shot, rupturing the huge weapon like a rotten fruit.

He squatted next to her, where she knelt. "Are you all right?"

Irene nodded. Smiled. He placed a hand on her shoulder.

He had never touched her before. She reached up and caressed the hand with her own. Feeling, with her long and slender fingers, the short ones, heavy with flesh and sinew, which held her shoulder so gently.

She pressed her face into his thick chest. His hand slid down her arm, his arm became a shield, his touch an embrace. Suddenly, fiercely, she pressed open lips against his muscular neck. Kissing, nuzzling. Her breath came quick and short. She flung her arms around him and drew him half-sprawling across her. Her left leg, kicking free of the long tunic, coiled down his out-thrust right leg. Her sandal scraped the bare skin of his calf.

For a moment—pure heat, bolting out of a stable like a wild horse—Irene felt Kungas respond. His hard abdomen pressed her own, desire meeting desire. But only for a moment. Kungas chuckled. The sound carried more delight than humor. Much more. *Much* more. It was the choked laugh of a man who discovers, unexpectedly, that an idle dream has taken real form. Yet, despite that little cry, his strong arms and body went rigid, pinning her—not like a wrestler pins an opponent, but simply like a man restrains a child from folly. Seconds went by, while his lips nuzzled her lovely, thick, chestnut hair. Irene felt his breath; heavy, hot at first, but cooling quickly.

She chuckled herself, then, as his restraint brought her own. "I guess it's not a good idea," she mumbled. "The Ethiopians would probably insist on watching."

"Worse, I'm afraid," he responded dryly, still kissing her hair. "They'd accompany us with drums. Placing bets, all the while, on when we'd stop."

Irene laughed outright. The sound was muffled against his chest.

"No," whispered Kungas gently. "Not for us, and not now. Passion always comes, after death's wings flap away. But it is cheap, and gone with the morrow. And you will wonder, afterward, whether it was you or your fear."

He chuckled again. Delight was still in that sound, but it was warm rather than ecstatic. "I know you, Irene. You would resent me. And what's worse, you would study books trying to find the answer."

"Think I couldn't find it?" she demanded.

She heard his soft laugh, rustling through her hair. Felt the little movement of his chest. Knew the economic subtlety she had come to cherish so. "I don't doubt you would. But reading takes so much time. I don't want to wait *that* long."

Smiling, she raised her head. The clear brown eyes of Greek nobility, looking past a long and bony nose, stared into eyes of almond, in a flat and barbarous face. "How long, then?" she asked.

Another muted roar swept the pavilion; and then another. But the Kushan's eyes never left her own. The destruction of Venandakatra's guns—the rubble of Malwa's schemes—the salvation of a dynasty—these were meaningless things, in that moment, for those two people embracing on a road.

"First, I must learn to read," he said. "Not before." His face was stiff, and solemn, but Irene did not miss the little twitch in his lips.

She smiled. "You are a good student, you know. Amazingly good."

Kungas' smile could have been recognized by anyone, now. "With such an incentive, who could fail?"

There was another roar, as a siege gun ruptured; and another. This time, Kungas did look.

"That's the last of them," he said. "We must be off, now, before they rally and Venandakatra sends more. We can make the coast, if we don't dawdle."

With easy grace, he rose to his feet and extended his hand. A moment later, Irene was standing at his side.

The realities of war had returned. Irene could see the sarwen and the Kushan troops forming their columns in preparation for the forced march to the sea, and the Ethiopian ships waiting there to carry them back to Suppara.

But Kungas did not immediately relinquish his grip on her hand. He took the time to lean over and whisper: "We will know."

Irene, grinning, squeezed his hand. "Yes. We will always know."

She burst into laughter, then. Riotous, joy-filled laughter. Ethiopian and Kushan soldiers nearby, hearing that bizarre sound on a bloody battlefield, looked her way.

For a second or two, no more. A woman, her wits frayed by the carnage. Nothing to puzzle over. Women were fragile by nature.

Chapter 19
PERSIA
Summer, 532 A.D.

"Can you disguise the entrance afterward?" asked Belisarius. He waved his hand, in a gesture which encompassed the valley. "The whole area, actually. Keep in mind, Kurush, there'll be more than ten thousand soldiers passing through here—*and* as many horses."

The Roman general turned his head, looking down at the river. The river flowed west by northwest. Like the valley itself, the river was small and rather narrow. The pass where it exited the valley was barely more than a gorge. They were almost in the foothills of the western slope of the Zagros, but the surrounding mountains seemed to have lost none of their usual ruggedness.

"I assume you'll be taking the horses out that way," Belisarius said, pointing toward the gorge. "By the time they pass through, the whole valley will be churned into mush. No way to disguise the tracks."

Kurush shook his head, smiling. "We won't try to

hide the tracks, Belisarius. Quite the opposite! The more Damodara's mind is on that gorge, the more he'll be diverted from the real exit."

Belisarius scratched his chin. "I understand the logic, Kurush. But don't underestimate Damodara and Sanga—*and* their scouts. Those Pathan trackers can trail a mouse. They won't simply trot after the horses, salivating. They'll search the entire valley."

Belisarius turned his head and studied the entrance to the qanat. The timber-braced adit was located about a hundred yards up the mountainside, not far from the small river which had carved out this valley. The sloping ramp, after a few feet, disappeared into darkness.

He hooked a thumb in that direction. "There'll be tracks there too," he pointed out. "No way to disguise *them*, either. Even if you collapse the entrance, the tracks will be all over the area. Ten thousand troops leave a big trail."

Kurush's smile widened. He shook his head. "You're worrying too much. We can cover the soldiers' tracks by running the horses through afterward. Everywhere except this immediate area. Then—"

The Persian nobleman leapt onto a small rock a few feet away. From that perch, he leaned over and pointed along the steep slope of the mountain. "This is mining country, Belisarius. Silver, mostly. There are small deposits in this valley."

He spread his hands apologetically. "Nothing more than traces, really, according to the miners I brought with me. But the miners will be gone before Damodara arrives. And I doubt very much if an army of Rajput cavalrymen will be able to tell him that the ore in the area isn't worth mining."

Aide made a mental snort. ***Rajputs?***

Belisarius chuckled. "Hardly! And their Pathans, outside of hunting, consider all forms of labor to be women's work."

The Roman general nodded. "Yes, that'll work. After we pass through, you'll have this whole slope turned into a mining operation. Cover our tracks with tailings." He pointed at the adit. "And I assume that you'll have your miners cover our tracks well into the qanat. Fifty yards should do it. Pathans are outdoorsmen. They won't be comfortable more than a few feet into that blackness."

Again, Belisarius studied the gorge at the far end of the valley. "All that will be left, after a few days," he mused, "are the tracks of Roman horses. Passing, by pure coincidence, through a mining area on their way into Mesopotamia."

He paused, thinking. "One thing, however. Those Pathans know their business, Kurush. You'll have to make sure—"

Kurush was grinning. "Yes, yes!" he interrupted. "I'll have the horses carrying sacks filled with dirt. Weighing about what a Roman soldier does. Their tracks will be deep enough."

Belisarius returned the grin with one of his own. "You've thought of everything, I see."

Kurush shrugged. Belisarius almost laughed. The modest gesture fit the Aryan sahrdaran about as well as a curtsy fits a lion.

His humor faded. "You understand, Kurush, that the hammer will fall on you? Once Damodara understands what has happened—and it won't take him long—he won't waste time trying to chase after me. He'll strike directly into Mesopotamia."

Kurush shrugged again. The gesture, this time, did not even pretend at modesty. It was the twitch of a lion's shoulders, irritated by flies.

"That is only fair, Roman, after all you've done for the Aryans."

Kurush sprang off the rock and strode over to Belisarius. He jabbed his chin toward the south, using his stiff Persian-cut beard as a pointer. "As soon as he gets the word, the emperor will begin retreating toward Babylon. He's on the verge of doing it, anyway, so it won't seem odd at all." Kurush scowled. "The Malwa have been pressing him very hard."

Belisarius eyed the sahrdaran. The Roman general had no difficulty interpreting Kurush's frowning face. He could well imagine the casualties which Emperor Khusrau's soldiers had taken over the past months. While Belisarius had been maneuvering with Damodara in the Zagros mountains all through the spring, Khusrau had been keeping the huge main army of the Malwa invasion penned up in the Tigris–Euphrates delta. The task would have been difficult enough, even without—

He decided to broach the awkward subject. "Has the rebellion—?"

Khusrau's frown vanished instantly. The Persian nobleman barked a laugh.

"The head of the emperor's half-brother has been the main ornament of his pavilion for two weeks, now." Kurush grimaced. "Damn thing was a mass of flies, by the time I left. Stinky."

His good humor returned. "Ormazd's rebellion has been crushed. *And* that of the Lakhmids. We took Hira almost two months ago. Khusrau drove the population into the desert and ordered the city razed to the ground."

Belisarius let no sign of his distaste show. He had never been fond of "punitive action" against enemy civilians, even before he met Aide and was introduced to future standards of warmaking.

But he did not fault Khusrau. By the standards of the day, in truth, driving the population of Hira out of the city before destroying it was rather humane. The Lakhmids had been Persian vassals before they gave their allegiance to the Malwa invaders. Most Persian emperors—most Roman ones, for that matter, including Theodora—would have repaid that rebellion by ordering the city's people burned inside it.

And let's not get too romantic about the Geneva Convention and the supposedly civilized standards of future wars, either, remarked Aide. **They won't prevent entire cities being destroyed, with their populations. Purely for "strategic reasons," of course. What difference does that make, to mangled children in the ruins of Coventry? Or to thousands of Korean slave laborers incinerated at Hiroshima?**

Kurush was pointing with his beard again, this time to the west.

"The emperor has instructed me to defend Ctesiphon, while he retreats to Babylon. I will have ten thousand men. That should be enough to hold our capital city, for a few months. Damodara does not have siege guns."

Kurush turned his eyes to Belisarius. There was nothing in the Persian's gaze beyond a matter-of-fact acceptance of reality.

"In the end, of course," he said calmly, "we will be doomed. Unless your thrust strikes home."

Belisarius smiled crookedly. "It is said that an army marches on its belly, you know. I will do my best to drive a lance into the great gut of Malwa, once you have drawn the shield away."

Kurush chuckled. " 'An army marches on its belly,' " he repeated. "That's clever! I don't recognize the saying, though. Who came up with it?"

Good move, genius, said Aide sourly. **This will be entertaining, watching you explain to a sixth-century Persian how you came to quote Napoleon.**

Belisarius ignored the quip. "I heard it from a Hun. One of my mercenaries, during my second campaign in the trans-Danube. I was rather stunned, actually, to find such a keen grasp of logistics in the mind of a barbarian. But it just goes to show—"

Father of lies, father of lies. It's a good thing my lips are sealed, so to speak. The stories I could tell about you! They'd make even Procopius' *Secret History* look like sober, reasoned truth.

Lord Damodara leaned back in his chair, studying Narses' scowling face.

"So what is it that bothers you, exactly?" he asked the eunuch.

"Everything!" snapped Narses. The old Roman glared around the interior of the pavilion, as if searching its unadorned walls for some nook or cranny in which truth lay hidden.

"None of what Belisarius is doing makes any sense," stated Narses. "Nothing. Not from the large to the small."

"Explain," commanded Damodara. The lord waved his pudgy little hand in a circular motion. The gesture included himself and the tall figure of the Rajput king seated next to him. "In simple words, that two simpletons like myself and Rana Sanga can understand."

The good-humored quip caused even Rana Sanga to smile. Even Narses, for that matter, and the old eunuch was not a man who smiled often.

"As to the 'large,' " said Narses, "what is the purpose of these endless maneuvers that Belisarius is so fond of?" The eunuch leaned forward, emphasizing his next words. "Which are not, however—*and cannot be*—truly endless. There is no way he can stop you from reaching Mesopotamia. The man's not a fool. That must be as obvious to him, by now—" Narses jabbed a stiff finger toward the pavilion's entrance "—as it is to the most dim-witted Ye-tai in your army."

"He's bought time," remarked Sanga.

Narses made a sour face. "A few months, at most. It's not been more than eight weeks since the battle of the pass, and you've already forced him almost out of the Zagros. Your army is much bigger than his. You can defeat him on an open battlefield, and you've proven that you can maneuver through these mountains as well as he can. Within a month, perhaps six weeks, he'll have to concede the contest and allow you entry into Mesopotamia. At which point he'll have no choice but to fort up in Ctesiphon or Peroz-Shapur, anyway. So why not do it now?"

"I don't think it's odd," countered Damodara. "He's used the months that he kept us tied up in the Zagros to good advantage, according to our spies. That general of his that he left in charge of the Roman forces in Mesopotamia—the crippled one, Agathius—has been working like a fiend, these past months. By the time we get to Ctesiphon, or Peroz-Shapur, he'll have the cities fortified beyond belief. Cannons and gunpowder have been pouring in from the Roman armories, while we've been countermarching all over these damned mountains."

Sanga nodded. "The whole campaign, to my mind, has Belisarius' signature written all over it. He always tries to force his enemy to attack him, so that he can have the advantage of the defensive. By stalling us for so many months here in the mountains, he's been able to create a defensive stronghold in Mesopotamia. It'll be pure murder, trying to storm Peroz-Shapur."

Narses stared at the two men sitting across the table from him. There seemed to be no expression at all on the eunuch's wizened, scaly face, but both Damodara and Sanga could sense the sarcasm lurking somewhere inside.

Neither man took offense. They were accustomed to Narses, and his ways, by now. There was a bitterness at the center of the eunuch's soul which was ineradicable. That bitterness colored his examination of the world, and gave scorn to his every thought.

Thoughts, however—and a capacity to examine—which they had come to respect deeply. And so a kinsman of the Malwa dynasty, and Rajputana's most noble monarch, listened carefully to the words of a lowborn Roman eunuch.

Narses leaned over and pointed with his finger to a location on the great map which covered the table.

"He will make his stand at Peroz-Shapur, not Ctesiphon," predicted Narses. "Belisarius is a Roman, when all is said and done. Ctesiphon is Persia's capital, but Peroz-Shapur is the gateway to the Roman Empire."

Damodara and Sanga both nodded. They had already come to the same conclusion.

Narses studied the map for a few seconds. Then:

"Tell me something. When the time comes, do you intend to hurl your soldiers at the walls of Peroz-Shapur?" He almost—not quite—sneered. "You don't have too many Ye-tai left, either, so the soldiers you'll use up like sheep at a slaughterhouse will all be Rajput."

Rana Sanga didn't rise to the bait. He simply chuckled. Damodara laughed outright.

"Not likely!" exclaimed the Malwa lord. He leaned over the table himself. The months of arduous campaigning had shrunk Damodara's belly enough that the movement was almost graceful.

Damodara's finger traced the Tigris river, from Ctesiphon upstream toward Armenia.

"I won't go near Peroz-Shapur." Another laugh. "Any more than I'd enter a tiger's cage. I won't try to besiege Ctesiphon either. I'll simply use the Tigris to keep my army supplied and move north into Assyria. From there, I can strike into Anatolia—or Armenia—while most of Khusrau's army is tied up fighting our main force on the southern Euphrates."

He leaned back, exuding self-satisfaction. "Belisarius will have no choice," pronounced Damodara. "All that work he's done to fortify Peroz-Shapur will be wasted. He'll have to come out and face me, somewhere in the field."

Narses' eyes left Damodara and settled on Rana Sanga. The Rajput king nodded his agreement with Damodara's explication.

"Ah," said Narses. "An excellent strategy. I am enlightened. *Except*—why hasn't Belisarius figured the same thing out himself? The man has never, to put it mildly, been accused of stupidity."

Silence. Damodara squirmed a bit in his chair. Sanga maintained his usual stiff composure, but the very rigidity of the posture indicated his own discomfort.

Narses sneered. "Ah, yes. You've wondered that yourselves, haven't you? Now and again, at least."

The eunuch relinquished the sneer, within a few seconds. He was too canny to risk offending the two men across the table from him. And, if the truth be told, he had a genuine respect for them.

"Let's leave that broad problem, for a moment, and move on to some seemingly minor questions. Of these, there are three that stand out."

Narses held up a thumb. "First. Why has Belisarius, since the very beginning of this campaign in the Zagros, always been willing to let us move north?"

Narses nodded toward the Rajput. "As Rana Sanga was the first to point out, many weeks ago." He gave another nod, this time at Damodara. "As you yourself remarked at the time, Lord, that makes no sense. It should be the other way around. He should be fighting like a tiger when we move north, and put up only token resistance when we maneuver to the south. That way, he would be keeping us from threatening Assyria."

Silence.

Narses held up his forefinger alongside the thumb.

"The second small problem. In all the skirmishes we've fought over the past months—even during the battle at the pass when his situation was desperate—Belisarius has never used his mercenaries. *Why?* He's got two thousand of the Goth barbarians, but he handles them like they were the only jewels in his possession."

Sanga cleared his throat. "Doesn't trust them, I imagine." The Rajput king scowled. "I don't trust mercenaries either, Narses."

The eunuch snorted. "Of course you don't!" Narses slapped his hand down on the table. The sharp sound seemed to fill the confines of the tent.

"*Belisarius has never trusted mercenaries,*" hissed Narses. The eunuch's eyes were fixed on Sanga like a serpent's on its prey. "He never has. He is well known for it, in the Roman army—which, as you know, is traditionally an army which uses mercenaries all the time. But Belisarius never uses them except when he has no choice, and *then* he only uses mercenaries as auxiliaries. Hun light cavalry, for the most part."

Narses jabbed at the map. "So why would he bring two thousand Goth heavy cavalry with him, in a campaign like this one? There's nothing in this kind of campaign which would keep a mercenary's interest. No loot, no plunder. Nothing but weeks and weeks of arduous marches and countermarches, for nothing beyond a stipend."

The eunuch laughed sarcastically. "Belisarius never would have brought Goth mercenaries along with him for the good and simple reason, if no other, that he would have known they'd desert within two months. Which brings me—"

He held up a third finger.

"Point three. Why *haven't* those mercenaries deserted?" Another sarcastic, sneering laugh. "Goths are about as stupid as the horses they ride, but even horses aren't that stupid."

Narses planted both hands on the table and pushed himself against the back of his chair. For just an instant, in that posture, the small old eunuch seemed a more regal figure than the Malwa dynast and the Rajput king who faced him.

"So. Let's put it all together. We have one of history's most cunning generals—who *always* subordinates tactics to strategy—engaged in a campaign which, for all its tactical acumen, makes no sense at all strategically. In the course of this campaign, he drags along a bunch of mercenaries he has no use for, and which have no business being there on their own account. What does that all add up to?"

Silence.

Narses scowled. "What it adds up to, Lord and King, is—*Belisarius*. He's up to something. Something we aren't seeing."

"What?" demanded Damodara.

Narses shrugged. "I don't know, Lord. At the moment, I only have questions. But I urge you"—for just an instant, the eunuch's sarcastic, sneering voice was filled with nothing beyond earnest and respectful pleading—"to take my questions seriously. Or we will find ourselves, in the end, like so many of Belisarius' opponents. Lying in the dirt, bleeding to death, from a blow we never saw coming."

The silence which now filled the tent was not the silence of a breath, held in momentary suspense. It was a long, long silence. A thoughtful silence.

Damodara finally broke it.

"I think we should talk to him," he announced. "Arrange a parley."

His two companions stared at him. Both men were frowning.

Narses was frowning from puzzlement. "What do you hope to accomplish? He'll hardly tell you what he's planning!"

Damodara chuckled. "I didn't imagine he would."

The Malwa lord shrugged. "The truth? I would simply like to meet the man, after all this time. I think it would be fascinating."

Damodara shifted his eyes to Rana Sanga. The Rajput king was still frowning.

Not from puzzlement, but—

"I am bound to your service by honor, Lord Damodara," rasped Sanga. "That same honor—"

Damodara raised a hand, forestalling the Rajput. "Please, Rana Sanga! I am not a fool. Practical, yes. But practical in *all* things." He chuckled. "I would hardly plan a treacherous ambush, in violation of all codes of honor, using Rajputs as my assassins. *Any* Rajputs, much less *you*."

Damodara straightened. "We will find a meeting place where ambush is impossible. A farmhouse in open terrain, perhaps, which Belisarius' scouts can search for hidden troops."

He nodded at Rana Sanga. "And you, King of Rajputana, will serve as my only bodyguard at the parley itself. That should be enough, I think, to protect me against foul play—and *will* be enough, I am certain, to assure Belisarius that he has nothing to fear. Not once he has *your* word of honor, whatever he thinks of my own."

The frown faded, somewhat, from Sanga's brow. But the quick glance which the Rajput king gave Narses still carried a lurking suspicion.

Damodara chuckled again. "Have no fear, Rana Sanga. Narses won't be within miles of the place."

"Not likely!" snorted the eunuch.

A week later, Damodara's dispatch rider returned with Belisarius' response.

"The Roman general wrote it out himself," the Rajput said, as he handed over the sealed sheet. The man seemed a bit puzzled. Or, perhaps, a bit in awe. "He didn't even hesitate, Lord Damodara. He wrote the reply as soon as he finished reading your message. I watched him do it."

Damodara broke the seal and began reading. He was surprised, but not much, to see that Belisarius' message was written in perfect Hindi.

When he finished, Damodara laughed.

"What's so amusing?" asked Narses.

"Did he agree?" asked Rana Sanga.

Damodara waved the letter. "Yes, he agreed. He says we can pick the location, and the time. As long as Rana Sanga is there, he says, he has no concerns about treachery."

The Rajput's face was stiff as a board. Damodara smiled, knowing how deeply Sanga was hiding his surge of pride.

He transferred the smile to Narses.

"As for the amusement—Belisarius *did* add a stipulation, Narses. He insists that you must be at the parley also."

The eunuch's face almost disappeared in a mass of wrinkles. Damodara's smile became an outright grin. The Roman traitor, in that moment, was not even trying to hide his own emotions. That great frown exuded *suspicion*, the way a glacier exudes chilliness.

"*Why me?*" demanded Narses.

Damodara shrugged. "I have no idea. You can add that to your list of unanswered questions."

Chapter 20

ADULIS

Summer, 532 A.D.

Seated on his throne, in what had been the viceroy's audience hall at Sana, Eon stared down at the crowd. Other than the dozen or so sarwen standing guard against the walls, and his immediate advisers—Antonina, Garmat and Ousanas—the people who packed the large chamber were all Arabs. The Arabs were gathered in clusters. Each cluster consisted of several middle-aged or elderly men, a middle-aged woman serving as a chaperone, and—

"Christ in Heaven," muttered Eon, "there's a *horde* of them. Did every single Arab in Mecca bring his daughter?"

Garmat, standing at Eon's left hand, whispered, "Don't exaggerate, King. That's not a horde of young women. Merely a large mob. As to your question—what did you expect? There are many tribes in the Hijaz, and each is comprised of several clans. They couldn't agree on a single choice, so every one of those clans sent its favorite daughter."

Eon's jaw tightened. "This is no time for humor, old man. How am I supposed to choose one? Without offending the others?"

Garmat hesitated. From Eon's other side, Ousanas whispered: "Have Antonina make the choice. She is from Rome. The Empire is very respected, but also very distant. The Arabs will accept her decision as being impartial."

Standing next to Ousanas, Antonina's eyes widened with startlement. Before she had time to register any protest, however, Garmat weighed in with his concurrence.

"That's an excellent idea. And because she's a woman, she can spend time alone with the girls before making her choice. That gives better odds of making a good selection than for you to just guess, looking at a sea of veils."

Eon looked up at Antonina. Whatever protest she might have made died under the silent appeal in those young brown eyes. An appeal, she realized, which was as much personal as political. So soon after the loss of his two beloved concubines, Eon was in no mental state to select a wife.

She nodded. "If you wish, King of Kings. But I would like to have several days to make the decision. As Garmat said, I can spend the time getting acquainted with the girls."

"Take as much time as you need," said Eon. The King rose from his throne. The faint murmurs in the room died away.

"As all of you know," he said, speaking in a voice loud enough to be heard throughout the chamber, "Axum has formed an alliance with the Roman Empire against the Malwa." Eon nodded imperiously toward Antonina. "This woman, Antonina, is the wife of the great general Belisarius. She is also an accomplished leader in her own right and is the head of the Roman Empire's delegation."

The room was silent. The absence of any whispers indicated the fact that everyone in the room was already quite familiar with Antonina's position. Eon had suspected as much, but wanted to give emphasis to her importance.

"I wish to have her select my wife from among your daughters," he announced. "There can be no suspicion of any favoritism, if the choice is made by Rome's envoy. She will spend a few days in the harem, in order to meet the girls, before making her decision."

Now, the room *was* filled with whispers. Antonina, listening carefully to the emotional undertone of the hubbub, decided that Eon's announcement was meeting with general favor.

Since the negusa nagast was clearly prepared to let the crowd's quiet little discussion continue for a bit, Antonina took the opportunity to inspect her surroundings. She had been rushed into the audience chamber the moment she arrived in Sana.

The viceroy's palace, judging from the evidence, suffered more damage from Eon's recapture of Sana than the city itself. The heavy stone architecture was still intact—Eon had used no gunpowder in his assault, simply the spears of the sarawit—but most of the walls were scorched. The palace walls had been adorned with tapestries, which were now nothing but ashes. Fortunately, the flames had been extinguished before they could do more than slightly char the heavy beams supporting the roof.

The rebel Abreha had made his last stand here. It hadn't been much of a stand, from the reports Antonina received. Once his Arab auxiliaries had been drawn away from Sana by Antonina's bait, Abreha's two rebel regiments had been forced to face the loyal Ethiopian sarawit unaided. Even sheltered behind Sana's walls, they had had no great stomach for the task.

When word came, from fleeing bedouin, that the Romans had shattered the Arab army at the oasis, most of Abreha's troops had mutinied. Only two hundred men from his own Metin regiment had remained loyal to him. The rest, and the entire Falha sarwe, had negotiated surrender terms with Eon.

The negusa nagast, filled with youthful fury, had not been inclined to grant anything beyond their lives. But Garmat's advice prevailed. The Falha sarwe had been reaccepted as a unit, with no repercussions. Even the men from Abreha's regiment who surrendered had gone unpunished, except that new officers had been appointed. The old ones were cashiered in disgrace.

Abreha and his remaining two hundred rebels had forted up in the viceroy's palace. The fighting had been ferocious, for about an hour, as spears flashed in rooms and corridors. But Abreha's two hundred had been overwhelmed by the loyal sarwen pouring through the palace's many entrances.

There had been no quarter given. Not even Garmat had recommended mercy, after the body of his friend, Sumyafa Ashwa, had been found. The former viceroy had been tortured by the Malwa agents who had advised Abreha in his rebellion. Whatever information the Malwa had extracted from the man had not come easily. Sumyafa had died under the knife.

The Malwa agents had been captured, along with Abreha himself, in the very audience chamber where Antonina was now standing. They had not been tortured, exactly. Ethiopians were not given to lingering forms of death-dealing. Still, the traditional Axumite way of punishing treason was savage enough. The traitors had been disemboweled and then strangled with their own guts. The latter was simply a gruesome flourish, since intestines are too soft to serve as a proper garrote.

Antonina wrinkled her nose. The stench had faded,

but it was still powerful. Most of the stone floor, even after hours of scrubbing, was stained with brown marks. Flies were buzzing about everywhere. They seemed to cover every inch of floor where someone was not standing.

Antonina stared at the crowd of Arab tribesfolk. All of them were standing on those brown stains—men, women, and young girls alike—with not a trace of squeamishness. Oblivious to the smell, so far as Antonina could determine. Occasionally, casually, they swatted away flies buzzing around their faces, but they ignored the insects crawling on the floor.

Those people were merchants, not bedouin—Meccans, mostly, although some were from Yathrib and Jidda—but they were still Arabs. Arabia was the land of the desert, and its people, over the centuries, had been formed by its harsh regimen. Those folk were much given to poetry, and could spend hours in town squares and bedouin camps engaged in cheerful banter and argument. And they could often be the most generous and hospitable people in the world. But they were not squeamish, not in the least. Ethiopia had repaid rebellion in the traditional coin. The Arab merchants standing before the King of Kings were simply congratulating themselves for having had the good sense to avoid the business.

Eon, apparently, decided that the Arabs had had enough time to think.

"If anyone has an objection, speak now," he commanded. The room fell silent. Eon waited, for at least a minute. There was no voice of protest. Antonina, watching for the little body twitches which might indicate uneasiness, could see none.

"Good idea, Ousanas," she murmured.

"I am a genius," agreed the former dawazz. "It is well known, in educated circles." Garmat snorted. "Not, of course, among decrepit former bandits."

He began to add something else, but fell silent. Eon was speaking again.

"Send your girls to the harem. Servants will show you the way. Antonina will join them shortly."

A moment later, the crowd was filing out of the room. The eyes of several dozen veiled young women were now peeking at Antonina. All of those eyes were curious. Some were shy; some bold. Some seemed friendly; some uncertain; a few, perhaps even hostile.

Those last eyes, she suspected, belonged to particularly comely girls. Vain creatures, who were filled with dark suspicion that an unveiled Roman woman, herself a beauty, would not be swayed by their good looks.

You've got that right, my fine fillies, she thought sardonically. *Forget all that nonsense. I'm looking for a young man's* wife. *That's a different business altogether.*

Antonina's task was simplified, from the very beginning, by her unspoken decision to seek a wife only among the clans of the Quraysh. All the tribes in the Hijaz had sent girls, but that was mainly a matter of pride. The Quraysh, sensibly, had neither objected nor made any demand for precedence. Still, the fact remained that the Quraysh dominated western Arabia. To pick a wife from any other tribe would offend them deeply. And, on the other hand, none of the other tribes would take it amiss if Antonina chose a Quraysh girl. They were expecting her to, in truth. They simply wanted their own precious daughters to be given formal consideration.

Which Antonina did. She was careful to spend as much time with girls from the other tribes as she did with those from the various clans of the Quraysh. That was not simply a matter of show, either. Concubinage was respected practice among Arabs. She intended to select several concubines for the negusa nagast, from among the non-Quraysh girls. She had not discussed the matter with Eon prior to entering the harem. Antonina knew the young King was not even looking forward to a wife, much less a gaggle of concubines. But he would yield to political necessity, when the time came.

Her name was Rukaiya, and she was from the Beni Hashim clan of the Quraysh.

Antonina dismissed her, at first. The girl was much too pretty—downright stunning, in fact—and, what was worse, very slender. Eon was the sole survivor of the Axumite dynasty, and Antonina wanted to take no chances with the royal line. Her friend, the empress Theodora, was also a slender woman. Theodora had almost died in childbirth, because of her narrow hips. The baby *had* died, and Theodora had never had another.

Antonina wanted a girl with big hips. Intelligent, also, and with a good temperament. But she wanted a girl who could produce royal heirs without a hitch. Lots of them.

But, as the hours went by on the first day, in conversations with the various prospects, she found her eyes being drawn toward Rukaiya. That was not because the Beni Hashim girl was *trying* to draw her attention. Rather the contrary. If anything, Rukaiya seemed almost to be avoiding her.

There was no way to do so, of course. Not in the harem which, other than its sleeping chambers, consisted of a single large room. The roof was open, and the center of the room was occupied by a shallow pool. The girls—almost fifty of them—were seated on benches. The majority were packing the benches which fronted the pool, where they would be most visible. But there were perhaps two dozen seated on benches ranged against the far walls.

At first, Antonina had thought those were the shy

ones. But, as she became introduced to all of them, she realized that most of the girls on the rear benches were from the non-Quraysh tribes. They knew perfectly well that they would not be chosen, and they had seen no reason to gasp for breath in the crush at the pool.

All except Rukaiya—who, though Quraysh, had clearly not chosen that self-effacing position because of any shyness. Antonina's attention was drawn to her, in fact, because she began noticing how often other girls, as the day went on, would scurry over and exchange words with Rukaiya.

Antonina could not hear those exchanges, but it didn't take her long to understand what was happening.

In the first few hours, anxious girls went to Rukaiya to settle their nerves. A few words spoken by a calm and friendly face seemed to do the trick. The girls would resume their seats at the pool, a bit more relaxed.

As the day wore on, Antonina noticed several other girls surreptitiously scurrying over to Rukaiya's bench. These, she thought, were downcast because they were not very pretty, and were looking for reassurance. The most beautiful girl in the room seem to give it to them. With words, for the most part. But Antonina also noticed the little hugs, and the hair-stroking, and the time Rukaiya held a softly weeping fifteen-year-old girl in her arms for several minutes. The girl, with her lumpy face and figure, obviously felt she was too unattractive to be a king's wife.

Which, in truth, she was. Antonina was not looking for beauty, first and foremost. But whoever she selected would have to be pretty enough to arouse the king's interest. Axum needed a stable dynasty. That meant heirs, which a homely queen might not provide.

But, although Antonina was impressed by Rukaiya, she continued to rule her out. For a while, as she listened to one or another girl chatter at her, Antonina mulled over the possibility of selecting Rukaiya for one of Eon's concubines. But she decided against that, as well. The daughter of the Beni Hashim was just *too* beautiful. Too attractive in all respects, for that matter. After hours in the harem, observing with her keen eyes and mind, Antonina couldn't fail to notice Rukaiya's ease of manner and excellent temperament.

All of which, of course, argued against her.

She's too skinny for a queen and too dazzling for anything else. Antonina didn't want to risk a situation where the King of Kings produced no legitimate heirs because he was besotted with a concubine.

She went to bed, the first night, with that conclusion firmly drawn. By the end of the second day, the firm conclusion was getting ragged around the edges.

The second day was a day for culling. In the course of it, Antonina—as gently as possible—made clear to most of the girls she talked to that they were no longer under consideration. Many of them took the news cheerfully enough, especially those who were not of the Quraysh. But there were others, of course, who were upset.

At least half of those, Antonina couldn't help but notice, immediately made a beeline for Rukaiya's bench. By mid-afternoon, the daughter of the Beni Hashim was surrounded by a cluster of other girls. It was, by far, the most cheerful group of girls in the harem. Whatever tears had tracked down those young cheeks were dried, and the girls were laughing at one of Rukaiya's soft-spoken jests. The girl seemed to have quite a wit, on top of everything else.

Antonina had still not exchanged a word with her. She had ruled Rukaiya out from the very start, and Rukaiya herself had made no attempt to get Antonina's attention. But the Roman woman knew full well what was happening at that bench.

✧ ✧ ✧

There are people in this world who have the knack for it. People who draw others around them, like a lodestone draws iron filings. The kind of people whom others, when they stumble and fall, automatically look to for help and guidance.

The kind of people, in short, that you like to see sitting on a throne—and rarely do.

Antonina shook her head. *Too skinny.*

By the morning of the third day, Antonina had narrowed her selection to three girls. She decided to spend the entire day in private conversations with those final prospects.

Rukaiya was not among them. Yet, when the time came for Antonina to make her announcement to the assembled girls in the harem, her tongue seemed to have a will of its own. After she finished naming the three finalists, the rebellious organ kept talking.

"And Rukaiya," her tongue blurted out.

Across the room, Rukaiya's head jerked up. The girl was staring at Antonina, wide-eyed. That was due to surprise, and—something else. Rukaiya, strangely, seemed distressed by the announcement.

That's odd, thought Antonina. Then, firmly, to her tongue: *And she's still too skinny.*

Antonina interviewed Rukaiya last of all. It was already late in the afternoon by the time the Beni Hashim girl entered the small sleeping chamber in the harem which Antonina was using for her private meetings.

As Rukaiya took a seat on a bench across from her, Antonina admired the grace in the girl's movements. There was something almost sinuous in the way Rukaiya walked, and slid herself onto a couch. Even the way the girl sat, with her hands modestly folded in her lap, had a feline poise to it. And her clear brown eyes, watching Antonina, had little in them of a sixteen-year-old girl's uncertainty and awkwardness.

Antonina returned Rukaiya's stare in silence, for a good minute or so. She was studying the girl carefully, but could read nothing in her expression. That beautiful young face might as well have been a mask. Antonina could detect none of the quick-witted liveliness which she had noticed for two days, nor the startled apprehension which had shone in Rukaiya's eyes the moment she heard herself named as one of the four finalists.

Let's clear that mystery up first, she decided.

"You seemed startled, when I named you," Antonina stated. "Why is that?"

The girl's answer came with no apparent hesitation. "I was surprised. You had seemed to pay no attention to me, the first two days. And I was not expecting to be selected. I am too skinny. Two men—their parents, actually—have already rejected me as a wife. They are worried I will not be able to bear children."

The statement was matter-of-fact, relaxed—almost philosophical. That was its own surprise. Most Arab girls, rejected by a suitor's parents, would have been heartsick.

The problem was not romantic. Marriage among upper-class Arabs was arranged by their families. Often enough, the man and woman involved did not even know each other prior to their wedding. But marriage was the destiny and the highest position to which an Arab girl could aspire. To be rejected almost invariably produced feelings of unworthiness and shame.

Yet Rukaiya seemed to feel none of that. Why?

Antonina was alarmed. One obvious explanation for Rukaiya's attitude was that the girl was so egotistical—so enamored of her own beauty and grace—that she was simply incapable of accepting rejection. She might be the kind of person who, faced with disappointment, always places the blame on others.

In the long history of the Roman Empire, Antonina reminded herself, there had been more than one empress with that mentality. Most of them had been disastrous, especially the ones whose noble birth reinforced their egotism. Antonina's friend Theodora, in truth, had the same innate temperament. But Theodora's hard life had taught the woman to discipline her own pride. A girl like Rukaiya, born into Arabia's elite, would have nothing to teach her to restrain arrogance.

"You do not seem upset by the fact," Antonina said. The statement had almost the air of an accusation.

For the first time since she entered the chamber, life came back to Rukaiya's face. The girl chuckled. Her face exuded a cheerful acceptance of the world's whimsies. The expression, combined with the little laugh, was utterly charming.

"My family is used to it. All the women, for generations, have been skinny. My mother's thinner than I am, and she was rejected four times before my father's family decided to take a chance on her."

Rukaiya gave Antonina a level gaze. "I am her oldest daughter. She has had three more, and two sons. One of my sisters, and one of my brothers, died very young. But not at childbirth. My grandmother had nine children. None died in childbirth, and six survived into adulthood. *Her* mother—my great-grandmother—had twelve children. She died before I was born, but everyone says she had the hips of a snake."

Rukaiya shrugged. "It just doesn't seem to matter, to us. My mother tells me that it will be very painful, the first time, but not so bad after that. And she is not worried that I will die."

Well, so much for that *problem,* thought Antonina wryly. *But I'm still puzzled—*

"You did not simply seem surprised, when you

heard me call out your name. You also seemed upset." Again, Antonina's statement had the air of an accusation.

The mask was back in place. Rukaiya opened her lips, as if to speak. It was obvious, to Antonina, that the girl was about to utter some sort of denial. But, after a moment, Rukaiya lowered her head and murmured: "I was not upset, exactly. It would be a great honor, to become the wife of the negusa nagast. My family would be very proud. But—"

She paused, then raised her head. "I have enjoyed my life. I am very happy, in my father's house. My father is a cheerful man. Very kind, and very intelligent."

Rukaiya hesitated, groping for words. "I have always known, of course, that someday I would be married and have to leave for another man's house. And there is a part of me that looks forward to that day. But not—" She sighed unhappily. "Not so soon."

Her next words came out in a rush. The girl's face was full of life, now, and her hands gestured with animation.

"I don't know what I would *do*, in another man's house. I am so afraid of being *bored*. Especially if my husband was a severe man. Most husbands are very strict with their wives. Since I was ten years old, my father has let me help him with his work. He is one of Mecca's richest merchants, and he has many caravans. I keep track of most of his accounts, and I write almost all his letters, and—"

Antonina's jaw dropped. She didn't think there were more than two dozen women in all of Arabia—and they were invariably middle-aged widows—

"You can *read*?" she demanded.

Rukaiya's own jaw clamped shut. For an instant, her young face reminded Antonina of a mule. A beautiful mule, true, but just as stubborn and willful.

The expression was fleeting, however. Rukaiya

lowered her head. Her quick-moving hands, once again, were demurely clasped in her lap.

"My father taught me," she said softly. "He insists that all women in his family must know how to read. He says that's because they might be widows, someday, and have to manage their husbands' affairs."

Again, the words started coming in a rush. "But I think he just says that to placate my mother. She doesn't like to read. Neither do my sisters. They say it's too hard. But I love to read, and so does my father. We have had so many wonderful evenings, talking about the things we have read in books. My father owns many books. He collects them. My mother complains because it's so expensive, but that's the one subject on which my father lays down the law in our house. Most of our books are Greek, of course, but we even have—"

She stopped talking, then, interrupted by Antonina's laughter. The laughter went on for quite a while. By the time Antonina finally stopped, wiping tears from her eyes, Rukaiya's expression of shock had faded into simple curiosity.

"What's so funny?" she asked.

Antonina shook her head. "The negusa nagast of Ethiopia is one of the world's champion bibliophiles. His father, King Kaleb, amassed the largest library south of Alexandria in his palace at Axum. In all honesty, I don't think Kaleb himself actually read any of those books. But by the time Prince Eon was fifteen, he had read all of them. I remember, when he came to Rome, how many hours he spent with my friend Irene Macrembolitissa—she *is* the world's greatest bibliophile—"

Antonina fell silent, staring at the girl across from her. Again, tears welled up in her eyes, as she remembered a friend she thought she would never see again.

Oh God, child, how much you remind me of Irene.

Memory made the decision. Memory of another

woman—intelligent, quick-witted, active—whose own life had been frustrated, so many times, by the world's expectations.

Fuck it. We have souls, too.

"You will be happy, Rukaiya," predicted Antonina. "And you will never, I promise you, be bored." Again, she wiped away tears; and, again, laughed.

"Not as that man's wife! Oh, no. You'll be keeping track of the King of King's accounts, Rukaiya, and writing *his* letters. He's building an empire and he's at war with the greatest power in the world. Soon enough, I think, you'll find yourself longing for a bit of tedium."

Finally, finally, the face across from her was nothing but that of a young girl. A virgin, barely sixteen years of age. Shy, anxious, uncertain, apprehensive, eager, curious—and, of course, more than a little avid.

"Is he—? Will he—?" Rukaiya fumbled, and fumbled.

"Yes, he will like you. Yes, he will be kind. And, yes, he will give you great pleasure."

Antonina rose and walked over. She took Rukaiya's face in her hands and fixed the girl's eyes with her own.

"Trust me, child. I know King Eon very well. Put aside all doubts and fears. You will enjoy being a woman."

Rukaiya was beaming happily, now. Just like a bride.

Chapter 21

Garmat did *not* beam happily, when he first saw Rukaiya.

"She's too skinny," he complained. Standing in his place of honor on the lower steps of the palace entrance, he turned his head and hissed in her ear: "What were you *thinking*, Antonina?"

Antonina's humor was a bit frayed, because of the heat. Standing under the bare sun of southern Arabia, wearing the heavy robes of imperial formality, was not enjoyable. So, for an instant, the decorum of a Roman official was replaced by the response of a girl raised on the rough streets of Alexandria.

"Piss on you, old fart," she hissed back. Then, remembering her duty, Antonina relented.

"I checked the family history, Garmat. All the women are slender, but none of them have had problems with it. Rukaiya's mother—"

There followed a little history lesson. Not so little, rather. Antonina had expected the issue to arise, so she had supplemented Rukaiya's own account with a more thorough investigation. Happily, the girl had not been sugar-coating the truth. For as many generations as clan memory went—which, typical of Arab tribesmen, was a *long* way back—only two women in that line had died in childbirth. That was better than average, for the day.

Her history lesson concluded, with all the solemnity of a Roman official, the Alexandria street urchin returned.

"So piss on you from a dizzy height, old fart."

"Well said," came Ousanas' whisper. The former dawazz—he still had no official title—was standing right behind them, on a higher step.

Antonina cocked her head a quarter turn. "You're not worried?" she whispered over her shoulder. Sourly: "I expected every man within fifty miles to be crabbing at me about it."

Ousanas' gleaming grin made a brief appearance. "Such nonsense. It comes from too much exposure to civilization and its decadent ways. My own folk, proper barbarians, never fret over the matter. Women drop babies in the fields, just like elands and lions."

Garmat, still tight-faced, began to mutter again. He was giving his own lecture, now, on natural history. Explaining, to a bird-brained Roman woman and an ignorant Bantu savage, the difference between passing a large human skull through a narrow pelvic passage and the effortless ease with which mindless animals—

He fell silent, stiffening with formal rigidity. The King of Kings was finally entering the square before the palace, where his bride and her party were waiting.

It was quite an entrance. Antonina, even after her years of exposure to Roman imperial pomp, was impressed. Axumites, as a rule, were not given to formality. But, when occasion demanded, they threw themselves into it with the wild abandonment of a people shaped by Africa's splendor.

Eon was preceded by dancers, leaping and capering to the rhythm of great drums. The dancers were garbed in leopard skins and cloaks of ostrich feathers. The drummers were clothed less flamboyantly. They wore shammas, the multilayered togas which were the usual costume worn by Ethiopians in the highlands. But these shammas were for ceremonial occasions. The linen was richly dyed, and adorned with ivory and tortoiseshell studs.

Behind the dancers and drummers came Eon's ceremonial guard. This body consisted of the officers of his regiment, and was much larger than normal. Eon had been adopted by three regiments, not the customary one, and all of them were present. Wahsi, Aphilas and Saizana, as commanders of the Dakuen, Lazen and the Hadefan sarawit, led the procession.

Here, Axum's more typical practicality made its reappearance. True, the soldiers were wearing ostrich-plume headdresses which were far larger and more elaborate than anything they would have worn in battle. But the weapons and light armor were the same practical and utilitarian implements with which the Ethiopian army went to the field of slaughter.

The soldiers were there, not so much to protect their king from assassins, as to remind the huge crowd packing the square of a simple truth. *Axum rules by the spear, when all is said and done. Do not forget it.*

Studying the crowd, however, Antonina could detect no signs of resentment in the sea of mostly Arab faces. The people of the desert, for all their love of poetry, were not given to flights of fancy when it came to politics. That rulers will *rule*, was a given. That being so, best to have a strong rule, and a firm one. That makes possible—possible—a fair rule as well.

Antonina decided she was reading the crowd properly. All the faces she could see were filled with no expressions beyond satisfaction and the pleasure of people enjoying a great spectacle. The measures which Eon had taken, the concessions which he had given the Hijaz even more than his leniency toward the bedouin rebels, had gone a long way to mollify southern Arabia to Ethiopian rule. The marriage about to take place, she thought, would finish the job. Arabs were as famous for their trading ability as they were for their poetry and their incessant political bickering. They knew a good bargain when they saw one.

Eon entered the square, now, and splendiferous royal pomp soared to the heavens.

"Good God," whispered Antonina, "is that thing *solid gold*?"

Garmat smiled. His usual good humor was back. "Of course not, Antonina," he whispered in return. "A chariot made of solid gold would collapse of its own weight. The wheels and axle, anyway."

Garmat bestowed a look of admiration on the vehicle lumbering into the square. "But there's plenty of gold on it, believe me. Enough gold plate to make it seem solid, even on the undercarriage." He made a little pointing gesture with his beard. "Those elephants aren't there just for show. The beasts have their work cut out for them, hauling the thing."

"Not to mention their own costumes," murmured Antonina. The four elephants drawing the chariot were cloaked in a pachyderm version of ceremonial shammas, not battle armor, but Antonina didn't even want to guess at the weight of ivory and tortoiseshell decorations.

Eon was riding alone in the open-backed, two-wheeled chariot. The chariot itself was patterned after the ancient war chariots of Egypt, which were designed for two men—one to control the horses, while the other served as an archer. But Eon did not require assistance. He had no reins to hold. The elephants were controlled by four mahouts. Those men, Antonina was relieved to see, were wearing nothing beyond their usual practical gear. The four elephants drawing Eon's chariot were *war* elephants, with the temperament to match. God help the crowd if the mahouts lost control of them.

Eon's own costume, to Antonina's eye, was a bit odd at first, until she realized she was seeing the usual Axumite combination of splendor and practicality. On the one hand, his tunic was made of simple, undyed linen. A Roman emperor—any Roman nobleman, for that matter, above the level of an equestrian—would have worn silk. But the utilitarian cloth was positively festooned with pearls and beads of red coral, and the threads which held the garment together were inlaid with gold.

His tiara, unlike the grandiose crowns of Roman or Persian emperors, was nothing more than a silver band studded with carnelian. The simplicity of the design, Antonina suspected, was to emphasize the importance of the four-streamered headdress which the tiara held in place. That was called a phakhiolin, by Ethiopians, and it was the traditional symbol of Axum's King of Kings.

She thought there was a subtle message in that headgear. Eon had already announced, the day before, that the capital of Axum was being moved to Adulis. The Arab notables gathered in the palace had reacted to the announcement with undisguised satisfaction. The decision to move the capital, those shrewd men knew, was the surest sign that their new ruler intended to weld them into his empire. The center of Axum, from now on, would be the Red Sea rather than the highlands—a center which was shared by Arabia along with Africa.

Today, gently, Eon was reminding them of something else. He still had the highlands, after all, and the breed of disciplined spearmen forged in those mountains. Their symbol, still, rode on the top of the negusa nagast's head.

His staff of office carried the same message. The shaft of the great spear was sheathed in gold, as was the Christian cross surmounting it. Sheathed in gold, and decorated with pearls. But the blade itself—the great, savage, leaf of destruction—was plain steel, and razor sharp.

The slow-moving chariot finally reached the center of the square. The mahouts brought the elephants to a halt, and Eon dismounted. In a few quick strides, he took his place next to his bride, and the wedding ceremony began.

The first part of the ceremony, and by far the longest, consisted of Rukaiya's conversion to Christianity. That went on for two hours. Long before it was over, Antonina, sweltering in her robes, was cursing every priest who ever lived.

In fairness, she admitted, the fault lay not principally with the priests. True, they were their usual long-winded selves, the more so when they basked in the warmth of such a gigantic crowd's attention. But most of the problem came from the sheer number of conversions.

Rukaiya was not converting alone. Everyone had known, of course, that the new Queen of Ethiopia would have to become a Christian (if she was not one already, as many Arabs were). Her own father, the day after Rukaiya's selection was publicly declared, had made his own announcement. He—and all his family—would convert also.

That had been a week ago. By the day of the wedding, well over half of the Beni Hashim had made the same decision, and a goodly portion of the other clans of the Quraysh as well. There were hundreds of people in the square—well over a thousand, by Antonina's guess—who were undergoing the rite alongside their new queen.

For all her sweltering discomfort, Antonina did not

begrudge them that ceremony. True, she suspected that most of the converts were driven by less-than-spiritual motives. Canny merchants, seeing an angle. But not all of them. And not even, she thought, any of them—not completely, at least.

Arabia was a land where religion seethed, under the surface. Most Arabs of the time were still pagans, despite the great success which Jewish and Christian missionaries had found there. But even Arabia's pagans, she knew, had a sense that there was a supreme god ruling the many deities of their pantheons. They called that god Allah.

As the conversion ceremony wound its way onward, Antonina's mind began to drift. She recalled a conversation she had had with Belisarius, before he left for Persia.

Her husband had told her of a religion which would rise out of Arabia, in what had been the future of humanity. Islam, it would be called, submission to the one god named Allah. The religion would be brought by a new prophet not more than a century in the future. A man named Muhammad—

For a moment, she started erect, snapped out of her reverie by a specific memory of that conversation. Her eyes darted to Rukaiya, standing in the center of the square.

Muhammad will also be from the Beni Hashim clan of the Quraysh. And, if I remember right, will have a daughter named Rukaiya.

She realized that her choice of Rukaiya, in ways she had not even considered, had probably already changed history. The Beni Hashim of Muhammad's future had not been Christians, except for a few. After today, they would be. How would that fact affect the future?

She slipped back into memory.

"Will it still happen, now?" she had asked Belisarius. "After all that's changed?"

Her husband shrugged. "Who's to know? The biggest reason Islam swept the Levant, and Egypt, was because the Monophysites converted almost at once. Voluntarily, most of them. Muhammad's stark monotheism, I think, appealed to their own brand of Christianity. Monophysitism is about as close as you can get to Islam, within the boundaries of the Trinity."

Belisarius scowled. "And after centuries of persecution by orthodox Christians, I think the Monophysites had had enough. They saw the Arabs as liberators, not conquerors."

Antonina spoke. "Anthony's trying—"

"I know he is," agreed Belisarius. "And I hope the new Patriarch of Constantinople will be able to rein in that persecution." Again, he shrugged. "But who's to know?"

Standing in the square, sweating in her robes, Antonina could still remember the strange look which had come to her husband's face.

"It's odd, really," he'd said, "how I feel about it. We have already, just in what we've done these past few years, changed history irrevocably." He patted his chest, where Aide lay in his little pouch. "The visions Aide shows me are just that, now. I can still learn an enormous amount from them, of course, but they're really no more than illusions. They'll never happen—not the way he shows me, anyway."

His face, for a moment, had been suffused with a great sadness. "I don't think there will ever be a Muhammad. Not the same way, at least. He might still arise, of course, and be a prophet. But if Anthony succeeds, I think Muhammad will more likely be a force regenerating Christianity than the founder of a new religion. That was how he saw himself, actually, in the beginning—until orthodox Christians and the Jews rejected him, and he found an audience among pagans and Monophysites."

Antonina had been puzzled. "Why does that make

you sad? I would think you'd prefer it. You're a Christian, yourself."

Belisarius' smile, when it came, had been very crooked. "Am I?"

She remembered herself gasping. And, just as clearly, could remember the warm smile in her husband's face.

"Be at ease, love. Christianity suits me fine. I've no intention of abandoning it. It's just—"

The look of strangeness, of strange *wonder*, was back on his face. "I've seen so much, Antonina," he whispered. "Aide has taken me millions of years into the future, to stars beyond the galaxy. How could the simple certainties of the Thracian countryside withstand such visions?"

She had been mute. Belisarius reached out and caressed her face.

"I am certain of only one thing," he said. "I can't follow half of Anthony's theology, but I know he's right. God made the Trinity so unfathomable because He does not want men to understand Him. It's enough that we look for Him."

His hand, leaving her cheek, swept the universe. "Which we will, love. Which we will. We are fighting this war, at bottom, so that people can make that search. Wherever the road leads them."

His gentle smile returned. "That's good enough. For a simple Thracian boy, raised to be a soldier, that's more than good enough."

Finally, it was ending. Antonina almost sagged from relief. She felt like a melting blob of butter.

She watched as Eon turned to Rukaiya and removed the veil. Then, she fought down a grin. The King of Ethiopia, for the first time, saw his new wife's face. He seemed like an ox, struck between the eyes by a mallet.

A little gasp—not so little, actually—went up from

the crowd. Some of that was caused by shock, at seeing a young woman unveiled in public. The Arabs had known it was coming, of course. Eon had made very clear that he was only willing to concede so much to Arab traditions. Ethiopian women did not wear veils, not even young virgins, and the King of Kings had stated in no uncertain terms that his new wife would follow Axumite custom in that regard. Still, the matrons in the square were shocked. Shocked, shocked! They could hardly wait to scurry home and start talking about the scandal of it all.

But most of the gasps came from Rukaiya's sheer beauty. The crowd had been expecting a pretty girl, true. But not—not *this*.

Within seconds, the gasps gave way to murmurs. Looks of shock and surprise were replaced by—

I will be damned, thought Antonina. *I didn't even think of that.*

"You are a genius yourself, Antonina," whispered Ousanas. "That is what a queen *should* look like. And will you look at the greedy bastards? Every one of those coin-counting merchants just realized there's no way the King of Kings is going to ignore his new Quraysh bride."

Garmat's opinion was otherwise. "She's too gorgeous," he complained. "We'll never be able to pry Eon out of bed." With a hiss: "What were you *thinking*, Antonina?"

Antonina ignored the old fart. She simply basked, a bit, in the admiring glances sent her way by the crowd. And she positively wallowed in the penumbra of another's admiration. Even at the distance, she could not misread Eon's face. That young face had been shadowed, ever since he found the mangled bodies of his concubines in the stones of the Ta'akha Maryam. Now, at last, she could see the shadow start to lift.

Like her husband before her, Antonina had come

to love Eon as if he were her own son. She realized, now that it was over, that she been guided throughout by a mother's instinct—not the calculations of a diplomat. She trusted that instinct, far more than she trusted the machinations of politics.

Garmat still didn't understand, but Ousanas did. The tall hunter leaned over and whispered: "A genius, I say it again."

Antonina shrugged modestly. "It's a good match. The girl's father, I think, will make an excellent adviser in his own right. And Rukaiya herself is very intelligent. She'll—"

"Not that nonsense," snorted Ousanas.

He sneered at Garmat. Ousanas' sneer was as magnificent as his grin. "Politics is a silly business. Games for boys too old to grow up." The famous grin made its appearance. "Wise folk, like you and me, understand the truth. As long as the boy is happy, he will do well. Everything else is meaningless."

That evening, at the great feast in the palace, Eon sidled up to her. He began to fumble with words of thanks and appreciation.

Antonina smiled. "She's very beautiful, isn't she?"

Eon nodded happily. "She's smart, too. Did you know she can actually *read*? And she's funny. Even before I lifted the veil I thought I would be enamored. She told a little joke, while the priests were droning on and on. I almost died, trying not to laugh."

He was silent, for a few seconds, admiring his wife. Rukaiya was the center of attention for the crowd—and had been, since the feast started. At the moment, she was surrounded by many of the young girls who had spent the days in the harem with her. Antonina, watching the ease with which Rukaiya handled that little mob of admirers—who had, not so long ago, been her rivals—congratulated herself once again.

She'll make a great queen.

The final reward came. Eon took her hand and gave it a little squeeze.

"Thank you," he whispered. "You have been like a mother for me."

Toward the end of the feast, Rukaiya sought her out. The young queen drew Antonina aside, into a corner of the great chamber. She clutched Antonina's hands in her own.

"I'm so nervous," she whispered. "Eon and I will be leaving, very soon. For his private chamber. I am so nervous. So scared."

Antonina smiled reassuringly, almost placidly. The expression was hard to maintain. She was waging a ferocious battle—not against giggles, but uproarious laughter.

What a lot of crap! Do you think you can fool me, *girl? You're not scared. You just can't wait to get laid, that's all.*

But a mother's instinct came to the rescue, again.

"Relax, Rukaiya. Forget what you might have heard. Most men, believe it or not, don't mount their wives like a bull mounting a heifer. They actually talk, first."

Some of them, anyway. Eon will.

Rukaiya's eyes were boring into her own, like a disciple staring at a prophet.

Hell with it. Antonina did laugh.

"Relax, I say!" She pried loose one of her hands and stroked the girl's cheek. Humor faded away, under the intensity of Rukaiya's gaze. Half-dreading; half-hopeful; half-eager; half-curious; half- . . .

That's way too many halves. This girl's got too many emotions going on at once.

"Trust me, Rukaiya," she said softly. "When the time comes, Eon will be very gentle. But it may not come as soon as you think. Maybe not at all, tonight."

Rukaiya's mouth gaped wide.

Antonina's hand went from the girl's cheek to her

lustrous, long black hair. Still stroking, she said: "Remember, girl, he recently lost concubines that he loved very much. It will be hard for him, too, when you are alone. He will be reminded of them, and be saddened. And he will be nervous himself. He's not a virgin, of course—"

She fought down a giggle. *To put it mildly!*

"—but he's still a young man. Not much older than you. In the beginning, I think, he will just want to talk."

Slowly, Rukaiya's mouth closed. The girl thought on Antonina's words for a time, as the Roman woman kept stroking her hair. The words, and the caresses, began to calm her.

"I know how to do *that*," Rukaiya announced. "I'm good at talking."

The next morning, at the breakfast feast, Garmat began grumbling again.

"What were you *thinking*, Antonina?"

The old adviser was sitting right next to her, in a position of honor near the head of the great table. Ousanas was seated on her other side. The two positions at the very head of the table, of course, were reserved for the King of Kings and his new queen. Judging from the fanfare of the drums, they were about to make their entrance.

"What were you *thinking*?" he repeated. "I just discovered the girl can read, on top of everything else. Wonderful. Two bookworms. They probably spent the whole night talking philosophy." He shook his head sadly. "The dynasty is doomed. There will be no heirs."

Eon and Rukaiya swept into the dining hall and took their seats. Ousanas took one glance at their faces and pronounced the obvious.

"You are a doddering old fool, Garmat. And Antonina is still a genius."

Yes, I am, she thought happily. *A true and certain genius.*

Chapter 22
PERSIA
Summer, 532 A.D.

"It looks like he's coming alone," said Damodara, squinting at the tiny figure in the distance. The Malwa lord cocked his head toward the tall Rajput standing next to him. "Am I right? Your eyes are better than mine."

Sanga nodded. "Yes. He's quite alone." The Rajput king watched the horseman guiding his mount toward them. The parley had been set on the most open patch of ground which Sanga's trackers had been able to find in this stretch of the Zagros. But the bleak, arid terrain was still strewn with rocks and small gullies.

"That is his way, Lord Damodara." Sanga's dark eyes were filled with warm admiration. "His way of telling us that he trusts our honor."

Damodara gave Sanga a quick, shrewd glance. For a moment, he felt a twinge of envy. Damodara was Malwa. Practical. He did not share Sanga's code of honor; nor, even, the prosaic Roman version of it possessed by Belisarius. But Damodara understood that code. He understood it very well. And he found himself, as he had often before, regretting that he felt no such certainty in the face of life's chaos.

Damodara was certain of nothing. He was a skeptic by nature—and had been, since his earliest memories as a boy. He was not even certain of the new gods which ruled his fate.

He did not doubt their existence. Like Sanga himself—the Rajput king was the only man who had ever done so beyond Malwa's dynasty—Damodara had spent time alone with Link. Damodara, like Sanga, had been transported into visions of humanity's future. He had seen the new gods, and the destiny they brought with them.

No, Damodara did not doubt those gods. He did not even doubt their perfection. He simply doubted their certainty. Damodara did not believe in fate, and destiny, and the sure footsteps of time.

Belisarius was close enough now for Damodara to make him out clearly. *That*, Damodara believed in. That, and the reality of the Rajput standing next to him in the shade of the pavilion. He believed in horsemen riding across stony ground, under the light of a mid-morning sun. He believed in the sun, and the rocks, and the cool breeze. He believed in the food resting on platters at the center of the low table in the pavilion. He believed in the wine which was in the beaker next to the food, and he believed in the beaker itself.

None of those things were perfect. Even the sun, on occasion, had spots. And they were very far from being certain, beyond the next few hours. But they were real.

Damodara was Malwa. Practical. Yet he had discovered, as so many practical men before him, that being practical was a lot harder than it looked. So, for a moment, he envied Sanga's certainties.

But only for a moment. Humor came to his rescue.

Damodara had a good sense of humor. Practical men needed it.

"Well, we can't have that!" he proclaimed. "A commander should have a bodyguard."

Damodara turned his head and whispered something to Narses. The eunuch nodded, and passed the message to the young Rajput who was serving as their attendant in the pavilion. A moment later, the youth was on his horse and cantering toward the Rajput camp a short distance away.

And so it was, by the time Belisarius drew up his horse before the small pavilion in which the parley would be held, that he discovered he would have a bodyguard after all.

Valentinian helped him down. The cataphract was not wearing any armor, beyond a light Rajput helmet, but he was carrying a sword slung from a baldric. And, of course, knives and daggers. Belisarius could see three of them, thrust into a wide sash. He did not doubt there were as many more, secreted away somewhere. Most men counted wealth in coins. Valentinian counted wealth in blades.

"How are you feeling?" asked Belisarius.

Valentinian's narrow face grew even more pinched. "Not too well, sir, to be honest. I stopped seeing double, at least. But my head still hurts, more often than not, and I don't have much strength back."

Valentinian glanced at the Malwa sitting in the open pavilion. They were out of hearing range. Damodara had politely allowed Valentinian to meet Belisarius alone.

"I'll do my best," he whispered, "if there's any trouble. But I've got to warn you that I'm not my old self. Not yet, anyway."

Belisarius smiled. "There won't be any trouble. And if there is, we'll have Sanga to protect us."

Valentinian grimaced. "Pity *those* poor bastards.

God, that man's a demon." Gingerly, he touched the light helmet on his head. "I don't ever want to do that again, I'll tell you for sure. Not without him tied up, and me using grenades."

Again, Valentinian glanced at the enemy in the pavilion. This time, however, it was a look of respect rather than suspicion.

"I've been well treated, general. Pampered like a lord, if you want to know the truth. Sanga himself has come to visit me, any number of times. Even Damodara." A look of bemusement came to his face. "He's actually a friendly sort of fellow, the fat little bugger. Odd, for a Malwa. Even got a sense of humor. Pretty good one."

Belisarius shrugged. "Why is that odd? The Malwa are humans, Valentinian, not gods." Belisarius gave his own quick glance at the pavilion. "Which is the reason, when the dust settles, that the new gods will find Malwa has failed them. They're trying to make perfection out of something which is not only imperfect by nature, but *must* be. Only imperfect things can grow, Valentinian. Striving for perfection is as foolish as it is vain. You can only create a statue—a thing which may look grand, on a pedestal, but will not stand up so well on the field of battle."

Belisarius brought his eyes back to Valentinian. "You swore an oath, I assume."

Valentinian nodded. For a moment, he seemed uncomfortable. Not ashamed, simply . . . awkward, like a peasant in the company of royalty. Men of Valentinian's class and station did not swear solemn oaths with the same practiced ease that nobility did.

"Yes, sir. They stopped putting a guard over me. But I had to swear that I would make no attempt to escape and that I wouldn't fight, except in self-defense. And I'll have to go back with them, of course, after this parley."

Valentinian's feral, weasel grin made its appearance.

"On the *other* hand, they didn't make me swear I'd keep my mouth shut." Another glance at the pavilion. "I've learned some things, General. Real quick: you were right about Damodara's arms complex. It's in Marv, just like Vasudeva thought it might be. They'll have their own handcannons soon enough. The Malwa have already started making them, in Kausambi. But Damodara's boasting that he'll have his own, made in Marv."

Belisarius shook his head. "He wasn't boasting, Valentinian—and he didn't tell you by accident. He knows you'll pass on the information. He wants me to have it."

Valentinian frowned. "Why would he do that?"

"Because he's a very smart man. Smart enough to understand something which few generals do. Sometimes a secret given away can serve as well as a secret kept. Or even better. He's probably hoping I'll try to make a raid on Marv, once he forces me out of the Zagros, rather than retreating into Mesopotamia. The city's in an oasis, and I'm sure he's got it fortified like Satan's jaws. We'd be eaten alive, trying to storm the place, and the few table scraps would be snapped up in the desert."

Valentinian squinted at him, as if he were seeing double. His hand, again, touched his helmet gingerly.

"Christ," he muttered. "How can you stand to think all crooked like that? My head hurts, just trying to follow." He made a little hiss. "And I *still* don't understand why Damodara would do it. He can't really think you'd fall for it."

Belisarius shrugged. "Probably not. But you never know. It's worth a try." He scratched his chin. "The man's a lot like me, I believe. In some ways, at least. He likes an oblique approach, and he keeps his eye on all the angles."

Another hiss came from Valentinian. "God, my head hurts."

Belisarius took Valentinian by the arm and began leading him toward the pavilion. As they neared, walking slowly, Valentinian remembered something else.

"Oh, yeah. Maurice was right about Narses, too. He's—"

Belisarius nodded. He had already spotted the small figure of the old eunuch in the shade of the pavilion.

He smiled crookedly. "I imagine, by now, that Narses is running the whole show for Damodara."

Valentinian grinned. It was an utterly murderous expression.

"Would you believe how successful that raid was? You know—the cavalry raid against the Malwa camp that you must have ordered, even though I never knew about it and I was right by your side the whole time."

Belisarius grinned himself. "A brilliant stroke, that was. So brilliant that my own memory is blinded."

Mine too, concurred Aide. Firmly: **But I'm sure you must have ordered it. And I'm *quite* sure the raid was a roaring success.**

"Killed every one of Damodara's top spies," murmured Valentinian. They were almost at the pavilion. "Vicious Romans slit their throats, neat as you could ask for."

They were entering the pavilion, now. Valentinian moved aside and Belisarius strode to the low table at the center. Damodara and Sanga nodded a greeting. Damodara was smiling; Sanga, stiff and solemn. Narses, sitting far back from the table, was glaring. But he, too, managed a nod.

Gracefully, with the practiced ease of his time in India, Belisarius folded himself into a lotus and took a seat on one of the cushions.

He saw no reason to waste time on meaningless diplomatic phrasery.

"What is the purpose of this parley?" he asked. The statement, for all the brusqueness of the words, was not so much a demand as a simple inquiry. "I can't see where there's any military business to discuss." He waved at Valentinian. "Unless you've changed your mind about his ransom."

Damodara chuckled. Belisarius continued.

"So what's the point of talking? You're trying to get into Mesopotamia, and I'm trying to stop you. Slow you down, more precisely. You've managed to drive me almost out of the Zagros—we're not so many miles from the floodplains, now—but I kept you tied up for months in the doing. That's bought time for Emperor Khusrau, and time for my general Agathius to build up the Roman forces in Mesopotamia."

Belisarius shrugged. "I'm going to keep doing it, and you're going to keep doing it. Sooner or later—sooner, probably—I'll give up the effort and retreat to Peroz-Shapur. Maybe Ctesiphon. Maybe somewhere else. Then we'll fight it out in the open. I imagine you're looking forward to that. But you won't enjoy it, when the time comes. So much, I can promise."

Damodara shook his head, still smiling. "I did not ask for this parley in order to discuss military affairs. As you say, the matter is moot."

Still smiling; very cheerfully, in fact: "And I don't doubt for a minute that you'll make it just as tough for us on flat ground as you have in the mountains."

Sanga snorted, as a man does when he hears another man announce that the sun rises in the east.

"I asked for this parley, Belisarius, simply because I wanted to meet you. Finally, after all these months. And also—"

The Malwa lord hesitated. "And, also, because I thought we might discuss the future. The *far* future, I mean, not the immediate present."

Bull's-eye. Am I a genius, Aide?

A true and certain genius, came the immediate

response. **But I still don't understand how you figured it out.**

Belisarius leaned forward, preparing to discuss the future. *Because Lord Damodara is a man. The best man of the Malwa, because he's the only one who doesn't dream of being a god. He follows the Malwa gods, true. But he is beginning to wonder, I think, how well his feet of clay will stand the march.*

"Lord Damodara—" began Belisarius. The general reached up and began unlacing his tunic. Beneath the cloth, nestled in a leather pouch, the future lay waiting. Like a tiger, hidden in ambush.

You're on, Aide.

There was no uncertainty in the response. Neither doubt, nor puzzlement.

I'll clean their clocks. Scornfully: **Polish their sundials, rather.**

Damodara—almost—took Aide in his hand when Belisarius made the offer. But, at the end, the Malwa lord shied away from the glittering splendor. Partly, his refusal was based on simple, automatic distrust. But not much. He didn't really think Belisarius was trying to poison him with some mysterious magical jewel. He believed, in his heart of hearts, that Belisarius was telling the truth about the incredible—*gem?*—nestled in his hand.

No, the real reason Damodara could not bring himself to take the thing, was that he finally realized that he did not want to know the future. He would rather make it himself. Poorly, perhaps; blindly, perhaps; but in his own hands. Pudgy, unprepossessing hands, to be sure. Nothing like the well-formed sinewy hands of a Roman general or a Rajput king. But they were *his* hands, and he was sure of them.

Sanga was not even tempted.

"I have seen the future, Belisarius," he stated

solemnly. "Link has shown it to me." The Rajput pointed to Aide. "Will that show me anything different?"

Belisarius shook his head. "Not at all. The future—unless Link and the new gods change it, with Malwa as their instrument—is just as I'm sure Link showed it to you. A place of chaos and disorder. A world where men are no longer men, but monsters. A universe where nothing is pure, and everything polluted."

Belisarius lifted his hand, his fingers spread wide. Aide glistened and coruscated, like the world's most perfect jewel.

"This, too, is a thing of pollution. A monster. An intelligent being created from disease. The worst disease which ever stalked the universe. And yet—"

Belisarius gazed down at Aide. "Is he not beautiful? Just like a diamond, forged out of rotting waste."

Belisarius closed his fingers. Aide's glowing light no longer illuminated the pavilion. And a Roman general, watching the faces of his enemies, knew that he was not the only one who missed the splendor.

He turned to Damodara. "Do you have children?"

The Malwa lord nodded. "Three. Two boys and a girl."

"Were they born perfectly? Or were they born in blood, and your wife's pain and sweat, and your own fear?"

A shadow crossed the Roman's face. "I have no children of my own. My wife Antonina can bear them no longer. In her days as a courtesan, after she bore one son, she was cut by a man seeking to become her pimp."

Those coarse truths, spoken by a man about his own wife, did not seem odd to his enemies in the pavilion. They knew the story—Narses had told them what few details the Malwa espionage service had not already ferreted out. Yet they knew as well, as surely as they knew the sunrise, that the Roman was oblivious to any shame or disgrace. Not because he was ignorant of his wife's past, but simply because he didn't care. Any more than a diamond, nestled with a pearl, cares that the pearl was also shaped from waste.

The shadow passed, and sunlight returned. "Yet that boy—that bastard, sired by a prostitute's customer—has become my own son in truth. As dear to me as if he were born of my own flesh. Why is that, do you think?"

Belisarius stared down at the beauty hidden in his fist. "This too—this monster—has become like a son to me. And why is *that*, do you think?" When he raised his head, the face of the Roman general was as serene as the moon. "The reason, Lord of Malwa and King of Rajputana, was explained to me by Raghunath Rao. In a vision I had of him, once, dancing to the glory of time. *Only the soul matters, in the end.* All else is dross."

Belisarius turned to Rana Sanga. "My wife is a very beautiful woman. Is yours, King of Rajputana?"

Sanga stared at the Roman. Belisarius had never met Sanga's wife. For a moment, angrily, Sanga wondered if Rome's spies had—

He shook off the suspicion. Belisarius, he realized, was simply making a shrewd guess. Looking for any angle from which to drive home the lance.

"She is plump and plain-faced," he said harshly. "Her hair was already gray by the time she was thirty."

Belisarius nodded. He opened his hand. Beauty reentered the pavilion.

"Would you trade her, then, for my own?"

Sanga's powerful fingers closed around the hilt of his sword. But, after an instant, the gesture of anger became a simple caress. A man comforted by the feel of an old, familiar, trusted thing. The finest steel in the world was made in India. That steel had saved him, times beyond counting.

"She is my life," he said softly. "The mother of my children. The joy of my youth and the certainty of my manhood. Just as she will be the comfort of my old age."

Sanga's left hand reached up, gingerly stroking the new scar which Valentinian had put on his cheek. The scar was still angry-looking, in its freshness, but even after it faded Sanga's face would remain disfigured. He had been a handsome man, once. No longer.

"Assuming, of course, that I reach old age," he said, smiling ruefully. "And that my wife doesn't flee in terror, when she sees the ogre coming through her door."

Again, for a moment, the fingers of his right hand clenched the sword hilt. Powerful fingers. Sanga's smile vanished.

"I would not trade her for a goddess." The words were as steely as his blade.

"I didn't think so," murmured Belisarius. He slipped Aide back into his pouch, and refastened the tunic.

"I didn't think so," he repeated. He rose, and bowed to Damodara. "Our business is finished, I believe."

Belisarius was a tall man. Not as tall as Sanga, but tall enough to loom over Damodara like a giant. He was a big man, too. Not as powerful as Sanga, to be sure, but a far more impressive figure than the short and pudgy Malwa lord sitting on a cushion before him.

It mattered not at all. Lord Damodara returned the Roman general's gaze with the placidity of a Buddha.

"Yes, I believe it is," he agreed pleasantly. Damodara now rose himself, and bowed to Belisarius. Then, he turned slightly and pointed to Narses. "Except—"

Damodara smiled. The very image of a Buddha. "You requested that Narses be present. I assume there was a reason."

Belisarius examined the eunuch. Throughout the parley, Narses had been silent. He remained silent, although he returned Belisarius' calm gaze with the same glare with which he had first greeted him.

"I would like to speak to Narses alone," said Belisarius. "With your permission."

Seeing the distrust in Damodara's eyes, Belisarius shook his head.

"I assure you, Lord Damodara, that nothing I will discuss with Narses will cause any harm to you."

He waited, while Damodara gauged the thing. Measured the angles, so to speak.

That was a beautifully parsed sentence, said Aide admiringly.

I had an excellent grammarian. My father spared no expense on my education.

Damodara was still hesitating. Looking for the oblique approach, wherever the damn thing was. That it was there, Damodara didn't doubt for an instant.

"I will give you my oath on it, if you wish," added Belisarius.

Oh, that's good. You're smart, grandpa. Don't let anybody tell you different.

Belisarius almost made a modest shrug. But long experience had taught him to keep his conversations with Aide a secret from those around him.

I am a man of honor. But I've never seen where that prevents me from using my honor practically. We Romans are even more practical than the Malwa. Way more, when push comes to shove.

The offer seemed to satisfy Damodara. "There's no need," he said pleasantly. Again, he bowed to Belisarius. Then, taking Sanga by the arm, he left the pavilion.

Belisarius and Narses were alone. Narses finally spoke.

"*Fuck you*. What do you want?"

✧ ✧ ✧

Belisarius grinned. "I just want to tell you your future, Narses. I think I owe you that much, for saving Theodora's life."

"I didn't do it for *you*. Fuck you." The old eunuch's glare was a thing of wonder. As splendid, in its own way, as Aide's coruscating glamour. Sheer hostility, as pure as a diamond, forged out of a lifetime's malice, envy and self-hatred.

"And what do I care?" demanded the eunuch. Sneering: "What? Are you going to tell me that I'm an old man, right on the edge of the grave? I already know that, you bastard. I'll still make your life as miserable as I can. Even while they're fitting me for the shroud."

Belisarius' grin was its own thing of marvel. "Not at all, Narses. Quite the contrary." He tapped the pouch under his tunic. "The future's changed, of course, from what it would have been. But some things will remain the same. A man's natural lifespan, for instance."

Narses glared, and glared. Belisarius' grin faded, replaced by a look of—sorrow?

"Such a waste," he murmured. Then, more loudly: "I will tell you the truth, Narses the eunuch. I swear this before God. You will outlive me, and I will not die young."

His crooked smile came. "Not from natural causes, anyway. In this world, which we're creating, who knows what'll happen? But in the future that would have been, I died at the age of sixty. You were still alive."

Narses jaw dropped. "You're serious?" For a moment, a lifetime's ingrained suspicion vanished. For that moment—that tiny moment—the scaled and wrinkled face was that of a child again. The infant boy, before he had been castrated and cast into a life of bitterness. "You're really telling me the truth?"

"I swear to you, Narses, before God Himself, that I am speaking the truth."

Suspicion returned, like a landslide. "Why are you telling me this?" demanded Narses. "And don't give me any crap. I know how tricky you are. There's an angle here." The eunuch's angry eyes scanned the interior of the pavilion, and the landscape visible beyond, as if looking for the trap.

"Of course there's an angle, Narses. I should think it's obvious. *Ambition*."

Narses' eyes snapped back to Belisarius.

"Such a waste," repeated Belisarius. Then, firmly and surely: "I forgive you your treason, Narses the eunuch. Theodora won't, because she cannot abandon her spite. But I can, and I do. I swear to you now, before God, that the past is forgiven. I ask only, in return, that you remain true to the thing which brought you to treason. Your ambition."

Belisarius spread his hands, cupped, like a giant holding an invisible world. "Don't think small, Narses. Don't satisfy yourself with the petty ambition of bringing *me* down. Think big." His grin returned. "Why not? You've still got at least thirty more years to enjoy the fruits of your labor."

Narses' quick eyes glanced at Rana Sanga. The Rajput king was standing outside, perhaps forty feet away. He and Damodara were chatting amiably with Valentinian.

"Don't be *stupid*," he hissed. "I cleaned up Damodara's nest, sure. He was sick and tired of Nanda Lal's creatures watching his every move. But—more than that?"

The great sneer was back in force. "This is a *Rajput* army, Belisarius, in case you haven't noticed. Those crazy bastards are as likely to violate an oath as you are. They swore eternal allegiance to the Malwa emperor, and that's that."

Belisarius scratched his chin, smiling crookedly. "So they did. But I suggest, if you haven't already, that you investigate the nature of that oath. Oaths are specific, you know. I asked Irene, last year, to find out for me just exactly what the kings of Rajputana swore, at Ajmer, when they finally gave their allegiance to Malwa."

The smile grew as crooked as a root. "They swore eternal allegiance to *the Emperor of Malwa*, Narses."

Belisarius began to leave. At the edge of the pavilion, just within the shade, he stopped and turned around.

"There was no mention of Skandagupta, by the way. No name, Narses. Just: *the Emperor of Malwa.*"

He almost laughed, then, seeing Narses' face. Again, it was the face of a young boy. Not the face of trusting innocence, however. This was the eager face of a greedy child, examining the cake which his mother had just placed before him in celebration of his birthday.

With many more birthdays to come. Lots of them, with lots of cake.

On the way back, riding through the badlands, Aide spoke only once.

Deadly with a blade, is Belisarius.

Chapter 23

The minute Belisarius entered the headquarters tent, he knew. The grinning faces of his commanders were evidence enough. Maurice's deep scowl was the proof.

He laughed, seeing that morose expression.

"What's the matter, you old grouch?" he demanded. "Admit the truth—you just can't stand it, when plans go right, that's all. It's against your religion."

Maurice managed a smile, sort of. If a lemon could smile.

" 'T'ain't natural," he grumbled. "Against the laws of man and nature." He held up the scroll in his hand and offered it to Belisarius. Then, shrugging: "But, apparently, it's not against the laws of God."

Eagerly, Belisarius unfolded the scroll and scanned its contents.

"You read it." It was a statement, not a question.

Maurice nodded, gesturing to the other officers. "And I gave them the gist."

Belisarius glanced at the faces of Cyril, Bouzes and Coutzes, and Vasudeva. A Greek, two Thracians, and a Kushan, but they might as well have been peas in a pod. All four men were beaming. Satisfaction, partly, at seeing plans come to fruition. Sheer pleasure, in the main, because they were *finally* done with maneuvers. Except for one last, long, driving march, of course—but that was a march to battle. That the march would end in triumph, they doubted not at all. Theirs was the army of Belisarius.

Not *quite* peas in a pod. The Kushan's grin was so wide that it seemed to split his face. Belisarius gave him a stern look and shook the scroll admonishingly.

"The helmets stay on until we're well into the qanat, Vasudeva. Any Kushan who so much as sheds a buckle, before we're into the passage—I'll have him impaled. I swear I will."

Vasudeva's grin never wavered. "Not to fear, General. We are planning a religious ceremony, once we're in. A great mounded pile of stinking-fucking-stupid-barbarian crap. We will say a small prayer, condemning the shit to eternal oblivion." He spread his hands apologetically. "By rights, of course, we should set it all afire. But—"

Coutzes laughed. "Not likely! Not unless you want to smother all of us in smoke. It'll be hard enough to breathe, as it is, with over ten thousand men humping through a tunnel. Even sending them through in batches, we'll be half-suffocating."

Satisfied, Belisarius resumed his examination of the scroll. He was not really reading the words, however. The message was so short that it did not require much study. Simply a date, and a salutation.

His gaze was fixed on that salutation, like a barnacle to a stone. Two words.

"Thank God, we're done with these mountains," stated Bouzes. "*And* those tough Rajput bastards!" agreed his brother happily.

Tears welled into Belisarius' eyes. "This message means something much more precious to me," he whispered. He caressed the thin sheet. "It means my wife is still alive."

Seeing the sheer joy in Belisarius' face, his commanders fell silent. Then, after clearing his throat, Cyril muttered: "Yes, sir. Very probably."

Belisarius gave the Greek cataphract a shrewd glance. Cyril's expression, he saw, was mirrored on the faces of the brothers and Vasudeva. Uncertainty; hope, for the sake of their general; but—but—

"Shit happens, in war," stated Belisarius, verbalizing their unhappy thoughts. "Maybe Antonina's dead. Maybe Ashot sent the message, telling us when the fleet would sail from Adulis."

He looked at Maurice. The chiliarch was grinning, now, as hugely as Vasudeva had done earlier. There was not a trace of veteran pessimism in that cheerful expression.

Belisarius smiled. "Tell them, Maurice."

Maurice cleared his throat. "Well, it's like this, boys. I only told you the gist of the message itself. Ashot might have sent *that*, sure enough. Could have sent it, standing over Antonina's bleeding corpse. But I really doubt the stubby bastard would have addressed the general as—and I quote—'*dearest love.*' Even if he is an Armenian."

The tent erupted with laughter. Belisarius joined in, freely, but his eyes were back on the scroll.

Dearest love. The two words poured through his soul like wine. Standing in a tent, in the rocky Zagros, he felt as if he were soaring through the heavens.

Dearest love.

They broke for the south two days later. Belisarius waited until the next cavalry encounter was over. Just a quick clash between thirty Romans and their equivalent number of Rajputs, in a nearby valley. No different from a dozen others—a hundred others—which had taken place over the past few months.

The encounter, as had usually been the case since the Battle of the Pass, was almost bloodless. Neither side was trying to hammer the other any longer. They were simply staying in touch, making sure that each army knew the location of its opponent.

No Roman was killed. Only one was seriously injured, but he swore he could make the march.

"It's just my arm, general," he said, holding up the heavily bandaged limb. "Just a flesh wound. Didn't even lose much blood."

Belisarius had his doubts. But, seeing the determination in the cataphract's face, he decided to bring him along. The army had just been informed, at daybreak, of their new destination. The wounded cataphract wanted to stay with his comrades. At worst, the man would not lose his strength for several days. That was good enough.

The general straightened up from his crouch. "All right," he said. He gave the cataphract a look which was not grim, simply stoic. "Worst comes to worst, you'll be in Rajput hands."

The cataphract shrugged. He was obviously not appalled by the prospect. Nor had he any reason to be. The conflict between the two armies, even before the battle in the pass, had been civilized. Thereafter, it had been downright chivalrous. The Rajputs would treat the man as well as Belisarius' soldiers had treated their own Rajput captives.

Remembering those captives, Belisarius shrugged himself. "Comes to it," he said, "I'll just leave you behind with the prisoners. Far enough into the qanat that Damodara won't find you until it's too late, and with plenty of food. You won't need water, of course."

The cataphract grimaced, slightly, at the mention of water. The spring runoff was long over, but the qanat was still at least a foot deep. For all their eagerness to quit the mountains, none of the soldiers were looking forward to a long march through a tunnel. Walking along narrow ledges on the sides, lest their feet become soaked by the water pouring through the center passage.

Maurice came up. "Now," he said. "Couldn't ask for a better time."

Belisarius nodded. It was only mid-morning of the day after the cavalry clash. The Rajput horsemen would have returned to their own army, bringing Damodara the news of the Roman whereabouts. They would not return for at least a day, probably two.

Long enough.

"Are the men—?"

"Mounted up, and ready," came Maurice's immediate reply. "They're just waiting for the order."

Belisarius took a deep breath, filling his lungs. "*Now,*" he said. Quickly, while the clean air of the mountains buoyed him up and stiffened his resolve. Soon enough, he would be gasping and sweating in damp, smoky darkness. One of thousands of men, stumbling through a tunnel eight feet wide, their steps barely illuminated by a few torches.

The Roman camp, within minutes, was a beehive of activity. Long files of mounted soldiers started down the valley, headed for another small valley two days' ride away. That valley was also a beehive of activity. Kurush and his miners had been preparing the deception for weeks, now.

Belisarius waited until the very end, before he mounted up and followed. It was odd, he realized, how much he was going to miss the mountains. Odd, when he thought of the many times he had cursed them. But the Zagros had been good to him, when all was said and done. And he was going to miss the clean air.

He drove out all regrets. Aide helped.

Think of the sea breeze. Think of gulls, soaring through blue skies. Think of—

The hell with all that! came Belisarius' cheerful

retort. *All I want to think about is Venus rising from the waves.*

And that was the thought that held him, through the miserable days ahead. His wife, coming to meet him from across the sea.

Dearest love.

At a place called Charax. A place where Belisarius would lance a dragon's belly; and show the new gods that they too, for all their dreams of perfection, still needed intestines.

Charax. Belisarius would burn that name into eternity.

But the name meant nothing to him. It was just the place where his Venus would rise from the waves. A name which was only important because a man could remember embracing his wife there, like so many men, over so many years, at so many places, had embraced their wives after a long separation. Nothing more.

So is eternity made, said Aide gently. **Out of that simple clay, and no other.**

Chapter 24

MAJARASHTRA

Summer, 532 A.D.

Irene whispered a few words into her agent's ear. The man nodded, bowed, and left the room. Irene closed the door behind him.

Kungas had ignored the interchange. Bent over the reading table in Irene's outer chamber, carefully writing out the assignment she had given him, Kungas had seemed utterly oblivious to the spy's arrival or his whispered conversation with Irene. But, the moment the spy was gone, Kungas raised his head and cocked an eye toward her.

Seeing the expression on her face, he turned away from the table completely.

"Is something wrong?" he asked.

Irene stared at him, blank-faced. Kungas rose from the chair. A faint frown of worry creased his brow.

"What is wrong?" he demanded.

Irene shook her head. "Nothing," she replied. "Nothing is *wrong*."

With the air of a woman preoccupied by something,

she drifted toward the window. Kungas remained in place, following only with his eyes.

Once at the window, Irene placed her hands on the sill. She leaned into the gentle breeze coming from the ocean, closing her eyes. Her thick, lustrous, chestnut hair billowed gently in the wind.

Behind her, unseen, Kungas' hands moved. Coming up, cupping, as if to stroke and caress. But the movement was short-lived. In seconds, his hands were back at his side.

Irene turned away from the window. "I need your advice," she said softly.

Kungas nodded. The gesture, as always, was economical. But his eyes were alert.

For a moment, as her mind veered aside into the hot place in her heart, Irene reveled in her own words. *I need your advice*. Simple words. But words which, except for Belisarius and occasionally Justinian, she had never spoken to a man. Men, as a rule, did not give advice to women. They condescended, or they instructed, or they babbled vaingloriously, or they tried to seduce. They rarely simply advised.

She could not remember, any longer, how many times she had said the words to Kungas. And how many times, in the weeks since the battle where they destroyed the guns, he had simply advised.

By sheer force of will, she jerked her mind back from that place in her heart. The fire was there, but it was banked for a time.

She shook her head, smiling.

"What is so amusing?" asked Kungas.

"I was just remembering the first time I met you. I thought you were quite ugly."

His lips made the little movement which stood Kungas for a grin. "No longer, I hope?"

She gave no answer. But Kungas did not miss the little twitch of her hands. As if she, too, wanted to stroke and caress.

Irene cleared her throat. "There is news. News concerning Dadaji's family. The location of his son has been found. The location where he *was*, I should say. It seems that several months ago Dadaji's son was among a group of slaves who escaped from his master's plantation in eastern India. The ringleader, apparently. Since then, according to the report, he has joined one of the rebel bands in the forest."

Kungas smacked his hands together. For an instant, the mask vanished. His face shone with pure and unalloyed delight.

"How wonderful! Dadaji will be ecstatic!"

Irene raised a cautioning hand. "He is in great danger, Kungas, and there is nothing I can do to help him. The Malwa have been pouring troops into the forests, since they finally realized they can no longer dismiss the rebels as a handful of brigands."

Kungas shrugged. "And so? The boy dies, arms in hand, fighting the asura who ravages his homeland. That is the worst. You think that would break Dadaji's heart? You do not really understand him, Irene. Beneath that gentle scholar is a man of the Great Country. He will do the rites, weeping—while his heart sings with joy."

Irene stared at him. Skeptically, at first. Then, with a nod, she deferred to his judgement. (And reveled, also, in that deferral.)

"There is more," she added. "More than news." She took a deep breath. "My spies found his wife, also. A slave in a nobleman's kitchen, right in Kausambi itself. Following my instructions, they decided it would be possible to steal her away. In Malwa's capital," she snorted, half-chuckling, "noblemen do not guard their mansions too carefully."

Kungas' eyes widened. In another man, they would have been practically bulging.

Irene laughed. "Oh, yes. She is *here*, Kungas. In Suppara." She nodded toward the door. "In this very house, in fact. My man has her downstairs, in the salon."

Now, even Kungas' legendary self-control was breaking. "*Here?*" he gasped. He stared at the door. Then, almost lunging, he began to move. "We must take her to him at once! He will be so—"

"*Stop!*"

Kungas staggered to a halt. For a moment, staring at Irene, he frowned with incomprehension. Then, his expression changed, as understanding came. Or so he thought.

"She has been disfigured," he stated. "Dishonored, perhaps. You are afraid Dadaji will—"

Irene blew out a breath—half-laugh, half-surprise. "No—no." She smiled reassuringly. "She is quite well, Kungas, according to my agent. Very tired, of course. He says she was asleep within seconds of reaching the couch. The journey was long and arduous, and her life as a slave was sheer toil. But she is well. As for the other—"

Irene waved her hand, as if calming an unsettled child. "My spy says she was not abused, not in that manner. Not even by her master. She was not a young woman, you know. Dadaji's age."

She looked away, her jaw tightening. "With so many young slaves to rape, after the conquest of Andhra, men simply beat her until she was an obedient drudge." Her next words were cold, filled with the bitterness of centuries. Greek women had been raped, too, often enough. And listened to Greek men, and Greek poets, boasting of the Trojan women. "Not even Dadaji will count that as pollution."

"*That is not fair,*" said Kungas harshly.

Irene took a deep breath, almost a shudder. "No, it is not," she admitted. "Not with Dadaji, at least. Although—" She sighed, shaking her head. "How can any man as intelligent as he be so stupid?"

It only took Kungas a second, perhaps two, to finally understand her concern.

"Ah." He stared out the window for a moment. "I see."

He looked down at his hands, and spread wide his fingers. "Tonight, the empress has called a council. She will finally decide, she says, which offer of marriage to accept."

The fingers closed into fists. He looked up at Irene. "You will state your opinion, then, for the first time. And you do not want Dadaji to refrain from arguing his, because he feels himself so deeply in your debt."

She nodded. Kungas chuckled. "I never imagined Rome's finest spymaster would hold herself to such a rigid code of honor."

Irene made an inarticulate, sarcastic noise. "I hate to disillusion you, Kungas. I do this not from honor, but from simple—" She paused. When she spoke again, the acid-tinged sarcasm was gone from her voice.

"Some, yes. Some." She sighed. "It is difficult to manipulate Dadaji, even for someone like me. It's a bit too much like maneuvering against a damned saint."

She reached up and wiped her face, restoring the spymaster. "But that is still not my reason. My reason is cold-blooded statecraft. Whatever decision the empress makes will be irrevocable. You know Shakuntala, Kungas. She is as intelligent, I think, as Justinian."

She barked a laugh. "She *certainly* has the willpower of Theodora." Then, shaking her head: "But she is still a girl, in many ways. If she discovers, in the future, that one of her closest advisers—he is like a father to her, you know that—withheld his advice on such a critical matter—" The headshaking became vigorous. "No, no, no. That would shake her self-confidence to the very roots. And *that* we cannot afford. She may make the wrong decision. Rulers often do. But her confidence must never waver, or all will be lost."

Kungas eyed her, head aslant. "Have I ever told you that you were a very smart woman?"

"Several times," she replied, smiling. She cocked her own head, returning his look of amusement with questioning eyes.

"You still have not asked," she said softly. "What my opinion is. We have never discussed the matter, oddly enough."

He spread his hands. "Why is that odd? I know your opinion, just as surely as you know mine."

He dropped his hands and lifted his shoulders. "It is obvious. I even have hopes, once we explain, that Dadaji will be convinced."

Irene snorted. Kungas smiled, but shook his head.

"You are too skeptical, I think." The thick, heavy shoulders squared. "But we will know soon."

He began to move toward the door, his head turned away. "I think it would be best, Irene, if you spoke first."

"I agree. It will strike the harder, coming from an unexpected source. You will follow, of course, when the time is right."

He did not bother to reply. There was no need. For a moment, never speaking, the man and woman in the room reveled together in that knowledge.

Kungas had reached the door. But Irene spoke before he could open it.

"Kungas." He turned his head. Irene gestured at the writing table. "You can read, now. Kushan, rather well, and your Greek is becoming passable. Your writing is still very crude, but that is merely a matter of practice."

His eyes went to the table, lingering there for a moment. Then, closed shut.

"Why, Kungas?" she asked. Her voice was calm, but

tinged with anxiety. And, yes, some pain and anger. "My bed has always been there for you. But you have never come. Not once, in the weeks since the battle."

Kungas reopened his eyes. When he looked at Irene, his gaze was calm. Calm, and resolute.

"Not yet."

Irene's own gaze was not so calm. "I am not a virgin, Kungas," she said. Angrily, perhaps—or simply pleading.

The Kushan's mask of a face broke in half. Irene almost gasped. She had never seen Kungas actually *grin*.

"I did not imagine you were!" he choked out. He lowered his head, shaking it back and forth like a bull. "Shocking news. Most distressing. I am chagrined beyond belief. Oh, what shall I do?"

As tense as she was, Irene couldn't restrain her laughter. Kungas raised his head, still grinning.

But the question remained in her eyes. He took a few steps forward, reached out his hand, and drew her head into his shoulder.

"I have this to do first, Irene," he said softly, stroking her hair. "I cannot—" Silence, while he sought the words. "I cannot tend to my own needs, while hers are still gaping. I have guarded her for too long, now. And this struggle, I think, is perhaps her most desperate. I must see her through it safely."

She felt his chest heave slightly, from soft laughter. "Call it my own dharma, if you will."

Irene nodded, her head still nestled in his shoulder. She reached up and caressed the back of his neck. Slender fingers danced on thick muscle.

"I understand," she murmured. "As long as I understand." She laughed once herself, very softly. "I may need reassurance, again, mind you. If this goes on and on."

She knew he was smiling. "Not long, I think," she heard him say. "The girl *is* decisive, you know."

Irene sighed, and ceased caressing Kungas' neck. A moment later, her hands placed firmly on his chest, she created a space between them.

"So she is," she murmured. "So she most certainly is."

Pushing him away, now. "Go, then. I will see you tonight, at the council meeting."

He bowed ceremoniously. "Prepare to do battle, Irene Macrembolitissa. The dragon of Indian prejudice awaits your Roman lance."

Gaiety returned in full force. "What a ridiculous metaphor! It's back to the books for you—*barbarian oaf!*"

Chapter 25

It was late in the night before Irene spoke. The council had already gone on for hours.

Irene craned her neck, twisting her head back and forth. To all outward appearance, it was the gesture of someone simply stretching in order to remain alert in a long, long imperial council.

In reality, she was just trying not to smile at the image which had come to her mind.

This isn't a "council." It's a—down, smile, down!—damned auction.

Her eyes, atop a rotating head, fell on the empress. Shakuntala was sitting, stiff and straight-backed, on a cushion placed on her throne. The throne itself was wide and low. In her lotus position, hands at her side, Shakuntala reminded Irene of the statue of a goddess resting on an altar. The girl had maintained that posture, and her stern countenance, throughout the session—with no effort at all, seemingly. That self-discipline, Irene knew, was another of Raghunath Rao's many gifts to the girl.

Irene's head twisting became a little shake.

Stop thinking of her as a "girl." That is a woman,

now. Not more than twenty, yes, and still a virgin. But a woman nonetheless.

In the long months—almost a year, now—since Irene had come to India, she had grown very fond of Shakuntala. In private, Shakuntala's imperious demeanor was transmuted into something quite different. A will of iron, still, and self-assuredness that would shame an elephant. But there was also humor, and quick intelligence, and banter, and a willingness to listen, and a cheerful acceptance of human foibles. And that, too, was a legacy of Raghunath Rao.

Not one of Shakuntala's many advisers doubted for a moment that the empress, should she feel it necessary, could order the execution of a thousand men without blinking an eye. And not one of those advisers—not for instant—ever hesitated to speak his mind. And that, too, was a legacy of Rao.

Irene's eyes now fell on the large group of men sitting before the empress, on their own plush cushions resting on the carpeted floor.

The bidders at the auction.

The envoys from every kingdom in India still independent of Malwa were there. Tamraparni, the great island south of India which was sometimes called Ceylon, was there. And, in the past two weeks, plenipotentiaries from every realm in the vast Hindu world had arrived also. Most of those envoys had brought soldiers with them, to prove the sincerity of their offers. The Cholan and Tamraparni units were quite sizeable. Suppara was packed like a crate, with soldiers billeted everywhere.

Whether smuggled through the blockade of the coast, or, more often, marching overland from Kerala, they had come. Kerala, ruled by Shakuntala's grandfather, was there too, despite his treacherous connivance the year before with a Malwa assassination plot against her. Shakuntala had practically forced its representative Ganapati to grovel. But, in the end, she had allowed Kerala to join the bidding.

Irene had never fully realized, until the past few weeks, the true extent of the Hindu world. She had always thought of Hinduism, and its Buddhist offspring, as religions of India. But, like Christianity, those religions had spread their message over the centuries. And, more often than not, spread their entire culture along with it.

Representatives from Champa were there, and Funan, and Langkasuka, and Taruma, and many others. The faces of those envoys bore the racial stamp of southeast Asia and its great archipelagoes but, beneath the skin, they were children of India in all that mattered. Nations sired by Indian missionaries, suckled by Indian custom, nurtured by Indian commerce, and educated in Sanskrit or one of its derivatives.

Even China was there, in the form of a Buddhist monk sent by one of the great kingdoms of that distant land. He, unlike the others, had not come to bid for Shakuntala's hand in marriage. He had come simply to observe. But men—not royal envoys, at least—do not travel across the sea in order to observe a stone. They come to study a comet.

Shakuntala's rebellion had shaken Malwa. The world's most powerful empire was still on its feet, and still roaring its fury. But it was locked in mortal combat with adversaries from the mysterious West—enemies who had proven far more formidable than the Hindu world had envisioned. And now, rising from the stony soil of the Great Country, Shakuntala's rebellion was hammering the giant's knees. If those knees ever broke—

The independent kingdoms of the Hindu world, finally, had shed their hesitation. They feared Malwa, still—were petrified by the monster, in fact—but Shakuntala had shown that the beast could be bloodied. Not beaten, perhaps. That remained to be seen. But even the vacillating, timid, fretful kingdoms of south India and southeast Asia had finally understood the truth.

Andhra had returned. Great Satavahana, the noblest dynasty in their world, was still alive. That empire, and that dynasty, had shielded south India and the Hindu lands beyond for centuries. Perhaps it could do so yet.

All of them had come, and all of them were bidding for the dynastic marriage. And the bidding had been fierce. In the weeks leading up to the council, the canny peshwa Dadaji Holkar had matched one proposal against another, scraping quibble against reservation, until nothing was left but solid offers of alliance. At the council meeting itself, in the course of the hours, Dadaji had compressed those solid offers into so many bars of iron.

Irene repressed a grin. Dadaji Holkar, low-born son of polluted Majarashtra, had outwitted and outmaneuvered and outnegotiated the Hindu world's most prestigious brahmin diplomats. Had any of them been told, now, that Dadaji himself was nothing but a low-caste vaisya—a mere sudra, in truth, in any land of India outside the Great Country—they would have been shocked from the tops of their aristocratic heads to the soles of their pure brahmin feet. Distressed also, of course, at the thought of the pollution they had suffered from their many hours of intimate contact with the man. For the most part, however, they would have simply been stunned.

It is not possible! He is one of the most learned men in India! A scholar, as well a statesman!

She could picture them gobbling their disbelief. *It is not possible! He is the peshwa of Andhra! How could great Satavahana—India's purest kshatriya—have been fooled by such a man? Not possible!*

Irene's fight to restrain her humor became transformed into something much grimmer. Something cold, and calculating, and—in its own way—utterly ruthless. She, too, could be an executioner.

Studying the brahmin diplomats seated before the empress, Irene's eyes began to glint. *I will show you what is* possible. *Fools!*

It was time. The envoys had presented their offers. Dadaji had summarized the situation. It only remained for the empress to make her decision.

Irene could not have explained the little movements she made, of head and hands and eyes, which drew Shakuntala's attention. Neither could the young empress herself. But the two women had spent many hours in private and public discourse. Irene knew how to signal the empress, just as surely as the empress understood how to interpret those signals.

Shakuntala's head turned to Irene. The empress' eyes seemed as bright as ever, probably, to most observers. But Irene could sense the dull resignation in that imperial gaze.

"I would like to hear from the envoy of Rome," stated Shakuntala. As always in public council, the empress' voice was a thing to marvel at. Youthful, true, in its timbre. But a fresh-forged blade is still a sword.

A faint murmur arose from the diplomats.

Shakuntala's eyes snapped back to them. "Do I hear a protest?" she demanded. "Is there one among you who cares to speak?"

The murmurs fled. Shakuntala's eyes were like iron balls. The Black-Eyed Pearl of the Satavahanas, she was often called. But black, for all its beauty, can be a terrifying color.

Black iron smote clay. "You would *protest*?" she hissed. "*You?*" The statue moved, slightly. A goddess, with a little gesture of the hand, dismissing insects.

"After Malwa conquered Andhra, and flayed my father's skin for Skandagupta's trophy, what did *you* do?"

The statue sneered. "You trembled, and quailed, and whimpered, and tried to hide in your palaces." The goddess spoke. "Rome—*only Rome*—did not cower from the beast."

Shakuntala's next words were spoken through tight teeth. "Doubt me not in this, you diplomats. If Malwa is slain, the lance which brings the monster down will be held in Roman hands. Not ours. Alone—not if all of us united—could we do the deed. Our task is to shield the Deccan, and do what we can to lame the beast."

The diplomats bowed their heads. Those brahmins, for all their learning, were insular and self-absorbed to a degree which Irene, accustomed to Roman cosmopolitanism, often found amazing. But even they, by now, knew the name of Belisarius. A bizarre name, an outlandish name, but a name of legend nonetheless. Even in south India—even in southeast Asia—they had heard of Anatha. And the Nehar Malka, where Belisarius drowned Malwa's minions.

Shakuntala kept her eyes on their bowed heads, not relenting for a full minute. Black iron is as heavy as it is hard.

During that long minute, while Indian diplomats—again—quailed and hid their heads, Irene sent a mental message to a man across the sea. He would not receive it, of course, but she knew he would have enjoyed the whimsy. That man had spent hours and hours with her, in Constantinople—days, rather—counseling Irene on her great task. Explaining, to a woman of the present, the future he wanted her to help create.

Well, Belisarius, you wanted your Peninsular War. I do believe you've got it. And if we don't have

Wellington, and the Lines of Torres Vedras, we have something just as good. We have Rao, and the hillforts of the Great Country, and—

Her eyes fell on a hard, harsh, brutal face.

—and we've got my man, too. Mine.

She gathered the comfort in that possessive thought, and transformed softness into hard purpose.

"Speak, envoy of Rome," commanded Shakuntala.

Irene rose from her chair and stepped into the center of the large chamber. Dozens of eyes were fixed upon her.

She had learned that from Theodora. The Empress Regent of Rome had also counseled Irene, before she left for India. Explaining, to a spymaster accustomed to shadows, how to work in the light of day.

"Always sit, in counsel and judgement," Theodora had told her. "But always stand, when you truly want to lead."

Irene, as was her way, began with humor.

"Consider these robes, men of India." She plucked at a heavy sleeve. "Preposterous, are they not? A device for torture, almost, in this land of heat and swelter."

Many smiles appeared. Irene matched them with her own.

"I was advised, once, to exchange them for a sari." She sensed, though she did not look to see, a pair of twitching lips. "But I rejected the advice. Why? Because while the robes are preposterous, what they represent is not."

She scanned the crowd slowly. The smile faded. Her face grew stern.

"What they represent is Rome itself. Rome—*and its thousand years.*"

Silence. Again, slowly, she scanned the room.

"A *thousand years,*" she repeated. "What dynasty of India can claim as much?"

Silence. Scan back across the room.

"The greatest empire in the history of India, the Maurya, could claim only a century and half. The Guptas, not more than two." She nodded toward Shakuntala. "Andhra can claim more, in years if not in power, but even Andhra cannot claim more than half Rome's fortune."

Her stern face softened, just slightly. Again, she nodded to the empress. The nod was almost a bow. "Although, God willing, Andhra will be able to match Rome's accomplishment, as future centuries unfold."

Severity returned. "*A thousand years.* Consider *that,* noble men of India. And then ask yourself: how was it done?"

Again, she smiled; and, again, plucked at a heavy sleeve.

"It was done with these robes. These heavy, thick, preposterous, unsuitable robes. These robes contain the secret."

She paused, waited. She had their complete attention, now. She took the time, while she waited, to send another whimsical, mental message across the sea. Thanking a harsh, cold empress named Theodora, born in poverty on the streets of Alexandria, for training a Greek noblewoman in the true ways of majesty.

"The secret is this. These are the robes *of* Rome, but they are not Roman. They are Hun robes, which we took for our own."

A murmur arose. *Huns? Filthy, barbarous—Huns?*

"Yes. Hun robes. We took them, as we took Hun trousers, when our soldiers became cavalrymen. Just as we took, from the Aryans, the armor and the weapons and the tactics of Persia's horsemen. Just as we took from the Carthaginians—eight hundred years ago—the secrets of war at sea. Just as we took, century after century, the wisdom of Greece, and made it our own. Just as we took the message of Christ from Palestine. Just as we have taken everything we needed—*and discarded anything we must*—so that Rome could endure."

She pointed her finger toward the north. "The Malwa call us mongrels, and boast of their own purity. So be it. Rome shrugs off the name, as an elephant shrugs off a fly. Or, perhaps—"

She grinned. Or, perhaps, bared her teeth.

"Say better, Rome *swallows* the name. Just as a huge, half-savage, shaggy, mastiff cur of the street wolfs down a well-groomed, purebred house pet."

A tittering laugh went through the room. Irene allowed the humor to pass. She pointed now to Shakuntala.

"The empress said—and said rightly—that if the monster called Malwa is slain, the hand which holds the lance will be Roman. I can give that hand a name. The name is Belisarius."

She paused, letting the name echo through the chamber.

"*Belisarius*. A name of glory, to Rome. A name of terror, to Malwa. But, in the end, it is simply a name. Just like this"—she fingered a sleeve—"is simply cloth. So you must ask yourself—why does the name carry such weight? Where does it come from?"

She shrugged. "It is a Thracian name, first. Given to his oldest son by a minor nobleman in one of Rome's farming provinces. Not three generations from a peasant, if the truth be told."

She fixed cold eyes on the crowd. "Yet that *peasant* has broken armies. Armies more powerful than any of you could face. And why is *that*, noble men of India?"

Her chuckle was as cold as her eyes. "I will tell you why. It is because Belisarius has a soul as well as a name. And whatever may have been the flesh that made the man, or the lineage that produced the name, the *soul* was forged on that great anvil which history has come to call—*Rome*."

She spread her arms wide, trailing heavy sleeves. "Just as I, a Greek noblewoman wearing Hun robes, was forged on that same anvil."

Irene could feel Theodora flowing through her now, like hot fire through her veins. Theodora, and Antonina, and all the women who had birthed Rome, century after century, back to the she-wolf who nursed Remus and Romulus.

She turned to Shakuntala.

"You asked, Empress of Andhra, my advice concerning your marriage. I am a Roman, and can give you only Roman advice. My friend Theodora, who rules Rome today, has a favorite saying. *Do not trample old friends, in your eagerness to make new ones.*"

She scanned the faces in the crowd, watching for any sign of understanding.

Nothing. The faces were transfixed, but blank with incomprehension. Except—Dadaji Holkar's eyes were widening.

Drive on, drive on. Strike again.

"Whom should you marry? To a Roman, the answer is obvious. You are a monarch, Shakuntala, with a duty to your people. *Marry the power*—that is the Roman answer. Marry the strength, and the courage, and the devotion, and the tenacity, which brought you to the throne and can keep you there. Wed the strong hand which can shield you from Malwa, and can strike powerful blows in return."

Scanned the faces. Transfixed, but—still nothing. Except Holkar. A wide-eyed face, almost pale with shock, as he began to understand.

Again, the hammerstroke. Even prejudice, in the end, will yield to iron.

"Do not wed a man, Empress. Wed a people. Marry the people—the *only* people—who never failed you. Marry the people who carried Andhra on their shoulders, when Andhra was bleeding and broken.

Marry the men who harry Malwa in the hills, and the women who smuggle food into Deogiri. Marry the nation that sent its sons into battle, not counting the cost, while all other nations cowered in fear. Marry the boys impaled on the Vile One's stakes, and their younger brothers who step forward to take their place. Wed *that* folk, Shakuntala! Marry that great, half-savage, shaggy mastiff of the hills, not—"

She pointed accusing fingers at the assembled representatives of the Hindu world's aristocracy.

"Not these—these purebred *lapdogs.*"

Accusing fingers curled into a fist. She held the fist out before her.

"*Then—!* Then, Shakuntala, you will hold power in your hand. True power, real power—not its illusion. Steel, not brittle wood."

She dropped her fist, flicking dismissive fingers. The gesture carried a millennium's contempt.

"Marry the Roman way, girl," she said. Gently, but with the assurance of Rome's millenium. "Wed Majarashtra. Find the best man of that rough nation, and place your hand in his. Let *that* man dance your wedding dance. Open the womb of India's noblest and most ancient dynasty to the raw, fresh seed of the Great Country. Let the sons born of that union carry Andhra's fortune into the future. If you do so, that fortune will be measured in centuries. If you do otherwise, it will be measured in years.

"As for the rest . . ." She shrugged. "As for what people might say, or think . . ." She laughed, now. There was no humor at all in the sound. It carried nothing beyond unyielding, pitiless condemnation. Salt, sown into soil.

"Let them babble, Shakuntala. Let them cluck and complain. Let them whimper of purity and pollution. Let them sneer, if they will. What do you care? While their thrones totter, yours will stand unshaken. And they will come to you soon enough—trust me—like beggars in a dusty street. Pleading that you might let the uncouth husband sitting by your side, and lying in your bed, lead their own armies into battle."

Finally—*finally*—everyone in the room understood. The envoys were gaping at her like so many blowfish. Dadaji's face, she could not see. The peshwa's head was bowed, as if in thought. Or, perhaps, in prayer.

She turned back to Shakuntala. The empress, though she was not gaping, seemed in a pure state of shock. She sat the throne, no longer like the statue of a goddess, but simply like a young child. A schoolgirl, paralyzed by a question she had never dreamed anyone would ever ask.

The Roman teacher smiled. "Remember, Shakuntala. Only the soul matters, in the end. All else is dross. That is as true of an empire as it is of a man."

Quietly, then, but quickly, Irene took her seat. In the long silence which followed, while envoys gasped for breath and a peshwa bowed his head—and a schoolgirl groped for an answer she already knew, but could not remember—Irene simply waited. Her hands folded in her lap, breathing easily, she simply waited.

Prejudice would erupt, naturally. Soon, the room would be filled with outrage and protest. She did not care. Not in the least.

She had done her job. Quite well, she thought. Holding the tongs in firm hands, she had positioned the blade to be forged. Prejudice would sputter up, of course, just as hot iron spatters. But the hammer, held in barbarous thick hands, would strike surely. And quench the protest of purity in the greater purity of tempering oil.

Kungas did not wait for the protest to emerge. Kushans were a folk of the steppes, and swift horses.

"*Finally!*"

He was standing in the center of the room, before anyone saw him rise.

"*Finally.*"

He let the word settle, ringing, as that word does. Then, crossing muscle-thick arms over barrel chest, he turned his head to the empress.

"Do as she says, girl. It is obvious. *Obvious.*"

The first mutters began to arise from the crowd of notables. Kungas swung his head toward them, like a swiveling cannon.

"*Be silent.*" The command, though spoken softly, brought instant obedience. The mask was pitiless, now. As pitiless, and as uncaring, as steppe winter.

"I do not wish to hear from *you*." The mask twisted, just slightly. But Satan, with his goat lips, would have been awed by that sneer.

"*You?* You would *dare?*" The snort which followed matched the sneer. Pure, unalloyed contempt.

Kungas swiveled his head back to Shakuntala. "I will tell you something, girl. Listen to me, and listen well. I was your captor, once, before I was your guardian. I knew the truth, then, just as surely as I know it now. The thing is obvious—*obvious*—to any but fools blinded by custom."

Again, he snorted. Contempt remained, augmented by cold humor.

"All those months in the Vile One's palace, while I held you captive. Do you remember? Do you remember how carefully I set the guards? How strictly I maintained discipline? You had eyes to see, girl, and a mind which was trained for combat. Did you see?"

He stared at the empress. After a moment, Shakuntala nodded. Nodded, not imperiously, but like a schoolgirl nods, when she is beginning to follow the lesson.

Kungas jerked his head at the notables.

"Against whom was I setting that iron guard, girl? *Them?*"

He barked a laugh so savage it was almost frightening.

"Them? Those purebred pets?"

The laugh came again, baying like a wolf.

"I did not fear *them*, girl. I did not watch so carefully because I was worried about *Chola*. Or Tamraparni, or Kerala, or—"

He broke off, waving a thick hand.

"I was your enemy then, Shakuntala. And as good an enemy, as I have been a friend since. I knew the truth. I always knew. I knew who would come for you. I knew, and I feared the coming."

For a moment, his eyes moved to Dadaji. The peshwa's face was still hidden. Kungas made a little nod toward that bowed head, as if acknowledging defeat in an old argument. "My soul knew he was there. I could sense his own, lurking in the woods beyond the palace. I never spotted him, not once, but I *knew*. That is why I set the guards, and held the discipline, and never wavered for a second in alertness. I never feared anything, except the coming of the panther. One thing only, I knew, could threaten my purpose. The Wind of the Great Country—that, and that alone, could sweep you out of Malwa's grasp."

His eyes returned to the empress. Clear, bright almond eyes, in a face like bronze. "And that Wind alone, girl, is what can keep you from the asura's claws."

He uncrossed his arms, and dropped his hands to the side. "Do as the Roman woman tells you, Shakuntala. Do that and no other. Hers is the advice of an empire which, for a thousand years, has never lost sight of the truth. While *these*—"

Again, the stiff, contemptuous fingers. "*These* are nothing but envoys from kingdoms long lost to illusion."

And now he too took his seat. And silence reigned

again. The envoys did not even murmur. The lapdogs had been cowed.

Irene held her breath. One voice, alone, remained to be heard. One voice, alone in that room, which could still sway the empress to folly. She dreaded that voice, and found herself praying that the man she had come to love had read another man's soul correctly. For perhaps the first time in her life, Irene prayed she was in error.

Shakuntala's face was as stiff as a statue's. But the exterior rigidity could not disguise—not from Irene; not from anyone in the room—the turmoil roiling beneath.

Irene was swept with pity. The girl's mind—and the empress *was* a girl, now—was locked tight. Sheer, utter paralysis. Shakuntala's deepest, most hidden wish was at war with her iron sense of duty—and now, a foreign woman had turned duty against desire. Cutting loose one with the other, true. But still leaving behind, to a girl who had never once seen their connection, nothing but a tangled web of doubt and confusion.

Shakuntala did what she could only do, then. She turned to the man who, more than any other, she had come to rely on to find the threads which guided her life.

"Dadaji?" she said softly, pleadingly. "Dadaji? You must tell me. What should I do?"

Irene's jaws tightened; her lips were pursed. That question had not been asked of an adviser, by an empress. That had been the question a daughter asks her father. A loving daughter, turning to a trusted father—seeking, not advice, but direction.

It was Holkar's decision, now. Irene knew that for a certainty. In her current state of paralysis and confusion, Shakuntala would obey the peshwa as surely as a daughter will obey her father.

Irene saw Dadaji's shoulders rise and fall, taking

a deep breath. He lifted his head. For the first time since Irene had read understanding in his eyes, she saw Dadaji's face.

The relief was almost explosive. She had to fight to let her breath escape in silence.

Before Holkar said his first word, Irene knew the answer. That was the face of a father, not a peshwa. A loving father who, like millions before him, could chide and train and discipline his daughter. But who could not, when the time finally came, deny her what she truly wished.

Dadaji Holkar began to speak. Irene, listening, knew that Kungas had read the man's soul correctly, and she had not. When all was said and done, and the trappings and learning were stripped away, Dadaji Holkar remained what he had always been. A simple, modest, kindly man from a small town in Majarashtra, trying to raise a family as best he could. Malwa had savaged his family, and torn his own daughters away. He would not, could not, do the same to the girl he had taken in their place.

Holkar's face had brought relief. Relief so great, that Irene barely listened to his first words. But after a few seconds, she did. And then, less than a minute later, was struggling not to laugh.

The soul of Dadaji Holkar was that of a father, true. But the mind still belonged to the imperial adviser. Once again, great Satavahana's lowborn peshwa would outmaneuver brahmins.

"It is difficult for you, Empress, I realize." Dadaji raised his hand, as if to ward off the peril which threatened his monarch. As best he could, that is—which, judging from the feebleness of the gesture, was precious little. "Your own purity—" He broke off, sighed, plowed forward. "But you must put the needs of your people first. As difficult as the choice may be, for one of your sacred lineage."

The peshwa, twisting sideways on his cushion, turned toward Irene and bowed.

"I listened carefully to the Roman envoy's words. As carefully as I could, even though my heart was beating rebellion. But my mind could not deny the words. It is true, what she says." Again, he sighed, as a man does when he cedes preference to duty. "If you place your obligation to your people above all else, thrusting aside your personal concerns, then you must indeed do as the Roman says. If you would marry power, Empress, then marry the man from the Great Country."

A faint murmur of protest began to rise from the envoys seated nearby. The barbarous Kushan had intimidated them, with his savage derision. The scholarly peshwa—a brahmin like themselves; or so, at least, they thought—could perhaps be reasoned with.

Dadaji thrust out his hand, palm down. The gesture, in its own way, was as contemptuous as Kungas' sneer. A sage, stilling the ignorant babble of village halfwits.

"*Be silent.*" Holkar fixed cold eyes on the gathered envoys. "What do *you* know of power?"

The peshwa was well into middle age, but he was still an active man. Dadaji rose from the cushion, as easily as a youth. He stared down at the envoys for a moment, before he began pacing back and forth. Hands clasped behind him, head tilted forward—the master, lecturing schoolboys. "You know nothing. The true ways of power are as mysterious to you as the planets."

Pace, pace, back and forth. "No country in India—not all of us put together—can field an army which could defeat Malwa in the field. That task is for the Romans, led by Belisarius. But he, too, cannot do it alone. Belisarius can lance the asura, but only if the demon is hamstrung. And *that*, we *can* do. But the doing will be difficult, and bloody, and costly. It will require courage and tenacity, above all other things."

He stopped, gazing down on Chola's envoy. "When Shakuntala's father, years ago, asked you for your help against Malwa, what did you do?" He waited for the answer. None came, beyond a head turned aside.

He looked upon Ganapati. "What did Kerala do?" he demanded. Ganapati, also, looked away.

Holkar's bitter eyes scanned the envoys. Most looked aside; some bowed their heads; a few—those from distant southeast Asia—simply shrugged. Their help had not been asked by Shakuntala's father.

But Holkar did not allow them that easy escape and, after a time, they looked away also. They knew the truth as well as he. Had Andhra asked, the answer would have been the same. *No.*

He flared his nostrils. "Power!" he snorted. "What you understand, *diplomats*, is how to manipulate power. You have no idea how to create it. Tonight, I will tell you. Or, rather—"

Again, he bowed to Irene. "I will simply repeat her words. Power comes from below, noble men of India. From that humble place, and no other. An empire, no matter how great—no matter how large its armies or well-equipped its arsenals—has no more power than the people upon whom it rests give to it. For it is they—*not you*—who must be willing to step forward and die, when the time comes. It is that low folk—*not you*—who have the courage to crawl upon a demon's haunch and sever its tendons."

He turned his back to them. Scornfully, over his shoulder: "While you, consulting your soothsayers and magicians, try to placate the beast in the hope it will dine elsewhere."

His hands were still clasped behind his back. For a moment, they tightened, and his back stiffened.

"Do not forget, noble men of India, that I am also Maratha. I know my people, and you do not. You scorn them, for their loose ways and their polluted nature. But you are blind men, for all your learning. As the Kushan says, lost in illusion."

He took a deep breath, and continued. "Today, Majarashtra trembles on the brink. Maratha sympathies are all with Shakuntala, and many of its best sons have come to her side. But most Maratha are still waiting. They will smuggle food, perhaps, or spy; or hide a refugee. But no more. Not yet. The heel of Malwa is upon their neck. The Vile One's executioners have draped their towns with the bodies of rebels."

Another deep breath; almost a great sigh. "It is not fear which holds them back, however, if you plunge into their hearts. It is simply doubt. They remember Andhra, true, and are loyal to that memory. But Andhra failed them once before. Who is to say it will not again?"

He turned his head to the northeast, peering intently at the walls of the chamber, as if he could see the Great Country beyond. "What they need," he said softly, "is a pledge. A pledge that the dynasty they have supported will never abandon them. And what pledge could be greater—than for the Empress of Andhra to make the dynasty their own? No Maratha has ever sat upon a throne. A year from now, the child of Majarashtra's greatest champion will *be* the dynasty."

His own face—soft, gentle, scholarly—was now as hard a mask as that of the Kushan.

"It will be done," he pronounced. "The empress, I am sure, will find her way to her duty. As will Rao." Then, spinning around, he confronted the envoys again. "But it will be done *properly*."

His smile, when it came, was as savage as Kungas'. "The empress will wed Rao in Deogiri, not here. She will dance her wedding dance in the Vile One's face, in the midst of a siege. Hurling defiance before

Malwa, for all to see. And *you*, noble men of India—you of Chola and Kerala and Tamraparni—will attend that wedding. And will provide the troops to escort her through the Vile One's lines."

The envoys erupted in protest. Outraged babble piled upon gasping indignation.

Holkar ignored them serenely. He turned back to his empress. Shakuntala was staring at him—blank-faced, to all appearances. But Holkar could sense her loosening self-control.

From the side of the chamber, Irene sent him an urgent thought. *End it, Dadaji. Give her space and time, before she breaks. The rest can be negotiated tomorrow.*

Apparently, telepathy worked. Or perhaps it was simply that two people thought alike.

"Marry Rao, Empress," decreed Dadaji Holkar. Then, in words so soft that only she could hear: "It is your simple duty, girl, and nothing else. Your dharma. Let your mind be at ease."

Those father's words removed all doubt. Shakuntala was fighting desperately, now, to maintain her imperial image. Beneath the egg-thin royal shell, the girl—no, the woman—was beginning to emerge.

Dadaji turned, but Kungas was already on his feet, clapping his hands.

"Enough! Enough!" the Kushan bellowed. "It is late. The empress is very weary. Clear the chamber!"

No envoy, outraged or no, wanted to argue with that voice. The rush for the door started at once. Within a minute, the chamber was empty except for Irene, Kungas, and Dadaji. And the empress, still sitting on her throne, but already beginning to curl. As soon as the heavy door closed, she was hugging her knees tightly to her chest.

Years of discipline and sorrow erupted like a volcano. Shakuntala wept, and wept, and wept; laughing all the while. Not the laughs of gaiety, these, or even happiness. They were the deep, belly-emptying, heaving laughs of a girl finally able—after all the years she had swallowed duty, never complaining once of its bitter taste—to wallow in the simple joys and desires of any woman.

Kungas stepped to her side and embraced her. A moment later, squirming like an eel, Shakuntala forced him onto the throne and herself onto his lap. There she remained, cradled in the arms of the man who had sheltered her—as he had again that day—from all the world's worst perils. Since the day her father died, and Malwa made her an orphan, Kungas had never failed her. The child found comfort in his lap, the girl in his arms, the empress in his mind. But the woman, finally out of her cage, only in his soul. Choked words of love and gratitude, whispered between sobs, she gave him in return. And even Kungas, as he stroked her hair, could not maintain the mask. His face, too, was now nothing but a father's.

Dadaji began to move toward the empress, ready to share in that embrace. But Irene restrained him with a hand.

"Not now, Dadaji. Not tonight."

Holkar looked back, startled. "She will want—need me—"

Irene shook her head, smiling. "Her wants and needs can wait, Dadaji. They are well-enough satisfied, and Kungas is there for her tonight. He will shelter her through her joy, just as he guarded her through despair. Tonight, Dadaji, you must give to yourself."

He frowned, puzzled. Irene began pulling him toward the door. "There is someone you must see. Someone you have been seeking, since the day she was lost. She should already be in your chambers."

By the time she opened the door, Dadaji understood. By the time she closed the door, he was already gone. She could only hear his footsteps, pounding down a corridor. It was odd, really. They sounded like the steps of a young man, running with the wind.

The lamps were lit, when Irene entered her own chambers. Her servants, knowing her odd tastes from months of experience, had prepared her reading chair. Tea was ready, steeping in a copper kettle. It was lukewarm, by now, but Irene preferred it so.

As always, her servants had taken several books from the chest and placed them on the table next to the lamp. The books had been chosen at random, by women who could not read the titles. Irene preferred it so. It was always pleasant, to see her choices for the night. Irene enjoyed surprises.

She sat and took a sip of tea. Then, for a few minutes, she weighed Plato against Homer, Horace against Lucretius.

None, in the end, fit her mood. Her eyes went to the door of her bedroom. A flush of passion warmed her. But that, too, she pushed aside. Kungas would not come, that night. Not for many nights still, she knew.

There was regret in that knowledge, and frustration, but neither anger nor anxiety. Irene knew her man, now. She did not understand him, not entirely. Perhaps she never would. But she did know him; and knew, as well, that she could accept what she did not understand. The same stubborn determination that had kept an illiterate to his books, week after week after week, would keep him away from her bed, for a time. Not until an empress was wed to a champion, and he gave away his girl to the man she had chosen, would Kungas be satisfied that he had done his duty.

So the man was. So he would always be. Irene, comparing him to other men she had known, was well content in her choice.

She arose and moved to the window. Felt the

breeze, enjoyed the sound of surf. She was happy, she realized. As happy as she had ever been. That understanding brought with it an understanding of her mood. And frustration anew.

She laughed. "Oh, damn! Where are you, Antonina? I want to get blind, stinking drunk!"

Chapter 26

THE ARABIAN COAST

Autumn, 532 A.D.

"How could I have been so *stupid*?" demanded Antonina, glaring over the stern rail of her flagship. She rubbed her face angrily, as if she might squeeze out frustration by sheer force. "I should have known they'd follow us, the greedy bastards. And we were bound to be spotted, once we came within sight of land. There's only one obvious reason a fleet of Ethiopian warships would be cruising along the southern coast of Arabia—we're going to pillage the Malwa somewhere. Damned carrion-eaters!"

Wahsi, standing next to her, was matching her glare with one of his own. Even Ousanas, on her other side, had not a trace of humor in his face.

"None of us thought of it, Antonina." Ousanas twisted his head, as if searching the deck of the Ethiopian warship for a missing person. Which, in a way, he was.

"I wish Garmat were here," he grumbled. "If there's anyone who knows how a bandit thinks, it's him."

Ousanas gestured at the Arab dhows which were trailing in the wake of Antonina's fleet. "He might figure out how to talk them into going away."

"I doubt it," said Antonina, wearily. She stopped rubbing her face and stared at the small armada. The dhows reminded her of buzzards following a pack of wolves. "The problem is, Ousanas, they're not really pirates. Just dirt-poor fishermen and bedouin, smelling the chance for loot."

"They'll ruin all our plans!" snarled Wahsi. "There'll be no way to keep this expedition a secret, with that gaggle of geese following us. Assuming they don't just sell the information to the Malwa outright."

Antonina was back to rubbing her face. With only one hand, this time, slowly stroking her jaw. Without realizing it, she was half-imitating her husband's favorite mannerism when he was deep in thought.

"Maybe not," she mused. "Maybe—"

She glanced up, gauging the time of day. "It'll be sundown, soon." She pointed to a small bay just off the port bow. "Can we shelter the fleet there, tonight?" she asked Wahsi.

The Dakuen commander examined the bay briefly. "Sure. But what for? You said you wanted us to stay out of sight of land once we got halfway down the Hadrawmat. We're there. We should be putting further out to sea. Make sure we're over the horizon during daylight, until we reach the Strait of Hormuz."

Antonina shrugged. "That was for the sake of secrecy. With them following us"—she pointed to the fleet of dhows—"there's no point. We have to keep *them* out of sight, too. No way to do that without talking to them. That's why I want to anchor in the bay. The dhows will follow, and I think I can set up a parley."

"A *parley*?" choked Wahsi.

Antonina smiled. "Why not?"

Wahsi was glaring at her, now. "Are you insane?

Do you really think you can *reason* with those—those—"

Ousanas' laugh cut him off. The laugh, and the huge grin which followed. "Of course she doesn't think that, Wahsi!"

The tall hunter beamed down at the short Roman woman. "She's not going to appeal to their 'reason,' man. Just their greed."

"Well spoken," murmured Antonina. She smiled demurely at Wahsi. "I'm a genius, remember?"

It took hours, of course. Long into the night, negotiating with a small horde of Arab chieftains and subchieftains. Each little dhow had its own independent captain, and each of them had an opinion of his own. Four or five opinions, as often as not.

"We cannot board those great Malwa beasts," snarled one of the village-notables-turned-pirate-captain. He spoke slowly, and emphatically, so that Antonina could follow him. Her command of Arabic was only middling. "The one time we tried—" He threw up his hands. "Butchered! Butchered! Only two ships came back."

"Butchered, butchered," rose the murmur from the crowd. The pavilion which Antonina had ordered erected on the beach was packed with Arab chieftains. All of them joined in the protest, like a Greek chorus.

Antonina responded with a grin, worthy of a bandit. "That was my husband's ship, I imagine."

The statement brought instant silence. Seventeen pairs of beady eyes were examining her, like ferrets studying a hen. Except this hen had just announced that she was mated to a roc.

Antonina nodded toward Ousanas. The hunter was squatting out of the way, in a corner of the tent. He had been there since the Arabs first entered. After a glance, none of them had paid him any attention.

The Roman woman's slave, obviously; beneath their notice.

Ousanas grinned and rose lazily. The tall hunter reached behind him and drew forth his great stabbing spear. Then, hefting it easily, he began rattling off some quick sentences in fluent Arabic. Antonina could only follow some of it, but the gist was not hard to grasp.

Simple concepts, really. *Yeah, that's right, you mangy fucks. I was there too.* (Here, two of the chieftains hissed and tried to edge their way back into the crowd. No translation was needed—they remembered Ousanas, clearly enough.) *It was almost funny the way you pitiful amateur pirates scuttled over the sides—the few of you who still could, that is, after we gutted and beheaded and disemboweled and maimed and mangled and slaughtered—*

And so on, and so forth. Fortunately, Ousanas concluded on a happier note.

So let's not hear any crap about what can and can't be done. You *couldn't do it, for sure. But nobody's asking you to. We'll do the serious work. All you've got to do is haul away the spoils.*

The fishermen/bandits had taken no offense at Ousanas' grisly taunts. But they were deeply offended by his last statement.

Again, Antonina had no difficulty interpreting the gist of their hot-tempered remarks.

What? Do we look like fools? Why would you do all the dangerous work and let us take the loot? Snort, snort. *Do you take us for idiots? Lies, lies.*

Antonina decided to interject the voice of sweet, feminine reason.

"Nobody said you'd get *all* the loot, you stupid oafs. Do we look like fools, ourselves?" She pointed imperiously at the fleet of Ethiopian warships moored in the bay. The ships were quite visible in the moonlight, since the tent flaps had been pulled aside to allow the cooling breeze to enter.

"*Those*, you ignorant dolts, are what are called *warships*." Snort, snort. "As different from your pitiful canoes as a lion from a sheep." Sneer, sneer. "You *do* know what a sheep is, don't you? You should. You've fucked them often enough, since you're too ugly to seduce a woman and too clumsy to catch one."

The Arabs laughed uproariously. Then, settling comfortably on their haunches, they readied for some serious bargaining. Clearly, the Roman was a woman they could do business with. A marvelous command of insult, even if her words were stumbling and prosaic. But allowances had to be made. Arabic was not her native tongue, after all.

Antonina clapped her hands, like a schoolteacher commanding the attention of stupid and unruly students. The Arabs grinned.

"The Axumite warships are quite capable of bringing down the Malwa vessels. The problem is—they're fighting ships. Not much room, with all the soldiers, to carry off loot." Her next words, Antonina spoke very slowly, so that imbeciles might be able to follow her simple reasoning.

"We . . . will . . . take . . . what . . . we . . . can. You . . . get . . . the . . . rest. Do . . . you . . . understand?"

Suspicion came back, in full force.

Why would you offer us charity? Are we fools? A trap! A trap! One of them began warning his fellows that the treacherous Romans and Ethiopians were trying to steal their dhows, but he was silenced by scowls. Insulting, that was, to their intelligence. The Arabs knew perfectly well the Ethiopians were about as interested in patched-together dhows as they were in camel dung. Still—

Why?

"We are at war with Malwa," was Antonina's reply. "We will strike their convoy, but we are not seeking loot as such. After we are done, we will sail east, to storm their fortress at Barbaricum. Burn it to the ground. In war, you must move quickly. We will not have time to plunder the entire convoy and make sure it is completely destroyed. We simply cripple it, take what we can—quickly—and be on our way. You will finish them off."

She leaned back, gazing on them serenely. Like a schoolteacher, satisfied that she had—*finally*—hammered home the simple lesson. "With your help, we strike the hardest blow at Malwa. With our help, you get much plunder. That's the bargain."

It took two more hours. But it was not really difficult. Most of the time was spent haggling over the peripheral details.

The Arabs would stay out of sight of land, like the Ethiopians. They would obey the orders of the flotilla commander. (Here, Antonina pointed to Ousanas; the hunter began honing his spear.) They would not wander off if they spotted a lone merchant ship. And so on, and so forth.

Not difficult. Those men knew a good bargain when they saw one. Even if they weren't geniuses.

Chapter 27

THE TIGRIS

Autumn, 532 A.D.

"You seem unhappy, Sanga," commented Damodara. "Why is that?"

The Malwa lord had drawn up his horse next to the Rajput king, on a slope of the foothills. Damodara gestured at the floodplain below them. A large river was clearly visible, a few miles in the distance, wending its slow way to the sea. "I should think you'd be delighted at the sight of the Tigris. *Finally*."

Rana Sanga rubbed the scar on his left cheek. Then, realizing what he was doing, drew away the hand. He was a king of Rajputana. Battle scars should be ignored with dignity.

Still frowning, Sanga twisted in his saddle and stared back at the mountains. The peaks of the Zagros front range loomed behind them, like unhappy giants. They, too, seemed creased with worry.

"Something's wrong," he muttered. Sanga brought his gaze back, staring down at the slope before them. The rolling ground was sprinkled with Rajput cavalrymen. Each cavalry platoon was accompanied by a Pathan tracker, but the presence of the trackers was redundant. The huge trail left by the Roman army would have been obvious—quite literally—to a blind man. Ten thousand horses, and as many pack mules, tear up soil like a Titan's plow.

"Why do you say that?" asked Damodara. "Are you still concerned that our advance scouts haven't made contact with Belisarius?" The Malwa lord shrugged. "I don't find that odd. Once Belisarius made the decision to retreat into Mesopotamia, he had every reason to move as quickly as possible. We, on the other hand, have been moving cautiously and slowly. He might have been laying an ambush."

Damodara pointed to the floodplain, sweeping his hand in a wide arc. "There's no way to set an ambush *there*, Rana Sanga. That land is as flat as a board. You can see for miles."

The Malwa commander eased back in his saddle. "We don't know where he is, that is true. Ctesiphon. More likely Peroz-Shapur. Somewhere else, perhaps. But that he is in the floodplain cannot be doubted. You could hardly ask for a clearer trail."

Sanga's lips twisted. "No, you couldn't. And that's exactly what bothers me." Again, he twisted in the saddle, staring back at the mountains. "In my experience, Lord Damodara, Belisarius is most to be feared when he seems most obvious."

Damodara felt a moment's irritation at Sanga's stubborn gloom, but he squelched it. He had learned not to dismiss Sanga's presentiments. The Rajput king, for all his aristocratic trappings, had the combat instincts of a wild animal. The man was as fearless as a tiger, but without a tiger's assumption of supremacy.

Damodara almost laughed at the image which came to him. A mouse the size of a tiger, with a tiger's fangs and claws, wearing Sanga's frowning face. Furious worry; fretting courage.

Sanga was still staring at the mountains. "I cannot help remembering," he said slowly, "another trail left by Belisarius." He jerked his head slightly, motioning to the floodplain below. "Just as obvious as that one."

He settled himself firmly in the saddle. Then, turning to Damodara, he said: "I would like your permission to retrace our steps. I would need several of my Pathan trackers and my own clansmen. You can spare five hundred cavalrymen for two weeks."

For the first time, a little smile came to Sanga's face. "For what it's worth, I don't think you need fear an ambush." The smile vanished. "I have a feeling that Belisarius is hunting larger game than us."

Frowning with puzzlement, Damodara cocked his head southward. "The only bigger game is Great Lady Holi's army." The Malwa lord, in Sanga's presence, did not bother with the fiction that Great Lady Holi was simply accompanying the Malwa Empire's main force in Mesopotamia. Sanga knew as well as Damodara that "Great Lady Holi" was a human shell. Within the exterior of an old woman rested the divine creature from the future named Link. Link, and Link alone, commanded that huge army.

"There are more than a hundred and fifty thousand men in that army, Rana Sanga," protested Damodara. "Even now that they have left the fortifications of Charax, and are marching north along the Euphrates, they can have nothing to fear from Belisarius. Military genius or not, the man's army is simply too small to threaten them."

Sanga shrugged. "I do not claim to have any answers, Lord Damodara. But I am almost certain that *that*"—he pointed to the trail left by the Roman army—"is a knife-cut on a horse's hoof."

Damodara did not understand the last remark, but he did not press Sanga for an explanation. Nor did he withhold his permission. Why should he? On the open plain, Belisarius posed no real threat to his army either. He could afford, for two weeks, to lose the services of Rana Sanga and five hundred Rajput cavalrymen.

"Very well," he said. Damodara paused, rubbing his lower back. "Probably just as well. The army is weary. While you're gone, we'll make camp by the Tigris. After six months of campaigning, the soldiers could use some rest."

Chapter 28

THE STRAIT OF HORMUZ

Autumn, 532 A.D.

Wahsi had been skeptical, at first. But, by the time the fleet reached the Strait of Hormuz, even he was satisfied that the Arabs would not give away the secret.

"Not until they discover they've been tricked, at least," he said to Antonina. The Dakuen commander pressed his shoulders against the mainmast, rubbing them back and forth to relieve an itch. The feline pleasure he seemed to take in the act matched poorly with the unhappy scowl on his face.

Wahsi had been gloomy since the start of the expedition. Like Maurice, Wahsi viewed "clever plans" with a jaundiced eye—especially plans which depended on timing and secrecy. Synchronization is a myth; stones babble; and nothing ever works the way it should. Those, for Wahsi as much as Maurice, were the Trinity.

"Doesn't really matter, I suppose," he grumbled sourly. "I'm sure half the crowd who watched us sail from Adulis were Malwa agents, anyway."

"Please, Wahsi!" protested Antonina. Smiling: "You exaggerate. Not more than a third of the crowd, at the most."

If anything, Wahsi's scowl deepened. Sighing, Antonina decided to retread old ground.

"Wahsi, they saw us sail *north*. Carrying the Theodoran Cohort back to Egypt."

"They won't believe—"

"Of course they won't!" snapped Antonina. "That's why I had my Syrians babble cheerfully in the markets that we had a secret plan to disembark at Aila and march into Mesopotamia. The Malwa will be looking for the truth beneath the illusion, and that should satisfy them. Especially when they see Ashot and the cataphracts—and the whole Cohort except for the gunners—unload from the ships and march inland." She giggled. "Koutina looked perfect, too, wearing that obscene replica of my obscene cuirass."

Wahsi was still scowling. Antonina sighed again.

Exasperated, now: "Do you really think Malwa spies in Aila are going to match numbers with Malwa spies at the other end of the Red Sea in order to make sure they have the same count of the ships in that huge fleet? Do you really think anyone saw twelve ships come about, after nightfall, and sail back? Do you really think Malwa agents can see in the dark? We were out of sight of land when we passed Adulis, and we stayed out of sight until we reached the Hadrawmat." She concluded firmly: "The only ones who spotted us were the Arab fishermen of the coast, and we've got them with us now."

Wahsi had no argument. But his expression was still mulish.

Ousanas, lounging against the rail nearby, had been following the conversation. When he spoke, his own face was more serious than normal.

"Still, Antonina, Wahsi raises a good point." Ousanas gestured with his head toward the flotilla of

Arab dhows trailing the Ethiopian warships. "What will they do, once they discover they've been swindled?"

Antonina shrugged. "They'll be very unhappy with me, I imagine. So what? They're hardly likely to attack *us*. Those flea-bitten bandits have no more stomach for taking on Ethiopian warships than Malwa ones."

Wahsi stopped rubbing his shoulders against the mast and stood erect. Hands planted on hips, he twisted and glared at the Arab dhows.

"I'll tell you what they'll do, Antonina. They'll be as grouchy as so many camels. And they'll be looking to get something out of all those windless days pulling on the oars. It won't happen until we're almost at Charax. The greedy bastards will keep hoping, till the last minute, that the Malwa convoy you promised them is just over the horizon. But by the time they finally realize that there is no Malwa convoy and never was, they'll also understand what you're really planning to do. They'll land and go looking for the first Malwa, to sell the information."

He turned back to Antonina, cocking his head. "Am I not right?" he demanded.

She responded with a cheerful grin "Yes, yes. *And then what*?"

Her question produced a moment's silence. Suddenly, Ousanas whooped a laugh.

"Of course! *Then*—" He whooped again. "*Then*, a bunch of dirt-poor Arabs, for whom haggling is both art and sport, spend twenty-eight years bargaining with a snotty Malwa official over the price. *Before* they tell the Malwa anything. By which time—" He beamed on Antonina approvingly. "It's all over, one way or the other."

He transferred the beaming grin to Wahsi. "The woman's a genius. I said it before; I say it again."

Even Wahsi managed a smile. "She's tricky, I give you that." Grudgingly: "Maybe. Maybe it'll work."

Then, back to scowling: "I *hate* clever tactics." For a moment, his eyes caressed the sight of his stabbing spear, propped against the rail nearby. He sighed, scratching his scalp. "You know what I wish? I wish—"

There was a sudden cry from the lookout perched in the bow. A stream of words followed, by way of explication. An instant later, Wahsi was capering about, cackling with glee.

Ousanas leapt onto the port rail, holding himself by a stay. Once he verified the lookout's claim with his own eyes, his grin erupted.

"Thy wish is granted, commander of the Dakuen!" he shouted gaily.

Even if she had been standing on the rail, Antonina would have been too short to see. "Is it really—?"

"Indeed so! Take heart, Antonina. Your name will not be cursed, in villages of the Hadrawmat, for a trickster and a cheat." Ousanas pointed dramatically at the northern horizon. "The Malwa convoy has arrived—just as you promised!"

Chapter 29

It was blind luck, of course. The westbound monsoon season, which would bring hordes of ships bearing supplies to the Malwa in Charax, would not begin for several weeks. At this time of the year, with the eastbound monsoon breathing its last, Antonina had not expected to encounter any ships sailing back to India.

It was even bad luck, in some ways. On balance, Antonina would have preferred to encounter no Malwa ships at all on her way into Charax. There was always the danger that her own flotilla would be too badly mauled in a sea battle to carry out her task. Had the Arab dhows not attached themselves to her fleet, she would have been tempted to let the Malwa convoy pass unmolested.

But when she muttered her misgivings to Wahsi, the Dakuen commander shook his head.

"That'd be pointless, Antonina. Those Malwa spotted us as soon as we spotted them. Sooner, probably, if they're keeping lookouts on those huge masts. They would have sent a warning back to Charax, on one of the galleys. We'd have had to attack them in any event."

The Malwa convoy was completely in sight, now. The convoy had been sailing from west to east, before the wind. The Axumite fleet, approaching from the south with the wind on the beam, was intercepting them at a ninety-degree angle.

Wahsi studied the enemy ships. The hulls of the great cargo vessels had emerged over the horizon, and they could see the sails of the two smaller galleys which were serving the convoy as an escort. The galleys were already furling their sails and unlimbering their oars, in preparation for battle.

"Arrogant shits," he snarled. "*Two* galleys? For a convoy that size?" His Axumite *amour propre* was deeply offended.

Ousanas chuckled. "They probably never expected to face Ethiopian warships, Wahsi. Not this year, at least." He hooked a thumb over his shoulder, pointing to the Arab ships. The dhows were already falling back and spreading out. The Arabs intended to stay well clear of the fighting, but be ready to swoop in for the spoils. "And two galleys are more than enough, to protect against that rabble. We beat off a fleet just as big with a single unguarded cargo vessel."

He studied the five cargo ships. "Big brutes, aren't they?"

"So what?" said Wahsi, shrugging. "We're not planning to board those wooden cliffs." He cast approving eyes on the Roman gunners readying their guns. "We'll just pound them into splinters, and let the Arabs do the rest."

Privately, Antonina thought Wahsi was being overly sanguine. Like most people who had little experience with cannons, Wahsi tended to have an inflated idea of their effectiveness. But she said nothing. This was no time for doubts. Not less than two hours before a pitched battle at sea.

She brought her own eyes to bear on the men and women of the Theodoran Cohort who were struggling to ready the cannons. But, unlike Wahsi's unalloyed admiration, hers was a knowledgeable gaze.

Too few. That was her main concern. The Ethiopian war galleys, unlike the ship which John of Rhodes had constructed a year earlier, were not designed for cannons. In the time allowed, before they left Adulis, her Syrian gunners had done what they could. But there was no way to overcome the basic design problem of the ships themselves.

Like almost all warships of the time, the Axumite craft were built for speed and maneuver. Only the prows were well braced. The rest of the ships were lightly built. And even the prows, on Axumite warships, were relatively flimsy. Ethiopian naval tactics were based on boarding. Their ships had no rams.

To make matters worse, the ships were built using the method which was common to the Mediterranean and the Erythrean Seas. Instead of starting with a sturdy skeleton of keel and ribs—that method, in Antonina's day, was only used by north Europeans—the Ethiopian ships were built of planks pegged or sewn together, with only a modicum of internal bracing added at the very end. The ships were not much more than wooden shells, really. The recoil from broadsides fired by five-inch guns would start breaking up the hulls after a few volleys.

Antonina's gunners had compromised by simply bracing the hulls directly amidships. Each Axumite craft had four guns, two on a side. Fearsome weapons, true, especially within a hundred yards. But two guns do not a broadside make.

For a moment, Antonina felt a deep regret that she had not brought John's gunship with her. At the moment, she would trade half the Ethiopian flotilla for the *Theodora.* But—

She made a mental shrug. Her decision had been the right one. The problem had not been technical. It would have been possible, though very difficult, to portage the *Theodora* from the Nile to the Red Sea. But there would have been no way to do it in secret, not with the huge workforce the job would have required. The Malwa would have been alerted to her plans. The only reason to haul the *Theodora* into the Red Sea would be to go after Malwa ships in the Persian Gulf. The Malwa probably wouldn't have deduced her ultimate goal—the idea of attacking Charax by sea was insane; it was the most fortified harbor in the world. But they would have surely beefed up the patrols in the Gulf, which would be enough to stymie her purpose.

A cry from the lookout cut through her half-reverie. After a few seconds, Antonina saw the cause. The two Malwa galleys were emerging from the enemy convoy, bearing directly on the Ethiopians.

"They're brave bastards," she said, half-admiringly.

Wahsi glanced at her, then sneered. "Brave? No, Antonina. They're just swaggering bullies, who've never faced Axumites at sea."

The Dakuen commander's gaze returned to the cannons. For just an instant, admiration was replaced by something which was almost resentment. Antonina choked down a laugh. Wahsi, she thought, was half-tempted to leave the cannons unused—just so he could prove to the Malwa how hopelessly outclassed they were.

But Wahsi was a veteran. Within seconds, he had apparently repressed the childish impulse. He turned to Ousanas and said: "I recommend that we simply blow them apart on our way into the convoy. But the decision is yours, *aqabe tsentsen*."

The term "aqabe tsentsen" meant "keeper of the fly-whisks." To Antonina's Roman sensibilities, it was a peculiar title for a man who was second only to the negusa nagast in authority. But the fly-whisk, along with the spear, was the traditional emblem of Axumite royalty. Three days after his marriage, the King of

Kings had bestowed the title on Ousanas. Other than the forces in Ethiopia itself, and the troops which Garmat commanded as the new viceroy of Arabia, Ousanas was now Axum's top military officer as well as the king's chief adviser.

Ousanas grinned. "Please, Wahsi! I am still the uncouth barbarian hunter of old. I know as much about sea battles as a hippopotamus knows of poetry." He made a grand, sweeping gesture. "I leave everything in your capable hands."

Wahsi grunted. "All that philosophy has not been wasted, after all." A moment later, he was shouting orders at his crew.

The flagship continued on its northerly course, still under sail. The other Axumite warships followed the lead. Antonina was surprised. She had expected Wahsi to order the sails reefed, and to unlimber the oars. Like all such craft of the time, Ethiopian warships usually went into battle with oars rather than sails.

At first, she assumed that Wahsi had given the order because he was leery of his ships' rowing capacity. One of the problems with fitting the ships with cannons was that a large section of the oarbanks was taken out of action. But then, as she saw the grim satisfaction on Wahsi's face, she had to choke down a laugh.

Wahsi was too much of a veteran to indulge himself in the childish fancy of fighting without cannons. But she thought he had found a substitute. He would defeat his enemy without even bothering to use his oars—much as a boy boasts that he can whip another with one hand tied behind his back.

As the galleys neared, Antonina's amusement faded. Apprehension came in its place. As superior as Ethiopian ships were, compared to Malwa vessels, there was still no way they could outmaneuver galleys while under sail.

She gave Ousanas a look of appeal. He simply

grinned. So, reluctantly, she opened her mouth, preparing to urge caution on the headstrong Dakuen commander.

Whatever words she would have spoken were drowned by Wahsi's sudden bellow. *"Fall off the wind!"*

Within moments, the ship turned to starboard and was running with the wind. Behind, one ship following the other, the fleet copied the maneuver.

Antonina held her breath. They were now driving across the oncoming Malwa galleys at what seemed a blinding speed. Collision was almost upon them—and the Malwa vessels, unlike their own, had cruel rams splitting the waves.

Only at the last instant did she realize the truth. The Malwa, oared, might be more maneuverable. But they were no faster, not with the Ethiopians sailing before the wind. The Axum warships would cross their enemies' bows at point-blank range.

The Syrian gunners were excellent. And, if Antonina had not been able to bring the *Theodora*, she *had* been able to bring its gunnery officer. The best gunnery officer in the world.

Eusebius' high-pitched screech rang out. The two five-inch guns on the port side roared, heeling the ship.

When the smoke cleared—

Two five-inch marble balls, fired at thirty-yards range, had split the galley's bow wide open. Both rounds must have struck within inches of each other, right on the ship's prow.

Once shattered, the heavy bracing which secured the ram acted like so many pile drivers hammering the thin planks of the hull. The Malwa ship opened up like a hideous flower, spilling men and blood into the sea.

The gruesome sight fell behind. The second Malwa galley came up, also to port. Not enough time had elapsed for the gunners to have reloaded, so Wahsi simply sailed on. A few seconds later, Antonina heard the guns of the next ship. Then, the third; and then, the fourth.

She did not turn her head to watch the results. There was no need. Not when she had Ousanas' and Wahsi's cheerful faces to serve as her mirror.

"More food for the fish," Wahsi pronounced. He turned his eyes back to the front. Beyond the bow, he could see the five great cargo ships, less than a mile away.

"Soon, now." He pointed. "Look. They've already set up their rockets."

As if his pointing finger had been a signal, a volley of rockets soared away from one of the Malwa vessels. Of the six missiles, five skittered half-aimlessly before they plunged into the sea. But one of the rockets held a straight course until it, too, plowed harmlessly into a wave two hundred yards distant.

Antonina was not relieved by the distance of the miss. This first volley had been a mistake, undoubtedly ordered by a nervous and rattled captain. The range was still too great for rockets to have any real hope of success. But the steadiness with which that one rocket had held its course could only mean one thing.

They've fitted them with real venturi. Some of the rockets, anyway. Just as Belisarius predicted.

She took a breath. "I think—"

Wahsi was already shouting the orders. A moment later, the Ethiopian crew was swarming over the ship, erecting the new rocket shields. Each Axumite ship was carrying almost two hundred soldiers. Most of those men, under normal conditions, would have been busy at the oars. But with the ships under sail, they were free for other work. The shields were erected within minutes.

As she watched, Antonina gave herself a silent

reproof. Wahsi's determination to fight under sail, she now realized, had not been the decision of a truculent male eager to show his mettle. The commander had foreseen the necessity to erect the shields quickly.

She glanced at Ousanas. The aqabe tsentsen, once again, was grinning at her. She grinned back, accepting the jeer in good humor.

I, too, when it comes to this, am nothing but an amateur. Let the professionals handle it.

She turned her eyes to the shields. Her own professional pride surfaced. She might not know anything about ships, but she *did* know gunpowder warfare. Better than anyone in the world, she thought. John of Rhodes might have a superior grasp of the theory, but not the practice.

Except my husband. After all these months fighting the Rajputs in Persia, I'm sure he's better than I am.

The thought combined pride and worry. Antonina had no idea if Belisarius was still alive. By now, he should have gotten the message she had sent him, telling Belisarius when she would leave Adulis for their rendezvous at Charax. That message would have been taken by fast horses to the nearest semaphore station, at Aila. From there, flashing up and down the line of semaphore stations which she and Belisarius had constructed the year before, the message would have reached Ctesiphon within a day. Persian couriers would carry it to Belisarius' army in the nearby Zagros, again using the fastest horses available.

But there had been no way for a message to be returned. Belisarius had told Antonina, once, of the almost-magical communication devices of future centuries. "Radio," one was called. Such devices were far beyond the technological capability of her time—and would be, even with Aide to guide them, for decades to come.

She sighed unhappily. To shake off her anxiety concerning Belisarius, she resumed her study of the shields.

Antonina had designed the shields herself, before she left Constantinople the year before. Not, of course, without advice from Belisarius—and plenty of help, when the time came to translate theory into practice, from the Syrians of her Theodoran Cohort. The gunners and their wives, being borderers born and bred, were excellent blacksmiths, carpenters and tanners. And whatever they couldn't handle had been done by the Ethiopian artisans and craftsmen whom King Eon had put at her disposal in Adulis.

Each Axumite ship had been fitted with iron hoops on the rails near the bow. A heavy wooden ridgepole was affixed to the mainmast. The ridgepole ran parallel to the ship's hull, right down the center, its end stabilized in the stem.

As soon as Wahsi gave the order, the Syrian gunners and the Ethiopian sailors began erecting the shield. While Ethiopians furled the sails, the gunners set sturdy wooden braces in the iron hoops along the rails. Each hoop had a bar welded across the bottom to hold the brace butts. The top end of each brace had a hole drilled through it. As the gunners lowered the braces toward the ridgepole, the Ethiopian sailors began threading rope through the holes. Within minutes, the tops of the braces were bound tightly to the mast-and-ridgepole structure. The end result was a sloping A-frame which covered the bow of the ship.

Other sailors were already tossing ropes over the ridgepole and braces. Quickly, with the speed of experienced seamen, the ropes were drawn tight. The A-frame was now lashed down. The ropes provided further strength, along with a filled-in framework.

The wives of the gunners, meanwhile, had finished hauling the special armor out of the hold. The spans of boiled leather, already precut and punched with holes, were stitched onto the pole-and-rope framework with thinner cord. The sailors began dowsing the leather armor with buckets of seawater.

Antonina moved to the bow along with Ousanas and Wahsi, admiring the handiwork. Wahsi did not share her enthusiasm. "Ugly," he groused. Through a viewing slit in the shield, the commander glared down at the bow-waves, which were noticeably smaller. "Slow. Clumsy."

"Ignore him, Antonina," said Ousanas serenely. The aqabe tsentsen pointed to the nearest Malwa vessel. The huge cargo ship was less than four hundred yards away. Kshatriyas could be seen scurrying about their rocket troughs. "Soon enough, he will be glad to have that shield."

Seconds later, the Malwa vessel was shrouded in rocket smoke. Six missiles came streaking across the water.

Five missed, most of them widely. But, again, the sixth missile sped straight and true. Antonina held her breath. She was about to discover if her inventor's pride was warranted.

It was. The rocket struck the sloping side of the shield and glanced off. The shield boomed like a giant kettledrum. The missile soared into the sky, exploding fifty yards overhead.

She blew out her breath, as a second relief came to reinforce the first.

No impact fuses, thank God. Belisarius didn't think they'd have them yet. Not for cargo vessels, anyway.

Theoretically, she knew, the shield should protect the ship even from rockets armed with impact fuses. Partially, at least. If the Malwa fuses were anything like the Roman ones, they were crude devices. A glancing impact might very well not be enough to trigger them—and, even if it did, most of the force would be spilled across the shield instead of punching through. The design would have been well-nigh useless, of course, against heavy cannon balls. But the Malwa had not yet equipped their ships with cannons. Not these ships, anyway.

"Good," grunted Wahsi. "It works." Grudgingly: "I didn't really think it would."

And why not? thought Antonina merrily. *It worked at Hampton Roads, didn't it?*

But she kept the thought to herself. Both Wahsi and Ousanas knew of Aide. Ousanas, in fact, was one of the few people in the world who had entered Aide's world of future vision. But they were not really comfortable with the knowledge. At the moment, in the midst of battle, they needed surety and solid ground. It was not the best time to launch into a discussion of visions.

Besides, I've got a reputation as a genius to maintain. Won't help that any, if I admit I got my design from a future ship called the Merrimac.

Another volley erupted from the Malwa ship. Then, seconds later, a flight of missiles soared off the deck of another enemy vessel.

Wahsi ignored the oncoming rockets. He stooped, sticking his head into the entrance of the shield, and bellowed orders. The orders were passed down to the steersman at the rear.

The Ethiopian ship began pulling toward the nearest enemy. Progress was slow, of course. The shield was not especially heavy, but it caught the wind like a giant drag. The oarsmen strained, grunting with every sweep of the oars, forcing the craft forward.

Fortunately, neither the seas nor the wind were heavy. Antonina had been told they wouldn't be, as a rule, this time of year. She was relieved to find the information accurate.

Slow progress is still progress. The Malwa convoy—all merchantmen, now that their escorts had been destroyed—were simply seeking to escape the Ethiopians. But the Malwa ships paid a price for their huge and ungainly design. They, too, crept along like snails.

Ousanas verbalized her own assessment. "We'll overtake them," he pronounced. "Soon, I think."

Chapter 30

"Soon" proved to be half an hour.

Half an hour after that, "soon" became "never."

Antonina, once again, discovered the First Law of Battle. Nothing ever works the way it should.

"Pull out, Wahsi!" she shouted, trying to make herself heard over the roar of the cannons and the shrieks of the rockets. "We can't sink them!"

Stubbornly, the Axumite commander shook his head. The headshake turned into a duck, as another flight of rockets soared overhead. But there was no damage. The Syrian gunners, after a few minutes of battle, had switched to cannister. The solid shot had proven ineffective, but the cannister kept the Malwa kshatriyas from the rail. They were not able to lower their rocket troughs far enough to bring the missiles to bear on the Ethiopian ships alongside.

"There's no point!" she shouted. "We could punch holes in that damned thing for a week, and it wouldn't make a difference. We can't sink it!"

Wahsi ignored her. He was leaning out of the shield, studying the rest of the battle. The huge

Malwa cargo ships were like buffaloes being torn at by a dozen lean wolves. The roar of cannon fire, mingled with the shriek of rocketry, rippled over the waves. Each Axumite ship was wreathed in gunsmoke; every Malwa ship had holes punched in its hull—and none of them, plain as day, was in any danger of sinking. The battle was a pure and simple stalemate.

While she waited for Wahsi to make a decision, Antonina snarled her own frustration at the Malwa ship looming above her, not twenty yards off.

It was an incredible sight, in its way. The hull of the Malwa ship looked like a sieve. At least a dozen five-inch marble cannonballs had punched holes through the thin planks. But—

I was afraid this might happen. Belisarius warned me that wooden ships, in the days of sail, were almost never sunk by cannon fire. The Spanish Armada was wrecked by a storm, not English guns. The only ship at the battle of Trafalgar actually destroyed by gunfire was the Achille, *after fire spread to its magazines. The rest were captured by boarders or lost during the storm which followed. Still, I had hoped—those ships, after all, were heavily built northern European craft. Not these cockleshells. But it doesn't matter. Wood doesn't sink. It's as simple as that.*

Another volley of unaimed rockets shrieked overhead. The Malwa were simply venting their own frustration. The missiles plunged into the sea hundreds of yards past the two Axumite vessels drawn alongside.

Wahsi ducked back under the shield. The leather was ragged now, where a few Malwa rockets had struck early in the battle. But that, at least, had worked as Antonina hoped. Even the one rocket which exploded when it hit the shield had spent most of its fury harmlessly. Only five rowers had been injured, none seriously.

"We'll do it the old-fashioned way!" shouted Wahsi.

He seized his spear and began bellowing new orders. The rowers drove the ship against the Malwa vessel. Grappling hooks were being dug out, and scaling equipment readied.

Antonina started to protest. This battle with the convoy had turned into an absurd distraction. They could break off now and still make it into Charax long before the convoy could bring the alarm. The last thing she wanted was to see the Ethiopian forces suffer heavy casualties in a boarding operation.

But the protest died on her lips. One look at Wahsi's face was enough. The Dakuen commander was in pure battle fury. He would have that convoy, by God—no matter what.

She glanced at Ousanas. The aqabe tsentsen shrugged.

The cannons, after firing a last volley of cannister to clear the rail, were being hastily drawn aside. With Wahsi in the lead, dozens of Axumite soldiers tossed their grappling hooks and began swarming up the side of the Malwa ship. Their battle cry—*Ta'akha Maryam! Ta'akha Maryam!*—rang with pure bloodlust.

"Forget it, Antonina," said Ousanas. "If Ezana were here—"

Ousanas glanced at the other Malwa ships. Already he could see other Ethiopian soldiers starting their own boarding operations. And, faintly, he could hear the same merciless words: *Ta'akha Maryam! Ta'akha Maryam!*

He turned back to Antonina. "Ezana was always the more cool-headed of the two. But I'm not sure even he would be able to restrain the sarwen. Not this far into the battle. Axum has the most ferocious navy in the Erythrean Sea. They didn't get that way by being timid."

Antonina sighed, and leaned against one of the poles bracing the shield. Her face was covered with sweat and the streaks left by gunsmoke. The interior of the shielded bow, under the heat of a mid-autumn afternoon, was a sweltering pit.

"Let's just hope, then," she muttered.

"Relax." Ousanas studied her with his intelligent eyes. "You're thinking about that other boarding operation, aren't you? Where we—Belisarius and his companions—slaughtered the Arab pirates who tried to storm our ship."

She nodded wearily. Ousanas gave her a reassuring little pat on the shoulder. "Relax, I say."

He paused for a moment, listening to the sounds of combat coming from the deck above. Then, very calmly: "Four things are different, here. First, the Arabs were facing a large force of Ye-tai escorting Lord Venandakatra. These cargo ships only have a handful of the murderous bastards. Second, the Arabs didn't have cannister to clear their way to the deck. Half of them died before they made it over the rail. Third, they were pirates, not Axumite marines. Finally—"

His great grin erupted. In the gloom of the shield's interior, it seemed to Antonina like a beacon. "And finally—fool woman!—*these* sorry Malwa bastards don't have your husband to save their hides."

"Or me," he added modestly, caressing the shaft of his spear. "*Especially* me, now that I think about it." He seized the great spear and began prancing about, feigning lunges and thrusts. "I was terrible! A fury! A demon from below!"

Antonina managed her own grin. Despite herself, Ousanas' antics were cheering her up. It was impossible to wallow in misery for very long around Ousanas.

There was a sudden surge in the battle clangor. Hurriedly, Antonina stuck her head out of the shield and peered up at the rail.

A moment later, a small flood of Malwa sailors and kshatriyas began diving overboard. Their own shouts of fear were pursued by the sounds of murder. *Ta'akha Maryam! Ta'akha Maryam!* One of the leaping Malwa, misjudging in his terror, landed on the rail of her ship. His body seemed to snap in half, not ten feet from her. The sound of the impact combined breakage and rupture—like sticks in a bag of offal, slammed against stone.

Antonina thought his back was broken. It was a moot point. Even before her bodyguards, Matthew and Leo, unlimbered their weapons, Ousanas pushed past her and stabbed the fallen sailor with his spear. The great leaf blade opened his chest and drove him over the side.

She craned her head up. Another—a Ye-tai warrior—had his back pressed to the rail, fighting an unseen opponent. Not two seconds after she spotted him, she saw a spear drive through his chest. The bloodied blade was sticking four inches out of his back.

The Ye-tai was driven half over the rail by the power of the blow. He toppled over, falling into the sea, the spear still sticking into his body.

Wahsi appeared at the rail, grabbing for the haft of the spear. Too late.

The Dakuen commander's face was contorted with rage. He shook his fist at the plunging body of the Ye-tai.

"That was my best spear!" he roared. "You stinking—"

Then, everything seemed to happen at once—and yet, to Antonina, as slowly as anything she had ever seen.

Wahsi's face was suddenly a mask of—not shock, so much as simple surprise. Then, he was flying through the air, soaring over the waves as if he were a bird. The Malwa rocket which had struck him right in the spine was carrying him out to sea like a gull. For a moment, his arms even seemed to be flapping.

But Antonina, seeing the burning fury pouring out of his back, knew that the man was already dead.

The burning gunpowder reached the warhead. The rocket exploded thirty yards from the ship and half as many above the waves. The largest piece of Wahsi which struck the water was his right leg. The rest of the Dakuen commander was simply a cloud of blood and shreds of flesh and bone.

"God in Heaven," she whispered. She turned a shocked face to Ousanas.

The aqabe tsentsen clenched his teeth. Then, without a word, he took his spear and raced toward the grappling ropes amidships. Within seconds, Antonina saw him swarming onto the ship.

At first, she assumed that Ousanas was just venting his own fury and battle lust. But then, hearing his bellowing roars, she realized that he was doing the opposite. The aqabe tsentsen was taking command, and dragging the sarwen away from their pointless revenge.

Literally dragging, in some cases. She saw Ousanas personally pitch three Ethiopian marines onto the rail. He had to rap one of them on the skull with the haft of his spear before the man started climbing down the ropes.

Blood was beginning to drip over the sides of the Malwa ship above her. Antonina didn't want to think about the carnage up there. At the best of times, Axumite sarwen were murderous in battle. Now, with their regimental commander slain, they were fury incarnate.

"What a waste," she whispered. "What a pointless, stupid waste."

She stared out at the patch of ocean where Wahsi had disappeared—what was left of him. There would be no point, she knew, in searching for the pieces of his body. The fish would get them long before they could be retrieved.

She wiped her face, smearing sweat and smoke and more than a few tears.

"What a waste," she whispered again. "What a stupid, stupid, stupid waste."

It took Ousanas fifteen minutes to get the Ethiopian soldiers off the Malwa vessel. By then, any Malwa was long dead except for the few who might have found a hiding place in the hold below. Ousanas had to bully a dozen sarwen from wasting time searching the cargo.

At his order, the Ethiopian ships cast off and began rowing toward the other ships being boarded. Soon enough, the aqabe tsentsen was repeating his actions, bringing the battle to a halt.

That did not prove difficult. All five Malwa vessels had been stormed. As Ousanas had predicted, Malwa cargo ships were simply no match for Axumite marines.

Wisely, Ousanas said nothing of Wahsi's death until the Ethiopian fleet had resumed its course up the Persian Gulf. The five Malwa vessels were left behind, wallowing in the waves. Already, the Arab dhows were closing in.

When the news was passed, from one ship to another, Ousanas had to reestablish his authority anew. He was forced to personally visit one of the ships crewed by men of the Dakuen sarwe, to beat down what almost amounted to a mutiny.

"Stupid fools," he snarled to Antonina, after clambering back aboard the flagship. "They were bound and determined to go back and see that not a single Malwa was left alive."

She looked at the cluster of Malwa ships, now several miles astern. The Arab dhows were tied alongside, like lampreys.

She shook her head. "That's—"

"Stupid!" roared Ousanas. The aqabe tsentsen

gestured angrily at the ships being plundered. "What do they think the Arabs won't do, that they would?" He glared astern. "Any Malwa cowering in a hold is having his throat slit, even as we speak."

Antonina grimaced. "Maybe not. They might capture them, in order—"

"Better yet!" bellowed Ousanas. "Better yet! We can lullaby ourselves to sleep, thinking of Malwa slaves hauling water for bedouin women."

He shook his head. "But they won't be so lucky, believe me. The ships were India-bound, Antonina. Loaded with booty from Persia. The sarwen grabbed some, but most of it was left behind. Those Arabs are now the richest men in the Hadrawmat. What do they want with some mangy Malwa slaves? They can buy better ones back home." He made a savage, slitting gesture across his throat. "Fish food, that's all."

Ousanas leaned on the rail, gripping the wood in his powerful hands. The anger faded from his eyes, replaced by sorrow.

"What a waste," he murmured. "What a stupid waste. All for a stinking convoy that was never anything more than an accidental diversion."

He shook his head sadly. "We cannot even do the rites. Nothing left."

Antonina placed her hand on Ousanas' shoulder and shook it firmly.

"That is also stupid. Of course we can do the rites. We are not pagans, Ousanas." What had become her husband's most treasured saying came to her mind. "Only the soul matters, in the end. We can pray for Wahsi's soul—and those of the other men who died."

Ousanas sighed, lowering his head. Then he snorted.

"*What* other men?" For a moment, his grin almost appeared. "Wahsi was the only casualty. The only fatality, at least."

Antonina's jaw sagged. Seeing the expression, Ousanas did manage a wan and feeble grin.

"I told you, woman." He tossed his head, sneering at the Malwa ships fading into the distance. "Sheep, in the hands of Ethiopian marines. Nothing but sheep. The only wounds were caused by Ye-tai, and even they could do no better. There are no soldiers in the world as good as Axumite sarwen, Antonina, in the close quarters of a boarding operation."

He rubbed his face. The gesture was sad, not weary. "Even the rocket which killed Wahsi was fired by accident. A gaggle of kshatriyas were trying to turn it around to face their attackers. The fuse was lit—one of them killed by a spear—he stumbled, fell, knocked the rocket trough askew—"

Ousanas waved his hand. "Stupid," he muttered. "Just one of those stupid, pointless deaths which happen in a battle. That's all it was."

Wahsi's death was far more than that, when the funeral ceremony was held the next day. By then, after hundreds of Ethiopian soldiers had whispered through the night, the sarawit had come to their own conclusions.

There was a part of Antonina, as she listened to the lays and chants—there were bards among the soldiers; amateurs, but good at their business—which thought the whole thing absurd. But that was only a part of the woman's soul, and a small one at that. The soul which stood at her center did not begrudge the soldiers their myth. By the time the expedition returned to Ethiopia, she knew, Wahsi would have entered Africa's own warrior legends. His death, leading a great sea battle, would become a thing of glory.

She did not begrudge the sarwen those legends. She would not have begrudged them, even if she weren't the leader of an expedition to rescue her husband from destruction.

But, since she was, she *certainly* didn't intend to start spouting nit-picking, picayune, petty little truths. Leave that for antiquarians and historians of the future.

Ousanas spoke her thoughts aloud.

"Pity the poor Malwa at Charax," he said cheerfully, as he and Antonina listened to the chants. "That stupid death has turned a shrewd maneuver against enemy logistics into a crusade. They would storm the gates of Hell, now."

Chapter 31

CHARAX

Autumn, 532 A.D.

When the captain of the unit guarding Charax's northeastern gate was finally able to discern the exact identity of the oncoming troops, he was not a happy man.

"Shit," he cursed softly. "Kushans."

The face of his lieutenant, standing three feet away, mirrored the captain's own alarm. "Are you sure?"

The captain pulled his eye away from the telescope mounted on the ramparts and gave his lieutenant an irritated look. "See for yourself, if you don't believe me," he snarled, stepping away from the telescope.

The lieutenant made no move to take his place. The question had not been asked seriously. It was impossible to mistake Kushans for anyone else, once they got close enough for the telescope to pick out details. If for no other reason, no one in Persia beyond Kushans bound up their hair in topknots.

The captain marched over to the inner wall of the battlement and leaned over. A dozen of his soldiers were standing on the ground below, their heads craned up, waiting to hear the news.

"Kushans!" he shouted. The soldiers grimaced.

"Summon the commander of the watch!" bellowed the captain. Then, more loudly still: "And hide the women!" The latter command was unneeded. The soldiers were already scurrying about, rounding up the slave women whom the guard battalion had dragooned into their service.

Not that those women needed any chivvying. Except for the cosmopolitan sprinkling typical of a great port, the women were Persian and Arab. Some had been captured during the sack of Charax when the Malwa first took the port. Others had been seized by one or another of the raiding columns which the Malwa had sent ravaging Mesopotamia over the past year and a half. They detested their captors, true. But they had even less desire to be seized by soldiers arriving at Charax after weeks on campaign. The garrison troops were foul and brutal, but at least they were no longer rampant.

Let the poor creatures in the military brothels handle these new arrivals. The women in the guard compound were even more determined than their masters to stay out of sight.

Satisfied that the necessary immediate measures were being taken, the guard captain slouched back to his post. In his absence, the lieutenant had manned the telescope.

"Good news," announced the lieutenant, his eye still at the telescope. "Most of that lot are prisoners. Must be ten thousand of them."

The captain grunted with satisfaction. That *was* good news. Excellent news, actually, and on two counts.

First, it meant that the Malwa had scored a big victory somewhere. The captain was relieved. Ever since the disaster at the Nehar Malka, followed by a year of frustration, the commanders of the Malwa army had been like so many half-lamed tigers, nursing wounded paws and broken teeth, and venting their anger on subordinates. A victory, thought the captain, would help to ease the sullen atmosphere.

Secondly, and more important for the immediate future, it meant that the Kushans would be kept busy. The slave laborers which the Malwa Empire's early victories in Mesopotamia netted had long since been worked to death, except for the women kept for the army's pleasure. Until the new prisoners were securely fitted into slave-labor battalions and set to work expanding the harbor, the Kushans would be needed to guard them. That meant they wouldn't have idle time on their hands, to go looking for the better women and wine which the garritroopers would have stashed away. They would have to be satisfied with the hags in the brothels, and the vinegar which passed for wine in the barracks.

He could see that an advance party of Kushans was cantering toward the gate. The main body of Kushans and their captives was not more than two hundred yards away.

The captain turned, looking for the commander of the watch. The sot should have arrived by now, to order the opening of the gates. In turning, the captain caught a glimpse of the soldiers standing by a siege gun positioned on the great firing platform appended to the wall. As always, the gun was pointed toward the desert. By now, the gun crew would have loaded the weapon with cannister. One of the soldiers was removing the firing rod from the furnace. The bent tip of the rod was glowing red, ready to be inserted into the touchhole.

Angrily, the captain shouted at him. His words were not orders. They were not even particularly coherent. Just a string of profanities. Hastily, the soldier quenched the rod in a nearby bucket.

"Fucking idiots," snarled the captain. Next to him, the lieutenant shook his head. "Just what we need," he groused. "Some stupid jackass to fire a load of cannister into a couple of thousand Kushans."

The lieutenant made for the ladder and began scurrying down. "I'll get over there," he said. "Make sure there aren't any other imbeciles roaming around loose." His head disappeared below the wall. "Kushans!" came his voice.

Again, the captain looked for the watch commander. Seeing the soldier he had sent on the search standing below—alone—he cursed under his breath. The soldier looked up, spread his hands, shrugged.

Not even sundown, and the bastard's already drunk.

The captain sighed. He hated taking responsibility for anything, much less opening the city's gate. But—

He eyed the oncoming troops. *Kushans. Hot, tired, thirsty, horny*—and *they just won a victory. I don't get that gate open, they'll come over the walls and—*

The thought was too gruesome to contemplate further. The captain bellowed new commands. By the time the advance party of Kushans arrived, the gates were open. Wide enough, at least, to admit a dozen horsemen. It would take another full minute to swing the huge, heavy gates completely aside.

To the captain's surprise, the leader of the Kushans clambered up the ladder as soon as he dismounted. The captain had expected him to join his fellows at the well below. The guards were already circulating among the new arrivals, flavoring the well water with wine poured from amphorae. Doing what they could to assuage the new arrivals, who would know full well that the garritroopers had good wine hidden somewhere about. Hopefully, the Kushans would be satisfied with the hospitality, and not go searching in the cellars.

"So let's be hospitable," muttered the captain to himself. He went to greet the Kushan climbing onto the rampart, hands outstretched.

"A great victory!" he cried, beaming from ear to ear.

The Kushan returned the grin with one of his own. "Better than you think," he replied. Proudly, the Kushan pointed to the oncoming mass of prisoners. "Those are Romans. Belisarius' men! We smashed them not six days ago. Routed them! Even got their horses."

The captain had wondered a bit, seeing so many of the prisoners still mounted. The majority were marching on foot, manacled in long chains, but there were at least four thousand captives who were simply manacled to their saddles.

Then again, if I were one of those Romans I wouldn't try to escape either. Horse be damned. Just like those crazy Kushans to make a game out of hunting you down. Gut you along with your horse and then drag you with your own intestines. Drag the horse too, probably.

The Kushan leader seized the captain in a hearty embrace. Gasping for breath, but not daring to complain, the captain studied the nearest prisoners. The first ranks were now within thirty yards of the gates. At the very forefront were two tall men. One of them was so huge he was almost a giant.

The captain grimaced. *Glad I didn't have to catch that monster! Let's hear it for garrison duty.*

To the captain's relief, the Kushan drew away from the bear hug and gestured toward the nearby gun platform.

"You *did* quench the firing rods?" he demanded. The Kushan's smile thinned, became less friendly. "We don't want any accidents now, do we?" The smile became *very* thin. "We wouldn't even bother looking for your women. Time we were done, you could fit one of those siege guns up your ass."

The captain shook his head hastily. Reassurances began pouring out of his mouth. To his relief, the friendly grin returned.

"Enough said!" exclaimed the Kushan. He seized the captain's arms and squeezed them reassuringly.

The first prisoners had reached the gate. They were being marched in ten abreast, with Kushan guards flanking them on both sides. The huge one at the fore, noticed the captain, really was a giant. He positively dwarfed the man next to him, even though that man was big himself.

The captain made a quick decision.

"Listen," he said softly, conspiratorially. "You come—" He glanced at the horizon. The sun was almost setting. "Tonight, after dark. Bring a few of your officers, if you want."

He gave the Kushan a friendly leer. "We'll have some fresh young women for you." He started to make a jocular shrug, but the Kushan's hands were still on his arms. "Well, they're not all *that* fresh, of course."

The prisoners were pouring through now, spilling onto the flat expanse inside the walls. The column barely fit the gate, even as wide as it was. The Kushans were chivvying the captives mercilessly, driving them in like a human flood.

"But they're better than the broken-down cunts in the brothels." Cackling: "Last week, half the crew of a cargo ship got through one of the bitches before they noticed she was dead."

He cackled again. The Kushan joined in the humor, laughing uproariously. Apparently, he found the thing so funny that he couldn't stop squeezing the captain's arms. The Kushan was very strong. The captain began to wince.

The wince turned into a gasp. A horse had kicked him in the stomach. The captain couldn't understand where the horse had come from.

He was on his knees. He didn't understand how he'd gotten there. And he saw, but didn't understand, how a sword was in the Kushan's hand.

The sword moved. The captain's vision was blurred, for an instant, as if he were being tumbled about in a barrel. He heard vague and muffled sounds, like shouts and screams filtered through wool.

When the captain's eyes refocused, his cheek was pressed to the stone floor of the rampart. A few feet away, blood was pumping out of the neck of a headless corpse. The noise was soft, rhythmic. *Splash. Splash.*

He just had time, before everything went dark, to realize that he was staring at his own body.

Chapter 32

"I thought, at first, that you'd moved too quickly," said Belisarius. He finished cleaning the blood from his sword and tossed the rag into a corner of the room. The tattered piece of cloth, torn from a Malwa soldier's tunic, landed soddenly on a large pile of its fellows. From the grisly mound of linen, a pool of blood was spreading slowly across the stone floor, reflecting the light from the lamps on the walls.

It was a large floor. The room had once been the audience chamber of Charax's viceroy, before the Malwa turned it into their military headquarters. But even that floor was now half-stained. The blood pooling from the heap of bodies in one corner had almost joined that spilling from the rags.

Vasudeva shrugged. "I had planned to wait, until everyone was through the gates. But there was always the danger of someone spotting something wrong, and besides—"

He shrugged again. Coutzes, sitting at a nearby table with his feet propped up, laughed gaily. "Admit it, maniac of the steppes!" The young Syrian general lifted his cup, saluting the Kushan. "You just couldn't resist! Like a wolf, with a lamb in its jaws, trying to withstand temptation."

Coutzes downed the cup in a single gulp. Then grimaced.

"God, I hate plain water. Even from a well." But Coutzes didn't even glance at the amphorae lining the shelf on a nearby wall. Belisarius had given the most draconian orders, the day before, on the subject of liquor. The general had seen what happened to an army, storming a city, if it started to drink. Troops could be hard enough to control, at such times, even when they were stone sober. It was essential—imperative—that Charax stay intact until the Roman army was ready to leave. Drunken troops, among their multitude of other crimes, are invariably arsonists. Let fire run loose in Charax, with its vast arsenal of gunpowder, and ruin was the sure result.

Belisarius slid the sword back into its scabbard. "I wasn't criticizing," he said mildly. "Once I realized what caliber of opponent we were facing, I was only surprised that you'd waited so long."

Bouzes came through the door. His sword was still in his hand, but the blade was clean. A few streaks indicated that it had been put to use; but not, apparently, in the past few minutes.

Coutzes' brother was scowling fiercely. "Where did they find this garbage?" he demanded. "Did they round up every pimp in India and station them here?" He seemed genuinely aggrieved.

Maurice, leaning against a nearby wall, chuckled. "What did you expect, lad?" He tossed his head, northward. "Every soldier worth the name is marching along the Euphrates, ready to fight Khusrau. The Malwa must have figured they could garrison a place this well fortified with anybody who could walk."

"Some of them couldn't even do that!" snapped Bouzes. "Half the garrison was already drunk, before we even started the assault. The sun hadn't gone down yet!" His scowl became a thing purely feral. "They won't walk now, for sure. Not ever."

"I *would* like as many prisoners as possible, Bouzes," said Belisarius. As before, his tone was mild.

Yes, agreed Aide. **The more enemy soldiers we can shove out the gates, the more mouths Link will have to feed. With nothing to feed them with.**

Bouzes flushed under the implied reproof.

"I tried, General." He gave a quick, appealing glance at the other commanders in the room. "We all tried. But—"

Maurice levered himself off the wall with a push of the shoulder and took two steps forward. Bouzes gave a small sigh of relief.

"Forget it, General," said Maurice harshly. "If there's five hundred of that scum left tomorrow morning to push out into the desert, I'll be surprised. There'll be no mercy for Malwa, this night. Not after the men found the torture chambers, and the brothels. Any Mahaveda priest or mahamimamsa who died by the blade can count himself lucky. The men are dragging most of them to the torture chambers, to give them a taste of their own pleasures."

"*Along* with any soldier they caught within sight of one of the brothels," growled Coutzes. "*Jesus.*"

Belisarius did not argue the matter. He had seen one of the brothels himself.

Roman soldiers were not, to put it mildly, the gentlest men in the world. Nor was "gallantry" a word which anyone in their right mind would ever associate with them. Any Roman veteran—and they were all veterans, now—had spent his own time in a military brothel, filing through a crib for a few minutes' pleasure.

But the scene in *that* brothel had been something out of nightmare. A nightmare which would have roused Satan from his sleep, trembling and shaken.

Long rows of women—girls, probably, though it was impossible to determine their age—chained, spread-eagled, on thin pallets. On occasion, judging from residual moisture, they had been splashed with a pail of water to clean them off. All the women were sick; most suffered from bedsores; many were dying; not a few were already dead.

No, Roman soldiers were not what a later age would call "knights in shining armor." But they had their own firm concept of manhood, nonetheless, which was not that of pimps and sadists. The women in the brothels were all Persian, or Arab, just like the women those soldiers had been consorting with since they began their campaign in Persia. Many Roman soldiers had married their kinsfolk. Among Persians, since the Malwa invasion began, the name of Charax had been synonymous with bestiality. Their Roman allies—friends and husbands, as often as not—had absorbed that notion, over the past year and a half. Now, having seen the truth with their own eyes, they would exact Persia's vengeance.

And besides, mused Aide whimsically, **they've spent the last six months fighting Rajputs. Can't do that, not even the crudest brawler recruited in Constantinople's hippodrome, without some of the chivalry rubbing off.**

Belisarius' eyes fell on the pile of corpses in a corner. The body of the Malwa garrison's commander was on the very top. Belisarius himself had put the body there, with a thrust through the heart, after the man had failed to stutter surrender quickly enough.

For just an instant, Belisarius regretted that sword thrust. He could have disarmed the man. Saved him for the torture pits.

He shook off the thought. Took a deep breath, and forced down his own rage, seething somewhere deep inside. This was no time for rage. If he was having a hard enough time controlling his fury, he could well imagine the mental state of his troops.

That fury can't be stopped, but it must *be controlled.*

He turned his eyes back on his commanders. All of them were staring at him. Respectfully, but stubbornly.

He forced a smile. "I'm not arguing the point, Maurice. But if it gets out of control, if the men—"

"Don't worry about it," interrupted Maurice brusquely, shaking his head. He pointed to the row of amphorae lining the shelf. "To the best of my knowledge, that's the only liquor left in Charax which hasn't already been spilled in the streets. More often than not, the men do it themselves before they're even ordered. No one wants any Malwa to escape because some bastard was too drunk to spot them. As for the women—"

He shrugged. Coutzes lazed to his feet and strode over to the shelf. As he began plucking amphorae and tossing them through a nearby window, he said: "The only problem there, general, is that any woman in Charax who's managed to stay out of the brothels—hooking up with a garrison unit, usually, or an officer—is throwing herself at a Roman soldier tonight." The first sounds of shattering wine flasks came from the street below. "Can't blame them. They'll do anything to get out of here. So would I."

Finished with the last amphora, he turned back, grinning. "Even if meant being called Coutzes the Catamite for the rest of my life."

Belisarius chuckled, along with his officers. "All right," he said. "I don't care about that. I don't expect my soldiers to be saints and monks. By tomorrow, we'll have regular camp followers. As long as the women are treated decently enough, and the men are kept from liquor, I'll be satisfied. We'll take the women with us, when we leave. Those who want, we'll try to reunite with their families."

"Most of them don't have any families left," grated Bouzes.

"Except us," added Maurice. The chiliarch's gray eyes were as grim as death. He hooked a thumb toward the window. Now that the sounds of breaking amphorae had ended, the screams could be heard again.

"I'm telling you, General—*relax*. That isn't the sound of a city being sacked by troops raging out of control, raping, drinking and burning. That's just the sound of an executioner doing his duty."

After a moment, Belisarius nodded. He decided Maurice was right. The focused fury of an army, he could control.

He slapped his hands together. The sharp sound echoed in the room, snapping his officers alert.

"Let's get to the rest, then." He turned to Vasudeva. "Where does it stand with the ships?"

Vasudeva stroked his topknot. The pleasure he so obviously took in the act almost made Belisarius laugh. "The last word I got from Cyril—maybe half an hour ago—was that all of the cargo ships had been seized. Except one, which managed to pull free from the docks before the Greeks could get to it. Most of the galleys, of course, escaped also."

The Kushan shrugged. "No way to stop them, before they reached the screen of galleys in the outer harbor. Not without firing rockets or flame arrows. So Cyril let it be. He says we've got more ships than we need, anyway, and he didn't want to risk an explosion or a drifting fireship."

"God, no!" exclaimed Bouzes. The young officer shuddered slightly. Charax was a city made of stone and brick. It would not burn easily, if at all. But it was also, for all practical purposes, a gigantic powderkeg. The port had been the arsenal for Malwa's intended conquest of Persia.

"The Greeks hadn't searched the ships yet,"

continued Vasudeva. "Although I imagine by now they've probably—" He broke off, hearing footsteps. Then, waving his hand: "But let's let him tell us."

Cyril was marching through the door. As soon as he entered, his eyes fell on the pile of corpses in the corner.

"Got off too easy, the swine," he muttered. Turning to Belisarius, he said: "We've started the search. Everything looks good. Lucky for us, none of the priests were stationed aboard any of the craft."

That had always been Belisarius' deepest fear. Some of the huge ships moored at the dock had been loaded with gunpowder. A fanatic priest aboard one of them, if certain of capture, would have ignited its cargo. The explosion might well have destroyed the harbor, along with the Roman escape route.

"Nobody else?" he asked.

Cyril smiled. "The only ones aboard were sailors. After we stormed a few of the ships, the rest negotiated surrender. Once we were sure all of them were on the docks, and the ships were secured—"

His smile was as grim as Maurice's eyes. "We gave them new terms of surrender. They weren't happy about it, but—" He shrugged. "Their protests were short-lived."

Another laugh swept the room. Even Belisarius joined in. There would be no mercy for Malwa from anyone, that night. A dog, barking in Hindi, would have been slaughtered.

Belisarius turned to Bouzes. Without being prompted, the young Thracian officer moved back to the window and began pointing to the walls beyond. The gesture was a bit futile. It was still long before sunrise. The darkness was unbroken except by slowly moving Roman squads, holding torches aloft in their search for Malwa hideaways.

"All of the siege guns have been seized and manned. I talked to Felix just twenty minutes ago."

He gave Cyril a half-apologetic glance over his shoulder. "Unlike the Greeks, who have plenty of seamen, Gregory doesn't have anyone who's fired guns that size. So he kept maybe two dozen Malwa gunners alive. Felix says they're babbling everything they know, faster than we can ask."

"Good," grunted his brother. "By tomorrow morning, we can fire a few test rounds. Using them for the shot."

Again, savage humor filled the room. And, again, Belisarius joined in.

Even Aide: **Why not? The British did, during the Indian Mutiny. Unlike them, we've even got a decent excuse.**

The bloodthirsty aura of that thought did not surprise Belisarius. He only wondered, for a moment, at the vastness of the universe. Which could produce, over the eons, such miracles as a crystal intelligence learning human wrath.

His eyes came back to Vasudeva. From experience with the Kushan since he entered the service of Rome, Belisarius had learned to use him as his executive officer in matters of logistics. Vasudeva was as proficient a lieutenant, in that complex work, as Maurice was on the battlefield.

Vasudeva tugged his goatee. "Everything's still a mess, of course. Will be, till at least tomorrow night. But I'm not worried about it."

He spread his arms, hands wide open, as if he were embracing a beloved but obese friend. "There were fifteen thousand men garrisoned here, permanently. Between their stores, and the huge stockpiles for the main army, the Malwa have bequeathed a treasure upon us. We don't really have to organize much of anything. Just grab what we need, load up the ships, and get ready to leave when the time comes. Won't take more than three days."

"The Malwa army should be back here by then,"

opined Cyril. "Their first elements, anyway. Enough to invest the city."

Maurice made a fist, and inspected his knuckles. "That'll be too late. Way too late. By the day after tomorrow, we'll be able to hold Charax against them. For three weeks, at the very least. A month and a half wouldn't surprise me. Although I don't want to think about our casualties, by then."

And now, all eyes were on Belisarius.

He smiled. Widely, not crookedly. All rage and fury vanished, as he remembered that other—much deeper—side of life.

"She'll come," he said. "She'll come."

Chapter 33

THE TIGRIS

Autumn, 532 A.D.

In the event, Lord Damodara lost Sanga's services for only nine days. On the morning of the tenth, the Rajput king strode into Damodara's pavilion and slammed the truth onto his commander's table.

Damodara stared at the object resting before him. At his side, he sensed Narses' start of surprise. A moment later, the eunuch hissed.

The "truth" was a helmet. A great, heavy, ungainly contraption of segmented steel plates. A Goth helmet, Damodara vaguely realized.

"We found a small mountain of the things," said Sanga, "along with all the other gear those mercenaries were wearing."

Damodara looked up. "Where?"

Sanga glowered at the helmet. "Do you remember that small valley we passed through, where the Persians had been mining?" He snorted. "I remember noticing how fresh the mine tailings were. I was impressed, at the time, by the courage and determination of the

Persian miners—to have kept working till the last minute, with a war raging about their heads."

"The tunnel!" explained Narses. "There was a tunnel there. A mine adit."

Sanga shook his head. "That is no mine, Narses. They disguised the first few dozen yards to make it look like one, but it is really an entrance to a qanat." He pointed at the helmet. "We found those about fifty yards in. Piled in a heap, as I said. It took us an hour to move the stuff aside, and go beyond. Thereafter—"

He pulled up a chair and sat down heavily. "From that point on, the trail is as clear as the one we have been following. Belisarius' entire army—I am as certain of it as I am of my own name—took that route. Hidden from sight underground, they marched to the south. They probably emerged, miles away, in another valley. Their Persian allies would have had fresh horses waiting for them."

He slapped the map with his hand. "*That* is why Belisarius was always willing to let us move north, but was so stubborn an opponent to the south. He was protecting the location of the tunnel. It must have taken them weeks—months—to prepare everything, even with help from the Persians. He could not afford to have us stumble upon his secret by accident, in the course of our maneuvers."

Damodara's eyes were wide open. His next words were almost choked out.

"Are you telling me that—" He waved his hand, weakly, as if to encompass all of time and space. "Everything we've done, for months—all the maneuvers and the fighting—even the battle at the pass—was a *feint*?"

Sanga nodded. "Yes, Lord. It was all a feint. Belisarius was buying time, yes. But he wasn't buying time for Emperor Khusrau, or his man Agathius in Peroz-Shapur. He was buying it for himself. Until the time was right, and the preparations were finished, and he could finally strike at his true target. Now that Emperor Khusrau's retreat has drawn our main army out of Charax, the Roman can drive home the death stroke."

"*Here,*" said Sanga. His finger speared a point on the map. "*At Charax.*"

Damodara's eyes, already wide, were almost bulging.

"That's insane!" he cried. "Charax is the most fortified place in the world! Even without the main army there, the garrison is still the size of Belisarius' army. Bigger! There's no way on earth he could storm the place—not even if he had siege guns."

Narses interrupted. His voice was dry and cold, like arctic ice.

"Have you ever heard of the Trojan Horse, Lord Damodara?" he asked. The Malwa lord twisted his head, transferring the incredulous gaze to Narses.

The old eunuch chuckled humorlessly. "Never mind. I will tell you the tale some other time. But you can trust me on this, Lord. *That*—"

He jabbed a finger at the helmet resting on the table. "*That* is a Trojan helmet." Narses laughed. There was actual humor in that laugh, mixed with rueful admiration.

"God, has the world even seen such a schemer?" He laughed again. "Those helmets, Lord Damodara, tell you the truth. They were discarded by Belisarius' two thousand Goth mercenaries, now that they no longer needed them to maintain the disguise. For those men were never Goths to begin with."

Damodara's mind finally tracked the trail. His eyes remained wide. His jaws tightened. The next words came between clenched teeth.

"There were two thousand Kushans in the army which Belisarius destroyed at Anatha last year. We always assumed they were slaughtered along with the rest."

Rana Sanga ran fingers through his thick hair. Then he, too, laughed—and, like Narses, his laugh was mixed rue and admiration.

"He used the same trick against us in India," mused Sanga. "Turned the allegiance of Kushans, and then left a false trail, so that the Kushans could do his real work."

Damodara was back to staring at the map. After a moment, his eyes narrowed.

"This still doesn't make sense," he said softly. He tapped his finger on the location of Charax. "I can see where he might get into Charax, using Kushans as his entry. And, certainly, once he got in—" Damodara snorted. "His soldiers, against garrison troops, would be like wolves in a sheep pen."

Slowly, the Malwa lord rose up, leaning on the table. His eyes went back and forth from Sanga to Narses.

"But then—how does he get *out*?"

Again, Damodara's finger tapped the map. This time, very forcefully, like a finger of accusation.

"Our main force is still not more than a few days' march away from Charax. Before Belisarius could finish his work of destruction, he would be surrounded by the largest army in the world. No way to escape. He couldn't even sail out on the cargo ships in the harbor. He couldn't get through the screen of war galleys stationed in the outer harbor. And not even Belisarius—not even behind *those* fortifications—can hold more than a few weeks against fifteen-to-one odds. Two months, at the outside."

Again, the jabbing finger. "It's a suicide mission!" he exclaimed. "Impossible!"

Sanga shook his head. "Why so, Lord? Belisarius is as courageous as any man alive. I would lay down my life for my country and honor. Why would not he?"

Damodara was shaking his head before the Rajput

even finished. "That's not the point, Sanga. For honor and country, yes. But for *this*?"

Sanga stared up at Damodara, as if he were gazing at a unicorn. Or a cretin.

"Lord Damodara," he said, speaking slowly, "do you understand what Belisarius will do? Once he is in Charax—"

Damodara slammed the table angrily. "I am not a fool, Sanga! Of course I know what he will do. He will destroy the entire logistics base for our invasion of Persia. He will leave a hundred and fifty thousand men stranded without food or supplies—*and* without means of escape. He will certainly destroy the fleet at anchor there. He will not be able to touch the war galleys outside the harbor, of course, but even if he could—" Damodara threw up his hands. "Those ships could not possibly transport more than two thousand men. Even including the supply ships on the Euphrates, we couldn't evacuate more than—"

Abruptly, Damodara sat down. His face was drawn. "It would be the worst military disaster in history. A death stroke, just as you said. Our army would have no choice. They would have to retrace the route taken by Alexander the Great, when he retreated from India to the west. Except they would have no provisions at all, and far more men to feed and water. Even for Alexander, that road was disastrous."

Gloomily, Damodara stared at the map. His eyes were resting on what it showed of the lands bordering the Persian Gulf. The map showed very little, in truth, because there was nothing there of military interest. Mile after mile after mile of barren, arid coastline.

His eyes moved up. "They can't even try to retrace the route we've taken, through the plateau. We're too far north. They'd have to fight their way through Khusrau's army. With no way to replenish their gunpowder."

"We could help," interjected Sanga quickly. "With

us striking in relief, we could open a route for them into the Zagros. Then—" His words trailed off. Sanga, unlike Damodara, was not an expert in logistics. But he knew enough to realize the thing was hopeless.

"Then—*what*?" demanded Damodara. "An army that size—through the Persian plateau *and the Hindu Kush*? We had a difficult enough time ourselves, with a quarter that number of men and all the supplies we needed."

He was back to staring at the map. "No, no. If Belisarius drives home that stroke, he will destroy an army of one hundred and fifty thousand men. Not more than one in ten will ever find their way back to India. The rest will die of thirst or starvation, or surrender themselves into slavery."

Again, he slammed the table. This time, with both hands.

"If! If!" he cried. "It still doesn't make sense! Belisarius would not pay the price!"

Sanga began to speak but Damodara waved him silent.

"You are not thinking, Sanga!" Damodara groped for words, trying to explain. "Yes—Belisarius *might* commit suicide, to strike such an incredible blow. But I do not think—"

He paused, and took a few breaths. "One of the things I noticed about the man, these past months—noticed and admired, for it is a quality I like to think I possess myself—is that Belisarius does not throw away the lives of his soldiers. Some generals treat their men like so many grenades. Not he."

Damodara gave Sanga a piercing gaze. "You say you would give up your own life, King of Rajputana. For honor and country, certainly. But for the sake of a strategic masterstroke?" He waited. Sanga was silent.

Damodara shrugged. "Possibly. Possibly. *But would you condemn ten thousand other men as well?*"

Sanga looked away. "I didn't think so," said Damodara softly. "Neither would Belisarius."

Not a sound was heard, for perhaps half a minute. Then, Narses began to chuckle.

"What is so funny?" demanded Damodara angrily. Sanga simply glared at the eunuch.

Narses ignored Damodara. He returned Sanga's glare with a little smile, and a question.

"Whom do you trust most of all in this world, King of Rajputana? If your life depended on cutting a rope, in whose hands would you want the blade?"

"My wife," came the instant reply.

Narses grinned. A second later, the eyes of Sanga and Damodara were riveted back to the map. And, a second after that, moved off the map entirely—as if, somewhere on the floor, they could find the portion which displayed Egypt, Ethiopia, and the Erythrean Sea.

They barely registered Narses' words. Still chuckling: "Now we know—*now*, at last we understand. Why Belisarius put his own wife in charge of the Roman expedition to Egypt and Ethiopia. You remember? We wondered about it. Why risk her? Any one of his best officers could have commanded that expedition. But if your life depended on it—yours and ten thousand others—oh, yes. Then, yes. Then you'd want a wife, and no other."

"How can any man think that far ahead?" whispered Damodara. "And even if he could—how could they coordinate their movements?"

Sanga crossed his heavy arms, and closed his eyes. Then, speaking slowly: "As to the first, he did not have to plan everything down to the last detail. Belisarius is a brilliant tactician as well as a strategist. He would have relied on himself to create the openings, where needed. As to the other, they have their semaphore stations. And—"

All traces of anger left his face. His eyes reopened.

"I have often noticed, from my own life, how closely the thoughts of a man and his wife can run together. Like the thoughts of no other person."

He took a deep breath and exhaled. "I believe Narses is right, Lord Damodara. At this very moment, I think Belisarius is destroying Charax. And—this very moment—his wife is bringing a fleet to clear away the war galleys and escort her husband and his men to safety."

The Rajput king stared at the map. "The question is—what do *we* do?"

He uncrossed his arms and leaned on the table. A long, powerful finger began tracing the Tigris. "We can do nothing to help the main army in the Delta. But the one advantage we have now is that Belisarius is no longer barring our way. We can strike north, into Assyria, and—"

"*No!*"

Startled, Sanga stared at Narses. The old eunuch rarely intervened in purely military discussions. And then, with diffidence.

Narses arose. "I say—*no*." He looked to Damodara. "This army is the best army in the Malwa Empire, Lord. Within a month—two, at the outside—it will be the *only* Malwa army worth talking about, west of the Indus. I urge you, Lord, not to throw that army away."

Narses pointed to the map. "If you go north to Assyria—then what? You could wreak havoc, to be sure. Possibly even march into Anatolia. But you are not strong enough, with your army alone, to conquer either Persia or Rome. And your army will suffer heavy casualties in the doing. Very heavy."

Damodara was frowning. "Then what do you suggest, Narses?"

The eunuch shrugged. "Do nothing, at the moment." He cast a glance at Sanga. The Rajput king was scowling, but there was no anger in the expression. He seemed more like a man puzzled than anything else.

"Do nothing, Lord," repeated Narses. "Until the situation is clarified. Who knows? The emperor may very well want you to return to India, as soon as possible. Not even the Malwa Empire can withstand the blow which Belisarius is about to deliver, without being shaken to its very roots. The Deccan rebellion rages hot. Others may erupt. You may be needed in India, very soon—not in Assyria. And, if so, best you should return to India—"

The last words were spoken with no inflection at all. Which only made them the more emphatic.

"*—with the best army in the possession of the Malwa dynasty. Intact, and in your hands.*"

Damodara's eyes seemed to widen, a bit. Then, his eyelids lowered.

"Narses raises a good point, Sanga," he murmured, after a moment's thought. "I think we must give it careful consideration."

His eyes opened. The lord straightened in his chair and issued commands.

"Have the men make camp, Rana Sanga. A strong camp, on the near bank of the Tigris. Not permanent, but no route-camp either. We might be here for several weeks. And begin the preparations for a possible march back across the plateau."

His eyes closed again. "It is true, what Narses says. Who knows what the future will bring? We might, indeed, be needed back in India soon."

Sanga hesitated, for perhaps a second or two. Then, with a little shrug, he rose and left the pavilion.

When he was gone, Lord Damodara opened his eyes and gazed at Narses. The gaze of a Buddha, that was.

"I have been thinking," he said serenely, "of what Belisarius said to me. When he swore that what he wished to discuss with you in private would cause no harm. To *me*, that is. As I think back, I realize it was a very carefully phrased sentence. Would you agree?"

Narses nodded immediately. His own face was as placid and expressionless as Damodara's. "Oh yes, Lord. That's the nature of oaths, you know. They are always very specific."

Damodara gazed at him in silence. Still, like a Buddha.

"So they are," he murmured. "Interesting point."

He looked away, staring at nothing. His eyes seemed quite unfocused.

"We will do nothing, at the moment," he mused softly. "Your advice is well taken, Narses. Nothing, at the moment. So that, whatever the future brings, Malwa's best army will be available for—whatever is needed."

"Nothing," agreed Narses. "At the moment."

"Yes. That is the practical course. And I am a practical man."

Chapter 34

CHARAX

Autumn, 532 A.D.

Belisarius peered between the shields which Anastasius and Gregory were holding up to shelter him. They themselves were crouching far enough below the battlements to be protected from the swarm of incoming arrows, but Belisarius had insisted on observing the siege personally. That meant sticking his head up, despite the unanimous disapproval of his officers.

"You were right, Gregory," he murmured. "They'll have their siege guns ready by tomorrow evening. But no sooner. As it is, they'll have to work through the night. If they try to fire them now, before they've laid stone platforms, the recoil will probably spill the guns."

Gregory refrained from any comment. Maurice, in his place, would have already been uttering sarcastic phrases. *I told you so* would have had been cheerfully tossed with *What? I am blind?* and *A commanding general has to risk his neck to play scout?*

But Maurice had a unique relationship with Belisarius. Gregory did not feel himself in a position to reprove his general. Even if the damned fool *did* insist on taking needless risks.

Belisarius ducked below the ramparts. Gregory and Anastasius lowered their shields, sighing with relief.

"We could sally," said Gregory. "Try to spike the guns. Probably couldn't get close enough, but we might be able to fire the carriages."

Belisarius shook his head. "It'd be pure suicide. The main body of the Malwa army hasn't arrived yet, but there are at least thirty thousand men out there. Ye-tai and Kushans, most of them, along with a few Rajput cavalry contingents."

Belisarius shook his head again. The gesture was almost idle, however. Most of the general's mind seemed to be concentrated elsewhere.

"Not a chance, Gregory. Not even if we sallied with every man we've got. The Malwa know as well as we do that those guns are the key to smashing their way into Charax quickly. That's why they cannibalized most of their supply ships in order to get them down here as quickly as they could. They probably hope they might retake the city before we destroy it completely."

Belisarius fell silent. His eyes were now turned completely away from the enemy beyond the walls. He was studying the interior of Charax. The city, like most great ports, was a labyrinth. Other than the docks themselves and the small imperial quarter where, in times past, the Persian viceroys had held court, Charax was a jumbled maze of narrow streets. At one time, from what he could tell, the city had been blessed with a few small squares and plazas. But over the years, the necessities and realities of commerce had made themselves felt. Charax was a city of tenements, warehouses, bazaars, entrepôts, hostels, inns, brothels, and a multitude of other buildings designed for handling sailors and their cargoes. The construction, throughout, was either mud brick or simple fill, plastered with gypsum.

Rubble, in short, just waiting to happen.

"If we can keep it from burning . . ." he mused. His thoughts ranged wide, traversing the centuries which Aide had shown him.

You are thinking of Stalingrad.

Belisarius scratched his chin. *Yes, Aide. How long did Chuikov's men hold out, in the ruins? Before the counteroffensive was finally launched?*

Longer than *we* will need. Fighting street by street is the most difficult combat imaginable, if you are not concerned with saving the city.

Belisarius grinned. The feral expression would have been worthy of Valentinian.

I'm planning to wreck it anyway. I was going to do it all at once, when we left. But there's no reason not to make a gala affair out of the business. Why settle for an evening ball, when you can hold dances every night? For weeks, if need be.

He made his decision, and turned to Gregory.

"How long would it take you to turn the siege guns around? *Our* siege guns, I mean—the ones facing the sea from the south wall. I want them facing into the city."

Gregory started. "What about—?" The cataphract paused. His eyes went to the south. From his elevation, on the ramparts of the northern wall, Gregory could see all the way across the city to the harbor beyond. The twenty Malwa galleys patrolling just outside the range of the seaward siege guns were clearly visible.

Gregory answered his own question. "Guess we don't really need them, against the galleys." He frowned for a moment or two, thinking.

"I'd need at least three days, general. Probably four, maybe five." Apologetically: "The things are huge. The only reason we could do it at all, in less than two weeks, is because I can use the dockside cranes—"

Belisarius patted his arm. "Five days is fine, Gregory. Take a week. You'll need to build new ramparts, don't forget. Protecting them from fire coming from *inside* the city."

Gregory's eyes widened. "You're going to let them in!"

Belisarius nodded. "They'll breach the walls, anyway, once the siege guns start firing. Rather than waste men trying to hold the wall against impossible odds, we'll just let them come in. Then—" He pointed to the rabbit warren of the city. "The more walls and buildings they shatter, the worse it'll get for them. We can set mines and booby traps everywhere. We'll retreat through the city, day after day, destroying it as we go. The Malwa will have to charge cataphracts and musketeers across the worst terrain I can think of. By the time they pin us on the docks, they'll have lost thousands of men. *Tens* of thousands, more like."

For a moment, Belisarius' normally calm face was set in lines of savage iron. "Even if Antonina never arrives, and we die here, I intend to gut this Malwa beast. One way or the other."

He rose up, in a half-crouch. "Let's do it," he commanded. "I'll have Felix replace you in command of the pikemen. He's due for another promotion, anyway. You concentrate on the siege guns. Once we get them turned around, it'll be the Malwa facing cannister. They'll never be able to get their own siege guns into the rubble."

Gregory studied the far-distant southern walls of the city, facing the sea. "They'll still have the range—"

Belisarius snorted. "With what kind of accuracy? Sure, a few rounds will hit the harbor. But most of them will miss, and those guns take forever to reload. Whereas the farther back they push us, the closer they get to our own artillery."

Gregory's grin became feral. "Yeah, they will. And before they get into cannister range—you know that idea you had, about chain shot?"

Belisarius had intended to leave immediately. But the enthusiasm on the gunnery officer's face was irresistible. And so, for a few pleasant minutes, a general and his subordinate discussed murder and mayhem. With great relish, if the truth be told.

Aide kept out of the discussion, more or less, other than the occasional remark.

Unwanted remarks, so far as Belisarius was concerned. He thought: **How did we crystals ever emerge from such protoplasmic thugs?** was snide. And **Can't we just learn to get along?** positively grotesque.

By the morning of the tenth day, the Malwa siege guns had completed their work of destruction. A stretch of Charax's northern wall two hundred yards wide was nothing but rubble. Twenty thousand Ye-tai stormed out of their trenches a quarter of a mile away and charged the breach. Squads of Kushans were intermingled with the Ye-tai battalions, guarding other squads of kshatriya grenadiers.

"They've finally learned," commented Maurice, studying the oncoming horde through a slit window. He was squatting next to Belisarius in a tower, less than two hundred yards from what had been Charax's northern wall. The elevated position gave both men a clear view of the battleground.

Belisarius was still breathing heavily from the exertion of his climb up the narrow stairs. He had arrived at the top of the tower just seconds earlier. Maurice had flatly refused to allow him up until the siege guns had ceased firing. The chiliarch hadn't wanted to risk a stray round killing the Roman commander.

Belisarius had tried to argue the point with his

nominal subordinate, but Maurice had refused to budge. More to the point, *Anastasius* had refused to budge. The giant had made clear, in simple terms, that he was quite prepared to enforce Maurice's wishes by the crude expedient of picking Belisarius up and holding him off the ground.

"What's happening?" demanded Belisarius. The general put his eye to another window. For a moment, he was disoriented by the narrow field of vision. The slit window had been designed for archers. At one time, until Charax expanded, the tower he was perched in had been part of the city's original defensive walls.

"They've finally learned," repeated Maurice. He poked a stubby finger into the window slit. "Look at them, lad. The Ye-tai are leading the charge now, instead of driving regulars forward. And they're using Kushans as light infantry to cover the grenadiers." After a moment, he grunted: "Good formation. Same way I'd do it, without musketeers."

He turned and grinned at the general. "I'll bet that monster Link is kicking itself in its old woman's ass. Wishing it hadn't screwed up with the muskets."

Belisarius returned the grin. Three days before, in one of the warehouses by the docks, the Roman soldiers had found two hundred crates full of muskets. The weapons were still covered with grease, protecting them from the salt air of their sea voyage. The Malwa Empire had finally produced handcannons, clear enough. And, just as clearly, hadn't gotten them to Mesopotamia in time to do Link any good. Belisarius suspected that Link had intended to start training a force of musketeers. Three of the crates had been opened, and the weapons cleaned. But the gunpowder *hadn't* arrived in Charax yet. At least, the Roman soldiers investigating the warehouses and preparing them for demolition hadn't discovered any.

The best laid plans of mice and men, said Aide. **I guess it applies to gods, too.**

Belisarius smiled. The muskets were all lying underwater, now, in Charax's harbor. The Roman musketeers had taken one look at the things and pronounced them unfit for use. Too crude. Too poorly made. Most of all—*not our stuff. Furrin' junk.*

In truth, Belisarius hadn't thought the Malwa devices were much inferior to Roman muskets. But he had allowed the musketeers their pleasant hour, pitching "furrin' junk" into the sea. He had as many muskets as he needed, anyway, and the escape ships would be crowded enough already. There were at least six thousand Persian civilians to be evacuated, along with the Roman troops.

The first wave of Ye-tai was already clambering over the rubbled wall. Volleys of grenades were sailing over their heads, clearing the way.

There was no way to be cleared, however. As soon as the siege guns began firing, Maurice had pulled back the troops on the wall. Those soldiers had long since taken up new positions.

"When?" asked Maurice.

Belisarius studied the assault through the slit window. What had been the northern wall was now an ant heap, swarming with Ye-tai. The soldiers were making slow progress, stumbling over the broken stones, but at least five hundred were now into the level ground inside the city.

If the Ye-tai hadn't been seized by the fury of their charge, they might have wondered about that level ground. An area fifty yards wide, just within the northern wall, had been cleared by Belisarius' troops. "Cleared," in the sense that the buildings had been hastily knocked apart. The sun-dried bricks hadn't been hauled away, simply spread around. The end result was a field of stones and wall stumps, interspersed with small mounds of mud brick.

They might have wondered about those mounds, too. But they would have no time to do so.

There were now at least a thousand Ye-tai packed into the level ground, along with perhaps two hundred Kushans and kshatriyas. The Malwa soldiers were advancing toward the first line of still-intact buildings. They were moving more slowly now, alert for ambush. Kshatriya grenadiers began tossing grenades into the first buildings.

"*Now,*" said Belisarius. Maurice whistled. A moment later, the small squad of cornicenes in a lower level of the tower began blowing their horns. The sound, confined within the stone walls of the tower, had an odd timbre. But the soldiers waiting understood the signal.

Dozens of fuses were lit. Fast-burning fuses, these. Three seconds later, the holocaust began.

The mud brick mounds scattered everywhere erupted, as the huge amphorae buried within them were shattered by explosive charges. The amphorae—great two-handled jugs—had been designed to haul grain. But they held naphtha just as nicely.

Some of the jugs were set afire by the explosions. Mud brick mounds became blooming balls of flame and fury, incinerating the soldiers crowded around them.

Most of the jugs did nothing more than shatter, spilling their contents. The naphtha they contained was crude stuff. Undistilled, and thick with impurities. Explosive charges alone were not usually enough to set it aflame. But the charges did send clouds of vapor and streams of smelly naphtha spewing in all directions. Within seconds, most of the Malwa soldiers packing the level ground were coated with the substance.

The next round of charges went off. Mines, disguised with rubble, had been laid against the walls of the nearest tenement buildings. They had been manufactured over the past few days by Roman troops working in the harbor's warehouses, smithies and repair shops.

The mines, too, were crude. Not much more than buckets, really, packed with explosives and laid on their sides. Some were copper kettles, but most were simply amphorae reinforced with iron hoops. Wooden lids held the charges from spilling out.

These mines were designed for incendiary purposes. As soon as the charges in the bases of the buckets were fired, combustible materials saturated with distilled naphtha spewed forth. Hundreds—thousands—of burning objects rained all over the ground before them, igniting the crude naphtha which already saturated the area.

Within seconds, hundreds of Malwa troops had been turned into human torches. All other sounds were submerged under a giant's scream.

"Jesus," whispered Maurice, peering through the slit. "Jesus, forgive us our sins."

Belisarius, after a few seconds, turned away. His face seemed set in stone.

"That should stop the charge," he said. "From now on, they'll advance like snails."

Maurice's gaze was still fixed on the human conflagration below. It could not be said that he turned pale, but his cheeks were drawn. He hissed a slow breath between clenched teeth.

Then, with a quick, harsh shake of the head, he too turned away.

He glanced at Belisarius. "Snails? They'll advance like trees growing roots, more like." Again, hissing: "*Jesus.*"

Musketeers began to clamber onto the tower platform and take their places at the arrow slits. Belisarius and Maurice edged through the soldiers and started descending the stairs. Both men were silent.

Vocally, at least. Trying to shake off the horror, Belisarius spoke to Aide.

That was what you meant, isn't it?

Aide understood the question. His mind and Belisarius', over the years, had entwined their own roots.

Yes. Wars of the future will not really be civilized, even when the Geneva Convention is followed. More antiseptic, perhaps, in the sense that men can murder each other at a distance, where they can't see the face of the enemy. But, if anything, I think that makes war even more inhumane.

It did not seem strange—neither to the man nor the crystal—that Aide should use the word "inhumane" as he did. From the "inside," so to speak. Nor did it seem strange that, having used the word, Aide should also accept the consequence. If there had been any accusation in the word, it had been aimed as much at himself as the men who fired the naphtha. Had it not been Aide, after all, who showed Belisarius the claymore mines of the future?

The question of Aide's own humanity had been settled. The Great Ones had created Aide and his folk, and given them the name of "people." But, as always, that was a name which had to be established in struggle. Aide had claimed his humanity, and that of his crystal clan in the human tribe, in the surest and most ancient manner.

He had fought for it.

Chapter 35

DEOGIRI

Autumn, 532 A.D.

Irene chuckled sarcastically. "Well, Dadaji, what do you think they're saying now?" She draped her right elbow over the side of the howdah, leaned back, and looked at the elephants trailing them in the procession. The Keralan delegation was riding in the next howdah. The sight of Ganapati's face was enough to cause her to laugh outright.

Holkar did not bother to turn his head. He simply gazed upon the cheering crowds lining the road and smiled beatifically. "No doubt they are recognizing their error, and vowing to reapply themselves to their philosophical studies."

Irene, her eyes still to the rear, shook her head in wonder. "If Ganapati doesn't close his mouth a little, the first strong breeze that comes along will sweep him right out of his howdah."

She craned her neck a bit, trying to get a better glimpse of the elephants plodding up the road behind the Keralans. "Same goes for the Cholan envoys. And the Funanese, from what I can see." Again, she shook her head—not in wonder, this time, but cheerful condemnation. "O ye of little faith," she murmured.

She removed her elbow and turned back into her own howdah. For a moment, Irene's eyes met those of the woman sitting across from her, nestled into Holkar's arm. Dadaji's wife smiled at her. The expression was so shy—timid, really—that it was almost painful to see.

Irene immediately responded with her own smile, putting as much reassurance into the expression as she possibly could. Dadaji's wife lowered her gaze almost instantly.

Poor Gautami! She's still in shock. But at least I finally got a smile from her.

Irene moved her eyes away from the small, gray-haired woman tucked under Holkar's shoulder. She felt a deep sympathy for her, but knew that any further scrutiny would just make Holkar's wife even more withdrawn. The problem was not that Gautami was still suffering any symptoms from her long captivity. Quite the opposite, in truth. Gautami had gone from being the spouse of a modest scribe in a Maratha town to a Malwa kitchen slave, and then from a slave to the wife of ancient Satavahana's peshwa. The latter leap, Irene thought, had been in some ways even more stressful than the first plunge. The poor woman, suddenly discovering herself in India's most rarified heights, was still gasping for breath.

Looking away, Irene caught sight of yet another column of Marathas approaching the road along which Shakuntala was making her triumphant procession toward Deogiri. The gentle smile she had bestowed on Gautami was transformed into something vastly more sanguine—a grin that bordered on pure savagery.

"Column," actually, was an inappropriate word.

"Motley horde" better caught the reality. At the forefront, whooping and hollering, came perhaps two dozen young men. Five of them were on horseback, prancing forward and then back again—the self-appointed "cavalry" of whatever village had produced them. The rest were marching—half-charging, say better—on foot. All of them were bearing weapons; although, in most cases, the martial implements still bore the signs of recent conversion. Hoes, mostly, hammered into makeshift polearms by the local blacksmith. But Irene could see, here and there, a handful of real spears and swords.

Coming behind the rambunctious young men were other, older men—ranging through late middle age. They, too, were all carrying weapons of one sort or another. Some among them, astride horses, even had armor and well-made bows and swords. Those would be what passed for kshatriyas in that village, nestled somewhere in the Great Country's volcanic reaches. Behind them, marching more slowly, came perhaps two or three hundred people. Women, children, graybeards, the sick and infirm, priests—Irene did not doubt for an instant that the mob comprised every person in that village, wherever it was, who could move on their feet.

The column reached the road and began merging into the throng spilling along both sides, as far as the eye could see. Irene did not look back again, but she knew that many of those people, once Shakuntala's procession had passed, would join the enormous crowd following the empress toward Deogiri. The Greek noblewoman had stopped even trying to estimate their numbers.

I had no idea the Great Country held this many people. It seems like such a barren land.

Dadaji must have sensed something of her thoughts. "Many of us, aren't there?" he remarked. Holkar swiveled his head, examining the scene. "I had not realized, myself. Nor, I think, had anyone. And that too will give them courage, when they go back to their villages."

A sudden roar drifted back from the crowd ahead. Moments later, the procession staggered to a halt. Dadaji leaned over the side of the howdah and peered forward.

"She's giving a speech again." He shook his head, smiling. "If she keeps this up—"

A huge roar drowned his words; then, like an undulating wave, it rolled through the crowd lining the road. In seconds, as the people near the howdah joined in, the noise became half-deafening. Most of those people could not possibly have heard any of Shakuntala's words, but it mattered not in the least. They knew what she had said.

For days, as her expedition to Deogiri moved through southern Majarashtra, the Empress of Andhra had given a single short, simple, succinct speech. By now, every Maratha within a week's horseback ride—a fast, galloping ride—knew its content.

Andhra is Majarashtra's bride.
My army is my dowry.
My husband will break Malwa's spine.
My sons will grind Malwa's bones.

It was not even a speech, any longer. Simply a chant, every one of whose words was known by heart and repeated by untold thousands—untold *tens* of thousands—of Marathas. By them—and by many others. The Great Country, for centuries, had served as a haven for people fleeing tyranny and oppression. The Marathas, as a people, were the mongrel product of generations past who had found a sanctuary in its hills and badlands. The new refugees who had poured in since the Malwa Empire began its conquest of India simply continued the process. Many of the voices chanting Shakuntala's phrases did so, not in Marathi, but in dozens of India's many tongues.

The roar faded. The procession lurched back into motion. Irene cocked an eye at Holkar. "You were saying, Dadaji?"

The peshwa shook his head, still smiling. "If she keeps this up, she'll be so hoarse by the time she gets to Deogiri that she won't be able to propose to Rao at all." His smile widened, became quite impish. "He still hasn't said 'yes,' you know? And he's hardly the kind of man who can be browbeaten—not even by *her*."

Irene grinned in return. "You don't seem greatly concerned. Good God! What if he says 'no'? *Disaster!*"

Holkar made no verbal response. The expression on his face was quite enough.

Irene laughed. "You should model for sculptors, Dadaji—the next time they need to carve a Buddha."

Holkar squeezed his wife close. "So I keep telling Gautami." He chuckled. "Stubborn woman! She persists in denying my sainthood."

"Of course I do," came the instant response. Irene almost gasped, seeing the woman's eyes. Still shy, still half-downcast, but—yes! Twinkling!

"What kind of a saint snores?" demanded Gautami.

My God—she told a joke!

"The girl has gone mad, Maloji," growled Rao, glaring down at the elephant leading the enormous—and utterly bizarre—"relief column" which was almost at the huge gate in Deogiri's southern wall. From his perch atop that wall, Rao could see Shakuntala clearly. The empress was riding alone on the lead elephant, standing completely erect in full imperial regalia.

"Look!" he cried, pointing an accusing finger. "She does not even have a bodyguard in her howdah!"

Serenely, Maloji examined the army of polearm-wielding Maratha peasants who flanked the howdah, just beyond the stiff ranks of Kushans who marched directly alongside the empress. His gaze moved to the ostrich-plumed black soldiers who came behind her elephant.

Then, scanning slowly, Maloji studied the various military units which trotted all over the landscape south of the walled city, alertly watching for Malwa enemies. He recognized the Cholan and Keralan troops, but could only guess at the exact identity of the others. There were perhaps three thousand of them in all, he thought. It was difficult to make a good estimate, however, because of the huge crowd of Marathas which seemed to fill the landscape.

Rao started pounding the top of the wall with his hands. "What is Kungas thinking?" he demanded.

Maloji leaned back, sighing satisfaction. "I never realized how many nations there are in this world," he murmured. Then, casting his glance sideways at the fretful man by his side, he chuckled.

"Relax, Rao!" Another chuckle. "I really don't think she's in any danger from the Vile One's army."

Now, an outright laugh. Maloji jerked his head back and to the north. "Ha! The Vile One has all his troops surrounding *his* camp, while he cowers in his pavilion. For all intents and purposes, *he* is the one besieged this day."

Rao was still slapping the wall. Maloji snorted.

"Stop this, old friend!" He reached over and pinned Rao's hands to the stones. "You are being foolish, and you know it. Another report came in from Bharakuccha just this morning. More Malwa troops are stumbling into the city, seeking a haven. Entire garrisons, as often as not, from some of the smaller towns. The whole land is seething rebellion. The Great Country is coming to a boil. There is no chance in the world that Malwa will strike at the empress. Not today, for a certainty."

Rao stared at him. For a moment, he tried to pry his hands from under Maloji's. But there was no great conviction in that effort.

"She is still insane," he muttered stubbornly. "This whole scheme of hers is insane. It . . . it . . ." He took a breath. "She is endangering her purity—her sacred lineage—for the sake of mere statecraft."

For a moment, Rao's usual wit returned. "A masterstroke, I admit, from the standpoint of gaining Maratha allegiance." Wit vanished with the wind; the deep scowl returned. "But it is still—"

"*Stop it!*" commanded Maloji. Suddenly, almost angrily, he seized Rao's wrists and jerked the man away from the wall.

Startled, Rao's eyes went to his. Maloji shook his head.

"You do not believe any of this, Rao. You are simply afraid, that is all. Afraid that what you say is true. Afraid that the girl who comes to you today is not the girl you longed for, but simply an empress waging war."

After a moment, Rao's eyes dropped. He said nothing. There was no need for words.

Maloji smiled. "So I thought." He released Rao's wrists, but only to seize the man's shoulders and turn him toward the stairs leading down to the city below. Already, they could hear the sound of the great gates opening.

"Go, go! It's long past time the two of you spoke." He began pushing Rao ahead of him. Majarashtra's greatest dancer seemed to be dragging his feet.

"And let me make a suggestion." Maloji chortled. "I think you'd better stop thinking of her as a 'girl.' "

They were alone, now. Even Kungas had left the room, secure in the knowledge that his empress was in the care of a man who was, among many other things, one of India's greatest assassins.

Rao stared at Shakuntala. It had been three years since he saw her last. And then only for two hours.

"You have changed," he said. "Greatly."

Shakuntala's eyes began to shy away, but came back firmly.

"How so?" she asked, straightening her back. Shakuntala's normal posture was so erect that she always looked taller than she was. Now, she was standing like an empress. Her black eyes held the same imperial aura.

Rao shook his head. It was the slow gesture of a man in a daze, trying to match reality to vision.

"You seem—much older. Much—" He waved his hand. The gesture, like the headshake, was vague and hesitant. He took a breath. "You were a beautiful girl. You are so much more beautiful, now that you are a woman. I do not understand how that is possible."

There was perhaps a hint of moisture in Shakuntala's eyes. But her only expression was a sly smile.

"You have not changed much, Rao. Except there is some gray in your beard."

Rao stood as erect as the empress. Harshly: "That is only one of the reasons—"

"*Be quiet.*"

Rao's mouth snapped shut. For a moment, his jaw almost sagged. He had never heard Shakuntala speak that way. The Panther of Majarashtra was as stunned as any of the pampered brahmin envoys who had also been silenced by that ancient voice of great Satavahana.

When Shakuntala continued, her tone was cold and imperious. "I do not wish to hear anything about your age. What of it? It has never mattered to me. It did not matter to me when I was a girl, held captive by Malwa. It does not matter to me now, when I am the Empress of Andhra."

She snorted. "Even less! No untested young husband would survive Malwa, so I would still be a widow soon enough."

Rao began to speak again.

"*Be quiet.*" Again, Rao's mouth snapped shut.

"I will hear no argument, Rao. I will listen to no words which speak of age, or blood and purity, or propriety and custom. I have made my decision, and I will not be swayed."

Imperial hauteur seemed to crack. Perhaps. Just a bit. Shakuntala looked away.

"I will not force you into this, Rao. You have only to say—*no*. Refuse me if you wish, and I will bow to that refusal. But I will hear no argument."

"If I *wish*?" he cried. Shakuntala's gaze came back to him, racing like the wind. In that instant, she knew the truth.

There was no hint of moisture in her eyes, now. The tears flowed like rain. She clasped her hands tightly in front of her. Her shoulders began to shake.

"I never knew," she whispered. Then, sobbing: "Oh, Rao—I never *knew*. All those years—"

Rao's own voice was choked, his own eyes wet. "How could I—?" His legs buckled. On the floor, kneeling, head down: "How could I? I only—only—"

She was kneeling in front of him. Cradling him in her arms, whispering his name, kissing his eyes, weeping softly into his hair.

Eventually, humor returned, bringing its own long-shared treasure.

"You must be off," murmured Rao. "This is most unseemly, for a virgin to be alone with a man for so long."

Shakuntala gurgled laughter. "I'm serious!" insisted Rao. "People will say I married a slut. My reputation will be ruined."

She threw her arms around his neck, kissing him fiercely, sprawling them both to the floor.

"Gods above," gasped Rao. "I *am* marrying a slut!"

Shakuntala gurgled and gurgled. "Oh, Rao—I've missed you so *much*. No one ever made me laugh so!"

She kissed him again, and again, and again, before pulling her face away. Her liquid eyes were full of promise.

"We will be wed tomorrow," she decreed. "You will dance the greatest dance anyone ever saw."

He smiled ruefully. "I will not argue the point. I don't dare."

"You'd better not," she hissed. "I'm the empress. Can't even keep track, any longer, of my executioners. But there must be hundreds of the handy fellows."

Rao laughed, and hugged her tight. "No one ever made me laugh so," he whispered.

Seconds later, they were on their feet. Holding hands, they began moving toward the door beyond which Kungas and an empire's fortune lay waiting.

At the door, Rao paused. A strange look came upon him. Shakuntala had never seen that expression on Rao's face before. Hesitation, uncertainty, embarrassment, anxiety—for all the world, he seemed younger than she.

Shakuntala understood at once. "You are worried," she said, gently but firmly, "about our wedding night. All those years of self-discipline."

He nodded, mute. After a moment, softly: "I never—I never—"

"*Never?*" she asked archly. Cocking her head, squinting: "Even that time—I was fourteen, I remember—when I—"

"Enough!" he barked. Then, flushing a bit, Rao shrugged. "Almost," he muttered. "I tried—*so hard.* I fasted and meditated. But—perhaps not always. Perhaps."

He was still hesitant, uncertain, anxious. Shakuntala took his head between her hands and forced him to look at her squarely.

"Do not concern yourself, Rao. Tomorrow night you will be my husband, and you will perform your duty to perfection. Trust me."

He stared at her, as a disciple stares at a prophet.

"Trust me." Her voice was as liquid as her eyes. "I will see to it."

"I thought I might try this one," said Shakuntala, pointing to the illustration.

Irene's eyes widened. Almost bulged, in truth. "Are you *mad*? I wouldn't—"

She broke off, chuckling. "Of course, you're a dancer and an acrobat, trained by an assassin. I'm a broken-down old woman. Greek nobility, at that. I creak just rising from my reading chair."

Shakuntala smiled. "Not so old as all that, Irene. And not, I think, broken down at all."

Irene made a face. "Maybe so. But I'd still never try *that* one."

A moment later, Shakuntala was embracing her. "Thank you for loaning me the book, Irene. I'm sorry I took so long to return it. But I wanted to know it by heart."

Irene grinned. She didn't doubt the claim. The young empress' mind had been trained by the same man who shaped her body. Shakuntala probably *had* memorized every page.

"And thank you for everything else," the empress whispered. "I am forever in your debt."

As Irene ushered Shakuntala to the door, the empress snickered.

"What's so funny?"

"You will be," predicted the empress. "Very soon."

They were at the door. Irene cocked her head quizzically.

Shakuntala's smile was very sweet. Like honey, used for bait.

"You know Kungas," she murmured. "Such a stubborn and dedicated man. But I convinced him I really wouldn't need a bodyguard tonight. I certainly won't need one after tomorrow, with Rao sharing my bed."

Irene was gaping when the empress slipped out the door. She was still gaping when Kungas slipped in.

He spotted the scented oils right away, resting on a shelf against the wall. "Don't think we'll need those," he mused. "Not tonight, for sure."

Then, catching sight of the book resting on the table, he ambled over and examined the open page.

"Not a chance," he pronounced. "Maybe you, Irene, slim as you are. But *me*?" He pointed to the illustration. "You think you could get a thick barbarian like me to—"

But Irene had reached him, by then, and he spoke no further words. Not for quite some time.

Irene liked surprises, but she got none that night. She had long known Kungas would be the best lover she ever had.

"By far," she whispered, hours later. Her leg slid over him, treasuring the moisture.

"I told you we wouldn't need oils," he whispered in reply.

They laughed, sharing that great joy also. But Irene, lifting her head and gazing down at Kungas, knew a greater one yet.

The mask was gone, without a trace. The open face that smiled up at her was simply that of a man in love. Her man.

Chapter 36

CHARAX

Autumn, 532 A.D.

"I don't understand what that monster is doing," snarled Coutzes. He ducked below the broken wall as another volley of arrows came sailing from the Malwa troops dug into a shattered row of buildings across the street. The arrows clattered harmlessly into another room of what had once been an artisan's shop. A leather worker, judging by the few tools and scraps of raw material which were still lying about.

Belisarius, his back comfortably propped against the same wall, raised a questioning eyebrow.

Coutzes jabbed his finger at the wall, pointing to the unseen enemy beyond. "What's the point of this, General? That *thing* is just throwing soldiers away. You watch. They'll fire one or two more volleys of arrows—none of which'll hit anything, except by blind luck—lob some grenades, and then charge across the street. We'll butcher 'em, they'll withdraw, and then they'll do it again. By the time we finally have to retreat to the next row, they'll be moving forward across hundreds of bodies as well as rubble."

The Thracian officer rubbed his face, smearing sweat and grime. "It's been like this for two weeks now. Our own casualties haven't really been that heavy. At this rate, it'll take them another month—at least!—to fight their way to the docks. And they'll have lost half their army—at least!—in the doing."

The scowl was back in full force. "I've heard of crude tactics, but *this*—?" For a moment, his youthful face was simply aggrieved. "I thought that *thing* was supposed to be superintelligent."

Belisarius smiled. The smile was crooked, but there was more of contempt in it than irony. "Link *is* superintelligent, Coutzes. But intelligence is always guided by the soul. Which Link has, whether it realizes it or not. Or, at least, it is the faithful servant of the new gods, and their souls."

Belisarius craned his head, staring up at the broken stones above him. "Those—" He blew out a sharp breath, like a dry spit. "Those *divine pigs* don't view people as human. Their soldiers are just tools. So many paving blocks on the road to human perfection. They look on a human life the same way you or I look on a blade. File the worn metal away, in order to get a sharp edge. And if the scrapings shriek with pain, who cares?"

Again, he blew out a breath; and, again, it was a spit. "As for the tactics, they make perfect sense—if you look at it Link's way. The truth is, the Malwa have already lost this army, and Link knows it. The monster knows we must have already destroyed all the supplies in Charax—or have them ready for destruction, at least."

"Which we have!" barked Coutzes.

Belisarius nodded. "So why bother with clever tactics? And they can't use the Ye-tai they have left as spearhead troops. Not any longer. After the casualties they've taken, they need those Ye-tai to maintain control of the regulars. If those poor bastards hadn't already been so beaten down—" Belisarius shook his head. "Most armies, by now, after what they've suffered, would have already mutinied."

He rubbed his hand against the rough wall behind his back. The gesture was accompanied by another shake of the head, as if Belisarius was contemplating the absurdity of trying to wear down stone with flesh.

"The truth is, Coutzes," he said softly, "what you're seeing is kind of a compliment. If I were an egotistical man, I'd be preening like a rooster."

Coutzes frowned. Belisarius' smile grew very crooked. "The one thing Link is bound and determined to do—the one thing it wants to salvage out of this catastrophe—is to obliterate *me.* Me, and the whole damned army that's caused Malwa more grief than all their other opponents put together."

Coutzes grinned from ear to ear. "You really think we've become that much of a pain in the ass to it?"

Belisarius snorted. "Pain in the *ass*? It'd be better to say—pain in the *belly*." He gave the young officer squatting next to him a look which was both serious and solemn. "Know this, Coutzes. Whether we survive or not, we have already gutted Malwa. Whatever happens, the invasion of Persia is over. *Finished.* Malwa can no longer even hope to launch another war of conquest. Not for years, at least. Link will try to salvage what it can of this army—which won't be much. But after the Nehar Malka, and Charax—"

He groped for an illustration. Aide provided it.

In not much more than a year, Belisarius, you have given the Malwa their own Stalingrad and Kursk. Link can only do, now, what Hitler did. Try to hold what it can, and retreat as little as possible. But it is the defender, from this day forward, not the aggressor.

Belisarius nodded. He did not attempt to provide his young subordinate with all the history which went behind Aide's statement, but he gave him the gist. "Coutzes, there will be another great war against evil, in the future—or would have been, at least. Aide just reminded me of it."

He had Coutzes' undivided attention, now. The young Thracian knew of Aide. He had seen him. But, like all of Belisarius' officers, he thought of the crystal being as simply the Talisman of God. A pronouncement from Aide, so far as Coutzes was concerned, was as close to divine infallibility as any man would ever encounter.

Belisarius smiled, seeing that look of awe.

What are you grinning about? demanded Aide. The facets flashed. For an instant, Belisarius had an image of a crystalline rooster, prancing about with unrestrained self-glory. **I think "divine infallibility" fits me to perfection. Why don't *you* understand that obvious truth?**

Again, the facets flashed. Belisarius choked down a laugh. The crystalline rooster, for just a split second, had been staring at him with beady, accusing eyes. A barnyard fowl, demanding its just due. A combed and feathered deity, much aggrieved by agnostic insolence.

Belisarius waved his hand, as much to still Aide's humor as to illustrate his next words. "There came a time in that war, Coutzes, when the armies of wickedness were broken. Broken, not destroyed. But from that time forward, they could only retreat. They could only hold what they had, in the hopes that someday, in the future, they might be able to start their war of conquest anew."

Belisarius snarled, now. "Those foul beasts—they were called Nazis—were never given that chance. Their enemies, after breaking them, pressed on to their destruction." He jabbed a thumb over his shoulder, pointing to the inhuman monster lurking somewhere behind the wall. "Link knows that history as well as I do. And the *thing*, whatever else, is bound and determined to see that neither I—nor any of the soldiers of this magnificent army—are alive to participate in any future wars. Or else, it knows full well—"

He rolled his eyes, following the thumb. His next words were whispered. A promise, hissed: "I *will* be alive, monster. And I *will* give you Operation Bagration, and the destruction of Army Group Centre. And I *will* give you Sicily and D-Day, and the Falaise Pocket—except *this* time, beast, the pocket will be closed in time."

He turned his eyes back to Coutzes. Fury faded, replaced by wry humor. "As I said, this frenzied assault is quite a compliment. Feeds my pride no end, it does. Just think, Coutzes. Great gods of the future, convinced of their own perfection, have set themselves the single task of killing one pitiful, primitive, imperfect, preposterous, ridiculous, pathetic Thracian *goddam fucking son-of-a-bitch.*"

Coutzes laughed. "Can't say I blame them!"

Another volley of arrows sailed overhead. Behind them came a volley of words—the sounds of Ye-tai bellowing commands. Coutzes popped his head over the wall. When he brought it down, he was frowning.

"I think—" He transferred the frown to Belisarius. "I want you out of here, General. They'll be starting the next assault any minute. A stray grenade—" He shook his head.

Belisarius did not argue the matter. He rose to a half-crouch and scuttled out of the room. In the roofless chamber beyond, Anastasius was waiting, along with the other cataphracts who were now serving as his additional bodyguards. Maurice had replaced Valentinian with two of them, after Valentinian's capture. The cataphracts chosen had not taken offense at that relative estimation of their merits compared to Valentinian's. They had been rather pleased, actually, at the compliment. They had expected Maurice to choose twice that number.

Anastasius snorted, seeing the general scurry into the room. But he refrained from any further expression of displeasure.

Belisarius smiled. "It's important for a commanding officer to be seen on the front lines, Anastasius. You know that."

As the small body of Romans hurried out of the shattered ruins of an artisan's former workshop, heading south toward relative safety, Anastasius snorted again. But, again, he refrained from further comment. He had been through this dance with Belisarius so many times that he had long since given up hope of teaching new steps to his general.

One of the other cataphracts, new to the job, was not so philosophical. "For Christ's sake, Isaac," he whispered to his companion, "the general could lounge on the docks, for all the army cares. Be happier if he did, in fact."

Isaac shrugged. "Yeah, Priscus, that's what I think too. But maybe that's why he's Rome's best general—best ever, you ask me—and we're spear-chuckers."

Priscus' response, whatever it might have been, was buried beneath the sounds of grenades exploding a few dozen yards behind them. The Malwa were beginning a new assault. Seconds later, the shouts of charging men were blended with musket fire and more grenade explosions. And then, within half a minute, came the first sounds of steel meeting steel.

The cataphracts did not look back. Not once, in all the time it took them, guarding Belisarius, to clamber through the rubbled streets and shattered buildings which were all that days of Roman demolition and Malwa shelling had left of Charax's center district. Not until they finally reached the relatively undamaged harbor which made up the city's southern area did the cataphracts turn and look back to the north.

"Besides," said Isaac, renewing their conversation, "what are you complaining about, anyway?" He thrust his beard northward. "Would you rather be back there again? Fighting street to street?"

Priscus grimaced. Like Isaac, he had become Belisarius' bodyguard only a few days before. The initial pair of bodyguards whom Maurice had selected to replace Valentinian had been replaced themselves, after the siege of Charax began. Maurice, determined to keep Belisarius alive, had made his final selection based on the most cold-blooded reasoning possible. Whichever soldiers among the bucellarii could demonstrate, in days of savage battle in the streets of Charax, that they were the most murderous, got the job.

Isaac and Priscus had been at the top of the list. They had earned that position in one of the most brutal tests ever devised by the human race. Neither of them had heard of Stalingrad, nor would they ever. But either of them, planted amongst the veterans of Chuikov's 62nd Army, would have felt quite at home. Language barriers be damned.

"Good point," muttered Priscus. He turned, along with Isaac, and plodded after Belisarius. The general was heading toward the heavy-walled warehouse where the Roman army had set up its headquarters. Priscus eyed the figure of his tall general, stooping into a small door. "At least he's got the good sense to leave before the blades get wet."

"So far," grunted Isaac. He tugged at one of the straps holding up his heavy cataphract gear. "Damn, I'm sick of walking around in this armor."

The cataphracts plodded on a few more steps. As they came to the door, Isaac repeated: "So far. But don't get your hopes up. Two weeks from now, three at the outside, the Malwa will have reached the harbor. You know what'll happen, when that day comes."

Priscus scowled. "Sallies, lance charges, the whole bit—with the general right in the middle of it. We'll wish Valentinian were here, then."

On that gloomy note, the two cataphracts stooped and forced their armored way through a door designed for midgets. The door led into what seemed to be a six-foot-long tunnel in the massive wall of the warehouse. The effort of that passage left them practically snarling.

Five minutes later, they were smiling like cherubs.

Chapter 37

As soon as Belisarius straightened after squeezing through the narrow passage, he saw Bouzes rushing toward him. Except for a well-lit area against the far wall, where Belisarius had set up his writing desk and map table, the interior of the cavernous warehouse was dark. Bouzes was in such a hurry that he tripped over some debris lying on the floor and wound up stumbling into Belisarius' arms.

"Easy, there, easy," chuckled Belisarius. He set Bouzes back up straight. "Things can't be that bad."

Bouzes muttered a quick apology. Then, pointing toward a door on the opposite wall: "Maurice says you've got to go up and see something. He told me to tell you as soon as you arrived."

Belisarius brow was creased, just slightly. "What's the problem?"

Bouzes shook his head. "Don't know. Maurice wouldn't tell me anything else. But he was very emphatic about it."

Belisarius strode toward the door. Behind him, he heard the heavy footsteps of his armored cataphracts following. The door, like the one he had just passed through, was low and narrow. Again, Belisarius had to stoop to pass through. Except for the huge doors designed for freight, the entire warehouse seemed to have been built by dwarves.

Once through the door, he clambered up a wooden staircase leading to the roof. As quickly as Belisarius was moving, the effort of negotiating the steep and narrow stairs was considerable, even for a man in his excellent condition and wearing only half-armor. He felt a moment's sympathy for his cataphract bodyguards. They'd be huffing by the time they made the same climb.

The staircase debouched into a small chamber. Again, Belisarius squeezed through a tiny door, and emerged into open air. Behind him, the northern wall of the warehouse reared up like a battlement. Ahead of him, the brick roof—braced underneath by heavy beams—formed a flat expanse stretching toward the sea. He could see the delta, glistening under a midday sun.

Belisarius had selected this warehouse for his headquarters because of its odd design. At one time, he suspected, the north wall of the building had been the outer wall of Charax. It was built like a fortification, at least—which might explain the tiny doors. When Charax expanded, and new walls were built, some enterprising merchant had simply built his warehouse against the six-foot-thick northern wall. The end result, so far as the Roman general was concerned, was as good a field headquarters as he could ask for. The massive north wall gave some protection from artillery while, at the same time, the flat roof provided him with a perfect vantage point from which to observe the delta.

He saw Maurice standing on the southern edge of the roof. There was no railing to keep someone from pitching over the side onto the docks thirty feet below, but Maurice seemed unconcerned. The chiliarch had apparently heard the squeaking of the door, for he was already looking at Belisarius when the general emerged onto the roof.

"Come here!" he hollered, holding up the telescope. "There's a new development I think you should consider."

Belisarius hurried over. As he made his way across the fifty-foot-wide expanse, he quickly scanned the entire area. From the roof, he could see all of southern Charax as well as the great delta which extended southward to the Persian Gulf itself, perhaps ten miles away. Charax had been built on the east bank of the largest tributary which formed the Tigris-Euphrates delta, on a spit extending south and west of the Mesopotamian mainland. The tributary could hardly be called a river. It was so broad that it was almost a small gulf in its own right. For all practical purposes, Charax was a port city which was surrounded by water from the west all the way around to its east-by-southeast quadrant.

His eyes scanned right, then left. He could see nothing that would cause Maurice such apparent concern. There were masses of Malwa troops on both banks of the tributary, but they had been there since the first few days of the siege. The Malwa had tried to position siege guns on those banks, where they could have fired into the harbor area, but had given up the effort after a week. The ground, as the reeds which covered the banks indicated, was much too soggy. The troops were there simply to keep the Romans from escaping while the main forces of the Malwa tried to hammer their way into the city from the north. They also kept the galleys patrolling the delta supplied with provisions.

He turned his eyes to the fore, looking for the galleys. Again, he could see nothing amiss. There had been upwards of twenty galleys stationed in Charax, when Belisarius broke into the city. Half of them had been on patrol, and all but three of the ones moored to the docks had managed to get free before Roman troops could seize them.

Since then, the Malwa had used the galleys to maintain a blockade. Belisarius' obvious escape route was to sail out on the cargo ships he had captured. But there was no way to get those ungainly vessels through a line of war galleys. The huge Malwa cargo ships might have been able to withstand ramming—some of them, at least—but the galleys were armed with rockets as well as rams. At close range, with no room to maneuver, rocket volleys would turn unarmored cargo ships into floating funeral pyres.

As it was, Belisarius' soldiers had been hard-pressed to extinguish the small conflagrations started on the moored ships by long-range rocket fire. Link was making no pretense of saving the cargo ships to evacuate the Malwa troops. Even though the vast majority of the rockets never came close to the docks, the galleys as well as the troops stationed on the banks had kept up a steady barrage since the beginning of the siege. Belisarius didn't want to think about the disciplinary measures which Link must be taking, to keep its troops driving forward into what, by now, even the dimwits among them must have realized was a suicide mission.

I'm sure that Link has promised the Ye-tai commanders that Malwa would save the Ye-tai, if the barbarians kept the regular troops under control.

Belisarius agreed with Aide's assessment. But, as he advanced toward Maurice, Belisarius could still see nothing in the delta to cause any concern. Outside of three galleys moored to a makeshift pier on the east bank, taking on supplies, the rest were on patrol. As usual, the Malwa kept five galleys close to the harbor, with the remainder spread out between one and two miles away.

When he came up to Maurice, the gray-haired chiliarch was studying the galleys themselves. His expression seemed one of grim satisfaction.

"They haven't seen it yet," he said. "Our elevation's better."

He handed Belisarius the telescope. Grim satisfaction was replaced by—

Before he even got the telescope up, in a motion so quick he almost gave himself a black eye, Belisarius knew. He only heard Maurice's next words dimly, through the rushing blood in his ears.

"Yeah, I thought you'd want to see it, lad. It's not often, after all, that a man gets to watch Venus rise from the waves."

Belisarius saw the glint before he spotted the masts. He had been looking for sails, until he realized there wouldn't be any. This close to their final destination, the Ethiopian warships would be advancing under oar.

But there was no doubt of what he was seeing. Belisarius was not a seaman, but he could tell the difference between a warship and a cargo vessel at a glance. The twelve vessels whose masts he could see, perhaps ten miles away, were obviously fighting craft. And he had enough experience, with perhaps a minute's study, to be able to distinguish the upperstructure of an Axumite warship from a Malwa galley.

"They're ours, all right," he muttered happily. "No doubt about it. But—" He brought the telescope back to the lead ship in the oncoming flotilla. There it was again. Something glinting.

He pulled the telescope away from his eye, frowning. Not worried, simply puzzled. "There's something odd—"

Maurice nodded. "You spotted it too? Something shining on and off, on the lead ship?" The chiliarch's eyes fixed on the horizon. "I saw it myself. First thing

I spotted, in fact. Still haven't been able to figure out what it is. Might be a mirror, I suppose, if Antonina wanted to signal—"

Both men, simultaneously, realized the truth. And both, simultaneously, burst into laughter.

"Well, of course!" shouted Maurice gaily. "She's Venus, isn't she? Naturally she's got the biggest damn brass tits in the world!"

Belisarius said nothing coherent, until he stopped leaping about in a manner which was halfway between a drunken jig and a war dance. Then, before the astonished eyes of the cataphract bodyguards who had finally puffed their way onto the roof, the *strategos* of the Roman Empire and the commander of its finest army—normally as cool as ice in the face of the enemy—began taunting the distant Malwa troops like an eight-year-old boy in a schoolyard.

"That's my lady! That's my lady!" was the only one of those expressions which was not so gross, so obscene, so foul, so vile, and so vulgar, that Satan's minions would have fled in horror, taloned paws clasped over bat-ugly ears.

In the hours which followed, as Maurice and Vasudeva organized the escape from Charax, Belisarius paid no attention to the doings of his army.

There was no need for him to do so, of course. The plans for the escape had been made weeks before Charax was even seized. Ever since the Romans had taken the city, a large portion of the soldiers had been working like beavers to get ready for departure. The cargo ships were loaded with provisions. The city was mined for final destruction. All that remained to be done was drive out the horses, collect the civilians, and organize the fighting retreat back to the docks.

The horses were driven out within the first two hours. Released from their holding corrals near the docks, the panicked creatures were driven through broken streets toward the Malwa lines. It was a task which the Roman soldiers carried out with reluctance but, perhaps for that reason, as quickly as possible.

Most of the horses would die, they knew. Many would be killed by the Malwa themselves, either because they were mistaken for a cavalry charge or simply from being struck by stray missiles or grenades. Others would break their legs clambering through the rubble. Most of the horses who escaped the city, except for those captured by the Malwa, would probably die of starvation in the desert and swamps beyond. And even those horses which found themselves in the relative safety of Malwa captivity would, in all likelihood, be eaten by the Malwa troops as they themselves became desperate for food.

But the only alternative was to destroy them along with the city. There was absolutely no way to load them aboard the cargo ships. Transporting large numbers of horses by sea was a difficult enough task, under the best of circumstances. It would be impossible for an army making a hurried escape under enemy fire. Given the alternatives, the Romans would drive the horses out. Some would survive in the desert, after all, long enough to be captured by bedouin.

So, at least, Belisarius had explained the matter to his troops. And, so far as it went, the explanation was not dishonest. But the general's ultimate reason for the choice had not been humanitarian. When he needed to be, Belisarius could be as ruthless as any man alive. He knew full well that as soon as Link discovered that enemy warships were approaching Charax, it would understand—finally—the full extent of Belisarius' plan. At which point Link would order an all-out, frenzied assault on Charax, driving the Malwa troops forward as if they were beasts themselves. Stampeding herds of horses, meeting those incoming human herds, would create as much confusion as possible—confusion which would delay the Malwa advance, and give the escaping Romans that much greater a chance to save their own lives.

It took even less time to organize the evacuation of the civilians. The civilians were all women. There had been a handful of male Persian civilians when the Romans took the city. Within a day, after the women told their tales, they had been executed along with the Malwa soldiers with whom they had collaborated.

The female civilians had been warned days in advance, and now were being rounded up. But there was hardly any "rounding up" to do. Since the Romans had arrived and freed them from Malwa subjugation, none of Charax's women had strayed more than a few yards away from a Roman soldier at any time of the day or night. That was from their own choice, not coercion. They had been like half-drowned kittens, desperately clutching a log for survival.

As poor women thrust into such a wretched state have done throughout history, the survivors of Malwa Charax had become camp followers of the Roman army. Depending on their age, appearance, and temperament, they had become concubines, cooks, laundresses, nurses—more often than not, all of those combined. And if their current status was dismal, by abstract standards, it seemed like a virtual paradise to them.

The Roman soldiers, crude as they might be, were rarely brutal to their women. Belisarius' soldiers, at least. Other Roman armies might have been. But, between Belisarius' discipline—to which they had long been accustomed—and their own horror at Malwa bestiality, the soldiers had conducted themselves in a manner which might almost be called chivalrous. So long, of course, as the term "chivalrous" is understood to include: vulgarity; coarse humor; the unthinking assumption that the women would feed them, clean up after them and do the washing; and, needless to say, an instant readiness to copulate using any means short of outright rape.

In truth, the social position of most of the women was no worse than it had been before the Malwa invasion. More licentious, true. But there was this by way of compensation: the new men in their lives had proven themselves to be tough enough to give those women a real chance for survival. That is no small thing, in the vortex of a raging war. Belisarius, through his officers, had already told the women that they would be reunited with whatever families they might still have. But, not to his surprise, the majority had made clear that they would just as soon remain camp followers of his army—*wherever* it went.

The difficulty in evacuating the women, therefore, was not in collecting them. Those women who could move were gathered on the docks sooner than anyone else. The problem was that, even weeks after the liberation of Charax, many of the women could *not* move. At least a third of the women who had been enslaved in the military brothels were still too weak or sick to move under their own power. Their evacuation posed a major medical undertaking.

That evacuation took three hours, before all the litters were carried aboard the ships. In the end, only twelve women were left behind, in the medical ward set aside for the most badly abused slaves. All of them were unconscious, and so close to death that moving them seemed impossible.

The Roman officer in charge of evacuating that medical ward danced back and forth, fretful and indecisive. A nurse, who had herself been chained in one of the brothels, whispered to a Kushan soldier. He handed her his dagger. The nurse, cold-faced, ordered everyone out of the ward, using a tone which Empress Theodora would have approved. When she emerged, five minutes later, her face was calm, her manner relaxed. She had even taken the time to clean the dagger.

All that remained was the fighting retreat of the soldiers holding the front lines. Under any circumstances in the world, other than the one in which he found himself, Belisarius would have overseen that retreat personally. His bodyguards would have been driven half-insane, from the risks he would have taken. But today—

Maurice did not even bother to discuss it with Belisarius. He simply carried out the task himself. The work was not beyond his capability, after all. In truth, Maurice probably led that retreat as well as Belisarius could have. And there was an added advantage, at least to the soldiers who served as *Maurice's* bodyguards. The grizzled veteran had a proper understanding of the proper place of a proper commanding officer in the middle of a battle, thank you.

So, in one of history's little ironies, the military genius who led what was arguably, up to that day, the most daring and brilliant campaign of all time, played no role in its dramatic conclusion. Never even noticed it, in truth. Instead, his eye glued to a telescope, the general found himself undergoing a brand-new experience.

He knew, abstractly, of the anguish Antonina had always undergone whenever he went off to war. And he had chuckled, hearing the tales from Maurice and Irene afterward, of the way Antonia spent the day after his departure.

He was chuckling no longer. Belisarius, watching his wife wage a battle at sea—right under his eyes, but beyond his reach or control—finally understood what it meant. To stare at a horse.

Chapter 38

"Stay *down*, Antonina," grumbled Ousanas. The aqabe tsentsen looked to Matthew, and pointed at the woman forcing her head past his elbow. "Sit on her, if you have to."

Matthew flushed. Then, gingerly, advanced his great paws toward Antonina's shoulders.

Antonina gave him a quick glare. For a moment, Matthew retreated. But only for a moment. The inexorable clasp of unwanted protection returned.

"All right—all right!" snapped Antonina. She stepped back perhaps half an inch. Peevishly: "*Now* are you satisfied?"

"No!" came the immediate response. "I want you *down*, fool woman. Any minute now—"

A stretched-out shriek drew Ousanas' eyes back to the front. Through a narrow slit in the flagship's bow-shield, he could see the first volley of rockets heading their way from the line of Malwa galleys ahead.

"And *now* has come." He stepped back two paces, pushing Antonina behind him. With a little wave, he gestured Gersem forward. Wahsi's successor stepped up to the slit, where he could see well enough to guide the battle.

"Remember, Gersem," said Ousanas. "All that matters is to destroy the galleys. Whatever the cost. If need be—even if ours are destroyed—we can find a place on Belisarius' ships."

The new Dakuen commander nodded.

A moment later, the sound of the first rocket volley came hissing by overhead. As soon as the missiles went past the bow-shield, Ousanas and Antonina craned their heads to watch their flight.

"Way too long," muttered Ousanas. "But they've all been fitted with venturi. Let's hope the shields stand up."

He brought his eyes down to the short Roman woman standing next to him.

"I will not have you dead, when Belisarius comes aboard this ship," Ousanas said. "Not that, whatever else."

"We might all—"

Ousanas clapped his hands. An instant later, as helpless as a doll, Antonina was lowered onto the deck. Matthew and Leo each held an arm and a leg. Their grip on her was as delicate as possible, under the circumstances, but Antonina was not mollified. The entire process was accompanied by her own monologue.

"You're dismissed! Discharged, d'you hear?" was the only one of her spluttering phrases which was not so vituperative, so vindictive, so intemperate and so utterly foul-mouthed that Ousanas howled with laughter, clasping his hands over his belly.

Once her butt had been firmly planted on the deck, Antonina broke off her tirade and glared up at Ousanas. "You think this is funny?" she demanded.

Still laughing, Ousanas nodded. An instant later—even in her outrage, Antonina was stunned by the speed with which Ousanas could move, without, seemingly, any warning or effort—the aqabe tsentsen was sitting right next to her. He beamed down upon her from a height which was now only measured in inches instead of feet.

"Hysterically so," he pronounced. His next words were drowned under the sound of another rocket volley screaming overhead. Again, he and Antonina craned their necks, watching the rockets' trajectory.

"Can't see where they hit!" complained Antonina. Scowling: "Can't see anything, in this ridiculous position."

Ousanas' grin returned. "Which," he said with satisfaction, "is the whole point. You don't *need* to see where they hit. And if *you* can't see the rockets when they hit, we can hope *they* will return the favor."

Antonina's scowl, if anything, deepened. "That's the stupidest thing I ever heard! Those rockets'll go wherever they want to go. You watch!" Deep, deep scowl. "Except we *won't* be able to watch because we can't see a damned thing so the rockets'll catch us by surprise and—"

The next volley of rockets caught them by surprise. The Malwa, apparently, had adjusted the angle of the rocket troughs perched in the bows of the oncoming galleys. The first signal of incoming fire which Antonina and Ousanas received was the sudden boom of rockets smashing into the bow-shield and caroming off to either side. They only caught glimpses of the missiles streaking past. Perhaps two seconds later, they heard the erupting warheads. Both of them knew, from the sound alone, that the rockets had exploded harmlessly in midair.

Antonina's displeasure vanished instantly. "Beautiful!" she cried. "Beautiful!"

She squirmed onto her knees, raising her head high enough to be able to see over the side of the ship. Ousanas made no objection. He even gave Matthew and Leo, squatting nearby, a reassuring little wave of the hand. The essence of the gesture was clear. *As long as the fool woman doesn't stick her head and her brass tits out where any Malwa can take a shot at her.*

Antonina's lips were pursed, now, with a faint worry. "One problem, though. I hadn't thought about it." She pointed forward. "We sure enough protect against bow shots. But the ricochets might hit one of the ships alongside. There isn't any shielding covering most of the ships."

Ousanas shrugged. "Won't matter, Antonina. Luck—good or bad—will happen as it will."

The bow shield bellied again under the impact of a new rocket volley. Again, the boom, almost like a drum; and, again, two missiles caromed by. And, again, exploded harmlessly over the waves.

Antonina, scanning right and left as she stared toward the stern of the flagship, was relieved by what she saw. The Ethiopian ship captains had already recognized the same danger and were responding. Charax's delta was several miles wide, giving plenty of sea room. The Axumite ships, advancing in a single line, were already spreading out.

Antonina watched several more rockets bounce off the shields on other ships and skitter past the entire formation. The angle of the shields, she realized, was so acute that only the worst possible luck could cause a rocket to carom sideways.

"The main thing," Ousanas continued—unlike Antonina, he had not bothered to watch the trajectories—"is that almost all the incoming rockets will be harmless. Once we get in ramming range, they'll stop firing."

He chuckled grimly. "Not even a fanatic Mahaveda priest will want to be in the bow of a ship plunging in for a ram."

Antonina turned back and hunkered lower. She

studied the figure of Gersem in the bow. The new Dakuen commander, still peering intently through a slit in the shield, suddenly seemed very young.

Ousanas, apparently, could read minds. "Relax. I picked *him*, even though he's the most junior of the sub-officers, because he's also the best seaman."

"Says who?" demanded Antonina. "You know as much about boats as I do about—"

"Says all the *other* sub-officers," came the serene reply. Ousanas stretched out his arms, pointing to the Axumite ships ranging alongside them to both port and starboard.

"That's true on all of them. Existing commanders, of course, weren't replaced. But until the boarding starts, command of each of those ships is in the hands of the most capable captain. Rank be damned."

Mention of "boarding" focused Antonina's mind elsewhere. She turned and smiled sweetly at Matthew.

"I forgive you. Now, please bring me my gun."

It was Ousanas' turn to scowl. "What do you need that thing for?" he demanded. "*You* aren't going to be storming across any decks."

Antonina shook her head. "Certainly not!" Again, she smiled sweetly. "Whole idea's absurd. Unladylike."

Matthew returned with his mission accomplished. Antonina cradled the monstrous weapon, like a beloved child.

"But you never know," she said serenely. "Shit happens, in a battle."

Ousanas, plain to see, was not a happy man. But he made no further protest. What counter-argument could he advance? Antonina had just pronounced the oldest of all veteran wisdoms. "Shit happens," Matthew and Leo echoed, like a Greek chorus.

Antonina saw Gersem grow tense. Tense. Tense.

She held her breath. She couldn't see a blessed thing forward, but she knew the line of twelve Axumite ships had almost met the fifteen Malwa vessels charging toward them. By now, the enemy would be up to full ramming speed.

Held her breath. Held her breath.

"Relax," said Ousanas. He seemed as stolidly serene as a lump of granite. "O ye of little faith. Malwa galleys? In an open fight at sea—against *Axumites*?"

He raised his head, like a wolf baying at the moon. "Ha!"

That cry of derision blended into Gersem's sudden shouting command.

Within a minute, both the derision and the stolid serenity proved justified. And Antonina, once again, made a solemn vow not to meddle in the affairs of professionals.

Gersem timed the order perfectly. The Malwa galley driving straight upon them—bow against bow—was within yards of a collision. The Ethiopian warship, with experienced rowers and steersman, suddenly skittered aside. Then, at Gersem's new command, drove it forward in a quick lunge. And then—new command, *bellowed*—the rowers on the ship's starboard side lifted their oars straight up in a quick and coordinated motion. The maneuver was a perfectly executed *diekplous*, as the tactic was called by the Rhodians who were the Mediterranean's finest naval forces.

Disaster struck their Malwa opponent. The captain of that ship, as was true of all Malwa captains, was inexperienced in sea battle. Inexperienced, at least, against a real navy. As powerful as the Malwa Empire was, it rarely faced a challenge at sea from other kingdoms. The principal duty of the Malwa Empire's navy was to protect its merchant ships against pirates.

Arrogance and brute force are a splendid way to deal with pirates. They are poor methods, however, against one of the finest navies in the world.

The Malwa ship came driving in at full ramming speed. The Malwa captain, seeing that his opponent's vessel had no ram, was almost chortling with glee. He would split the enemy's prow in half, back away, and then finish them off with rockets. Once crippled, the enemy craft would no longer be able to hide behind that bizarre and infernally effective shield.

At the last possible moment, the Malwa captain ordered his rowers to slow the ship. No captain in his right mind will ram at full speed. The force of the collision might rupture his own bow. At the very least, his ram would be driven too deeply for extraction. Proper ramming tactics require: a full-speed lunge to get within ramming range as soon as possible; a sudden slowing of the ship with backthrust oars; then, in the last few feet, a simple collision. Ram splits hull, but is not wedged; back off, repeat if necessary.

Good tactics, classic tactics. But the Malwa captain never considered the possibility that his opponent would know those tactics just as well, have long since determined the proper counter, and have a captain, and rowers, and a steersman who were far superior to himself and his crew.

At Gersem's command, the Ethiopian ship sidled away from the ram. By the time the Malwa captain realized he was going to miss his strike, Gersem had ordered his ship into a forward lunge. The Malwa captain began screaming new commands to his confused rowers and steersman—

It was too late. The diekplous was done. The Malwa galley drifted inexorably forward. The Ethiopian ship, oars raised out of harm's way, drove down the side of the Malwa craft not more than two feet distant—starboard against starboard, practically scraping the hulls—smashing and shattering every Malwa oar it encountered. Which, given the Malwa crew's confusion and inexperience, was almost all of them.

The Malwa galley, as a vessel, was instantly crippled. Even worse was the damage to the crew. The oarbutts, flailing and splintering and hammering, killed only one man outright. But almost half of the Malwa galley's starboard rowers suffered broken bones, cracked skulls, and crushed ribs—and all of them were bruised and stunned. All order and discipline in the vessel collapsed, as the shouting commands of the officers were buried under screams and groans.

The port-side rowers gaped at the scene. And then, gaped wider at the sight of two five-inch cannon barrels approaching. Seconds later, many of those gaping mouths were swept out of existence entirely. Axumite marines were pouring over the side before the smoke cleared. Again, the murderous cry erupted: *Ta'akha Maryam! Ta'akha Maryam!*

The combat which followed lasted not more than five minutes. Six Malwa sailors escaped by diving over the side. One of them, a good swimmer in superb physical condition, would make it to the bank of the delta several miles away. The rest would drown, sharing the grim fate of their fellow crewmen.

In Charax's delta, Malwa would get no more mercy from Ethiopia than it had gotten from Rome in the city itself.

Antonina, huddling safely in the hull of her flagship, clasped the handcannon more tightly still. It was not fear which produced those whitened knuckles. Simply horror, at the sounds of unseen butchery not more than fifteen feet away. Cries of fury; cries of pain. Spears splitting flesh; sundering bone. Soft groans, and hissing agony, and death gurgling into silence.

All was silent, now, except the waves against the ships, and grunting exertion. Silent—except for the sodden noise of spears plunging, again and again, into corpses. Slaughter made certain, and certain, and certain. Once only, a low voice, filled with satisfaction: *Ta'akha Maryam.*

"I told you," said Ousanas serenely. The aqabe tsentsen, as had been true throughout the battle, had never so much as moved a hand. "O ye of little faith."

In the battle as a whole, Axum suffered the total loss of only one ship. It was a grievous loss, because the entire crew went with their vessel when the Malwa galley they were boarding suddenly erupted. What happened? No one would ever know. An accident, perhaps. Perhaps a fanatic priest.

Five other Axumite warships suffered major casualties. Numbers will tell, even against experience. Not every Axumite captain maneuvered as skillfully as Gersem. And, with twelve Axumite ships facing fifteen opponents, three Malwa galleys were left free to strike where they would.

Malwa's sea captains might have been arrogant and incautious, but they were by no means cowards. All three of those unharmed vessels rammed Axumite ships. Tried to, at least. One of the Malwa galleys was so badly bloodied by well-aimed cannon fire that it drew off—drifted off, rather; its captain and steersman slain, along with a third of the crew. The other two rammed, and then boarded.

But the final result, even there, was the same. The Malwa advantage in numbers was not enough—not even if they had been doubled—to offset the experience and ferocity of Axum's spearmen. The only difference was between a fight lost—badly lost—and an outright slaughter.

At Ousanas' command, the Axumite line reformed and advanced again toward Charax. The city's harbor was less than three miles away, now. Sharp-eyed Ethiopian lookouts reported that the Roman troop vessels were beginning to leave the docks.

There were only eight ships left in the Axumite fleet. In addition to the one destroyed outright, Ousanas had decided to abandon the two which had been rammed and one other which had been badly mauled. None of the three ships were in any danger of sinking, but they had been damaged enough to make them useless in combat. The sarwen on the three crippled vessels transferred quickly to other Ethiopian warships, filling out those crews which had suffered heavy casualties.

Eight ships, now, not twelve—but there were only five Malwa galleys left.

"Look at 'em," snorted Antonina, studying the enemy ships. "And they say women can't make up their minds!"

Ousanas grinned. "What you observe, Antonina, is a modern version of being caught in a myth. Between Scylla and Charybdis."

The commander of the Malwa inner squadron seemed to be torn by indecision. Or perhaps, as Ousanas said, he was simply caught between two monsters. At first, the five galleys headed toward the oncoming Ethiopians. Then, seeing the Roman ships casting loose from the docks, they headed back. The principal assignment of those galleys, after all, was to keep Belisarius and his men from escaping.

Then, seeing the first of the gigantic explosions which began to destroy what was left of Charax, the little Malwa fleet simply drifted aimlessly.

What to do? What to do? The harbor area was as yet untouched by either flame or gunpowder fury. The Malwa flotilla's commander knew that Belisarius would not set off the final round of explosions until he saw his way clear. With the rest of Charax a raging inferno—there had been naphtha mixed with the demolition charges—there was no possibility the oncoming Malwa army could reach the docks before the Roman ships were well into the delta. Where—

The Ethiopian warships were within a mile of the inner squadron. They would reach the Malwa galleys in less than ten minutes, long before the Roman troopships would be within effective rocket range.

Eight against five, now—and the flotilla commander had seen the carnage when the odds had favored Malwa.

Suddenly, from the eastern bank of the delta, signal rockets flared into the sky. Green, green, white. Within thirty seconds, all five Malwa galleys were pulling for the shore. Taking the only sensible course, when caught between monsters. *Get out of the way.*

"Will you look at them go?" chortled Antonina a few minutes later, watching the Malwa galleys scuttling eastward. "Jason and his Argonauts couldn't have made better speed."

Ousanas grinned. "Well, of course! What else can they do?"

He pointed straight ahead. The view was open, now. Already, the shields were being removed and the pole framework dismantled. The fleet of Roman troop vessels was completely clear of the harbor, which was beginning to burn fiercely. A rippling series of explosions shattered the docks themselves.

"To one side," Ousanas announced, "they have the famous general Belisarius, leading his fearsome men. To the other—*worse yet*!"

He began prancing about, lunging with his spear. "They face *me*! I was terrible, terrible—a demon!"

Antonina burst into laughter. "You spent the entire battle sitting on your ass! Fraud! Impostor!"

Ousanas shook his head. "That's because I understand the proper place of a commander in battle, woman." Scowling: "And what does that have to do with anything, anyway? It's the soul that matters, not the paltry flesh. Everybody knows that!"

He bared his teeth at the fleeing galleys. "The soul

of Ousanas, that's what terrified them!" A majestic, condescending wave of the hand. "The sarwen helped, of course. A bit."

Antonina began to make a bantering rejoinder when something caught her eye.

Someone, rather. The nearest Roman troopship was less than two hundred yards away. A soldier was perched on the very tip of its bow. A tall man, he seemed to be. And he was waving wildly.

A moment later, Antonina was teetering on the very bow of her own ship, waving frantically, screaming incoherent phrases.

Jumping up and down, now. Ousanas barely managed to grab her before she fell over the side.

"Antonina! Be careful! In that cuirass, you'll drown in two minutes."

Antonina paid him no attention at all. She was weeping now, from sheer joy. Still waving her arms and screaming. And still jumping up and down. Small as she was, and for all his great strength, Ousanas had some difficulty in his newfound task.

"Marvelous," he growled. "Once again, I have to save a fool Roman woman from destruction."

Chapter 39

In the event, Ousanas wound up saving the fool Roman general. When the troopship was almost alongside Antonina's craft, Belisarius—he was leaping about himself, hollering his own ecstasy—slipped and fell over the side.

Antonina shrieked. Ousanas, by main force, hurled her back into Matthew's arms.

"Keep her here!" he bellowed. An instant later, Ousanas split the water in a clean dive.

He found Belisarius in less than fifteen seconds, floundering about, gulping for breath as he tried to unlace his armor. Fortunately, the general was an excellent swimmer and—more fortunately still—was not wearing full cataphract gear. Had he been, Belisarius would already have been dragged under. But the half-armor was heavy enough, and awkward to remove.

"Hold still," snarled Ousanas. He tucked his arm under Belisarius and began towing him to Antonina's ship. Belisarius instantly relaxed, using only his feet to help keep him afloat.

"Nice to see you again, Ousanas," he said cheerfully.

Ousanas snorted. "Tell me something, Belisarius." He paused for a breath. His powerful strokes had already brought them almost to the ship. "How did you Roman imbeciles manage to conquer half the world?"

Pause for a breath. They were alongside, now. Eager hands were lifting Belisarius out of the water. "Personally, I wouldn't let you out of the house to fetch water from a well. You'd fall in, for sure."

He got no answer. The Roman imbecile was already in the arms of Venus.

About ten minutes later, Belisarius and Antonina finally pried themselves apart. Belisarius winced.

"You have *got* to get rid of that cuirass," he muttered, rubbing his rib cage. He eyed the device respectfully. "It's even deadlier than it is obscene."

Antonina grinned up at him. "So take it off, then. You can do it. I know you can." The grin widened. "Seen you strip me naked, I have, faster than—"

"Hush, wife!" commanded Belisarius. He frowned with solemn, sober disapproval. The expression, alas, fell wide of its mark. Antonina's grin grew positively salacious.

"Oh sure, soldier, tell me the thought never crossed your mind. That's just a cudgel, stuck in your trousers, in case you're ambushed by footpads."

Belisarius burst out laughing. Antonina's eyes quickly studied the immediate area.

"Bit primitive," she mused, "but we could probably manage on one of the rowing benches, as long as you refrain from your usual acrobatics." She cast a cold eye on the small crowd surrounding them. "Have to get rid of the spectators, though. Tell you what. You're the general. You order 'em overboard and I'll shoot the laggards."

Her last remarks had not been made sotto voce. Rather the opposite. The small crowd grinned at her. Antonina tried to maintain the murderous gleam in her eye but, truth to tell, failed miserably. The giggles didn't help.

"Guess not." The sigh which followed would have provided the world with a new standard for melancholy. If she hadn't kept giggling.

Belisarius swept her back into his arms. Into her ear he whispered: "As it happens, love, I've arranged accommodations on the troopship. The captain's cabin, in point of fact. Reserved for our exclusive use."

"Let's get to it, then!" she hissed eagerly. "God, am I glad I married a general. Love a man who can plan ahead."

He sighed himself, now. There was genuine melancholy in the sound.

"Not quite yet," he murmured. "Tonight, love, tonight. But there's still work to be done."

Startled, she drew back her head and stared up at him. "It *is* done!" she protested.

Antonina swiveled her head, scanning the ships which seemed to fill the delta. "Isn't it? Didn't you get everyone off the docks?"

Belisarius smiled. "Oh, *that's* done. To perfection. Best planned and executed operation I've ever seen, if I say so myself." For a moment, he seemed a bit embarrassed. "I'll have to remember to compliment Maurice," he mumbled.

He drove past that awkward subject. "But there's something left, yet. Something else." His smile changed, became quite cold and ruthless. "Call it dessert, if you will."

Antonina was still staring at him in confusion. Belisarius turned his head. When he spotted Ousanas, he motioned him over with a little nod.

"Are you in charge?" he asked.

Ousanas grinned, as hugely as ever. "Is not King Eon

a genius? Didn't I always say, when I was his dawazz, that the boy would go far? Make wise decisions—especially with regard to posts and positions?"

Belisarius chuckled. "Did you notice anything odd, in those last moments before our escape?"

Ousanas spoke without hesitation. "The signal rockets. Those galleys didn't flee. They were *summoned* to the shore. I did not understand that. I had expected them to launch a final desperate attack."

Belisarius' smile was no longer cold. It was purely feral. "Yes. That *is* interesting."

He said nothing further. But it only took Ousanas four seconds to understand. The aqabe tsentsen swiveled his head, staring at the far-distant piers where the five Malwa galleys were now moored.

"It is well known," he murmured, "that wounded animals make easy prey." He turned back to Belisarius. Predator grin met carnivore smile. "Ask any hunter, Roman. The best way to hunt is from a blind."

"Interesting you should mention that," purred Belisarius. "I was just thinking the same thing myself."

Chapter 40

THE GREAT COUNTRY

Autumn, 532 A.D.

On the day of the wedding, Kungas took command of all military forces in Deogiri. Rao, being the groom, naturally did not object. Neither did the various envoys and military commanders from the many kingdoms now allied with Shakuntala. They were intimidated by the Kushan, first of all. But even if they hadn't been, they would have been more than happy to let him take the responsibility.

More than happy. The truth was, the envoys were delighted. Now that they had had enough time to absorb the new reality, and get over their initial shock and outrage at Shakuntala's unexpected decision to marry Rao, the envoys were quite pleased by the whole situation. Well-nigh ecstatic, in fact.

All of the kingdoms which they represented had been petrified by Malwa. Their decision to seek the dynastic marriage with Andhra had been driven by sheer necessity, nothing more. They had approached the project with all the enthusiasm with which a man decides to amputate a limb in order to save his life.

Shakuntala had spurned their offers. Since the decision had been hers, she could hardly cast the blame on *them*. If they hadn't been diplomats, they would have been grinning ear to ear. They had the benefits of an alliance with resurgent Andhra—*without* the shackles of a dynastic marriage. If things turned out badly, they could always jettison Shakuntala in an instant. It wasn't as if *their* crown prince was married to the crazy woman, after all.

So let the rude, crude, lewd and uncouth Kushan barbarian take the responsibility. A low profile suited them just fine.

The forces now under Kungas' command were huge and motley. Deogiri was as crowded, that day, as any city in teeming Bengal. Under different circumstances, Kungas might have been driven half-mad by the chaos. But, probably not, given the man's unshakably phlegmatic disposition.

And *certainly* not, under the circumstances which actually prevailed.

His opponent, Lord Venandakatra, commander of the forces besieging Deogiri, was not called the Vile One by accident. A different man might have been called Venandakatra the Cruel, or Venandakatra the Terrible; or, simply, the Beast. But all of those cognomens carry a certain connotation of unbridled force and fury. They are the names given to a man who is feared as well as hated.

A vile man, on the other hand, is simply despised. A figure of contempt, when all is said and done.

On that day—*that* day—the Vile One was as thoroughly cowed as any commander of an army could be. And everybody knew it.

Venandakatra's own soldiers knew it. Throughout the day-long festivities in Deogiri, the Vile One never emerged once from his pavilion. His soldiers, from his top commanders down to the newest recruit, were as familiar as any Indian with what had now become a staple of the storyteller's trade. The tale of how a great Malwa lord's lust for a new concubine slave had been frustrated by a champion. Unrequited lust, no less, to make the story sweeter.

Today, that beautiful girl—once a slave and now an empress—would give herself to the man who had rescued her from Venandakatra. Right in front of the Vile One, dancing her wedding in his face. Taunting him with the virgin body that would never be his. Not now, not ever.

The Vile One, in his pavilion, gnashed his teeth with rage. Rage, seasoned with heavy doses of shame and humiliation. His soldiers, who despised the man not much less than his enemies, found it difficult not to laugh. They managed that task, of course. None of them were so foolish as to even smile—not with Venandakatra's spies and mahamimamsa prowling the camps and fieldworks. But they were about as likely to launch an assault on Deogiri, that day, as so many giggling mice would attack a lion's den in order to assuage Lord Rat's wounded vanity.

Kungas spent a pleasant day rubbing salt into the wound. He rotated all the various troops under his command across the northern battlements facing Venandakatra's pavilion and the bulk of his forces. Allowing Malwa's soldiery, if not the pavilion-enclosed Vile One himself, to see the full panoply of forces which were now arrayed against them.

By popular acclaim, the four hundred spearmen of the Dakuen sarwe were rotated through no less than three times. Partly, that was due to the exotic and splendid appearance of the Ethiopians. Black men from a far-off and fabled land—blacker than any Dravidian—sporting savage-looking spears and jaunty ostrich-feather headdresses. Mostly, however, it was due to the crowd's glee at the sight of four hundred bare asses, at Ezana's lead and command, hanging over the battlements in Malwa's face.

Better was still to come. By mid-afternoon, the wedding ceremony itself was finished and the bride and groom began to dance.

Shakuntala danced first. By custom, the husband should have done so. But the empress had decreed otherwise. Shakuntala was a wonderful dancer, in her own right, but she was not Rao's equal. No one was. So, she went first. Not because she was ashamed of her own skill, but simply because she wanted the people watching—and the world which would learn from their telling, in the years to come—to remember Rao in all his glory.

Her dance, in truth, was glorious itself. Shakuntala did not dance in the center square of the city, where the wedding had taken place. She did so on the top battlements of the northern wall, on a platform erected the day before, after hurriedly changing her costume.

When she appeared on the platform, the crowd gasped. Shakuntala had shed her elaborate imperial costume in favor of a dancer's garb. Her pantaloons, for all that they were tastefully dyed, bordered on scandal.

Yet, the crowd was pleased. At first, as she began her steps, they assumed that Shakuntala was simply taunting her enemy. Prancing, in all her youth and beauty, before the creature who had once dreamed of possessing her.

Which, of course, she was. Dancing, by its nature, is a sensuous act. That is as true for an elderly man or a portly matron, creaking and waddling their way through sober paces, as it is for anyone. But there is nothing quite as sensuous, dancing, as a young woman as agile as she is beautiful.

Shakuntala was both, and she took full advantage.

It was well for Venandakatra that he never saw that dance. The Vile One would have ground his teeth to powder.

But, as Shakuntala's dance went on, and transmuted, the crowd realized the truth. Taunting her enemy was a trivial thing. Amusing, but soon discarded.

The Empress Shakuntala was not dancing for the Vile One. She was not, even, dancing for Andhra. She was dancing for her husband, now. The sensuousness of that dance, the sheer sexuality of it, was not a taunt. It was a promise, and a pledge, and, most of all, nothing but her own desire.

They had wondered, the great crowd. Now, they knew the truth. Watching the bare quicksilver feet of their empress, flashing in the wine of her beloved's heart, they knew. Statecraft, political calculation—even duty and obligation—were gone, as if they had never existed.

Andhra had married the Great Country, not because its own past required the doing, but because that was the future it had chosen freely. The future that it *desired.* When she finished—in defiance of all custom and tradition—the crowd burst into riotous applause. The applause went on for half an hour.

It was Rao's turn, now, and the crowd fell silent. His reputation as a dancer was known to all Marathas. But most of them had never seen it with their own eyes.

They saw him now, and never forgot. The tale would be passed on for generations.

He began, as a husband. And if his dance was not as purely sensual as Shakuntala's had been, no one who saw it doubted his own heart.

The dance went on, and on. And, as it went, slowly transformed a man's desire for a woman—the life she would give him, the children she would give him—into a people's desire for a future.

It was Majarashtra's dance, now. The Great Country was pledging its own troth. Love was there, along with desire. But there was also courage, and faith, and hope, and trust, and determination. Majarashtra danced to its yet-unborn children, as much as it danced for its bride. It was a husband's dance, not a lover's. Every step, every gesture, every movement, carried the promise of fidelity.

Then, the dance changed again. The crowd grew utterly still.

This was the great dance. The terrible dance. The long-forbidden but never-forgotten dance. The dance of creation. The dance of destruction. The wheeling, whirling, dervish dance of time.

There was nothing of hatred in the dance. No longer. Love, yes, always. But even love receded, taking its honored place. This was the ultimate dance, which spoke the ultimate truth.

That truth, danced for all to see, held the crowd spellbound. Silent, but not abashed. No, not in the least. Every step, every gesture, every movement, carried the great promise. The crowd, understanding the promise, swelled with strength.

Empires are mighty. Time is mightier still. Tyrants come, tyrants go. Despots tread the stage, declaiming their glory. And then Time shows them the exit. People, alone, endure and endure. Theirs, alone, is the final power. No army can stand against it; no battlements hold it at bay.

It was over. The dance was done. A husband, taking his bride by the hand, led her into the chamber of Time. The people, watching them go, saw their own future approaching.

Once in the chamber, Rao's surety vanished. There was nothing left, now, of the superb dancer who had paced his certain steps. Stiff as a board, creaking his way to the bed, his eyes unfocused, Rao seemed like a man in a daze.

Shakuntala smiled and smiled. Smiling, she removed his clothes. Smiling, removed her own.

"Look at me, husband," she commanded.

Rao's eyes went to her. His breath stilled. He had never seen her nude. His mind groped, trying to wrap itself around such beauty. His body, rebelling against discipline, had no difficulty at all.

Shakuntala, still smiling, pressed herself against him, kissing, touching, stroking. His mind—locked tight by years of self-denial—was like a sheet of ice. His body, now in full and wild revolt, felt like pure magma.

"You made a pledge to my father, once," Shakuntala whispered. "Do you remember?"

He nodded, like a statue.

Shakuntala's smile became a grin. She moved away, undulating, and spread herself across the bed. Rao's eyes were locked onto the sight. But his mind, still, could not encompass the seeing.

"You have been neglectful in your duty, Rao," Shakuntala murmured, lying on the bed. " 'Teach her everything you know.' That was my father's command."

She curled, coiled, flexed.

"I never taught you *that*," Rao choked.

Arched, stretched. Liquid, smiling. Moisture, laughing.

"You taught me how to read," she countered. "I borrowed a book." Coiled, again; and arched; and stretched. Promise, open.

" 'Hold back *nothing*,' " she said. "That is your duty."

Denial shattered; self-discipline vanished with the wind. Rao moved, like a panther to his mate.

In the corridors beyond the chamber, servant women waited. Older women, in the main; Marathas, all. When they heard Shakuntala's wordless voice, announcing her defloration, they grinned. In another virgin, there might have been some pain in that cry. But for their fierce empress, there had been nothing beyond ecstasy and eager desire.

The thing was done. The pledge fulfilled. The promise kept.

The women scurried through the halls, spreading the word. But their efforts were quite needless. Shakuntala had never been a bashful girl. Now, becoming a woman, she fairly screamed her triumph.

The young men heard, waiting in the streets below. They had mounted their horses before the servants reached the end of the first corridor. By the time Majarashtra's women emerged onto the streets to tell the news, Majarashtra's sons and nephews had already left. By the time the dancing resumed, and the revelry began, they were carrying the message out of the gates and pounding it, on flying horseborne feet, in every direction.

The land called Majarashtra had been created, millions of years earlier, when the earth's magma boiled to the surface. The Deccan Traps, geologists of a later age would call it; solemnly explaining, to solemn students, that it had been perhaps the greatest—and most violent—volcanic episode in the planet's history.

Now, while Deogiri danced its glee, the Great Country began its new eruption. Dancing, with swift and spreading steps, the new time for Malwa. The time of death, and terror, and desperate struggle.

Malwa's soldiers already detested service in Majarashtra. From that day forward, they would speak of it in hushed and dreading tones. Much like soldiers of a later army, watching evil spill its intestines, would speak of the Russian Front.

Belisarius had planned, and schemed, and maneuvered, and acted, guided by Aide's vision of the Peninsular War.

He already had his Peninsular War. Now, he got the Pripet Marshes, and the maquis, and the Warsaw Ghetto, and the mountains cupping Dien Bien Phu, and the streets of Budapest, and every other place in the history of the species where empires, full of their short-memoried arrogance, learned, again, the dance of Time.

Time, of course, contains all things. Among them is farce.

Shakuntala's eyes were very wide. The young woman's face, slack with surprise.

"I thought it would— I don't know. Take longer."

Looking down on that loving, confused face from a distance of inches, Rao flushed deep embarrassment.

"I can't believe it," he muttered. "I haven't done that since I was fourteen."

Awkwardly, he groped for words. "Well," he fumbled, "well. Well. It *should* have, actually. Much longer." He took a breath. *How to explain?* Halting words followed, speaking of self-discipline too suddenly vanished, excessive eagerness, a dream come true without sufficient emotional preparation, and—and—

When Shakuntala finally understood—which didn't take long, in truth; she was inexperienced but very intelligent; though it seemed like ages to Rao—she burst into laughter.

"So!" she cried.

He had trained her to wrestle, also. In an instant, she squirmed out from under him and had him flat on his back. Then, straddling him, she began her chastisement.

"*So!*" Playfully, she punched his chest. "The truth is out!"

Punch. "Champion—*ha!* Hero—*ha!*" Punch. "I have been defrauded! Cheated!"

Rao was laughing himself, now. The laughs grew

louder and louder, as he heard his wife bestow upon him his new cognomens of ridicule and ignominy. The Pant of Majarashtra. The Gust of the Great Country—*no!* The *Puff* of the Great Country.

Laughter drove out shame, and brought passion to fill the void. Soon enough—very soon—the empress ceased her complaints. And, by the end of a long night, allowed—regally magnanimous, for all the sweat—that her husband was still her champion.

Chapter 41

THE STRAIT OF HORMUZ

Autumn, 532 A.D.

A monster fled ruin and disaster. Licking its wounds, trailing blood, dragging its maimed limbs, the beast clawed back toward its lair. Silent, for all its agony; its cold mind preoccupied with plans for revenge. Revenge, and an eventual return to predation.

A different monster would have screamed, from fury and frustration as much as pain and fear. But that was not this monster's way. Not even when the hunter who had maimed it sprang, again, from ambush.

Though, for a moment, there might have been a gleam of hatred, somewhere deep inside those ancient eyes.

Chapter 42

Belisarius started to speak. Then, closed his mouth.

"Good, good," murmured Ousanas. The aqabe tsentsen glanced slyly at Antonina.

She returned the look with a sniff. "*My* husband is an experienced general," she proclaimed. "*My* husband is calm and cool on the eve of battle."

Ousanas chuckled. "So it seems. Though, for a moment there, I would have sworn he was about to tell experienced sea captains how to maneuver a fleet."

Belisarius never took his eyes off the approaching flotilla of Malwa vessels. But his crooked smile did make an appearance.

"What nonsense," he said firmly. "The idea's absurd." He turned his head, speaking to the man standing just behind him. "Isn't it, Maurice?"

Maurice scowled. "Of course it is. You'd spend ten minutes, before you got into it, telling Gersem which way the wind's blowing. After spending half an hour explaining what sails are for."

"It's the general's curse," muttered Belisarius. "Surly subordinates."

"After spending two hours describing what wind is in the first place," continued Maurice. "And three hours—" He stuck out a stubby finger, pointing to the sea around them. "Oh, Gersem—look! That stuff's called *water*."

Ousanas and Antonina burst out laughing. Belisarius, for all his ferocious frown, was hard-pressed not to join them.

After a moment, however, the amusement faded. They *were* hunting a monster, after all. And they were no longer lurking in ambush, hidden in a blind.

Behind him, Belisarius heard Maurice sigh. "All right, all right," the chiliarch muttered. "Fair's fair. You were right again, general. But I still don't know how you figured it out."

"I didn't 'figure it out,' exactly. It was a guess, that's all. But we had nothing to lose, except wasting a few days here in the Strait while the rest of the cargo ships carried the troops to Adulis."

Belisarius pointed north, sweeping his finger in a little arc. They were well into the Strait of Hormuz, now. The Persian mainland was a dim presence looming beyond the bow of the huge cargo vessel.

"That's about the worst terrain I can think of, to try to march an army through, without a reliable supply route. Any size army, much less that horde Link's got."

Maurice snorted. "Not much of a horde now! Not after we got done with them."

Belisarius shook his head. "Don't fool yourself, Maurice. We inflicted terrible casualties on them, true. And God knows how many died in the final destruction of the city. But I'm quite sure two thirds of the Malwa army is still intact." He grimaced, slightly. "Well—*alive*, anyway. 'Intact' is putting it too strongly."

He paused, studying the oncoming Malwa vessels. There were six ships in that little flotilla. The five galleys which had avoided the Ethiopians in the delta were escorting a cargo ship. That vessel, though it was larger than the galleys, was far smaller than the huge ship Belisarius was standing upon.

The general interrupted his own discourse. Leaning back from the rail, he shouted a question toward Gersem. The Axumite commander was perched in the very bow of the ship, bestowing his own intense scrutiny on the enemy.

"Three hundred tons, Belisarius!" came the reply. "Probably the largest ship they had left."

Belisarius chuckled, seeing Gersem's scowl. The Malwa vessel had been used as a supply ship on the Euphrates. The Ethiopian, a seaman, was half-outraged at the idea of using such a craft for a river barge. And he was already disgruntled, having been forced to captain this great, ugly, clumsy, ungainly Malwa vessel—instead of one of the Ethiopian warships which formed the rest of his fleet.

Belisarius returned to the subject. "Link has to try to save as many of those soldiers as it can, Maurice. It can save a few of them—they'll be Ye-tai, to a man—by using what's left of the supply ships on the river. But the only way to salvage the main forces is to use the supply fleet at Bharakuccha, waiting for the westbound monsoon. Thirty ships, according to the report Antonina got from Irene. Irene wrote that report just before she left Suppara, not many days ago. The ships were already loading provisions."

Mention of Irene's report brought a moment's silence, as the four people standing at the rail joined in a heartfelt smile of relief, delight, and bemusement. Relief, that they knew Irene was still alive to write reports. Delight, at the report itself. And bemusement, at the workings of fate.

Irene had written that report more out of sentiment than anything else. The odds of getting it into Antonina's hands were well-nigh astronomical. But—

why not? There were no secrets in the report, after all, to keep from Malwa. And the captain of the Ethiopian smuggling ship had sworn—scoffing—that he could get the message through the Malwa blockade and back to Axum. Whether it would ever reach Antonina, of course, he could not promise.

In the event, that smuggler's ship had encountered the Ethiopian flotilla waiting at the Strait to ambush Link. The message had found its way into Antonina's hands the day before.

"I'd like to have been at that wedding," mused Belisarius. "Just to finally see Rao dance, right before me."

He closed his eyes, for a moment. He *had* seen Rao dance, but only in a vision. In another time, in another future, Belisarius had spent thirty years in Rao's company. He admired the Maratha chieftain—imperial consort, now—perhaps more than any other man he had ever known. And so, for a moment, he savored Rao's joy at being—finally, in *this* turn of the wheel—united with his soul's treasure.

Antonina spent that moment savoring another's joy. Irene was her best friend. She had been able to discern a subtle message contained within the depiction of political and military developments. Kungas had figured a bit too prominently in those sober sentences. *Quite* a bit too prominently, measured in sheer number of words. And why in the world would Irene, glowingly, take the trouble to describe an illiterate's progress at his books?

Uncertain, not knowing the man herself, Antonina had raised her suspicions with Belisarius. Her husband, once he realized what she was hinting at, had immediately burst into laughter.

"Of course!" he'd exclaimed. "It's a match made in heaven." Then, seeing her doubting face: "Trust me, love. If there's a man in the world who wouldn't be intimidated by Irene, it's Kungas. As for her—?"

Shrugging, laughing. "You know how much she loves a challenge!"

The moment passed, soon enough. Within an hour, they would be in battle again.

"So what would Link do, Maurice? Would it send subordinates to organize the supply effort, while it led the march back to India?" Belisarius shook his head. "I didn't think that likely. No, I was almost sure Link would want to get to India itself, as fast as possible. Why else hold back the surviving galleys, at the last minute, in the battle of the delta? One of them, certainly; perhaps two. That would have been enough to send subordinates with a message."

He pointed at the cargo ship nestled among the Malwa galleys. They were less than two miles away. He was smiling, not like a man, but like a wolf smiles, seeing a fat and crippled caribou.

"*That*, my friends, is not a subordinate's ship. *That* is the best Link could do, replacing Great Lady Holi's luxury barge in Kausambi."

The smile vanished completely. Nothing was left, beyond pure ferocity.

"I own that monster, now. *Finally.*"

Belisarius' quiet, seething rage brought hidden, half-conscious thoughts to the surface. For the first time, Aide realized Belisarius' full intentions. Sooner, perhaps, than Belisarius did himself.

No! he cried. **You must not! It will kill you!**

Belisarius started. There had been sheer panic in that crystalline voice.

What is wrong, Aide? Forcefully: *We're not going to have this argument again. I've led charges in battle, often enough.*

That was different! You were fighting men, not a cyborg. Men who wanted to live, as much as

you. Life means nothing to Link—not even its own!

Long minutes followed, while Belisarius waged a fierce argument with Aide. His companions, from experience, understood the meaning of his silence and his unfocused eyes. But, as the minutes passed, they grew concerned—none more so than Antonina. Not since they first encountered Aide, and he transported Belisarius into a vision of future horror, had she seen her husband spend so much time in that peculiar trance.

When he finally emerged, his face was bleak. Bleak, but bitterly determined.

Belisarius pointed to the Malwa cargo ship in which, if he was correct, Link was waiting. The ship was not more than a mile distant, now. Already, kshatriyas were erecting rocket troughs on the deck.

"There is something you should know. Aide just explained it to me. There is a reason the new gods choose women as the vessels for Link. Great Lady Holi, today. If she dies, Link will be transferred into the person—the body, I should say—of her niece, Sati. She is probably still in Kausambi. If Sati dies, there will be another girl, in that same line. Somewhere in Kausambi also, in all likelihood."

He paused, groping for a way to translate Aide's concepts. The effort was hopeless. Words like "genetics" and "mitochondrial DNA" would mean nothing to his companions. He barely understood them himself.

He waved his hand. "Never mind the specifics. Link is part machine, part human. The machine part, the core of it, is somewhere in India. Probably in Kausambi also. Its consciousness is passed, upon her death, from one woman to her successor. The new Link, once it's—'activated,' let's call it—has all the memories of the old one, up till the time she last—" Again, he groped for words. "Communicated with the machine."

He paused. Maurice, eagerly, filled the void. "You know what that means?" he demanded. The chiliarch gripped the rail fiercely, glaring at the enemy ship. "What it means," he hissed, "is that if we kill that old bitch, the Malwa will be thrown into complete confusion. The new Link—what's her name? Sati?—won't know what's happened since Holi left. That's been a year and a half, now! It'll take her months—*months*—to get things reorganized."

He turned from the rail, eager—*eager*. "God, General, that's *perfect!* We *need* that time, ourselves. Sure, we won this battle. But our troops are exhausted, too. We need to refit, and hook back up with Agathius and the Persians, and send another mission to Majarashtra, and—"

He stumbled to a halt. Maurice, finally, saw the other side of the thing.

Antonina had understood at once. Her face was pale.

"You *can't* board that ship! Link will commit suicide! It has no reason not to. It's not human, it's just a—a *vessel*. A tool." She almost gasped. "It'll *want* to! The last thing it can afford is to be captured."

All of them, now, understood the implication. *So why not take its enemy with it?*

"It'll have that ship rigged," muttered Maurice. "Doing it right now, probably. Ready to blow it up once you're aboard."

Antonina ignored him. She was pale, pale. She knew that expression on Belisarius' face. Knew it all the better because it was so rare.

"*I don't give a damn*," he snarled. "I've been fighting that monster for four years. I'm tired of tactics and strategy. *I'm just going to kill it*."

Protest began to erupt, until a new voice spoke.

"Of course we will!" boomed Ousanas. "Nothing to it!"

All eyes fixed upon him. The aqabe tsentsen

grinned. "Under other circumstances, of course, the deed would be insane. Foolish, suicidal!" He shrugged. "But you forget—you have *me*!" He began prancing around, lunging with his spear. "Terrible! A demon!"

Antonina was not amused, this time. She began to snarl a response, until she suddenly realized—

Ousanas was not prancing any longer. He was simply smiling, as serene as an icon.

"No, Antonina," he said softly, "I am not joking with you now. It is a simple fact"—again, he shrugged—"that I am the best hunter I know."

He pointed his finger at Link's ship. Not more than half a mile away, now. "Think clearly and logically. The monster cannot possibly have enough gunpowder to blow up the entire ship. It would only have brought defensive weapons. Rockets, grenades. It will set them to destroy its own cabin, after the boarding party arrives. That will take time."

He hefted his huge spear, as lightly as if were a mere twig. "Underneath, I think. Somewhere in the hold."

He turned to Belisarius. "You are determined, I imagine, to lead the boarding party yourself."

Belisarius' only answer was a snarl. Ousanas nodded. "*Do it, Roman*. Take your best men. I will see to the rest."

The argument still raged, but the issue was settled. Between them, Belisarius and Ousanas beat down all protest. Not even Anastasius—not even when ordered by Maurice—was prepared to stop the general. He remembered Valentinian, unyielding, on a mountainside in Persia. And knew that the champion's own general, this day, would do no less.

By then, the Ethiopian warships were already engaging the Malwa escort galleys. The battle was not quite as swift as that in the delta. Not quite. The

Malwa had seen the diekplous, and tried to avoid it. But, while their caution prolonged the outcome, it did not change it. It simply made it the more certain. In less than ten minutes, the five galleys had been boarded and their crews slaughtered. The Ethiopians lost only one of their craft to ramming. Even then, they were able to rescue the entire crew before the ship finally foundered.

Belisarius, however, observed none of it. He had been engaged, throughout, in a new argument. Which he lost, just as surely and inevitably as he had won the first.

"*All right!*" he growled, glaring at his wife. Then, heaving a great sigh: "But you stay behind, Antonina— d'you hear? I won't have you in the front line!"

Her stubborn look faded, replaced by an insouciant smile. "Well, of course! I had no intention of *leading* the charge." A very delicate snort. "The whole idea's ridiculous. Unladylike."

Chapter 43

The monster waited. Patiently, with the sureness of eternal life. Not its own—that was meaningless—but that of its masters.

Everything was finished, now, except revenge. The deck of the ship was a carrion-eater's paradise. Firing from the height of their own huge craft, with those powerful bows, the cataphracts had swept all life away. The kshatriyas at the rocket troughs, and their Ye-tai guards, were nothing but ripped meat.

No loss. The rocket volleys, in the short time they lasted, had been futile. The enormous vessel upon which the monster's great enemy came had simply shrugged off the missiles. There had not been many to shrug off, in any event. Most of the rockets had been taken into the hold. They would soon be put to better use.

The monster waited, satisfied. Next to it, squatting by the throne, an assassin held the gong which would give the signal to the priests waiting below. The creature, like the priests and the special guards, was a devotee of the monster's cult. The assassin, when the monster gave the order, would do his duty without fail.

The monster waited. Cold, cold. But, perhaps, somewhere in those depths, glowed an ember of hot glee.

The monster had been fighting its great enemy—its tormentor—for four years. Today, finally, it was going to kill it.

The monster idled away the time in memory. It remembered the trickery at Gwalior, and the cunning which crushed Nika. It remembered an army broken at Anatha, and another destroyed at the Nehar Malka. It remembered the catastrophe at Charax.

Come to me, Belisarius. Come to me.

Chapter 44

Silently, Ousanas crept through the hold, watching for the guards. *Listening* for the guards, more precisely. The hold was as dark as a rain forest on a moonless night.

Ousanas had waited for the sun to go down before he entered the hatch leading into the hold from the ship's bow. The horizon was still aglow with sunset colors, but none of that faint illumination reached into the ship's interior.

There had been guards waiting by the entrance, of course. Two, hidden among the grain-carrying amphorae lashed against the hull. Excellent assassins, both of them. Ousanas had been impressed. Before the feet of the Ye-tai corpse even touched the deck of the hold the assassins had been there, knives flashing. The blades had penetrated the gaps in the corpse's Roman armor with sure precision.

Excellent assassins. They had realized the truth with their first stabs, from feel alone. They were already withdrawing the wet blades by the time Ousanas dropped the rope holding the corpse upright and leapt through the hatch. But that was too late. Much too late. Ousanas crushed the first assassin's skull with a straight thrust of his spearbutt's iron ferrule. The blade did for the other.

He left the spear with them, still plunged into an assassin's chest. It would be knifework from here on. The hold was cramped, full of amphorae and sacks of provisions. No room there for Ousanas' huge spear.

He waited for a few minutes, crouched in the darkness, listening. There should have been a third guard somewhere nearby, to support the two at the entrance if need be.

Nothing. Ousanas was a bit surprised, but only a bit. The finest military mind in the world had predicted as much.

Ousanas smiled. It was a cold smile but, in the darkness, there was no one to see that murderous expression. Link's assassins were the ultimate elite in Malwa's military forces. And therefore—just as Belisarius had estimated—suffered from the inevitable syndrome of all Praetorian Guards. Deadly, yes. But, also—arrogant; too sure of themselves; scornful of their opponents. Well-trained, yes—but training is not the same thing as combat experience. Those assassins had not fought a real opponent in years. As Praetorian Guards have done throughout history, they had slipped from being killers to murderers.

Ousanas started moving again. Slowly, very slowly. He was in no hurry. Belisarius would wait until Ousanas gave the signal. The Roman general and his companions were perched on the stern, far from the cabin amidships. If the explosive charges went off, they should be able to escape unharmed. Even wearing armor, they could stay afloat long enough for the Axumite warships surrounding Link's vessel to rescue them.

For Ousanas himself, of course, things would be worse. Fatal, probably. The once and former hunter, now lieutenant to the King of Kings, cared not in the least. He had become a philosophical man, over the years. But he had always been a killer. He had walked alongside death's shadow since he was a boy.

Ousanas had his own scores to settle. He had admired King Kaleb, for all that he never spoke the words. Eon's father had possessed none of his son's quick wit. Still, he had been a good king. And Ousanas had been very fond of Tarabai and Zaia, and many of the people crushed in the stones of the Ta'akha Maryam.

Your turn, Malwa.

Black death crept through the hold. Two more murderers died by a killer's blade.

"I'll go first, General," stated Anastasius. The giant's heavy jaws were tight, as if he were expecting an argument.

Belisarius smiled. "By all means! I'm bold, but I'm not crazy. Link's guards are about the size of small hippos."

Anastasius sneered. "So am I." He hefted his mace. Huge muscles flexed under armor. "But *I* haven't spent the last few years wallowing in the lap of luxury."

"You will now," came Antonina's cheerful rejoinder. "Of course, given your philosophical bent, I'm sure you're planning to give it all away."

Anastasius grinned. When the Roman army seized Charax, they had also seized the Malwa paychests—not to mention the small mountain of gold, silver and jewelry which that huge army's officers had collected. The riches had been left behind in Charax when Link's army marched out of the city. Needless to say, it had *not* been left behind when the Romans sailed out.

Every soldier in Belisarius' army was now a wealthy man. Not measured by the standards of Roman senators, of course. But by the standards of Thracian,

Greek and Syrian commoners—not to mention Kushan war prisoners—they were filthy, stinking, slobbering rich. Belisarius was a bit concerned about it, in fact. He would lose some of those veterans, now. But he wasn't too concerned. Most of the veterans would stay, eager to share in the booty from future campaigns. And for every man who left, seeking a comfortable retirement, there would be ten men stepping forward to take his place. Other Roman armies might have difficulty finding recruits. Once the news spread, Belisarius' army would be turning them away.

But that was a problem for the future. For now—

There came a sound, from below their feet. A faint, clapping noise, resounding through the hull. Like a firecracker, perhaps.

"That's it!" bellowed Anastasius. A moment later, the huge cataphract was charging toward the cabin. Right behind him came Leo and Isaac, Priscus and Matthew. Belisarius and Antonina brought up the rear.

Your turn, monster.

When Ousanas finally reached his goal, he waited in the darkness only long enough to make sure he had a correct count of the opposition.

The area of the hold amidships, directly under Link's cabin, had been hastily cleared of amphorae and grain sacks. In the small open area created—perhaps ten feet square—two priests and an assassin were crouching. The area was lit by two small lamps. One of the priests was holding a cluster of fuses in his hands. The other, a striker. The assassin's head was cocked, waiting for the signal to come from his master in the cabin above.

For a moment, Ousanas admired Malwa ingenuity. He, like Belisarius, had thought they would disassemble the rockets and jury-rig explosive charges under the cabin. Link's minions had chosen pristine simplicity, instead. True, there were grenades attached to the wooden underdeck. The fuses had been cut so short they were almost flush. But the rockets had simply been erected, like so many small trees, pointing directly upward. As soon as the fuses were lit, the cabin above would be riddled by two dozen missiles. The backblast from the rockets would ignite the grenades.

There was no reason to wait. Silently, slowly, Ousanas pulled the pin of his grenade. Then, with a quick and powerful flip of the wrist, he tossed the explosive device against the far wall of the hold. The grenade had been disassembled, its charge removed, and then reassembled. But the impact fuse made a very satisfactory noise in the confines of the hold.

Startled, the Malwa looked to the sound. The assassin realized the truth almost immediately. But "almost," facing a hunter like Ousanas, was not quick enough. The assassin's heart was ruptured by a Roman blade before he had his own dagger more than half-raised. He did manage to gash the African's leg before he died. Ousanas was quite impressed.

The priests never managed more than a gasp. Ousanas did not take the time to withdraw the blade from the assassin's back. If Belisarius had been there, watching, he would have seen an old suspicion confirmed. Ousanas *was* stronger than Anastasius. The aqabe tsentsen simply seized the priests' necks, one in each hand, and crushed the bones along with the windpipes.

Before he even lowered the bodies to the deck, Ousanas could hear the thundering footsteps of the cataphracts charging the cabin. Then, the door splintering, as Anastasius went through it like a hurricane. Then—

The hunter was grinning now. As always, in darkness and gloom, those gleaming teeth seemed like a beacon.

Good-bye, monster.

✧ ✧ ✧

Anastasius was off balance when the first guard swung his tulwar. For that reason, he was unable to deflect the huge blade properly. Instead, his shield broke in half.

The guard gaped. That blow should have flattened his opponent, if nothing else. The guard was still gaping when Anastasius' mace crushed his skull.

Another guard swung a tulwar. Anastasius sidestepped the blow. Not as nimbly as Valentinian would have done, of course, but far more quickly than the guard would have ever imagined a man of Anastasius' size could move.

Anastasius might have slain that guard, easily, with another stroke of the mace. But he wanted to create some fighting room in the confines of the cabin. He could see four more guards crowding behind. So, instead, he dropped his mace and seized the guard in a half-nelson. Then, rolling his hip, he flung the man into his oncoming fellows.

Quickly, Anastasius lunged aside, pressing himself against the wall of the cabin. He would retrieve his mace later. For now, he simply needed to let his companions pass.

Leo came next, through the shattered door, roaring like an ogre. Truth be told, Leo was almost as dimwitted as the nickname "Ox" implied. So, as always in battle, he eschewed complicated tactics. And why not? He'd never needed them before.

He didn't need them this time, either. By the time Isaac and Priscus and Matthew forced their own immense and murderous bodies into the cabin, Leo had already killed one guard and disabled another.

The rest died within half a minute. The battle, for all its fury—eleven huge men hacking and hammering each other in a room the size of a small salon—was as one-sided as any Belisarius had ever seen.

He was not surprised. Watching from the doorway, Antonina peeking around his arm, Belisarius witnessed one of the few battles which went exactly according to plan.

He had known it would. Anastasius was the only Roman who matched the size of Link's special guards. But the others matched them in strength, if not in sheer bulk. And they, unlike the guards, were *not* a pampered "elite." They were the real thing. Swords and maces, wielded on battlefields and the cruel streets of Charax, went through the tulwars like fangs through soft flesh.

Silence, except for the ringing gong held in an assassin's hands. Then, *silence*, as Matthew's sword decapitated the gong holder.

Belisarius stepped into the room, staring at Link.

The monster was dying, now. With its inhuman intelligence, Link had already assessed the new reality. There would be no rockets coming through the floor, killing its great enemy. No grenades, to obliterate what might be left.

Link had been prepared for that possibility. So it had taken its last, pitiful revenge.

A jeweled cup slid out of the monster's hand. The body of an old woman—the monster's sheath—was already slumping in the ornate, bejeweled chair. An old woman's head lolled to the side.

It was a quick-acting poison. But there was still a gleam in those wizened eyes. A small gleam of triumph, perhaps. If nothing else, the monster's great enemy would not take its life.

Antonina shoved Belisarius aside. She sprang forward, raising her ugly and ungainly and detested handcannon.

Trusted weapon, now.

"*Fuck you!*" she screamed. Left hammer; rear trigger; fire. The first shot blew the monster's heart through its spine, spinning Antonina half-around. She spun back in an instant.

"*Fuck you!*" Right hammer; front trigger; fire. The

second shot splattered the monster's brains against the far wall.

Antonina landed on her butt, driven down by the cuirass.

Her ass hurt. Her hands hurt. Her arms hurt. Her shoulders hurt. Her breasts hurt.

She raised her head, grinning up at her husband. "God, that feels great!"

Belisarius beamed proudly at his cataphracts. "That's my lady," he announced. "That's my lady!"

EPILOGUE
An interruption and a conclusion

The monster came to life. As the soul which had once inhabited a young woman's body was obliterated, the monster groped for consciousness.

The moment of confusion was brief.

Disaster was the first thought. *There has been a disaster.*

The monster examined its memory, with lightning speed. *Nothing. All was going well. What could have happened?*

There came an interruption.

"Are you all right, Lady Sati?"

A woman—plump, young, rather pretty—was staring at the monster, her face full of concern. "You seem—ill, perhaps. Your eyes—"

The monster's thoughts, as always, raced with inhuman speed. In an instant, she had the interruption categorized. One of Lady Sati's maids. Indira was her name. She had developed a certain closeness with her mistress.

That could be inconvenient. More interruptions might occur.

The monster swiveled its head. Yes. The assassins were at their post.

Kill her.

By the time the knives ceased their flashing work, the monster's thoughts had reached a preliminary conclusion.

Belisarius. No other explanation seems possible.

There was no anger in the thought. There was nothing in the thought.

A command and a choice

"Are you insane?" demanded Nanda Lal, the moment he strode into Venandakatra's pavilion. "Why have you not already begun the withdrawal?"

The Vile One clenched his jaws. Any other man but Nanda Lal—and the emperor, of course—would be caned for using that tone of voice to the Goptri of the Deccan. Caned, if he were lucky.

But—

Venandakatra controlled his rage. Barely. He thrust a finger at the ramparts of Deogiri. "I will have that city!" he screeched. "Whatever else, I will take it!"

Nanda Lal seized the Vile One by a shoulder and spun him around. Venandakatra was so astonished—*no one may touch me!*—that he stumbled, almost sprawling on the carpet. Then, he did sprawl. Nanda Lal's slap across the face did for that. Physical power, partly—the Malwa Empire's spymaster was a strong man, thick with muscle. But, mostly, Venandakatra's collapse was due to sheer, utter shock. No one had ever laid hands on Lord Venandakatra. He was the emperor's first cousin!

But, so was Nanda Lal. And the spymaster was in plain and simple fury.

"You idiot," hissed Nanda Lal. "You couldn't take Deogiri even when it was possible. *Today?*"

Angrily, the spymaster pointed through the open flap of the pavilion. Beyond lay the road to Bharakuccha. "I had to fight my way here, you imbecile! With a small army of Rajputs!"

He reached down, seized Venandakatra by his rich robes, and hauled him to his feet. There came another buffet; hard open palm across flabby cheek.

"If you move now—fool!—we can still extract your army with light casualties. By next week—the week after, for a certainty—half your soldiers will be dead by the time you reach Bharakuccha."

Contemptuously, Nanda Lal released his grip. Again, Venandakatra collapsed to the carpet. His mouth was agape, his eyes unfocused.

Nanda Lal turned away, clasping his hands behind his back. "We can hope to hold Bharakuccha, and the line of the Narmada. The large towns in the north Deccan. That is all, for the moment. But we *must* hold Bharakuccha. If it is lost, our army in Mesopotamia will starve."

His heavy jaws tightened. Nanda Lal opened his mouth, as if to speak further, but simply shook his head. The spymaster was not prepared to share his still-tentative analysis of the likely situation in Mesopotamia. His *fears* about Mesopotamia. Certainly not with Venandakatra.

"Do it," he commanded. He tapped the sash holding his own robes in place. An imperial scroll was thrust into that sash. "I have the full authority here to do anything I wish. That includes ordering your execution, Venandakatra."

He turned his head, glowering down at the sprawled man at his feet. "The scroll is not signed by the emperor alone, by the way. It also bears Great Lady Sati's signature."

Venandakatra's shock and outrage vanished instantly. His face, already pale, became ashen.

"Yes," grated Nanda Lal. "Great Lady *Sati*."

The spymaster looked to the northwest, through the open flap.

Quietly: "The siege of Deogiri is over, Venandakatra. By tomorrow morning, this army will be on the road to Bharakuccha. That is a given. The only choice you have is whether you will lead it. Or simply your head, stuck on a pike."

A desire and a decision

"Where do we stand with the new warships?" asked the King of Kings, striding into the room which served Axum as its war center.

Rukaiya looked up from her table in the center of the room. It was a large table, but little of its expanse was visible. Most of it was covered with scrolls and bound sheets of papyrus.

The queen pointed to the sheet in front of her. "I was just finishing a letter to John of Rhodes, thanking him for the last shipment of guns. We have enough now to outfit the first two vessels."

"Good, good," grunted Eon, coming up to the table. "I want to get them out to sea at once, so we can start ravaging the supply fleet as soon as it leaves Bharakuccha."

He leaned over and nuzzled his wife's hair. Smiling, she reached up and drew his head alongside her own. "There is more good news," she whispered.

Eon cocked his eyebrow. Rukaiya's smile widened. "We'll call him Wahsi, of course, if it's a boy. But you really should start thinking about girls' names, too."

A question and an answer

Kungas rose from the bed and padded to the window. Planting his hands on the sill, he stared out over Deogiri. The city was dark, except for the lamps glowing in one of the rooms of the nearby palace.

His lips twitched. "It's a good thing for him that he has an understanding wife."

Irene levered herself onto an elbow. "What? Is Dadaji working late again?"

Seeing the Kushan's nod, she chuckled. " 'Understanding' is hardly the word for it, Kungas. She'll be sitting there herself, you know that. As patient as the moon."

Kungas said nothing. Irene studied him, for a moment, reading the subtle signs in his face.

"What is it, Kungas?" she asked. "You've been preoccupied with something all night."

Kungas tapped the windowsill with his fingers. Irene stiffened, slightly. That was as close as the Kushan ever came to expressing nervous apprehension.

"What is it?" she demanded. "And don't tell any fables. You've got the jitters, I know you do. Something which involves me."

Kungas sighed. "There *are* disadvantages," he muttered, "to a smart woman." He turned away from the window and came back to the bed. Then, sitting on the edge, he gave Irene a level stare.

Abruptly: "I spoke to Kanishka and Kujulo today. About Peshawar, and my plans for the future."

She nodded approvingly. Kanishka and Kujulo were the key officers in the small army of Kushans serving Shakuntala. Irene had been pressing Kungas for weeks to raise the subject with them.

"And?" she asked, cocking her head.

"They have agreed to join me. They said, on balance, that they thought I would make a good king."

Again, he sighed. "Nonetheless, they were critical. Rather harshly so, in fact. They feel that I have neglected the first requirement of a successful dynasty."

He looked away. "They are quite correct, of course. So I promised them I would see to the matter immediately. If possible."

Irene stared at him, for a moment. Then she bolted upright, clutching the sheets to her chest.

"*What?*" she hissed. "You expect me—*me*, a Greek noblewoman accustomed to luxury and comfort—to go traipsing off with you into the wilds of Central Asia? Squat in some ruins in the middle of mountains and deserts, surrounded by barbarian hordes and God-knows-what other dangers?" Her eyes were very wide. "Be a queen for a bunch of Kushan mercenaries with delusions of grandeur? Spend the rest of my life in a desperate struggle to forge a kingdom out of nothing?"

Other than a slight tightening of his jaws, Kungas' face was a rigid mask. "I don't *expect*," he said softly. "I am simply asking. Hoping."

Irene flung her arms around his neck and dragged him down. Within a second, the huge, heavy bed was practically bouncing off the floor from her sheer energy. Quiver, shiver; quake and shake.

"Oh, Kungas!" she squealed. "We're going to have so much *fun*!"

A reminder and a distinction

When he finished reading the letter from Emperor Skandagupta, Damodara turned his head and stared at the Tigris. For a moment, his gaze followed the river's course, north to Assyria—and Anatolia, and Constantinople beyond. Then, for a longer moment, the gaze came to rest on his army's camp. It was a well-built camp, solid, strong. Almost a permanent fort, after all the weeks of work.

"That's it, then," he said softly. "It's over."

He turned to the man at his side, folding the letter. "Prepare the army, Rana Sanga. We have been summoned back to India. The emperor urges great haste."

Sanga nodded. He began to turn away, but stopped. "If I may ask, Lord—what is to be our new assignment?"

Damodara sighed heavily. "Unrest is spreading all over India. The Deccan is in full revolt. Venandakatra has been driven back into Bharakuccha. He is confident that he can hold the city unaided, though he can't reconquer Majarashtra without assistance. That will end up being our task, no doubt. But first we must subdue Bihar and Bengal, while the emperor rebuilds the main army. He expects the Romans to attack our northwest provinces within a year. Two years, at the outside."

Sanga said nothing. But his face grew tight.

"It appears that you will be meeting Raghunath Rao again some day," mused Damodara. "After all these years. The bards and poets will be drooling."

Damodara studied Sanga closely. Then said, very softly: "The day may come, Rana Sanga—*may* come—when I will have to ask you to remember your oath."

Sanga's face, already tight, became as strained as a taut sheet. "I do not need to be reminded of honor, Lord Damodara," he grated harshly.

Damodara shook his head. "I did not say I would ask you to *honor* your oath, Sanga. Simply to remember it."

Sanga frowned. "What is the distinction?"

There was no answer. After a moment, shrugging angrily, Sanga stalked off.

Damodara remained behind, staring at the river. He found some comfort, perhaps, in the study of moving water.

A concern and an explanation

"I am your obedient servant, Lord," said Narses, bowing his head.

As soon as Damodara left the tent, Narses' face broke into a grin. "We're on," he muttered, rubbing his hands.

Ajatasutra looked up from the chess board. "What are you so excited about?"

Narses stared at him. The grin faded, replaced by something which bordered on sadness.

"You have become like a son to me," said Narses abruptly.

Ajatasutra's face went blank. For a moment, no more. Then, a sly smile came. "That's not entirely reassuring, Narses. As I recall, the last time you adopted a spiritual offspring you tried to murder her."

Narses waved his hand. "Not right away," he countered. "Not for many years, in fact. Besides—"

The eunuch sat on the chair facing Ajatasutra. He stared down at the chess board. "Besides, the situation isn't comparable. *She* was an empress. You're just a poor adventurer."

Ajatasutra snorted. Narses glanced at the small chest in the corner of the tent. "Well—relatively speaking."

The assassin crossed his arms over his chest and leaned back in the chair. "Why don't you just come out with it, Narses? If you want to know my loyalties, ask."

The eunuch opened his mouth. Closed it.

Ajatasutra laughed, quite gaily. "Gods above! I'd hate to live in your mind. You just can't do it, can you?"

Narses opened his mouth. Closed it.

Ajatasutra, still chuckling, shook his head. "Relax, old man. Like you said, I'm an adventurer. And I can't imagine anybody who'd provide me with more adventures than you."

Narses sighed. "Thank you," he whispered. His lips twisted wryly. "It means a great deal to me, Ajatasutra. Whether I'm capable of saying it or not."

Ajatasutra eyed the eunuch, for a moment. "I'm puzzled, though. Why the sudden concern?"

The assassin nodded toward the entrance of the tent. "I didn't catch any of your conversation with Damodara. But I did hear his last sentence. 'You do not have my permission to do anything, Narses.' That sounds pretty definite, to me."

Narses cackled. "What a novice! A babe in the woods!" He leaned forward. "You really must learn to parse a sentence properly, Ajatasutra. 'You do not have permission,' my boy, does not mean the same thing as: 'I forbid you.' "

Ajatasutra's eyes widened. Narses cackled again. "It's mate in six moves, by the way," the eunuch added.

A greeting and a grouse

There was not much left of Charax, when Belisarius and Antonina returned from Adulis a few weeks later. But the Persians had managed to salvage enough of the docks for their ship to be moored.

Emperor Khusrau was there to meet them, along with Baresmanas, Kurush and Agathius. The Persians were beaming happily. Agathius was not.

Politely, the Persians allowed Agathius to greet the

general first. The Duke of Osrhoene limped forward, aiding his wooden leg and foot with a pair of crutches. "Fine mess you left me," he grumbled, the moment Belisarius came up to him.

Belisarius glanced around, frowning. "What did you expect? You knew I was going to wreck the place."

"Not *that*," snorted Agathius. "It's all the irate letters I've been getting from the empress. Theodora is demanding to know how I could have been so careless. Letting the Persians get their hands on gunpowder technology."

"Oh—*that*." Belisarius clapped Agathius on the shoulder. "You covered for me, I trust?"

Agathius shrugged. "Sure, why not? I still know how to bake bread, when I get cashiered in disgrace." Gloomily: "Assuming she lets me keep my head."

Belisarius turned to Antonina. "The two of you have never met, I believe. Antonina, meet one of my finest generals. Agathius, this is my wife. She is also, I might mention, Theodora's best friend."

Agathius extended his hand. "Well. It's certainly a pleasure to meet *you*."

A regret and a cheer

Much later that night, after Khusrau and his entourage left, Belisarius stretched lazily.

"There's something to be said for having Persians as allies," he announced. His admiring eyes roamed about the lavishly furnished pavilion which the Aryan emperor had provided for them.

Antonina grinned. "Cut it out, soldier. Since when have you given a damn about luxuries? You just like the idea of dehgans hammering away at somebody else, that's all."

Belisarius returned the grin with one of his own. "True, true," he admitted. "Fills me with pure glee, it does, thinking about the Malwa trying to retreat with those mean bastards climbing all over them."

After a moment, his amusement faded. Within a very short time, it was gone completely.

"It's not your fault, love," said Antonina gently.

Belisarius blew out his cheeks. "No. It isn't. And if I had to do it over again, I wouldn't hesitate for a minute. But—"

He sighed. "Most of them are just peasants, Antonina. Not more than twenty thousand will ever make it back to their families in India. Khusrau and Kurush will harry them mercilessly, all the way to the Indus valley." He rubbed his face. "And if Eon's new warships can keep the Malwa from landing supplies on the coast, there won't even be ten thousand survivors."

It's not your fault, said Aide.

Belisarius shook his head. "That's not the point, Aide. Antonina. I'm not concerned with fault. Malwa is to blame for the death of their soldiers, just as surely as they are for the crimes those soldiers committed while they were in Persia. No one else."

His hands curled into fists. "It's just—"

Belisarius turned his head, staring into the flame of a lamp. "It's just that there are times when I really wish I could have been a blacksmith."

Silence followed. A minute or so later, Maurice came into the pavilion. The chiliarch gazed on his general, still staring at the lamp.

"Indulging in the usual triumphal melancholy, are we?" he demanded.

Belisarius, not moving his eyes from the lamp, smiled crookedly. "Am I really that predictable?"

Maurice snorted. He advanced into the pavilion and placed a hand on Belisarius' shoulder.

"Well, cheer up, lad. I've got some good news. I'm expanding your bodyguard. You'll be leading a huge allied army on your next campaign. Got to have a more substantial bodyguard. Nothing else, the Persians will be miffed if you don't."

Belisarius scowled. "For the sake of Christ, Maurice. If you give me a Persian-style bodyguard I won't be able to see my hand in front of my face."

Maurice chuckled. "Oh, I wasn't thinking of anything that elaborate. Just going to add one more man, to give Anastasius, Isaac and Priscus a bit of a break. The new man's here, by the way, right outside the pavilion. I'd introduce you, except that it would be purely ridiculous. And I don't want to have to listen to him muttering about stupid formalities."

Belisarius was out of his chair and gone in an instant.

"See?" demanded Maurice. "Didn't I say I'd cheer him up?"

An accusation and a reproof

"He just let me go, General," said Valentinian. The cataphract hooked a thumb over his shoulder, in the direction of the Persian camp. A wild revelry seemed to be going on. "He let all the Roman prisoners go. He told me to tell you that was in exchange for the Rajput prisoners you left in the qanat."

Belisarius scratched his chin. "That I can understand. But why *you*? I offered him a fortune for your ransom."

Valentinian's narrow face creased into a grin. "If I survive long enough, General, I'll be asking you to remember that ransom. When you decide on a suitable retirement bonus."

Belisarius smiled, nodding. "That I will, Valentinian. You can be sure of it."

There was still a question in his eyes. Valentinian shrugged. "I really don't know, General. But he did say something strange, when I left."

Belisarius cocked his eyebrow. Again, Valentinian shrugged.

"Meant nothing to me. Kind of silly, I thought. But the last thing Damodara said, just as I was getting on the horse, was that he hoped you were a man with a proper respect for grammar."

Belisarius laughed, then. The laughter went on so long that Valentinian started muttering.

That sounded like "cryptic fucking clowns" to me, pronounced Aide.

Me too, replied Belisarius, still laughing. *But I'm sure we must be mistaken. Be terribly disrespectful of the high command!*

Certainly would! The facets flashed. The crystalline rooster reappeared, its beady eyes filled with accusation. **Speaking of which—**

The laughter went on and on. Maurice and Antonina emerged from the tent.

"We're in trouble, girl," announced Maurice. "Deep trouble. That drooling idiot's supposed to lead us all to final victory."

Antonina stiffened. "Watch your mouth! That's my husband you're talking about." She frowned. "Even if he is a fucking clown."